TRADER

~1884~

TRADER 1884

Promontory Press
www.promontorypress.com

ISBN: 978-1-77374-114-7

Cover and Typeset designed by Edge of Water Design, edgeofwater.com
Interior Artwork Copyright © 2024 Sara Dahmen
Printed in the United States
0987654321

To my beloved husband and joyful children,
who let me trade time with them to write instead.

TRADER

~1884~

FLATS JUNCTION SERIES
BOOK 5

SARA DAHMEN

CHAPTER ONE

Kate

March 3, 1884

If an establishment is called The Prime Inn, one would think such a place was fine enough, if not the very best a town has to offer. It's all right there in the name. Prime. Excellent. Very suitable for a citified gentleman who has seen more of the world than I ever will, especially judging on his fine accent. He reminds me a little of the Fawcett brothers, with their tight English vowels and overlong use of the letter *h*. He's clearly traveled far and come further to land in our tiny dot on the map. Even with the railroad, Flats Junction is often overlooked. I should be sure we make a good impression, at the very least.

It's why I bring Mr. Thomas Smith to The Prime Inn.

Instead, all I see are worn floorboards as we step inside, clean filed to the bone-tan of grains about to collapse, with uncountable scuffs and gouges in the surrounding pine on the windowsills and the planks of the walls, which would be better off if at least whitewashed if not papered. The bar's drinks are grimy with dust and smudgy fingerprints, and even the chairs in the main lounge look hard-worked and weary from too many patrons. I'm finding it hard not to make excuses for something called 'prime', but when I turn to speak to Mr. Smith he's only smiling as if this is the best place on earth.

"It's not much," I say, reminding myself at the last minute not to use the word *ain't*. "But it'll do you for as long as you're in town." I'm fishing, like any proper shopkeeper would do, but he doesn't seem to mind at all, and latches himself onto it as if it was an opening to talk on his life's story. Which it is, because that's my point. News is gold, half the time.

"I'm incredibly beholden to you, ma'am," he says, pulling off his tall hat. It's so new I'm near sure it crinkles with any movement. "And very pleased to make your acquaintance."

"Call me Kate," I say at once. The way he speaks all fancy-like makes discomfort crawl along the backs of my arms. "Everyone does."

"Hiya Kitty!" Joe Greenman calls, coming out from around the back room. He settles worn elbows on his bar counter and grins. I scowl at him, but he only fixes his eyes on the newcomer and nods. "Needing a room, then? 'Preciate the business."

"This is the best inn in Flats Junction," I say, wishing I don't sound so defensive. "And this here is Thomas Smith. Just in on the morning train."

The gentleman reaches to shake Joe's hand. "Doctor Smith, at your service."

My eyebrows shoot up so fast I'm sure they'll get lost in my hair or get stuck up there at any rate. Another doctor? What will Pat have to say about this? Will he be like old Doc Gunnarsen who ran off any competition at once, or will he be glad for the help? That is, assuming this fellow wants to stick around.

"Give him the best room, Joe," I say. I lift my chin and look down my nose. He once again ignores my manners and only has eyes for Thomas Smith.

"Lucy can take you up and get you settled," he says, then twists at the waist to shout for the Brinkley's youngest and only unmarried daughter.

She appears so fast, I'm sure she's been listening on the other side of the backroom door and hustles herself out while trying to take off an oily apron. Lucy's the only Brinkley girl with black hair, but has the same blue eyes as all her family, straight from Susan's side. With a quick shy nod and a single flick of her wrist, she beckons Mr.—Doctor—Smith to follow. He does, with a long backward glance in my direction.

It doesn't do much on me. I'm used to men's looks. They try to figure on me, whether I'm married or widowed, important or only a busybody … white or something more. At least, I like to think it's the last one, though every time I look in the mirror I'm reminded that there's no fooling the nose and hair, or even the shape of my eyes and slant of my cheeks and jaw. I'm part Sihasapa, and anyone who claims they can't see it is just lying.

As soon as the new doctor is out of the room, I whirl on Joe and cross my arms.

"What?" he asks, lifting his hands. "I swear he'll get the best room, just as I said."

"There's no such thing as a best room in this entire building," I say, strolling up to the opposite side of the bar and letting my gaze crawl over the bits of fine touches, which are too few and far between to my liking. There's a mirror along the back of the bar, but it's foggy from no polishing, and there should be more wax mashed into the bar wood itself, not even thinking on covering the bare windows with curtains or putting down some rugs.

"What are you getting at, Kitty?" Joe presses. "I know that look. I spent too many years sitting right behind you in school to know you're thinking on something."

"Oh, is that such a surprise, then?" I shoot back. Then I force my shoulders down and move my fingers so they're not so stiff. Joe was never one who chased or yelled or used slang or other even less kind words. He always went straight to the inn to help his pop as soon as lessons were over. He didn't have time to walk ten paces behind me and use insults like *homemade sin* or *speckled pup*.

"I'm only thinking on some ideas," I tell him honestly. "This place used to be prime back when Gil ran it, but neither of you were up for making it pretty."

"It ain't no woman's parlor," Joe grouses.

"But just think if it was very fine," I insist. "Suppose we partnered on it and bring in the best foods, and make this a worthy stop to everyone traveling around these parts. We could make a good spot of cash."

Joe's eyes go round as he leans over the bar toward me. I lean in, too. We might as well get started on some business discussion from the start.

"I ain't selling you a stick of this place," Joe says lowly. "And I don't need no help. 'Sides, you can't afford it. You've had to rebuild your General and share profits with Yves, and don't think word hasn't got round of how you helped young Helena Salomon get herself set up making dresses covered in ribbons. Your hands are in enough for a woman, and there's the end of it."

"I—"

"And there's the time for the breakfast," Joe says suddenly, pushing back and walking away. "I'll take good care of the new gentleman, don't you worry."

I'm left standing in the empty front room, though the tinkering of Joe's coffee pots and the shuffle of feet upstairs reminds me that soon enough the room will be filling up with the other boarders. As much as I want to catch Doctor Smith and ask him any number of questions, I suppose I'm dismissed and then some.

It stings.

And while I'm very used to being stung, it doesn't take the bite away all the same. When I exit The Prime Inn into the pale morning haze, I'm filled up with annoyance and frustration and something tighter, like ambition that's been squeezed and turned into heat. Wrapping my shawl closer against the dampness of early March, I take only one step toward the General and change my mind. If I can't sidle myself into The Prime Inn quite yet, maybe I can make some headway into rising Flats Junction in another place. I could stop at The Golden Nail and ask Trusty Willy to buy some newfangled machine. Maybe one of those fancy ice boxes Helena saw out east would do well. Willy's mother could do something fine in her menus, something like a cold dessert. Toot Warren would like that, I think, and she'd be grateful to me for the idea. And then, as my footsteps move faster south down Alley Road toward Main

Street, I force them to slow. What am I thinking, running around trying to do these little pokes? We'd need to get in ice if I convince Toot and Willy to get an ice box in Flats Junction. And worse, Elaine Warren will want figures on cost overall, and everyone knows Willy won't buy anything without her say-so anyhow. I don't know how much it takes to get ice out west. Will it even make a difference?

I could figure it out …

Or maybe I'll figure on a better plan, one that'll change more than Trusty Willy's back kitchen and The Golden Nail's food offerings.

So instead, I turn myself back around and head back up to First Street and head east, until I hit the old cooperage and take stock on whether Yves is awake and able to discuss any plans other than his own.

No one sits outside, not even Arnold with his ebony eyes and blue-white teeth, who watches everyone coming and going, buying goods they'd normally get from me. Well, which folks will get from me again, when I've set up the General at last and have my grand opening. That's part of why I'm here, too. I need to talk about the future with Yves. He's going to have to shut down his operations here, and I mean to make sure he doesn't create mischief afterward. Last thing I need is the wild posse running around, breaking train rails I haven't approved, and making it too hard to get to Flats Junction at all.

The cooperage is still quiet, and I reckon the lot of them are sleeping off a night of drink and crowing their feats.

As I press open the door, the rough, weather-beaten plant feels like a worn river rock under my palm, all bumpy and smooth from uncountable hands. Maybe I'll come back later, when the fire in my belly to do something—change anything—has died down a bit. That might be best, anyway.

But I've already forgot that Matthias is awake.

He's there alone, puttering behind the make-shift counter, poking at the beaten book that serves as the posse's made-up ledger.

"Oh," I say. "Sorry."

He looks up briefly, nods, and goes back to his slow marking. Not for the first time I'm glad the man says about five words a year. At least he won't ask me about the soup he brought me this morning after I left Doc and Jane Kinney's house, which I didn't bother to eat. It's stone cold now, and the dumplings like mush. I'll toss it when I get home, and no one'll be wiser.

I've already plumb forgot Doc Kinney just had a baby, too.

I must really be riled to forget such things.

No. It just means I've better things to do than coo over a newborn or gush about a man bringing me soup. I'm no fool. Yves owes his place in Flats Junction because I offered him one. His posse is smart to try and butter me up when they can at the very least.

"I was looking for Yves," I explain, feeling silly speaking to the flat air in the empty ad-hoc mercantile. It's impossible not to take stock of what they've kept on hand while my General gets finished up and re-stocked after the fire. Only a bit of canned milk, and looks like only a small few sacks of tobacco and white sugar cones. He's stocked up on the oysters and canned herring, and the little tins of peppermints. I'll be glad when my own goods are put in place—the bolts of fabrics and glass jars sparkling with horehound and licorice and lemon drops … It would have been faster in the rebuilding, but a good portion of the folks didn't help. I'd counted on more help … Oh, and I couldn't ask everyone to hold off on their own businesses just to help me. There's that, too. And maybe some didn't mind shopping at Yves's in the meantime, though I like that notion the least.

Matthias only shoots a glance to the back room when I mention Yves's name. The notion of the entire posse sleeping sprawled out in that living space gives me visions I don't want to see in life. I continue my slow stroll around the room, noting the way they've stacked the flour in such a manner that the bottom two sacks will turn blue with mildew on the packed earth, and the barrels of canning salt are rusting along the corners of the bands.

"Think he'll be awake soon enough?" I ask, once I'm near enough to Matthias that I can speak without being overly loud.

Matthias shrugs once, then nods briefly. Everything about the strongman reeks of efficiency and economy. His movements, his lack of words, even his precise marks in the ledger. I suppose that's the German way. My father would have been pleased to work with him.

But I'm not working with Matthias. I'm working with the posse leader.

"Well, if he thinks to come my way—"

"What is zee wish, Kate?"

Yves walks out from the living space tucking in his striped shirt and bending his suspenders so far out that I think they'll snap in half. His hairless head gleams with leftover sweat from sleeping in a room packed with bodies, and his pale eyes are still lined with pink as he gazes up at me. I squash the pressure that I should hunch myself so I'm not so tall around him, but now's not the time to be anything but tall and brash.

"I've come to talk about the Fort," I say.

Yves considers, then gestures me over to the side of the counter that isn't taken up by Matthias's bulk. The scratch of his pencil on the soft paper sounds like nails sliding down silk and makes me want to yank it away if only to stop the itch down my spine.

"What about zee Fort? Zee Army is good for business, is it not?" Yves asks. He suddenly turns to Matthias. "Where is zee coffee? You are to have it ready, no?"

Without a flinch or signal of any normal emotion, Matthias heads over to the potbelly stove in the corner and slides the grate to stoke the fire and pours water from a pail into a dented coffee pot. Everything is done carefully, and with minimal noise, but Yves still growls. I'd make an excuse for Matthias—that maybe he hadn't had the brew ready because he was getting soup for himself and me, too, but maybe … maybe that would only make Yves more annoyed, and I wouldn't want that, now.

"There are new recruits coming in every day," I say, bringing Yves's rheumy gaze back to me. As his eyes wander up and down, I shove my pins up higher into the bun and continue as if he isn't gawking. "I just came from the depot myself now, and I'm here to say there are going to be far more men in Fort Randall than there has been for years."

"Why do you suppose zat is so?" Yves wonders. Spittle forms in the corner of his mouth, and he pulls out a long European knife to start on his fingernails. Each is filled with a gooey brown slime. What has he been doing?

Eating molasses straight from the barrel?

"I don't know, and I don't care," I say. "I'm saying there's more money and action to be made with working an angle with the Army than before. You might want to capitalize on it, is all."

He does not change his pattern, but his voice gets brittle, like ice ready to break at the start of spring. "Are you trying to get rid of me, Katherine?" His use of my full name feels too intimate, like he slapped me across the chest. "But zee business here is only just started. It has not yet been the full year."

"No, I'm not getting rid of you," I say at once. "I'm trying to think on how you could make more money, once my General opens back up shortly, and people come shop by me instead. You'll be missing your cash."

"Oh, so this is zee way you take care of me and mine?"

"I'm just thinking of everything. For the good of Flats Junction and all who live in it."

He begins to use the knife to pick at the tar stuck between his teeth. It's a dark color, and I can't tell if it's rot or just old meat. My nose curls up just the same, and I wince just a bit when he knicks his gums and a trickle of blood fills the space under his tongue, so that when he next talks, the ruby drops spray out on the wood between us.

"And here I thought we were to live in zee town forever," Yves said calmly. "Zat is what you said to everyone. It is why we have stopped our wild riding and made a home here."

"Maybe some of your … ah, folks will want to get back on the prairie again," I suggest, limping over the word to describe the posse. They're not a family, and I don't know exactly what ties them together other than time and habit, but I can't imagine they're all too happy by sitting in one place all these past months. I know I get stir crazy all the time myself. It's probably why I meddle in town business more than a woman really should do. "Maybe you'll find the Army will pay double for your goods, and make it worth your while to have business there. You're a businessman, Yves. Negotiate with the commander, and you'll be living like kings."

Yves glances around the makeshift store, with its uneven shelves and unorganized goods. I can't tell if he minds the clutter and lack of finesse or even proper shelves on the walls for the smaller items. Does he compare his little store to my grander one?

Did he think I'd want him selling dry goods after I re-opened?

He finds my gaze again and a small smile flits across the very corners of his mouth. Tilting his head to the side, exposing the raw cords of his scrawny neck, he shakes his head.

"I do not think we will be needing zee Fort as much as you think, Miss Kate. Business here is fine."

"And when it's not?"

"Well, as you say, maybe some of the gang misses zee prairie. Maybe they want to see how zee rails are holding up. What nice things are brought west for here. You see?"

Oh, I see. I do see. Damn the man. How can he not see that I'm offering him a way to keep making money while giving me my livelihood back? Why would he have to sabotage any engines or rails? It would help us both if they are left alone! My heart feels like it popped up to the back of my mouth, and spit of my own fills my throat. Why do I always have to be making these deals with devils?

I know part of the answer to that question, and I don't reckon I'll answer it.

"I don't think the Army would take kindly to anyone causing trouble with the rail," I remind him. "It's different than it was a year ago. Like I said, more presence now, for whatever the reason. More men coming in."

"But zen they will need me more, if zee rails are unreliable."

It's talking in circles. Pulling myself up to my full height, I purse out my lips. Maybe he'll think I'm giving in, and I don't nod or shake my head as I walk out and into the fresher air without a glance at Matthias and not even waiting on the coffee. Let Yves stew on it all a bit. If he sees it a different way, he might even come to think of it as his own idea and follow it up.

If he could be reined in, if he could be controlled just a bit … I could see how I could rule through Yves. It would work if he didn't notice, or if he didn't care, but he would, damn him. He's been wily from the start, even back when my father Percy ran the town.

That's the gist of it, really.

I want to run the town, too.

But better than Percy.

Make Flats Junction bold and big, as important as Deadwood, with crystals hanging from lanterns in all the inns, fine bathtubs and two-story houses that are real and not just flat fronts. We already got us two churches. If I can figure on it, we can get ourselves a steady schoolteacher at last—Harriet only shows when the pigs aren't giving Alan too much trouble and half the town won't send their kids when she's there. There will be oysters and a bakery. I could … I could get in electricity, and …

And make this a place I won't mind living in for the rest of my life.

I've never stepped outside of Flats Junction, and I never will.

Not because I can't take that train out, but when I'm gone, where will I go? I've got no one waiting on me on the other side of the rails. No livelihood. No man. Flats Junction is the only place I can do what I wish, without beholden to a husband, and still have more power and more say than most anyone else.

Now that I think on this, as I walk south once more to the back of the General, I think I will go back to Yves in a few days. I'm sure we can come to some arrangement, as he's liable to like the idea that he's important. He's just like the other men, though less content to work in the shadows.

Bern Masson's face floats across my thoughts. Bern, walking Jane home well before she stole Doctor Kinney from me. Bern, meeting me across candlelight in my back room, hatching plans. Bern, refusing to dance with me, because no matter what happened, he had no interest in tying himself to a woman with my heritage. Bern, as he died at the end of a rope …

Bern, riding his fast horse 'round Flats during the July races.

Just as I think of those races, half a dozen horses go tearing right past me, making my new bright skirts whip and spin, catching on my ankles and flapping mud high into the spring sky. It's the Svendsen cowboys, ripping and yelling, but something in their shouts sounds like panic and fear.

I catch Moses Thompson at the back, his deep brown eyes and skin near the same color as his hat and horse. If it weren't for the faded red shirt, he'd look like a night rider coming out of the Black Hills themselves with the devils of the underworld after him.

He notices me just as they pull past, and I cup my hands to shout.

"What is it?"

"The cows at the ranch!" he yells. "A whole passel of 'em just dropped down dead!"

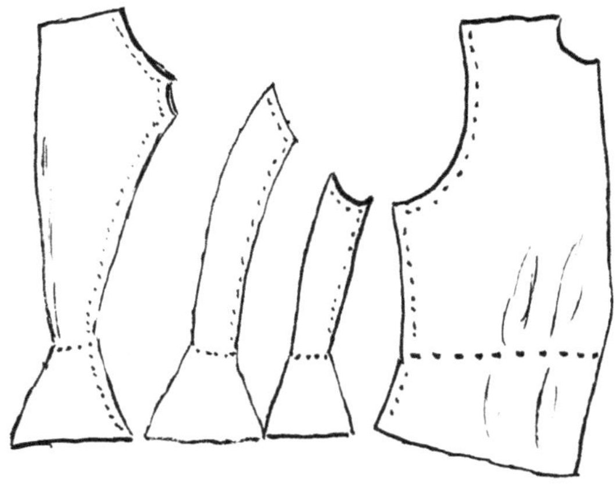

CHAPTER TWO

Helena

March 7, 1884

If I squint my eyes just so … very, very carefully, I can make sure that the pattern will line up perfectly when I put the seam together. Though I'd never tell my mother, the hours in her tinsmith shop have given me a very tight eye for the work with cotton and calico, muslin and silk. It's a strange and tiny and secret power in my blood, that tells me when I'm off an eighth of an inch or no. She'd be proud, but again, I'll never say so.

The pattern itself is easy enough to manage, as it's a brilliant plaid in yellow and pink and blue. If I'm fast enough between other dress orders, I'll have it well ready by the Independence Day celebrations. If, I guess, we have them this year in Flats Junction. The last one was simply awful for Kate and her General store, and also for the doctor and his poor wife. At least they hanged the man what done it. I mean, *who did it*. And now we should be safe, as it should be. I've never felt more safe than I do with the edges of the prairie all around me.

What I don't like exactly about the dress I'm making is the fact that it's for me. It'll be mine. I didn't pay for the thread or the cloth itself. Kate did. It's her money I'm using and her goods going to myself instead of a paying customer.

But I tell myself that wearing this fine dress, in the most fashionable cut—daring, my mother will say—will only advertise the dressmaking shop here behind the Fawcett house. It'll only bring more customers, so that Kate'll make back her investment and then some, and all the town women will look like they stepped out of a fashion plate. It'll be behind the fashion, as it is, but they don't have to know exactly how fast the cut of a sleeve or the yards in a bustle change. Oh, won't Elaine Warren and Sadie Fawcett be drooling? They'll want something the same—better! All I'm doing is showing what's possible, and that even if we're living in the dusty west, we can still be citified with our petticoats. Besides, me making my own dress and using it is no different than my mother making her own pots and pans and having them used in her own kitchen. Someone's got to make my clothes, and why not me?

I guess I just don't like feeling beholden with the very clothes I make myself.

Did my mother feel beholden when she started working her trade? I find it hard to imagine her under anyone's thumb.

She must have some sense when I'm thinking on her, though, because she opens the door to my tiny shop without knocking. Maybe a mother doesn't ever knock. Maybe she thinks because she gave me birth, she has some sort of hold over me forever. I wonder if that might change if I'm ever married. Maybe she won't want to walk in on me in undress then, and she'll give me some privacy. Even though I've now grown up enough, established this little business, she still thinks the door is only like my bedroom, which always gives her access to me.

"Helena? Still working?" she asks, though it's obvious I am, sitting at my bench behind the like-new sewing machine Elaine Warren had brought over from out east. My fingers go stiff, and my eyes feel stuck, as if I'm caught doing something naughty. And then I shake myself, lifting my chin in the way the haughty shop girls do out in the eastern cities, and remember that Mother has no idea the fabric I'm using is for myself alone.

"Until the last of the light goes," I say. But I put down the needle and shove the plaid silk off to the side anyway, because it feels strange to keep working when she's here watching. I can work without stopping when anyone else is in the shop—Doc Kinney's wife, Mrs. Fawcett, and even Mrs. Painter, the Reverend's wife with her sour moods, but I can't do it when it's Mother.

"Brought you bread and stew."

Mother pushes aside my scrap bag and the empty ribbon spools to set a small cast iron pot on the bit of bare space. It's the one table in my little space, which fits the sewing table with its oiled machine and my cot, which doubles as a table for goods during the day. Spools of ribbon hang from wooden dowels along the wall, and the shelves circling the leftover wall space are stacked with whatever fabrics don't fit in Kate's General. Shimmering pale peaches and frothy pinks, soft pastels for newborn christening gowns and a raw satin in bloodred that I plan to use for trim on the next gown Elaine Warren orders all wait for my fingers.

"It's hard not to dream of what it will be, isn't it?" Mother asks, her gaze following mine as it wanders across the goods in the early evening glow. "How you'll build it. It lives in your hands, in your mind. Impossible to let go, once you have the idea."

"Yes," I admit. A swell, like a bubble in the Flats Basin River, stuck under the ice and swelling up as it melts, rises behind my ribcage and fills the space around my heart. "It's exactly like that, Mother."

"Hm." Marie Salomon strolls the five paces up and then back along the bed, gazing up at the patterns I've hung, their precious paper shapes fluttering carefully with her steps. "These are much like mine."

"I know."

"And you use what? An allowance of fabric?"

"A quarter inch for skirts, more for a bodice."

She nods, and I can fairly see her do the calculations of geometry in her mind. Turning back to the greasy covered kettle, she jerks her chin at it. "Eat it up while it's warm enough, and I'll take the dishes back home."

"You're not supposed to have to feed me," I grumble, reaching for the cover. Mother hands me a spoon from her apron. "I'm a businesswoman in my own right."

"And with what kitchen?" she scoffs, glancing at the meager space. It's small, that's for sure, and even with all the tender care Sadie Fawcett put into fixing up her summer house, it's still just a little room that is mostly for dressmaking and the rest a place to sleep.

"I go to Matt Winters' mess," I say. "And I can pay my own way."

Mother's eyes go up, and she waves a hand for me to dig into the stew. I do, then choke. It is not too hot, but there's not a speck of seasoning in it, and I can taste the way the meat is near gone off and the potatoes are the staleness of last year's harvest.

"Sorry," Mother says.

"Did you make this?" I ask, glaring up at her. "What are you doing, cooking?"

"*Babcia* made it," she says.

"Then why is it so terrible?"

"Helena!" she admonishes, but then her shoulders go up and down. "I know. She forgot to put in the herbs. I was going to bring a sachet, but then I remembered I had to put out the soldering furnace, and Natan was slow bringing in water, and …" She grimaces. "I'm sorry."

The apology hangs awkwardly in the air between us. I don't know how to answer it. It's as if she sees me as a near equal, or at least is trying to treat me like one.

"It's not like Grandma to make something gross," I say, and go back to chewing. It's better than nothing, and at least it's free.

"Berit is losing her touch," Mother says. She fingers one of the velvet trimmings, but her scarred hands snag on the soft threads on the end and she quickly pulls her hands into the folds of her dress. "That is, your grandmother is elderly, and at least she still is able to move about and cook for us all."

I nod and eat as quick as I dare while holding my breath so I don't taste the bland near-rancid flavor of the old carrots. At least it's filling, and by the time I'm scraping the bottom I'm more than full.

Mother takes down several of the patterns carefully, laying them out on my bed, turning them one way and other as she attempts to put together the edges.

"Which way is it?" she mutters. "It doesn't make sense, these pieces. *Co do cholery* … what the hell …"

I put the spoon inside the pot and close the lid before joining her. "Like this." I put the skinny pieces between the curved, with the larger panel in front. "It's half a bodice."

"All these pieces!" she exclaims. "In my day, there were three! Front, side and back!"

"Well, things are different now."

She slides a glance sideways at me and shakes her head. There's gray shot through the wild black hair she has, the tight curls showing silver at her roots. It makes time suddenly feel solid and hard, like pebbles stacked and teetering.

"So different," she says, pulling out the words. The faint leftover Polish accent in her tone is more obvious when she does so. "Just like the fine pressed tin goods you brought back from that Dover Stamping company."

I shift the precious patterns over and sink onto my cot. It's the first time Mother has even given me the slightest opening about what I've done and what I've seen. Who else will listen? Who else will care?

"It was fantastic," I tell her. "The machines they have for the work—it's nothing like we'll see here. They take up a whole room, multiple rooms, and they move with steam and speed … but it will help you, won't it? And I saw the great rooms of girls sewing fashion, so many women can wear the fine patterns. There are dress shops, too, of the finest seamstresses, who are able to get the first look at the fashions from Europe. They even make sample dresses for the windows, because they have so much more cloth—lace that no one will wear here, it's too fine."

"Sadie'd wear lace," Mother mutters.

"She'd love the shops," I admit. "And…they'd love her."

She gazes at me for a moment. "You miss it?"

"I made friends at the shops—the shop girls and some of the seamstresses." I shrug, my mind whirling with the grandness of the city, and the lines of buildings where the modiste ladies live. "I miss them, yes. But they send patterns when they can, for a small price, and I remake them here. It's like being part of it all, from a distance."

"Yet it's nothing like," Mother reminds.

My spine goes rigid. "Well, then. Eventually, I will hire shop girls, too, and I'll maybe open something bigger than this."

Mother holds up her hand, her mouth a thin line. "And so? You think you can pull all of the east coast here to Flats Junction?"

I stand, and don't bother to clear my dress. "Why not?"

"You can't," she says simply, looking around my tiny space again.

"Why not?" I repeat.

"Because you are beholden to Sadie Fawcett for the very bed you sleep in and the roof over your head. Elaine Warren for your precious machine. And Kate Davies … Kate for the goods, from the thread to the needle and more. How can you think to grow like this?"

"Elaine gets dibs on the first new fabrics. She's nearly repaid in full for her machine. And Sadie is the same—the finest patterns go to her first. And Kate …" I frown. "She'll be repaid eventually as I make money from the frocks and such."

Mother shakes her head. It bothers me, that she can't see beyond my bit of debt. She's not me—she doesn't understand my planning!

"It's not just fancy dresses for the finest ladies here," I say. "You didn't let me finish. There's Fort Randall, too."

Mother pauses, her breathing stops completely. Then she tries to smile, though it doesn't reach her dark eyes. "What about the Fort?"

"There's plenty of menfolk there who probably need repairs to trousers and shirts. And new shirts, too, and long underwear for the winter. I can do all of that without needing Kate Davies."

"It's not near as glamorous," Mother says wryly. She begins to place the patterns back on their nail, but does them in the wrong order. I'll fix it later. "But it's not done."

"What? A woman building her own business? You did, years ago."

"Under duress," she says.

"But you kept with it, even after getting married," I press. "You liked it. You still do."

"I'm married!" Her voice is a little explosion in my tiny room. "It was hard, yes, but easier now. A married woman has protection. She can go to places like the Fort … with her man! Just because Flats Junction has become a place to know on the maps does not mean a woman can go anywhere she likes, do what she likes. No one has that kind of freedom."

"Kate does. She does great things in town, unbeholden to any man."

"Kate never leaves Flats Junction. She won't. She can't." The truth hanging in Mother's words has weight. I fight against it, as if I'm tangled in a spider's web. And she doesn't stop there. "And she's likely far more unhappy than you think."

"Well, I'm going to do it different," I say, feeling the words crystalize in my bones. It's a promise to myself. "I've seen more than any of you."

"Oh, so?" Mother picks up the pot. Inside, the spoon makes a faint clattering. "You are not the only one who has seen the Atlantic Ocean. Mrs. Kinney has lived in Boston, the doctor, too. I myself spent near two decades in Chicago. It'll take more than a few weeks out east—even if you did so alone—to create something from nothing."

"You don't think I can do it!" The fine hairs on my arms rise, fighting the tight cuffs that ride almost to my elbows. I don't know what to do with this … to realize she has no faith in me, or my choices. Doesn't she have faith—belief—in me, in the future, in what I can create?

"I want you to succeed," she says at once. "I only want you to understand you cannot bend the world to your view. It can't—not as quickly as you'd like."

"I'll figure it out," I tell her. "And what it will take to do so."

It's a promise again, and one I don't know how to follow up. When she leaves, the sunlight goes with her, and I'm only left with the echo of it.

CHAPTER 3

Jane

March 9, 1884

Anew child does not take his mother's mind into account when he wails. He simply wishes heat or a shoulder, a dry cloth or more milk. I stare into Andrew's tiny face, screwed up in a squall that tells me nothing. Knowing I cannot understand, that I don't know what ails him, eats at every fiber stitching me together. It drives me to near madness, the unknowing. As his fists flail in circles and his gums glisten in his tiny mouth, and his eyes curve into the half-moons of his father's when he smiles, I stare at his face and try to figure what could possibly upset him this time. It is a mystery I must solve every other hour, and yet I consistently fail. Pulling my son onto my shoulder, I walk from the surgery to my husband's office and let my eyes run over the familiar titles in English and German and even one in Hungarian. Though I cannot read them, they remind me that I am more than a wet nurse to a newborn and have some knowledge in my bones beyond a leaking bosom and a sore bottom.

When I stroll with him back into the kitchen, Esther has two more bundles of fringed sagewort up, the fine lacy fronds already drooping on the woody stems. She glances over her shoulder, the steely braid brushing the entirety of her back, and, without a single shift in the planes of her face, smoothly takes Andrew from me.

"Do I look so uncertain?" I ask, sinking to the bench at the kitchen table.

"You look like all mothers do," she says. "It is only that you have yourself, and me, to keep him contented."

"I suppose it's not done to have a nursemaid here," I muse. "Or a nanny."

"That is not what I mean. It is that you have no family. No aunts or cousins, no sisters or grandmothers to hold the babe. My people always had more arms than children to go around, so someone was always willing to comfort a little one, and it gives the mother time to rest, to eat, to sleep. Eat now, Jane, before he needs you again."

She jerks her chin at yesterday's second loaf and the jar of milky butter from the Brinkleys sitting on the table. I slice two pieces and bite into the chewy centers with relish, and watch Esther pour tea out for me with one hand, as she keeps Andrew propped and whimpering with her other.

"You'll learn," she tells me, amusement coloring her rich voice as she catches me staring, big-eyed and bewildered. "Everyone learns, even if they think they will not."

"What do you suppose kept Patrick all night?" I ask, redirecting my thoughts to yet another thing I cannot control. Perhaps this is why I am on the edge of a knife, all this unknowing. I didn't think I was so out of practice, but then again, I have never been a mother, either. It may keep any woman particularly snappish. "He rarely misses breakfast at least."

"He is glad to be called to the Brinkley farm," Esther reminds me. "But I'm sure he'll be home soon. The cattle must be very sick."

Shoving the last of the bread between my back teeth, I haul myself up to start breakfast, in the chance he will be back to eat it fresh. As I do, I'm reminded that I'm not completely back to myself when a wave of dizziness catches the corners of my vision. Blinking fast, I steady myself and then put on the skillet to heat. The blacking of the oven glitters against the oily cast iron, and I turn to the prepared potato bread dough. It rose well over the previous hours, and the specks of dried rosemary show between the pale tan of it.

"Patrick ought to manage," I say, more to myself than to Esther. "He worked with animals for years in Boston, he's said."

"Yes," Esther says, stroking Andrew's back in the same rhythm that she takes each step across the kitchen, back and forth in front of the east-facing window.

"I just hope it's nothing like the black measles," I say. I wince after I say so, remembering as I speak that Esther's husband died of it.

She does not cringe, though, and only lifts her free shoulder. "Some diseases are different for different people, and same for animals."

My mind suddenly spins at her implication. Slipping the bread into the oven to bake, and glancing at the sun and the small clock in the kitchen, I figure even if Patrick arrives soon, there will be the old bread, and we can pull hard cheese and eggs, too, to add to his morning meal. Wiping my hands on the sides of my apron, I turn back to Esther as she pivots to me.

"You're saying there's a difference in how things spread. To whom they spread. And how. For cows, yes, maybe, but for people, too."

"I'm not saying anything," she says evenly. "I am not a person of science as Patrick is, nor even you with all your reading. But the coming of the Europeans has changed the patterns. Not just here, but everywhere. Even as some things remain the same, others shift. It could be why the cattle are dying at the very least."

Andrew gives a soft fuss, but it is one I know much better than the others. Sitting back at the table, I reach up and she places him softly in my arms. My breasts surge, the nipples going hard and the bumpy trickle of milk rushing forward so quickly I barely have time to unbutton my dress bodice and pull down my corset and chemise. What I would give for one of the nursing corsets with the rounded cut-outs! Andrew knows the curve of my elbow and the smell of warmth attached to me these days, and curls in to suckle with a sweet sigh. Brushing the pads of my fingers along the fine whisps of dark hair curling at the nape of his neck, I melt into this delicate, intimate embrace.

Esther goes go hang more sagewort, and speaks to it, though the words are for me. "*Pȟežíȟóta waštémna.* Women's medicine, for baths. You will find it growing in dry earth, though I have planted some in my old garden. It grows wild easily; you will be able to harvest it many places."

Her hands twist the twine with movements that defy my sight, so quick and confident that I can only envy the surety. She says there are always names of knots and even if they differ among folks, they are always the same. She has even shown me several over the past few years, but they do not stick in my mind as they do hers, and I must be shown the same simple ties over and again. Perhaps not everyone has a mind alike, to her point—things are different for some, and not all bodies and brains are easily classified.

 My days are often numbered by the knocks that come at the door, one of the true hallmarks of a doctor's existence—and mine, by marriage. This knock is fast and quick, pounding in staccato stamps, and comes a second time just as soon. It bodes an emergency, especially this early in the morning, and Esther and I trade glances. With Patrick still out, there's only a small chance I will be helpful.

And none will take Esther at all.

I button up my bodice, and Andrew fusses, but his belly has some milk, and he will be quiet long enough. Handing him to Esther, I'm able to get to the front door before the knock comes a third time.

When I swing open the door, I don't recognize the youth waiting on the other side of the screen. He's scrawny and built of bones and wires, as are many children who work the land, but he is not shoeless and he wears a wool coat that is not patched.

"Yes?" I ask. I've learned to answer the door this way. It is neutral. I do not make it worse by asking 'what's wrong' because perhaps there is nothing truly wrong or upsetting. I do not ask 'what is it' because that would be uncountably rude. Or worse, I do not say 'the doctor is not here' because it can make everything worse.

"Ma'am," he says, yanking off his hat at the last moment. "This the doc's place, yeah?"

"It is. Won't you come in?" I open the screen door. It doesn't scrape along the porch as it used to—Thaddeus Salomon made sure to sand it when he helped rebuild after the fire. "I've some bread and butter if you like."

The young man steps in, but only just inside the door. He shakes his head. "Can't stay, ma'am. If the doc can be woke, I'm to take him out to the homestead. My little brother's poorly, and getting worse by the hour. It's been four days. Please, ma'am." He rotates his hat counter-clockwise as he speaks, round and round.

"I'm very sorry," I tell him. "Doctor Kinney has not yet come home all night."

"Oh." The skinny shoulders droop several inches. "Should I wait?"

My hands itch to grab some of Patrick's medicine and my own vials of herbs and tinctures and oils. At the same time, my limbs and bosom ache for Andrew and the comfort of home. Well, I suppose there's little to be done but to put on the mantle I have worked to wear.

"No," I say. "No use in waiting if your little brother is so ill. I'm the doctor's wife, and I'm a nurse. Let me gather my medicines and child and we'll be off. Have you a horse?"

"Brought the one," he says. "Bossy can take us both. He's a big 'un."

"Are you sure you won't wish to have bread?" I ask, moving toward the surgery. "We have a few minutes if you'd like to go on through to the kitchen and cut a slice. I'll be quick."

He gives in at last, and walks toward the light in the back of the house. I turn to the left and enter Patrick's surgery, which I now know as well as if it were my own: the embroidered linens, stitched by his Aunt Bonnie, waiting on the operating table, the cabinets of medicine in brown and green and blue bottles, the lesser used tools, sparkling silvery in the grey morning. I choose the silver nitrate and iron pills, and a smaller bottle of the carbolic acid, in case the illness is one of sepsis instead of viral. The doorway darkens, and I turn to see the young man, who has a hunk of bread in each palm.

"There's an Indian woman what's in your kitchen," he says solemnly.

"Yes, that's Esther Davies," I say briskly. "Come along." Whisking past him, I march back into the warmth of said kitchen and into the pantry, where my own roll of pocketed leather holds the rest of the herbal medicines I've gleaned from my months learning from Esther. I suddenly, acutely, understand the challenge Patrick faces near every time he walks out the door. How does one prepare for the unknown, when preparation can be the key to life and death?

As soon as I've gathered my items in my small satchel, leftover from my Boston days and now doubling as a nursing bag, I take Andrew from Esther. She has no possible way to keep him fed and I have no notion for how long I'll be gone.

"Have you had enough? Take another," I say, echoing how Anette Zalenski might press food on a guest. He pushes his hands down the side seams of his pants and shakes his head, eyes wide and worried.

"Let Patrick know I've gone to the—" I glance at the young man. "Where?"

"The Woodman homestead," he says. "I'm Ben, the eldest."

"There," I say. Tucking Andrew at an angle with my shawl feels awkward as I juggle the bag in my left hand, but there's no sense in asking for help, as I will have much more to manage shortly. "Please tell the doctor where to find me when he has a moment."

"It's not terrible far," Ben Woodman says, glancing very briefly at Esther, and then away, as if his eyeballs will scorch if he looks overlong. "Twenty minutes north and westerly, closer to Svendsen's."

We ride on his horse at least the twenty minutes, and longer as we go. Andrew would be upset with the lack of milk, but for the gait of Bossy the overly high horse. I wonder what I shall do when I arrive and he demands to be fed, and I consider how I might drape my shawl carefully so I might feed him on the side. Can I manage it so one hand is free? I have done so before, when baking, so I'm certain it can be managed in some respects, though it makes me feel much less like a nurse more like an imposter as we arrive at the Woodman homestead.

It›s not much—the usual house with plank siding and several outhouses and barns made of sod and hay, with meager fencing of rocks and twigs holding in livestock. Yet it's not a poor place, given the two glass windows on either side of the front door and the full second story on the house as well.

Ben tells me it's only his little brother Perry who has been ill. No one else has come down with the sickness the past few days, either, not beast or family, but as we arrive, I suddenly have a fearful dread pile in my lungs. Suppose the illness is catching, in the end? Have I doomed my infant son to the putrid air, where the disease lives, waiting to flood into a new body? Suppose I set Andrew down and he rolls into a rag of blood, which poisons his?

It›s too late now.

And if I am truthful, and if I mean to be a nurse or using the medicine I have slowly gleaned from Esther, then I must get used to bringing my children with me. There will be no other choice, not for many years.

A woman does not have the luxury of departing without a thought, like her menfolk.

When we dismount, Mrs. Woodman is waiting for us, the front door yawning open even with the spring chill in the air. Her face is still fresh and strong and young for all her children, and the hard life on the prairie, but the tight lines between her eyes and along the edges of her nose give away the anxiety of a mother with an ailing child. Will I have such a look later in life, where my woes are so easily read on the lines and contours of my jaw?

I drape my shawl around Andrew's tiny face. He's already begun to root, as if he knows our journey is done, and it will only be a few minutes before his thin fussing begins anew. Perhaps this will work in my favor—that I must nurse him as I speak with the mother and keep my breast from the eyes of the father. Andrew himself will be hidden under cloth and against my bosom, and though I am uncertain yarn and cloth will keep out humors and infected vapors, perhaps if I don't touch anything or do not put him down … but suppose I do? Suppose I must set down my infant, and when I pick him back up, he has come down with the fever and illness little Perry suffers?

"Where's the doc?" Mrs. Woodman asks, peering behind me, and then toward Ben as he walks the horse to the barn. "He still coming?"

"No, Ma," Ben calls. "He's not been home, his missus says."

"I'm Jane Kinney, the doc's wife," I say, letting a smile fill my face and hide my trepidation. This cannot be harder than the surgeries I've assisted Patrick with in the previous years. I tell myself this to let the smile lift into my eyes, hoping to reassure. "The doctor did not return home after a house call last night, but I have left a message so he will follow me here when he returns. In the meantime, I have some years of experience, and perhaps I can at least relieve your son's pain for a bit until Doctor Kinney arrives." I hope he arrives …

A shadow crosses over her, and her shoulders hunch. "He's near beyond pain now."

She lets me in, and I juggle my baby to keep him calm while I get some understanding of the illness and whether there is a chair to sit on, or if I must nurse at the bedside.

The home is not large, but surprisingly clean given how many people are crammed in. It's newer than some, too, with knotted pine wood planks that cannot have more than two seasons of wear—grey on the edges with streaks of yellow in the center yet. A loft is filled with the tousled heads of the other children, and the husband is nowhere to be seen—I must assume he is already far into his morning chores. The child Perry is on bedding made of two square bales of hay smashed together and covered with linens in front of the hearth, as if keeping him warm will stave off the violent chills he might be suffering.

When I approach, though, I fight everything inside of my blood to keep from recoiling, and I hug Andrew so tight that he gives a squeak.

Perry cannot be more than seven years old. The boy Ben says he is too young for much responsibility, and the boy's job is to mostly keep track of the family's dogs in the fields and woods on their property. Little Perry wanders often, but the family never worries, as he is always with their three hounds, or on the outskirts of the cattle pen, where the dogs often are sent to watch over the livestock, especially in the evenings when the coyotes prowl most often. He's small and round-faced, with the same long and lean look of his big brother.

But the limbs are listless, and the fingers are a mottled grey-black. Worse is the mouth, which looks as if it has pulled back from the teeth with decayed flesh. As the boy pants, his tongue lolls out thick and furred, and his gums look as if they, too are receding.

Patrick has mentioned this, described it in detail, and I have read about it in *The Collected Works* of Dr. P.M. Latham, but to see gangrene in the flesh is far more terrifying than I ever could imagine.

Fearing the worst, I glance at the boy's skin, and see the telltale black flecks blooming across his arms and neck, buried under his skin, but no less obvious.

It is the black measles.

Swallowing the sticky bile clawing up my throat and filling my cheeks, I turn to Mrs. Woodman and offer her a sympathetic grimace.

"I see what you mean—he is indeed beyond pain right now. How long has he been so ill?"

She shrugs, and wearily goes to her cupboards to pull out tin cups. "A couple days, maybe."

Biting back the retort that she might have asked for Doctor Kinney sooner, I nod, and pull a chair from the table without asking. Sinking down, I give her an apologetic look.

"I'll have to feed my infant."

She gestures and nods, the understanding between two mothers something I believe I'll never take for granted, and then pours me water from a tin pitcher. I re-open my bodice for Andrew, keeping him well under the protective layer of my shawl, and steel myself for another view of Perry.

His chest rises fast and low. It is too fast. Surely there must be a fever, and there will be aches, and perhaps even some discomfort in his belly. I try to recall everything Patrick and Esther describe about the disease, and whether anything Patrick tried has helped. But I can only think of all his losses to black measles, the low success rate he's had, and the defeat he's suffered when battling it.

One glance at Mrs. Woodman has me firm my resolve. She stares at Perry as if her own heart will give out if he dies, and I believe I can understand that horrible fear, for I live with my own source of it in my arms now. How would I fare if I lost my son? Or worse, one who has spent years under my eyes, growing and delighting, and then snatched away? I know children pass away often—I do not know a single mother in Flats Junction who has not lost a child or more—myself included. But I do not believe the loss gets easier with practice. And who knows how many this woman has already lost in infancy?

Yes, Patrick has not had much success fighting black measles, but I have other medicines in my bag that he does not, and perhaps one of them will work. It is worth attempting.

When Andrew is full and drowsy, I place him on the Woodman's bed to sleep, and approach Perry again. I force myself not to focus on the disgusting flesh of his mouth and fingers and toes, and instead open my case and pull out the leaves of big sagebrush and dried rosemary. What had Esther said? The rosemary will … kill a fever? And sage for the gums, to be sure. It should heal wounds. That I recall.

"May I trouble you for some hot water to make a few teas?" I ask Mrs. Woodman.

"Tea?" She looks doubtful. "For you?"

"For Perry," I say. "Some of the herbs from my garden can help."

She does as I ask, and I pull out the swamp milkweed as well, which Esther made from boiling the leaves with water, then adding it to lard and heating it. She says any animal fat will work as well as lard, and while I don't know if there's any hope for the boy's skin, there is nothing to do but try.

Cringing inside, I begin to rub the ointment into his toes. The flesh is spongy and feels wrong under my fingers. It must be painful still, as Perry makes tiny noises, though they are more whispering rasp than gasps of pain.

My stomach clenches with my clumsy handling of this—though I keep my hands busy, I know deep down there is too little to be done, and all of it too late. I cannot ease his sharp breath, or the fever that burns him. When

Mrs. Woodman brings me hot water, and I steep the sage leaves, Perry cannot even swallow much, and it dribbles out of the sides of his damaged mouth.

If I were alone, I would wring my hands and shake my head, but it will do only harm and worry Natalie Woodman if I say it is a lost cause … even if it is.

The hours roll by, and Perry's lungs slowly collapse into themselves. Soon the fast breathing turns to slower and less often, and his skin turns a yellowy ash.

"Is there anything else to be done?" Natalie asks at last. She has kept herself active as well, feeding her other children and her husband, none of which have much to say to me. They all glance fearfully at Perry, though the daughters coo over Andrew when he is awake.

I rise from the prickly straw of the makeshift cot, but keep an eye on Perry instead of Mrs. Woodman. From above, it is clear he is not doing well at all. The sight tickles at my memory, tugging at a long-forgotten thread I've tucked far away.

"I've used what I've brought," I say honestly. "Now we just wait."

But as I speak, Perry gives one hard exhale, and in the ringing silence afterward, the heat of shock, dismay, and disbelief makes the blood running in the veins behind my ears feel tight, as if my head is constricting and my body protesting. I want to grab Andrew and run all the way back to town. I want to shake the little boy and make him breathe again. I want …

I did not want to fail.

Not like this.

"Oh, baby," Mrs. Woodman says, her gaze glued to Perry's still frame. "It's over, ain't it, Mrs. Kinney? He's gone."

She sinks to the ground by the hay bales and gathers the boy up, ignoring the putrid pieces of his skin and pressing his face into her neck to rock him. The wrongness of it, of seeing a little boy without the spark of life, sends another rack of tremors through my body, and it's all I can do not to rush to Andrew to make sure he still breathes.

Before I can offer a word of comfort to the grieving mother, there's barking and voices outside the door, which opens with Mr. Woodman and Patrick speaking lowly as they enter.

I turn, pressing my hands to the sides of my thighs to avoid running to the doctor and begging for my own embrace. His eyes meet mine across the kitchen and in a moment he knows. His shoulders sink, and the bags under his eyes seem heavier, weighing on the usual spark in his blue eyes.

Pulling off his Stetson and running a hand through his dark hair, he turns to the father and claps him on the shoulder.

"I'm sorry, Nathan."

"Sor—" Mr. Woodman suddenly understands, his haggard frame winding itself inward as his head swings from Patrick to his kneeling wife. Without another word, he clumps in muddy work boots over to where his son drapes against his mother's shoulder, eyes half-open and bones sagging, and puts a shaking hand on Perry's head.

I say nothing more as Patrick speaks to the parents about contacting him should any others come down with the black speckled spots, and I gather up Andrew as Patrick grabs my satchel. He takes our babe in his arms so I might ride more comfortably, and I think perhaps he only wants to reassure himself as well that Andrew is hale and healthy. When we are both on Patrick's horse and halfway back to Flats Junction proper, I finally break my silence.

"How are the cattle?"

He does not move, and for a moment, I think the doctor has fallen asleep on horseback. I twist to glance at him, and am surprised at how utterly exhausted he looks. He must not have had a single moment of sleep at the Brinkley farm.

"Not all are dead," he says at last. "But it is not over yet."

"Will you be able to help?"

"I don't know, Janie," he says. In the late afternoon, the light is warmer than the cold sorrow in his voice. "I thought things were lookin' up at last. That we were findin' a place here. I know how to fight most of the diseases and illnesses folks catch, but this … with the cows and now black measles already, this early? I just don't know."

"No one expects miracles, Patrick," I say, but I realize I expect just that— that the herbs from Esther would be some sort of wonderful discovery. It would solve so many troubles, to be able to win against the unknown illness.

"They do, though," he says quietly.
He's right.
I have a taste for it, too, now.
I understand what it is to hope to find one.

CHAPTER 4

Kate

March 10, 1884

A grand opening should be grand. And while I don't want to be beholden to anyone to make it so, there's only so much a single body can do to make it fancy and fine, so I take myself to Helena and our dress shop behind Sadie and Tom Fawcett's house and open the latch without knocking.

"Miss Davies!" Helena says, looking up and around the bulk of Elaine Warren. Elaine looms over the sewing machine, all ownership and swelling up with pride, though her bosom has a fair chance of being caught up in the needle and spinning wheel if Helena takes to pressing the treadle by accident.

"Kate," Elaine says, turning at once. "I heard you're planning on a very fine party when you mark your store as fully finished at last."

"Hard to believe it's been so many months," I say. The words are gritty between my teeth, smashing like tiny rocks and grinding. "You know I'm still open some, but this will be making it official, and I'm bringing in particular items."

Elaine's eyes gleam under her steely hair. "Like what?"

"Ah … a new wringer machine." I haven't ordered this yet, though I saw it in a catalogue last year. But if she says she wants it, I'll send for it, and only tell her it was delayed.

"What about one of them newfangled ice boxes?" she asks, leaning forward. It's like she read my mind. Wasn't I just speculating on this the other day?

"I didn't think you'd be up for the expense."

"Well," she says. "Willy's been wanting one for years, but his ma said no."

"And what about you?"

Her eyes go crafty and she near leers. "I don't take my orders from Toot, even if she does do the cooking at the Nail. 'Sides, it's his birthday this summer."

I guess I am better at knowing the folks of Flats Junction than I even figured. I'm nodding before I'm talking, doing the numbers on how soon I might get one out, and if I do, should I just go and order two? Joe might be up for one once he hears Trusty Willy has an ice box at The Golden Nail. I might be able to split the cost and wiggle my way in to fixing up the Prime Inn after all if I play it just so. Percy always did say there's a back door to anything, if only you're looking sideways.

"Are you finished with your order?" I ask Elaine, gesturing for her to go back to Helena. "Or picking up?"

"Came to check on the machine," she says. I give her credit not to call it *my machine*. She doesn't need to, really. Everyone knows she invested in it, bringing the first one to Flats Junction and making Helena even more effective as a seamstress as I had originally planned. Granted, such a gift does not come without expectations. Even Helena can understand that.

"Missus Warren, I should be getting the latest patterns in the next mail delivery on the train," Helena says. Her voice is always a strange mixture of certainty and submissiveness. I wish I could copy it, as it suits well. "I'll be sure to let you know when it arrives."

Elaine swells up further and a grin traces across her jowls before she nods and sweeps out of the tiny space. I spin toward Helena and raise my eyebrows at her simplistic pose.

"Am I to believe you will only get a singular pattern?" I ask.

She raises her eyes to mine. "I didn't think you would mind."

"What of the grand opening of the General?" I ask. "Is there something special to be done? A new skirt or a fancy sleeve?"

"I'll wait to hear from my friends," Helena says. "They find it especially a delight to tell me what is in fashion, as if that makes them part of something outside of their own city. All of them think I'm wild, to live out here, where there are savages and bandits."

"Mmm," I say, fingering a piece of very thin lace, which is also thick at the same time. It is woven with cotton thread that has not been bleached, and the detailing reminds me of spider webs and the lines of leaves. "And do you write them that it is so?"

"I might embellish it a bit," she admits, and meets my eyes straight. "They seem to find it very wicked to learn about cowboys and hangings."

I go on and ignore her jabs about Bern Masson's death, and instead pluck at a bright plaid poking out from one of her baskets. "This is pretty."

"Yes," she hedges. Her fingers pause over the rustling silk, and then she comes around to kneel by her cot. Pulling out another box, she opens it with something like reverence. She is very careful when she unfolds the fabric, which has been covered by pale brown tissue that crinkles and cracks in the little room. I'm about ready to touch the shimmering cloth, but she makes a fast and hard sound, so I jerk back real quick.

"I bought this, not knowing when I'd use it, but it was too pretty not to bring some back," she says. "It's called faille—from France."

The soft blue begs to be felt with all that fine delicate ribbing, but I hold off. She seems to think it's especially fine, and I've never heard of it myself, neither. I bet Elaine and Sadie Fawcett haven't, too.

"It's plain," I say, my eyes darting over to the bright plaid.

"It's meant to be, so the details show," she says. "I'd pair this with rose silk, maybe in the waistcoat, black velvet ribbons and I bet I can even come up with one of the little black felt hats. If only there was time to get a pink ostrich feather for it …" Her eyes go glassy with the dreamy look, and I find myself wondering how she'll cut it all to look so fine.

"I might be able to get some in from Chicago," I say slowly. "Maybe."

She focuses again, and runs one tip of a prickly finger along the aqua softness. "I would do it in the tighter style, which isn't very … accommodating to fast walking. But you will cut the finest figure in Flats Junction."

"You've the pattern for it?" I ask.

"I don't need one exactly for it," she says. "I remember enough. It was in one of the fashion plates just in. No one had made it yet, it was just in from Paris. It'll only be difficult because we'll have to make you a bustle."

"No one wears those," I dismiss.

Her eyebrows go up, and a small smirk makes the corners of her mouth go up and down as she tries hiding it. "They do in the cities, the fashionable girls. It's back, I promise you, and different than before. It's not a bunch of draping fabric, but there's a structure that ties to your waist and goes backward. It's rigid. Mother might have to help construct it."

The idea of Marie Salomon helping build my undergarments makes me pause. But then the notion of walking out of the General store on the official grand opening in a pristine, French designed dress has me nodding and agreeing, even though I still can't see the final design in my mind. But Helena is ecstatic, and she takes a few more measurements of my waist and bosom to add to the list she keeps on me and sends me off to order the promised ostrich feathers.

Then there's nothing for it but to take my foolish self to the post office and send a note to the mercantile in Yankton and Chicago for the feathers.

Nancy Ofsberger, the postmistress, looks at me with her mouth wide open as I dictate the letter, so much so I can see she's a back molar that's going grey and can smell how she's been drinking dark tea all morning without eating breakfast to wash it down.

"You're wanting what?" she asks, her big blue eyes going so wide I'm afraid they'll pop outward and never go back in. "How's somebody going to go kill themselves a pink ostray-ch?"

"I don't believe they are different colors," I say, hoping I sound like I know something of the world. I should've had Helena put in the order instead. "I think it's dyed, like any fabric."

"Who's gonna buy these fancy-fine trimmings, anyhow?" she says, still looking a tad bit shocked as she goes back to scribbling.

"No one," I say. "They're for me. For the Grand Opening."

"Oh, tell on, I've heard everyone talking on that," she says.

"Good." Let them chatter on, and with Nancy knowing the feathers are for me, now even that will be added into the excitement. She'll make sure of it.

"That all said," she says, glancing slyly at her sleeping father-in-law in the corner rocker. "At least it's legal."

"What's not?" I ask.

Nancy leans forward over her counter, mussing the corner of the paper with my letter with her wide shoulders and hanging bosom. I suppose that happens after suckling five children, though. Bosoms give up and get tired, even with corsets.

"Some folks 'round here are using ways not to get knocked up no more," she half-whispers. There's no one else in the post office save me and her and the sleeping old George, who's hard of hearing even when he's awake. "Contraceptionals … all of that sort of thing."

"You mean rubbers?" I ask bluntly.

Nancy yanks back, as if my bald words are catching and might stick to her. But I'm not so innocent as someone might think. I've had a few men in my bed, not that I've used such things when I did. But I'm aware.

She turns a peachy-red, and huffs, then folds my letter up and twists the sides so it's nice and snug. "Well, them things is illegal to send by mail," she says. I think she's more miffed I'm not shocked and awed than anything. "Government says."

I can only guess one person who might be asking for such items, and I'm surprised Patrick Kinney thinks to stave off children for him and Jane, especially when they've married so late in life and need to keep moving if they want a house full.

The weight of time on my own shoulders suddenly nudges my mind, reminding me of my own silent bedroom and quiet life when the General door is locked and there's nothing but a lantern light and old coffee to keep me company.

"That new Doc Smith has set up a box, too," Nancy says. She leers for a moment. "With that eye patch, he's sure a dashing charmer. Looks like a pirate."

"A pirate!" My mouth feels like it'll burst with the laugh I'm holding in. "Don't let him hear you say that. We don't want to run him off. He says he wants to stay."

"Oh, so he says. He comes by every other day to chat, mind. A good sort of man, to spend time with us regular folks. *He's* not ordering illegals," she says.

"He seems a serious doctor," I agree.

"Might be, though he's yet to get a single letter come through."

"Maybe it's just slow, coming from out east."

"Well, and this all reminds me," Nancy remembers, her finger twirling. "You've a letter yourself."

She takes it out of the larger of the boxes in the wall behind her, slots and holes built by Douglas before he died. The envelope is open, and I give Nancy a tired glance as I turn it around. She pretends not to notice I can tell she's snooped, but I suppose I'm glad she treats me and my mail no different than any other in Flats Junction.

Besides, all irritable itchiness disappears when I see who's finally writing me back.

Black Hills Corporation.

"They're from Deadwood," Nancy says, nodding at the letter. "But they ain't sure Flats Junction is worth their trouble."

"Thank you," I say, letting tartness round out my voice as I depart before she can give up more of the letter's contents. I unfold the paper as fast as I can on the front step of the post office and frown as I scan it, then go back and work careful like over the words. They use a fine cursive and big vocabulary, but after the third time through I've figured on it.

As Nancy says, the businessmen in Deadwood have indeed brought electricity to Deadwood, and now would be up for considering an expansion of their influence. I'd written them on a whim, on a half idea. Nancy had thought my letter too short to be worth sending when I'd brought it over, but I didn't want her re-writing it and messing it up. I might not have the fine penmanship, nor know the fancy words and curls to a capital W, but it was important they heard from me directly first.

To be truthful, I didn't even believe they'd respond to a woman writing.

But maybe they're like me, and looking for a way to make another dollar and build a bigger world for themselves, and they'll work with anyone who's serious.

And I am.

I'm ready to build something so big that even without children holding my name and nose, I'm leaving behind roots and legacy. So, who now would want electricity? Fort Randall, I'd bet. Would Joe allow electric lights at the Prime Inn? Could I convince Elaine and Toot to put some into The Golden Nail?

Another truth is I'll need support from someone folks'll listen to, and there's only one old man left in Flats Junction that harks back to my father's time. Before I can second guess myself again, my feet head off easterly toward the Brinkley farm, where their ranch spreads out wide and takes up all the grazing land northeasterly, too. I even make it past the Svendsen bunkhouse without Moses Thompson spying me, and without Jane calling out for me to stop in to see the new babe or my own mother.

Yet as I place my boots in the shallowest ruts of the road, there's a crunch behind me, as a man's boots scuff the smaller rocks that aren't mucked up with dirt.

I spin, and take in the tall line and hard shoulders of Doctor Thomas Smith himself, who looks a bit out of place in the rugged new spring of the prairie, with his shiny top hat and well-cut suit. The eyepatch makes him look dashing and frightening, and a bit over-manly, but I don't know if I want to see what his eye socket looks like under it. How many years has he lived without an eye? How can he do doctoring with only the one working?

"Doc Smith," I say, smiling a bit and nodding up at him. "What brings you out this way?"

He steps next to me, offering his arm in a gentleman's way. I wonder if I should take it, and how, but he helps by tugging up my palm and putting it through his elbow, like a thread through a needle hole. It feels very fine and city-like to stroll this way.

"I admit I saw you walking," he says, tipping his hat an inch lower. "And I thought perhaps you would not mind the company again, if not some sort of protection."

"Ha!" I cough up the laugh. "It's the west, and everyone here knows me on sight. I'm not in real danger."

"Is that so?" he says mildly, but I can't read him. Maybe it's because he's new and I don't know him well, or because he's got on that mask men wear when they feel unsettled. I've only known a few men who don't wear such a thing, and instead give the world their immediate thoughts. One is Thaddeus Salomon, who I'm sure looks angry even when he's bedding Marie, and the other is Pat, who now only really looks at Jane …

"… to turn back, if you wish," Doc Smith says, looking back toward Flats Junction. His steps slow, but I pull him on.

"I'm off to see Old Henry Brinkley," I tell him. "He's like the mayor here, ever since my father passed, and most everyone will listen to what he agrees."

"And what are you hoping to accomplish with his backing?"

"I'm hoping he'll go with me on bringing in electricity to Flats Junction." The idea feels too huge now that I'm saying it out loud. I sneak a glance up at Doc Smith, who is keeping his eye mostly on the road. I wonder if he thinks it ridiculous, that a half-breed like me is making up such grand plans.

"Electricity here would be extraordinary," he says. But he doesn't say it like it's an impossibility, which I like more than I expect. "It could change lives."

"Speaking of change, why did you come here? It must be different—a change, as you say—from the big cities. You fixing to keep heading west, then?"

"I suppose you could say I'm interested in seeing what the west holds for doctors and medicine. The cities are overcrowded with physicians, and the politics that go with them. I'd rather try my hand where I'm needed. Where a hospital is needed."

His notion lands on me like a thunderbolt, and my steps trip over themselves. I'm glad for his arm, so I don't take a knee in the muck of spring, and yet he seems to understand what I'm gasping on about, because he turns to me while we walk and smiles so wide it makes the creases around his mouth go deep and dark.

"You are pleased with the thought of a hospital?"

"Pleased? It would make our dot on the map a big one!"

"Indeed," he says. "Certainly."

"And we'd definitely be needing that electricity, then," I say, warming up fast to the idea. The way my heart's going, too, makes me think I might go sideways if I don't drink a glass of water soon enough. A hospital! I hadn't even thought of something so large, so permanent!

"That would be ideal," he says. He's all calm and mild, as if he hasn't just tipped my mind upside down!

"And the commander would be happy, too, having such a medical place only ten miles from Fort Randall." All the ideas come racing down from the top of my head, through my neck and across the back of my shoulders. I suddenly feel so powerful with all my notions, how I can see the spread of Flats Junction five years into the future, that I'm sure if I lift up, I might be as bright as the sun. It's like filling up with so much energy I'm like to crackle if I open my palms.

"Then I suppose we are like-minded," Doc Smith says. The way he speaks this makes my stomach clench. I want to believe that he thinks so, that he's not just saying these fine words because they're what a gentleman would say in a dressed-up parlor. "Now, is this the place?"

We're at the Brinkley's already. The walk is always faster than I think, with the farm only a half mile east of the town, and I lead Doc Smith over to the largest of the houses on the ranch, which is where Old Henry and Susan live yet, even with their children all fanning out and building up their own little homes nearby. The farm itself has the road running through it, with four other houses on the property and an unending stretch of farm fields that hits the end in the distance, where the fences mark the near edge of the Svendsen ranch. Sometimes I think if they had their way, they'd start their own town right here on their land, but it'd only be full of relations, which would be troublesome in the end.

Old Henry Brinkley, the patriarch of the Brinkley clan, reclines on the porch just like Horeb and Gilroy do when the weather is fine. He is an average man, balding, slightly paunchy and reaching eighty. How he has lived so long with all of the heavy, hard work of farming, I'll never know, and it's probably beyond doctoring know-how, too. Susan's a stout woman with snow-white hair, who has also somehow survived the birth of eleven children and likely a few miscarriages. She is waiting for us too by the time we reach the porch.

"How have you all been?" I ask.

"Fine enough, excepting for my gout," Old Henry complains, reciting his one trouble. His hands fold over his round belly and his gouty feet prop up on a small block of wood.

From inside the house, the smell of hot bread and roasting onions trails from the half-open door. There's no way around noting how the Brinkleys are wealthy, and successful, with so many heads of cattle I cannot keep track of the count. They have somehow reached a truce with the equally wealthy Svendsens – and for all I've lived in Flats Junction my entire life, there has never been a direct quarrel between the two men in charge. The cowboys and farmhands, however, tend to have some issues on occasion, and the jokes can turn to legend, like the time Hank Martin fell asleep visiting Fortuna's brothel, but he didn't know Thunder, the oldest and most grizzled of the local hired hands, had come in between and had both Tilly and Meggie at the same time, but promised Hank'd pay their wage later. Hank woke, not remembering a thing, but sandwiched between two very buxom naked women demanding money. The way Fortuna tells it, she had him work in the kitchen for the entire next weekend he was in town just to help pay it off.

"What can we do you for, Kate?" Old Henry asks comfortably.

"First, you might like to meet Doctor Thomas Smith," I say, waving my hand at Doc Smith to come up the stairs. "He's been in a few days from out east."

"Another doc, eh?" Old Henry eyes up Doc Smith with bleary eyes. "What makes this one any different?"

"I'm certainly nothing like your Doctor Kinney," Doc Smith says.

My body pauses, and I wonder just how much this doctor has learned about Flats Junction in these past days. He says Patrick's name so casual, without any surprise, as if he has no trouble coming into a town where another doc's territory is staked. It's like he's not even worrying on competition.

Maybe he doesn't plan to stay after all, then.

My chest deflates just a bit at the thought that his big dream of a hospital was only conversation after all.

Susan disappears inside the house, and comes back almost immediately with some cold tea and biscuits, but I cannot stomach the food while I'm staring at Henry's feet.

I'm no trained nurse or physician, and I've seen some blood being around Patrick's surgery that the sight of it doesn't bother me so bad. But gout? I want to gag. The joints of Henry's toes and ankles are red and swollen, the skin stretched so tightly that it makes my own ache in response.

"Have you tried a poultice for it?" I ask as I jerk my chin at his feet, thinking to some of the herbal treatments Widow Hawks used to make when we all lived under a single roof.

"If I may?" Doc Smith bends down to one knee smoothly and picks up Old Henry's foot swift and light. Henry hisses through his teeth, but lets the doctor touch his skin. It would make Patrick's teeth grind to see how Doc Smith swoops in, especially with Pat trying to get healing on Henry's ailments and only allowed to help with the cattle and the youngest Brinkley's wife.

"We always did bread soaked in milk," Susan offers.

"Does it work?" Doc Smith asks, inspecting the other foot, too.

She shrugs and puts a hand on Henry's sloping shoulder. "Sometimes. Only it's gotten so bad nothing works."

"It's not any worse than usual," the old farmer argues, settling his arms further over his stomach.

"Hm," she hums her disapproval. "You can barely walk anymore."

"If I might offer a suggestion," Doc Smith says, getting up and looming over Old Henry. He does it in a bent-over way, though, not with menace. I watch him open his jacket and pull out a pad of paper and a pencil stub. "There is a place further west, a Doctor Hunter manages it. He has proprietary ownership of an ancient healing water source, which you can purchase and drink against all sorts of ailments—rheumatism, colic, gout. If I may write to him, perhaps he might ship a bottle or two for you, so you don't have to make the journey beyond the Bozeman Pass."

"Healing waters, you say?" Old Henry squints. "Well, it ain't hacking off my feet, so that's a start. Send for it, and I'll drink it."

"Very good," Doc Smith jots in his small book and tucks it back. He gives me a small nod, and gestures forward, and I'm reminded that this whole trip is for my own ends. Maybe his offer to help the gout will put Old Henry in a fine mood to listen more than usual.

"I've been thinking on a grand plan," I say, trying to find my footing. "Thought you might like to hear of it first off."

"The bread is done, as is the meal," Susan interrupts. She opens up the door, and spreads her doughy fingers. "Perhaps you might like to have your midday meal with us and speak on it inside. After a while, the spring air gets a bit chilly anyway."

I shrug at Doc Smith and Susan leads me through the back door and into the farmhouse kitchen. Behind us, I can hear the doctor helping Old Henry get to standing.

I've never been inside the main house. Like everything else in Flats Junction, the building is made of wood. Always wood. But it's faded and soft, and the inside has the peaty, deeply weathered scent of a thousand fires and even more meals. And Susan has decorated right fine, too. Creamy, flower curtains brace the walls around each small window, and there are oval rugs near the hearth. She's had a bread oven built in next to the fireplace, and the stove is immense. As I gaze at the fifteen iron skillets hanging on the wall, I almost laugh aloud. So many! For such a big family! That's what wealth looks like.

And there's richness in the plump bedding in the side room and the down in the pillows. But it's more than that. It's a life, all tangled up and earthy, and more than I'll ever know.

We sit at the big table, which looks strange with so many chairs so empty, and Susan explains how it's spring planting and everyone's eating out in the fields these days. I'm glad for it, because it means I only have to explain my news to the ears of two Brinkleys instead of getting the opinions of all of them at the once.

It's only tea and bread with cheese and onions for lunch, but it's good and the onions are new and sweet and layered with salt and a dash of cinnamon.

"I'm working to bring in the Black Hills Corporation," I tell him. "For electricity in Flats Junction. Anyone can latch onto it. Just think—lights in all the inns, the eateries, the churches—."

"And who's paying for such a thing?" Henry asks, slapping butter on his second slice of bread. It spreads like milk, the cream new and not yet set.

"Each business here. And perhaps the Fort. And … the new hospital would need it, too."

"The *what?*" Old Henry near chokes on his bite. "For *what?*"

I spare Doc Smith a tiny glance, but he's placing onions on his own bread in a very careful way, as if each one is something surgical. I wish he'd join in and speak on his topic, as he'd know more about the plans, but I figure I can manage the beginnings.

"Well, if Flats Junction is able to support electricity, it can have a hospital built."

"Now see here, just because I'm fine drinking some fancy medicine here and there don't mean I'm up for listening to a sawbones, let alone two of 'em!" Old Henry puts down his knife with a hard snap.

Susan meets my gaze, but I don't know her well enough to tell if she wants me to keep talking or stop.

"You're the mayor—or near enough like—and if you want to see this town on the map, we need to grow it. I'd do it myself, but no one listens—."

"Oh, we listen fine to you sometimes," Old Henry growls. "And things burn, people get near killed, and a man gets hung. Now you wanting, what? My place in town? No one'll listen to you, girl, no matter who your papa was."

This is not working at all how I thought it might go, though I'm thinking I didn't really know how it would, and maybe the bit about the hospital was too fast, and too outlandish.

I push up from the table, leaving half the meal there. Doc Smith shoves a big chunk of his bread in and stands in a rush as well.

"Well, just think on the electricity," I say. My voice is high—too high— but this means more to me than I can explain. I need to build this up. This is bigger even than owning the General or helping Helena's business or taking over half the Prime Inn. This is … forever.

Doc Smith and I are only just off the porch when there's a ruckus and a shout and the banging of too many hooves moving too fast. I turn while walking, and the doctor does so too. There's no reason not to be nosy now that we're out here.

Most of the Brinkley brothers and a bunch of their hired hands are rushing in from one of the fields. Even with the bit of distance, I see Mitch is the first to lift himself up out of the saddle and wave a hand, and by the time he and his brothers get to the porch, he's sliding off his mount to rush up the porch and past his waiting mother. His shout is loud enough I can hear it carry past the old rattling fall grass and spring flowers.

"It's worse!" he shouts into the house. "Pa—so many head are plumb dead."

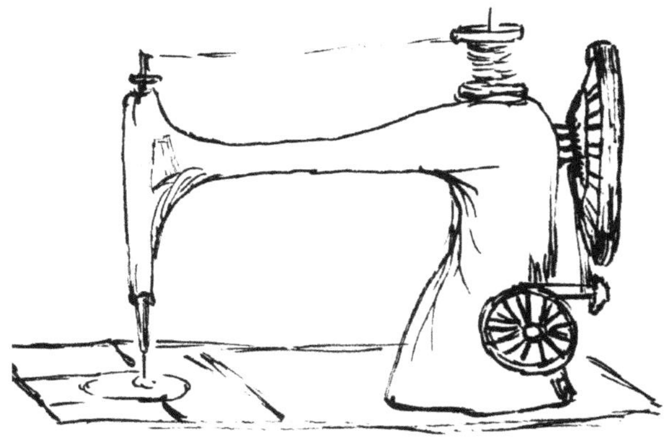

CHAPTER 5

Helena

April 4, 1884

For how much he works, Doctor Patrick Kinney is not a very wealthy man. Hardy has told me that it's because the doctor takes payment in all sorts of ways—leeks and next year's seed, recently butchered chicken and milk and promises. And yet he's pre-paid me in cash for a lovely new bodice for his wife. A secret, I guess, until it's time for me to fit her proper to it. Still, it's … oh, romantic. I pluck a small piece of fuzz from the lavender trimming, and turn the pale yellow sleeves inside out to add a thin band of lace to the sleeves. Imagine a husband ordering a wife some clothes! My own father never bought

Mother anything, though the small tools he makes her for Christmas make her eyes shine as if it's the grandest gift a woman could get.

As I jerk the needle through the calico lining, the door to my tiny kingdom opens, and the spring air blows in Hardy, as if he's appearing just as I thought of him.

I look up at him through my eyelashes as he steadies himself, as if unsure if he can move at all in a place that is so obviously feminine—spools of ribbon colored like a rainbow or zipping with strips in various colors, velvet and satin, silk and muslin. But he gets his bearing quick, and slowly strolls the couple of steps toward the sewing machine. Slipping his hands into his pockets, he watches, silent and patient, and for a bit I keep on stitching just to see how long he waits.

Hardy didn't last too long as my father's apprentice in the blacksmith shop, and it's a good thing too as he had no touch for the iron or bellows. Anyone with eyes could see that, and my two younger brothers will take over for Father sometime anyway when he decides to let them. Hardy was more helpful when my brother Kaspar was hurt in the General's fire, putting on plaster and medicine so that Kaspar could rejoin Father and Natan at the forge eventually, healed up at last except for thick scars he'll wear for life. It was a smart trade, not that anyone asked me my thoughts, but Hardy just can't stop walking around with a little smile under the early blonde beard he's working on, and he's got it on now as he watches my fingers.

"Doc Kinney's teaching me how to sew up skin," he says suddenly. "It's near the same as what you do there."

The notion of sewing up muscle with thread makes me gag deep in my throat, but I swallow the extra spit and look up at him at last.

"Do you want some pointers and advice, then?" I ask.

"No, no," he says quick and fast, the pale skin turning a deep pink quickly, and then just as fast fading. "Just … making conversation and so."

"I hope you're not here to pick up the doc's order," I say. "I told him it'd take a bit, plus I need Mrs. Kinney in for a final fitting."

"He didn't send me," he says. His fingers dig deeper into his pockets as he rocks back onto his heels.

My eyebrows go up. "Just stopping for a chat? I didn't think apprentice docs had free time to spare."

"Mrs. Kinney says I might sometimes see friends. She says a boy should still sometimes be a boy," he explains.

"So you're on your way to see Kaspar and Natan, then?" I bite off the end of the thread and flip the bodice back around.

"I ah … thought I'd see you. First, like," he says, his eyes glancing about, bouncing from shelf to cot. There's nowhere for him to sit but on that cot, and he seems unable to take the seat. Then I think on how it would be, to have a young man setting himself on my own bed where I sleep, and I realize I'm blushing foolish, too.

"How has it been, since," he starts, stops, swallows loud and goes on. "Since you went east and then come on back."

"Mother and Father have not smacked me for it yet," I say lightly. "Mother's even pleased with the tin pieces I brought back from the stamping company."

He dips his head, and the old small grin flits back. "They were fine pieces, what we saw in that catalogue."

"I'm glad you showed me," I tell him. "I've never been able to thank you before, but that made things better for me when I got back home."

"Did it?" He suddenly flares a brilliant red, but it's the light in his pale eyes that shines more than his cheeks. "Oh, I'm … plumb thrilled on that, Helena."

"I wouldn't have made it half as far had you not told me the tricks of city travel, too," I say, feeling strange to finally talk about our quiet conversations, spoken in fits and spurts in the weeks we lived under my parents' roof.

He shrugs his shoulders up, holds them, and lets them drop fast. "Riding the rails was harder, I'd guess, than the fancy fine railcars you used with Kate's dime. But it helps to know how it all works."

I put down the sewing and look up at him, truly look. Now that I've a few minutes alone with him at last, for the first time in months, I pull up the list of questions I'd thought while going east to gather patterns and build relationships with a modiste or dressmakers in the cities. It would have been impossible, scary, beyond my knowing had he not told me the way of the world.

"You jumped rail cars from Chicago to Flats Junction," I repeat. "Why? I never asked you why you came here."

"I wasn't planning on here, exactly," he says, looking longingly at the cot one more time. "It was just … I was heading west to find my pa."

"What? So … you're not an orphan?"

"Oh, no, as far as I know, I am. He's likely dead, anyhow," Hardy says, looking a bit miserable for a moment, and then shrugging again. "But no one knows, so I figured I'd just see what I could find. Then Miss Kate offered me the apprenticeship idea with your Pa, and I thought it might be good to learn myself a trade."

"What's his name?"

"Who?" he asks, shifting his footing.

"Your Pa."

"Same as mine, I guess."

"Well, there's no one round here called Hardy, except you," I remind him.

"My ma used to call me by it." He looks down at the tips of his boots, which have a rim of mud around the ankles, where he must have stepped in a puddle and let the mud from it dry. "Gerhardt Wagner is the formal, but …" He brings up his gaze to meet mine. "It's too fine a name for someone like me."

"When you're a doctor, you'll use it," I say firmly, and poke another length of thread through the needle head. "It'll sound grand then—Doctor Gerhardt Wagner. Doc Wagner." The words roll around my tongue and tingle. It does sound grand. And it's near unbelievable that this chunk of a young man will use it, with his head of thick yellow hair and sausage fingers and easy blush. Though come to think of it, he never gets red when I've seen him help Doc Kinney, the few times they're visiting Sadie Fawcett's boys across the yard. He looks earnest then, and serious. It might just be believable, then.

"I hope I do build up a practice like Doc Kinney," he tells me. "I'd like a house with a surgery room, and an office, just like his. And a medical kit from out east. He's saving up for a microscope, too, and I'd get me one of them, too, maybe newer and better. Oh, and I'd have a nurse to help, and a cabinet just for patient folders, and a whole stock of medicinals …"

I'm seeing it in my mind, too, as he talks about it, though I'm seeing it with the curtains at the windows and the rugs by each door, and the smell of baking beans from the kitchen. I'm just about to tell him, when I realize how it'll sound, me daydreaming along with him, and I screw my mouth shut before I give any ideas I'm not ready to offer.

It makes me feel just a bit dizzy, too, to realize what I'm thinking on.

Really, he's just like me, talking up the future, and goals for a bigger life. I'm like that too. I'm building up a business for dresses and gowns like Flats Junction has never seen the like. That's all it is, kindred business folks, thinking ahead …

"Speaking on what the future might bring," I interrupt. "Kate says the new doc in town, Doc Smith, wants to build a hospital here."

Hardy's eyes go wide, and he pulls out his hands as if to clench something, but has nothing to grab, so he just holds onto his elbows tight.

"A hospital?" he whistles. "For us all to work in?"

"I don't know if it's for all the doctors," I say, realizing I might have spoken too soon on this. "And it's just talk right now."

"How does Kate think to tell you this?" he asks.

"I meet her for dinner once a week, to go over the business," I say, waving my hand around the small, packed room. "She is the biggest investor in the seamstress endeavor, after all."

Hardy chews on his bottom lip, then twists it, all glimmer of his grin gone. "Ought I … should I be telling this to Doc Kinney? I don't want to upset him."

"Maybe not?" I hedge, wishing now it wasn't so free and easy to tell Hardy anything jumping into my mind. "Wait and see, it might come to nothing." I glance down at Jane Kinney's bodice, and my eyes fall on the tiny clock I string to my waist, the face hardly visible in the fast fading spring evening. "Speaking of, I'm late. You've got to go."

I stand and clear my skirts.

"Go where?" he looks around the room, as if it might suddenly expand out.

"As I said, I'm meeting Kate for dinner at the Nail, as we do each week." It's our second week doing so, as it is, but Hardy doesn't have to know this.

Besides, I'm strangely hot with him here now. It's probably because I just told him something that maybe should be kept quiet. "And you were going to see my brothers."

"Oh. Right," he says. His eyes stay down, though he moves to the door. "I'll walk you. The Nail's near enough your folks."

"I can go myself. It's not far." I want him gone, fast, before he can see how I twitch with him only a few feet away. "I should freshen up and put on a hat, maybe, and …" I cast about for more excuses to pile on, but Hardy seems to read me as well as a book and pushes the door open to let himself out.

"If you're sure. I can wait, otherwise," he says slowly. "Whatever you're thinking, Helena."

"Go, go," I wave. "I've lived here my whole life and even managed not to get lost in Chicago and Dover and Boston … I can walk a hundred yards."

That settles him. He still looks like he might want to stay, but he must feel me pushing at him to go, because with another glance back he heads out into the pale twilight.

I do put on my small straw hat, even if I'm just going to the Golden Nail. The hat itself makes me think of farms and spring, and I've put a new thin velvet ribbon around the brim the color of a robin's egg and a summer sky, so it feels fresh and smart and new again.

Going out into the early night gives me time to inhale the smell of spring, too. New churned mud that smells like dirt instead of ice, and there's the greenness in the breeze too, from the early prairie grasses that will soon spread outward from the ends of town. There's the waft of the usual stench from Alan Lampton's pig farm and the shoveling out of Rusty's livery boxes, but overall it just smells like possibilities.

I'll build something just like Kate. Like Mother did, but different. My own.

I can do as I please, and I don't need a man to help me, even if I don't mind talking to Hardy when I see him—.

Two sets of hands grab my upper arms—one set for each bicep—and another clamps dirty fingers over my lips. They smell like old cornbread and tobacco, and they're clumsy so I have enough space to inhale and rip a scream straight out of the bottom of my ribcage.

"Hush, shhhh," the voice to my left says, pressing his palm over my mouth now instead. "Shh, pretty thing, we're just here to enjoy th' sights afore we go sign ourselves over to th' gov'ment."

My little brothers are both my size, and I've had to wrestle them all my life, but I'm out of practice, and besides, these are men, and they smell of piss and beer and the sharp spice of whiskey gone sour.

Someone laughs, and I realize there's a third standing right in front of me, one hand holding a bottle of booze and the other creeping far too close to the fastenings of his pants. I pull and struggle and yank, but all I can do is make a soft sound that is more suggestive of love than terror. My head pounds, and I feel like I might pass over sideways with the speed of the blood under my bones, and how I feel hollow and dizzy doesn't help it. Where's my strength? Where's my heel, I can stamp one, maybe the other—they won't punch, will they? A lady—I'm a lady!

"Take her to the other side of the liv'ry," he drawls, finding the first button and flicking it open. "It's darker there."

"It's certainly not dark enough for this, and the like," someone says, high above us all.

In the gloom, it's a cowboy, all blacker than black, against the strange half-night around us. I can't tell the voice or face, or even the horse, but as he's up high and has a gleaming bit of a silver pistol at his side, the other men fall off me as if I have plague.

I stumble, but I'm caught up by the elbow and pulled up to the saddle fast, my petticoats tangling. One tears … maybe two. The sound of seams stretching is lost in the grumbling of the three men who back off.

"Get yourselves some vittles at Matt's mess hall," the cowboy says. "Right here at the corner. Sounds like you boys could use some food in your bellies, as it were."

As the horse starts moving, I glance back from my strange seat on the mount. I can't see the faces of the men, but one steps closer to Matt Winters's mess, and the buttery light of the window falls on a uniform.

"You safe? Not hurt? I can swing you to Doc Kinney's if you be," the cowboy says, sounding calm against the violence.

"Just a bit rattled," I manage, trying to stop the tremors in my hands. It's like it's stuck in my shoulders, and I wish I could go back, lock my door and hide under my bed. "Thank you."

I twist to see the face of my rescuer and am just able to make out the ebony jawline and flash of blue-white teeth under the wide brim. Moses Thompson catches me staring and nods his head.

"Where you off to tonight, Miss Helena?" he asks. "The smithy?"

"The Golden Nail," I say.

"Then we're right near there, as it were," he says, slowing his horse.

He helps me down, careful and gentleman-like, and even with him near, and his gun, too, I don't like that I'm so glad he follows me into the noisy, bright dining hall of the Nail. I pause to blink, and then to find Kate. The tavern is rowdy at the least of times—always has been. Mother says when it was the Rusty Nail back in the 60s that it was worse, because it was the only big place to get a decent drink in town, plus Toot Warren is arguably the best overall cook in Flats Junction. Her son, Trusty Willy, roars orders back to her while Elaine mans the bar and brings out orders four at a time, balancing plates on her wide hands and against her massive bosom. The many lanterns on the walls and tables make the room feel flush with rose and gold light, and the smell of oily potatoes and fried meat fills the room to the roof. I'm suddenly very desperate for a small beer and a heaping plate of food.

Kate waves at me from a table smack in the middle of the room, and as I walk toward her, she goes from pleased to frowning. It's only when I arrive at my chair that I realize Moses has followed me in, quiet as a shadow and so careful his boots don't thud.

"What do you want?" she asks, looking up at him and crossing her arms.

"Seeing Miss Helena to you," he says, and pulls up an empty chair to sit between us.

Kate's lips curl and her long straight nose wrinkles. "You did. Now you can go."

"No can do, as it were," he tells her, and raises two fingers to Trusty Willy. "I'll stay and see you both home safe."

"Why?"

"Mischief afoot tonight," he says.

Kate's eyes slide over me. "What happened?" She skims a glance over my rumpled hair, and I twitch my skirts to make sure the petticoats aren't ripped so bad they're trailing the ground.

"New recruits for Fort Randall. Fresh off the train today, I'd guess," he says. "No woman's going around alone with men like that on the roam, and the like."

Kate looks very annoyed, and sips her drink, but says nothing more to Moses.

Elaine grabs several beers from her husband and plunks two on our table before moving on without a word toward Gil and Horeb who sit next to us and are both eating with enthusiasm. Moses salutes me, then Kate, and downs half his beer in one huge gulp.

I try mine, and the familiar hoppy, watery flavor washes the clogged scream stuck in my throat and slips down into my belly. My hands are steady again, and I remind myself that nothing really happened. I was rough-grabbed, is all. Nothing more. Not even a spot of blood. All is well. I'm fine. Everything's fine.

Even as my heart slows at last, I try to name the sinking in my body, like I'm weighted down with sorrow.

Is it sadness? Or fear?

Maybe it's disappointment.

Maybe because Mother might be right after all. I'm an unmarried young woman in a rough place, with an unrealistic understanding of how I might be able to live the life I want … but where on earth can a woman do as she pleases safely?

Is there ever such a place?

CHAPTER 6

Jane

April 8, 1884

"I will depart before *čhaŋwápe ǧí-wi*, the brown-leaves moon. If I go before September, it will give me enough time to travel to the Fort and find my family from there and be settled to help with any harvesting," Esther says calmly, as she walks back and forth with Andrew on her shoulder. His tiny face, with cheeks that seem overly large for his rosebud mouth and dot of a nose, burrows further into the warm skin of her neck. She pats him almost absently, swaying so gently it is as if she is singing inside, a hum I can almost hear.

I catch the ladle from the root stew just before it splashes into the pot, but the surprise careens through my muscles. It is a very careful effort that keeps me from trembling when I twist from the stove to look at her.

"You have decided a day, then."

"I have stayed with you each season, from one fall to another, and then some," she says. "There is no more I can remember, or teach you, of my people's ways with the plants and medicines. It was never my family's way to capture and keep such knowledge. It fell to others to hold onto it, so I only know a little."

A little? She has taught me more about weeds and flowers and seeds and how to crush them, squeeze their oils and juice, and more—the information she has poured into me overflows, and it's all I can do to scratch it out in my little notebook before it all falls out of my ears. Even with her patience, and her repeating, I still am sure I have only managed to capture a fraction of what lives in her mind.

"I'm afraid I still don't want to see you go," I tell her. "How shall I manage? The house, the food, the gardens, the babe, and helping Patrick with some patients … and Hardy as an apprentice, too …" The words jump out, even though I know in some ways it is an unfair plead. Many women in Flats Junction do exactly that! They run taverns and post offices, volunteer at church and organize picnics, all while cooking, cleaning, gardening, and raising ten children. Anette Zalenski, Mary Brinkley, Grete Fawcett—I could list dozens.

"I cannot beg you to stay where you do not wish to live," I tell her, going back to the soup and stirring the chunks of potatoes with the droopy early onion greens. "But I hope you have always felt welcome with me—with Patrick."

"Always," she says. Her voice is warm and low, and it's all I can do not to suddenly give in to tears. What will I do when I don't have her to tell me what happens next? When I don't have an understanding of a flower or forgot to write down a remedy or something that must never be used for something else? Who will help me pull the bread from the oven when Andrew is crying, or meet me in the middle of the beans in the garden? The thought of being without her suddenly feels terrifying and lonely.

The front door cracks and then creaks as Patrick enters. His boots pace briskly between study and surgery, and the sound of water sloshing makes me hurry to grab the bread and jam out of the pantry, making sure not to look too close at the boards under the shelves in case I spy a mouse. My nerves are much stronger than they once were, but now that I know I'll soon manage this kitchen alone once again, I feel jumpier.

I've known Esther planned to leave me for months now. This is not a surprise.

Why does the decision, now that there's a timeline, make me tremble?

My hands shake again as I put bowls and plates on the table, and then steady as I carry over the glistening iron pot. The soup smells of dried parsley and salt, and the sweetness of canned tomatoes. A jar of last year's pickled beets rounds out the meal, which will only get better now that spring rides closer each week. Yet now I hope for the time to creep, if it means I have Esther with me.

"I'll take him," Patrick says immediately upon entering, reaching for Andrew. He copies Esther's hold, propping up our son so he can sleep and burp at the same time. I envy Patrick's ease with children, the casual way his large hands cover most of the baby's body. Perhaps with time, I will become as comfortable. Or perhaps he naturally is so, with his years minding babes in the Boston slums, and his constant desire for a family of his own. A seed of warmth unfurls in my chest, when I remind myself that I have given him this at last.

Esther goes out for fresh water to drink from the backyard and to see if there are small lettuces to pick, and Patrick slips himself into a seat on the bench at the kitchen table. With one hand, he deftly begins to slide jam onto the heel of the bread, which is the closest he can reach without jostling the sleeping infant.

I put the spoons and forks out, but when I hand him his set, he stops me with a grip on my fingers.

"You're quiet," he states. His blue eyes cut into my brown ones, and I feel stripped and exposed. How can he notice the smallest details about me after a full day observing others?

"Am I?" I say. The evasive answer is so obvious he doesn't move, and continues to hold me captive across the table, waiting. "It's only Esther is leaving. She said before September."

"We've known she would go. It's nothin' new." He runs a thumb across my knuckles and stares up at me. "What else has happened?"

"Nothing else. It's been the same type of day as the previous."

"Janie."

"I can't think of any other reason for my … quietness."

He lets me go, but his eyes unpeel me as he bites into the bread crust. It crunches loudly in the kitchen. Or perhaps I simply notice every little sound now, my hearing heightened by motherhood.

"Have you been to see Tina Brinkley's little one, their youngest with the bit of a rash that's healin'?" he asks suddenly.

I shake my head as I reach for tin cups.

"What about Grete's two girls, the ones who both have the chapped hands?"

He must notice my pause, because I don't get to answer negative before I hear him stand up and come behind me.

"Jane, look at me."

I turn around, uncertainty ripping into my heartbeat. When I look up at him, into that calm, expressive face with all its fine lines in the corners of mouth and nose, I see a doctor looking back, not a husband. If it were not for him still holding onto our son, I would think he was about to tell me something stern about medicine.

Instead, he reaches out to pull me into a one-armed embrace. "You don't have to be afraid. There's nothin' you could have done."

I start to pull back, but he keeps me tight, our hip bones bumping through all the layers of my skirts and petticoats and his leather vest.

"What are you talking about?" I manage, my cheek smashed into his chest.

"The little boy. Perry Woodman. He was too far gone, and it was black measles."

"I haven't even thought of it!"

"But you have. Ever since, all these weeks, you've become quieter and silent. You aren't askin' questions at the table. Are you even readin' up on medicine in the journals anymore? You can't just stop—I can't let you, either. You have to keep workin' with patients. But it's only natural to feel out of sorts and grievin' over the first one you lose."

"But I …" I swallow my words as they rise, bubbles of denials that would be hollow and untrue. Is this what bothers me, more than Esther leaving? Is it because I feel unsteady and uncertain now, in a trade I was beginning to truly feel as my own?

"I've noticed," he says gently. "Of course I have. What good would I be as a husband and a doctor if I can't see such things?"

"It wasn't … I didn't really think it's affected me," I tell him. "I've been so busy with spring. Getting the seeds in, the garden ready, and thinking perhaps the chickens from Marie at last."

"Sometimes that's part of it." He lets me go to grab the tin cups. "Sometimes you don't even realize you're feelin' it for a good long while. But luckily for you, you've me, and besides, not goin' to see patients is a sure-fire way to know if that's what might be ailin' you."

"I'm sorry," I say, following him and spooning out soup into everyone's dish. "I hope I hasn't caused you anxiety."

"Not anxiousness, no," he says. Then his eyes take on their old sparkle. "Only I mostly noticed because you've been less inclined to meet me under the sheets."

"Paddy!" I whack him on the shoulder. "Not in front of the children!"

"I'm only sayin' that's how we get more of them."

Esther reenters, her hands filled with early lettuce and the water bucket slung over her forearm. She shakes her head at us, and I feel hot redness climb my neck. How much has she heard?

"Where's your apprentice, by the way?" I suddenly round on Patrick, hoping to cover my fluster. "Did you lose him?"

"No, no, he wanted to pop over to see if Helena Salomon wants a walk to her dinner."

"Very gentlemanly of him." A shiver rises the hairs on my legs and arms. The rumors about Army recruits attempting to ruin the young woman have spun wildly throughout town in the past weeks. Some say she was caught undressed in the creek, and others that they attacked her right in Sadie's backyard. Others say there were two, others say four, but I've heard the story direct from Marie herself, and know the way of it. Knowing what actually happened does not make it any better. If anything, knowing there's reality behind the torrid talk is frightful, as it means the town is getting rowdier instead of more civilized.

"Speaking of, though, I was hoping we might walk over after dinner hour," Patrick says, as I sit next to Esther and pick up my spoon. "I've a bit of a surprise for you at Helena's."

My head comes up. "What? For … why?"

It's not my birthday, nor the anniversary of our wedding. Patrick is not an overly romantic man most of the time—though he can be when he wishes—and such trivial dates have never interested him even if I mark their passing.

"As I said … I've noticed you're quieter," he says simply.

"I shall watch the babe," Esther says.

It is a reminder again that soon enough I will not have such a luxury, and I stamp down the panic deep into my stomach. Meeting Patrick's eyes, I nod and pull a smile, knowing he must be able to read into all the layers I'm offering him in it. He smiles back, and tucks into the food and bread, and I can only hope there is enough left over for Hardy when he gets in.

He doesn't arrive before we finish our meal, and Patrick and I meet him instead as we step off the porch.

"Did you walk around the entirety of the town before droppin' Helena off at the Nail?" Patrick asks, but his voice is light and nearly teasing.

Hardy turns the color of summer roses, making the yellow of his hair brighter. His round shoulders go up and down.

"I decided to wait on her, in case she'd run into trouble on the way back. But after a while, Miss Kate says she'll be sure Helena gets back fine and safe and I should go on for my own supper."

"Is Helena even at the dress shop, then?" I ask.

"Oh, sure, or soon enough. They was mostly done, I just got the feeling

Miss Kate wanted to speak to Helena without me there." He shrugs again and heads toward the house.

"We can wander over," Patrick says to me, then tosses to Hardy. "Esther is inside with the babe, and your supper is on the table, though the soup isn't too hot anymore."

"I'm glad for the vittles, Mrs. Kinney," Hardy says, looking suddenly very hungry, as a growing young man often does. It's a peaky paleness around the corners of their ears and below their cheeks, as if they are suddenly close to starving.

We walk very slowly in the early evening. The sun sets later and later now, and the prairie looks like it's washed in peach and silver as the light fades. The grasses are thigh high, and the birds are all back and trilling and swooping at early insects. Patrick folds my arm through his, and under my palm the heat of his body reaches me and then spreads up and down, so my womb squeezes with the memory of lovemaking. He's right—I have been less attentive to him at night, wrapped in my own brooding, even if I did not have a name for it. I have been mourning my first loss. I shall have to remedy our lack of relations soon. Tonight, perhaps.

Around the back of Sadie and Tom Fawcett's house is the summer house, where Helena has built the little dressmaking business, thanks to the investment of Kate for the goods, the ribbons, the patterns, and even sending Helena out east for learning the details of the trade and forging relationships. How Kate thought of that—to get into direct contact with the dressmakers in the big cities and forge relationships—to ensure that the dressmaking business in Flats Junction would be the best in the Dakota Territories is nothing short of brilliant. I suppose it speaks to how cunning she is. It may be why she has run the General with such success, too. It takes a peculiar, forward-thinking mind to do such daring plans.

As we pass the window where Sadie, Tom, and their boys are visible eating, I hear the sound of water hitting wood.

"Don't look right, unless you want to see Rusty takin' a piss on his livery walls," Patrick mutters.

I don't look, and only blindly nod when Rusty hails us and returns to the livery's very ripe interior. A half-dozen horses snort when he enters, their muffled welcome sounding as if they know him. And, I suppose they must.

"Is she home yet?" I ask, peering at the small windows. In the half-light, it's difficult to see if there's a lamp lit or not.

Patrick stops moving next to me mid-step. His arm turns to rock, is rigid so fast I take the next step without him and jerk backward by his solidness. If a man could truly freeze, Patrick would be stuck to the earth as a pillar of ice.

I look about, wondering if Helena's attackers now circle us, but only see a man in a top hat detach from the long shadows of Alan's pig farm. He is nothing unusual other than he seems to be dressed more city-fine that most men in Flats Junction. A stranger, then, who has only surprised Patrick.

But my husband still refuses to move, and I suddenly worry he has forgotten to take a breath as well.

"Patrick?" I tug his arm a bit. "Come on, we'll knock."

He does not move an inch, so I rip my arm from his elbow to rap on Helena's door myself.

"Jane. Come here."

The timbre of Patrick's voice is unlike any I've heard from him in the years and emergencies we've struggled through—it is panic and shock, disbelief and terror—and I step back to his side just as the gentleman nears. As he tips his head back, the patch over his left eye forces me to swallow the small cry, but he doesn't seem to notice me at all.

"You … you?" Patrick sounds strangled. "W—how?"

The man steps close—not too close, but enough that it feels as though he looms. He's a few inches taller than Patrick, and his hat makes him look even taller.

"I thought I'd try my hand at working outside the city," the man says easily, his words slippery and smooth. "What are the odds? Likely slim, I suppose."

"How did you choose this? Here?"

"Boston is not so very big, and you forget we both know the MacHughs.

Perhaps your location was mentioned in passing. It's hard to remember the details."

"Why?" Patrick presses. He still has not moved one inch.

"This is a big wide land. Plenty of room for many doctors, especially one like me who wishes to set up hospitals—they're what this country needs to be truly civilized—and I aim to do it here." The man has a strange accent—Boston and England all mangled together—and his mouth curls up at the corners as he looks my husband up and down, and then, at last, turns to do the same to me. "You've found a wife, then, Paddy?"

Patrick attempts to put a step between me and the man, but can't seem to find his footing, and instead only sways.

"I'm Jane Kinney," I say, lifting my chin. "Who are you?"

"Doctor Thomas Smith, at your service," he says, tipping the brim of his hat.

Patrick sniffs softly, and the man—Doctor Smith—looks hard suddenly, lean and overly eager. He bends closer to stare into Patrick's face.

"Pop off it, Paddy," he croons. It's a taunt laced with something like memory, and it unleashes my husband in a fury I never would have believed he holds inside. It lashes out, as if it lives under his skin and in his bones.

Patrick flies at Doctor Smith—fists up and arms wide just like a boxer—and the man seems to have been hoping for the same, for he goes back on one leg and flings up his own block before taking a swing at Patrick's ear.

"Stop it!" My voice sounds high and shrill. "Stop! Patrick—no!" Am I screaming? Or yelling? Both?

Flesh smacking into flesh has a dead, thick sound, and both men seem well-matched. I have never seen a fight in the slums, but I imagine it is something as awful as this—fists and kicks, grunts and muffled yells. They tear at one another, both hats flying, pockets flailing, and even legs are used to try to force one another into the soft spring ground of Sadie's backyard. It takes an instant for flecks of blood to go, and another before the sound of cartilage snapping, and yet no one seems to see or hear them or me—until shouts from the Fawcett house match those coming from the north.

It feels as though Patrick and Doctor Smith have been fighting an hour, but it must only be a minute before Rusty, Tom Fawcett, and Alan Lampton arrive and tear the two men apart.

"That upset, are you, 'Doc' Kinney?" Doctor Smith says, panting between each syllable. "Don't like the idea of a hospital, eh?" His lip is cracked both top and bottom, and the patch over his eye is gone, leaving the saggy, wrinkled eyelid for all to see. A bloom on his jaw swells, and I don't want to know how his ribs feel. He's held back by Alan, who is wearing his long underwear and boots, but is quite strong from wrestling pigs all day, every day. Tom Fawcett has Patrick, both arms twisted behind his back, and Rusty stands in the middle, his grizzled beard torn in one chunk where he must have caught a bit of the fight.

"A hospital—yes!" Patrick wheezes. His nose looks swollen, and there's a trickle of blood under his earlobe, plus one eye is already turning colors. "But not run by the likes of you!"

"Why not?" Doctor Smith says. He strains a little from Alan's hold, leaning back toward Patrick. "At least with me, people might not die so quick … surely by now everyone here knows you kill more than you save!"

It's too much for Patrick. He wrests out of Tom's hands and shoves Rusty out of the way so he can attack Doctor Smith again. Alan, surprised, releases Doctor Smith, and the two doctors are at it again, though with less vigor as both are hurt and aching. In the fray, the mud flies up and hits my neck and face, and a booted foot—though I could not say whose—flings out and knocks the side of my knee.

I go down, catching myself with my left hand. The stones outside Helena's doorway dig into my palm, slicing the lines and my shoulder jars into my collarbone.

Neither man notices at first—they seem intent on killing each other—and it's Rusty who once again forces his way between Patrick and Doctor Smith, pushing both so hard on the chest that they stumble backward. Rusty's not young, but he holds down horses for a living, and is more efficient than I would expect a man who's half-drunk most of the time in breaking up the fight.

It's only then that Patrick notices me on the ground, though Tom Fawcett has stepped over to help haul me out of the dirt.

"Jane—are you hurt?" Patrick asks at once, turning away from the other doctor. Out of the corner of my eye, I see Doctor Smith's shoulders sag, and he bends over with his hands on his knees. Perhaps the worst of it is over, then.

"Nothing to worry on," I say, closing my fist over the laceration in my hand. "But you—you're bleeding."

Patrick suddenly seems to feel the blood down the side of his neck. He touches it and then looks up at Doctor Smith.

"You're not serious," he says to Doctor Smith. The comment is so flat I can't tell if the argument is resolved or only beginning. "You're not buildin' a hospital here. There's no reason for it. Flats Junction is too small. And I haven't heard a thing. How long have you even been in town?"

"Since early March, a month or so. Long enough to make some inquiries."

Patrick glances over at Rusty and Alan, and then at Tom Fawcett. "That is ... but how have I heard nothin'?"

Rusty looks at his boots, and Alan scratches the back of his head and glances at the sky. Tom Fawcett draws himself up, smoothing back his hair and adjusting his cuffs carefully before answering Patrick in his clipped British accent.

"It has been discussed here and there. And Doctor Smith has indeed seen me at the bank twice now as we discuss the potential paperwork and collateral needed for the funds."

Patrick's mouth, which thankfully does not look destroyed, hangs open. I find myself staring at our neighbors, too. It feels like a betrayal at the very least.

"Why has no one said anything?" My mind flickers through all the folks who would know—Marie, Kate, Anette—and then I realize I have not gone out much since Perry Woodman died on my watch. I suppose there wasn't much time to speak on this, and a delicate topic at that.

"Well ... we didn't want to upset the doc," Alan says.

"And it's not a complete deal, so's how I heard it," Rusty agrees, shifting his feet.

They are embarrassed, huffing and staring at anything but us. Perhaps they did not want to upset me, or anger the doctor, though I suppose now the story of Patrick's fight will spread faster than most news. Or perhaps people simply don't care to tell us, if they don't trust medicine, science, or Patrick himself. Maybe they think Doctor Smith will be a different kind of doc. A better one.

Patrick's ribcage heaves under his coat and shirt, and he seems to favor one side of his body over another. I hold onto his arm again, if only to keep the men from fighting a third time.

"I shall get my husband home, then," I say. "I appreciate the help." Jerking my chin stiffly at Rusty, Alan, and Tom, I walk with Patrick back around the Fawcett house. Sadie stands as close to her kitchen window as she can without smashing her gown against the glass, and her eyes are wide. Through it, she mouths 'Are you well?' and I shrug and tilt my head at the same time. I'm certain she will get the news straight from Tom when he goes in, and I will spend the next week trying to set the story properly.

When we get back to the house, Patrick gives up holding himself together and half-folds himself in order to limp up the porch and into the house.

"Hardy! We need you!" I call, suddenly very relieved to have the apprentice under my roof in a way I have not yet felt since he arrived. "Hurry, now!"

He flies from the kitchen, a linen still tucked into his shirt collar, which falls off as soon as he enters the hallway.

"Who is it?" he asks.

"Doctor Kinney," I say shortly, which makes him pause and gape, before following me into the surgery. Behind him, the shadow of Esther holding Andrew flits against the yellow light of the lantern candles.

Patrick groans as I help him onto the slab, the bleached white cotton with its fine edges sewn in his Aunt Bonnie's hand rumpling as he winces and lays back. I take a moment to stare at him, uncertain why I feel so loose and ungainly. I realize that this is likely the first time he's ever been on his own operating table – or maybe any surgical table – and he must bow to me to heal him. Me, who has only become a nurse here by trial and error and necessity.

I spin to Hardy, who is still stuck at the doorway, his eyes over-round, and the last of the day's bread in his hand, squeezed and smushed with his clenching.

"Hot water to wash off the blood, and a bar of soap."

"Right. Right! I know that!" He bolts back down the hallway, his footsteps sounding like a massive animal with his newly minted man's body.

This gives me a moment to bend over my husband and frown into his one open eye. The other is swollen, with blackening skin blooming a deep purple around it. He surely has a cracked nose, then, and perhaps a rib or two. But I find I only can glare at him.

"Do you think you might tell me why you wished to beat a man you've just met?" I ask.

"Don't harp on me now, woman," he says. "At least give me a spot of whisky to take off the edge. You'll have to reset my nose."

"Damn your nose."

He pauses his fidgeting against the pain at my cuss. My cheeks feel puffy with the hot bloom. Have I ever sworn in my life? And in front of him? I don't think I have. Perhaps this is a sign the west has entered my bones at last.

Patrick shifts, then jerks at the pain of the movement. "It's the Irish temper, aye?"

"It's more than that," I insist. "I've seen you drunk, and angry, and upset, but never this … violence."

"Maybe it's the west itself, makin' a fool of me," he counters, echoing my own recent musing. Then his body melts into the table, and he sighs. "I'm not bein' fair to you, am I, Janie?"

I leave his side to find the clean cloths. I don't believe there's much by the way of medicine that will heal him other than rest and time, unless there are injuries I can't see. Men and their fists generally don't do much lasting damage, though I don't like that he had to limp home.

"Wife," he says. "Come here."

I turn, but do not take his offered hand. Grime and bits of drying blood stick to the lines inside his palm, and I wonder if it's his or Doctor Smith's.

"We'd said no more secrets," I remind him. "We'd said there was nothing between us."

"There isn't!" he says, the old heat coming back into his words. The fire in the tone makes my shoulders bend and relax. If he can still be passionate, he is not so very hurt, then.

"You know him," I say, the realization filling into my mind as I speak. "You know each other. What happened?"

"I took his eye is what," Patrick admits.

"You?" My hands squeeze the bandaging cloth so tight that my fingers lose their feeling for a moment, sending the tingles of pins down my knuckles. His knuckles, on the other hand, are split open and swollen. One looks like it caught the worst of a button.

"Back in Boston, during my apprenticeship, before I went to work for Doc Stassen in the hotel stables. Before Mr. McClure died. Before Aunt Bonnie and I went west."

"So you weren't … fleeing the law for attacking him back east?" I ask. "He's not here to bring vengeance?"

He tries to sit up to his elbows and fails, laying back down with a hand to his left side. "Jesus, Mary and Joseph. He got at least two."

"Patrick, I won't even bother to help you if you don't answer me."

His eyebrows go up briefly. "Makin' demands now, are you?" He rubs his chest and scrunches up his eyes before rubbing at the blood on his neck. I can see now it's not his ear but a deep scratch behind it.

"Stop that," I say, stepping to grab his hand down. "Hardy's bringing water and I'll clean it up and put a bit of iodine on it." Our precious store of iodine as it is, and a surge of frustration pours into my limbs as I stare down at him.

"I suppose he found me by speakin' to one of our mutual acquaintances," Patrick sighed. "Bobby MacHugh or his wife, maybe … You want to know if he's here to run me out? To be true, I don't know. I took his eye, and I even helped Bobby steal away Tara, though I don't think she minded. Thomas used my good name to save himself, and it ended up bein' a fair reason enough for me to be unwelcome in many homes in Boston thanks to his lies. There was nothin' left but to leave and find work. I just didn't think he'd bother the trouble to find me."

"But why do you suppose he has hated you so much to follow you?"

"I'm sorry, Doc Kinney," Hardy says from the door. How long has he stood and listened? I wave him in, and he enters carefully with the pot of water in the tin coffee pot. Steam twirls out of the spout as he brings it to the side table next to the sterilized tools. Thank heaven I won't have to try my hand with any of those.

"What are you sorry for?" Patrick asks. "You couldn't have stopped the brawl."

"No—only I knew about Doc Smith bein' in town. And his ideas for a hospital and all. Helena told me. She says Kate's helping move the plan along, too." Hardy pauses in the middle of the room and only looks at the floorboards, which I keep scrubbed clean with just the right amount of water and lye.

"Why didn't you think to say somethin'?" Patrick asks. He grimaces as he tries to sit again, and succeeds, though not without coming up short of breath.

"I didn't know if I should. What if it was just the rumors? And I … I didn't want to upset you or the missus," he adds. His misery radiates out, and his earnestness with it, and while I'm further annoyed at his lack of reporting, I try to understand. He has only lived with us a few short weeks and does not know my nature or Patrick's. If anything, it shows restraint—this is not a young man who will grow up contributing to incorrect information. It is a good trait in a future physician, and I can only hope Patrick sees it that way, too.

He's already nodding, looking resigned. "It seems all of Flats Junction was afraid to speak to me on this matter. Am I such an ogre, then?" He waves his hand at Hardy. "Go on and finish your meal, Hardy. Mrs. Kinney can see to cleanin' me up."

The boy near flees the room, leaving me alone with my husband again.

"What can one say, in this instance with a new doctor coming in?" I pour the water into the waiting ceramic bowl, dipping the cloth in and scrubbing the soap on it before going for Patrick's neck. "Perhaps it's a sign they respect you, and don't wish to rile you. And many do not know the connection between you and Doctor Smith, or you'd have heard of it. If anything, it's a wonder he hasn't started his own gossip and rumors about you."

Patrick looks pensive, only shuddering a bit as I move to his knuckles. "Maybe he already has."

"To what end?"

He does not answer at first, and just winces as I finish cleaning his skin.

"I'm thinkin' Thomas knows deep down he's not a good doc," Patrick says quietly. "He doesn't even like being a doctor or workin' with people. The way he'd look at blood and fluids, and the flesh of … I think he just wants power, in all the ways. In any of the ways he can grasp it. Havin' a way to boss folks around as a physician is just one of them."

"But why the rancor to you?"

"I don't know, Janie," he sighs. He takes off his Stetson. In the moon and starlight, his blue eyes look cut of glass. "Maybe he's just … jealous that it comes easier to me, the doctorin'. Maybe he thinks if he can be rid of me, he'll feel better inside. Isn't that why folks try to destroy others? Because they don't like it when others are happy, and they are not?"

"It cannot be only his eye or even Tara, as you have said. Men lose eyes in brawls all the time, and there are other women in the world."

Patrick only sighs. "Well, we can't risk losin' too many patients to him as it is," he says slowly. "We'll maybe work to ingratiate with Fort Randall. They'll be happy to get some help from a proper doctor."

"The Army has mostly brought trouble wherever they go. To us and to Esther's people," I say, shaking my head. "Though your notion has merit. They'd pay well, perhaps."

"Well, it's either that or find a cure for what ails the cattle. Or the source of the black measles. If we beat Thomas at that, there'd be no reason to run me out of Flats Junction."

I pause and find his eyes. "It won't come to that, would it? You've been here longer!"

He shakes his head, then closes his one good eye and rubs his forehead against what must be a looming headache. "I know it seems a lost battle, my love. But it's that or we very likely may have to strike out and start over somewhere else. I've seen how it goes."

"Hm." I shake my head once, briskly, to dislodge the thousands of fears crowding in, not least of which I have no notion how difficult it would be to pick up house with an infant. "Well, at least tell me why we were going to the dressmaker's in the first place."

He cracks a small grin. "I've got Helena doin' a bodice for you, to match your yellow dress. It's not a full new gown, but … it's just a bit of something to lift you up."

I stare at him. To use some of our hard cash on something frivolous! And yet … my heart feels hot and lighter than it has in days. I had not realized how much the shadow of little Perry Woodman's death laid over me … and Patrick by default.

"That's quite romantic of you," I tell him, and bend to press a kiss carefully to the side of his mouth. "See, you are a good husband as well as a good doctor."

These conversations are so rare now between us, what with the comings and goings of life, Hardy underfoot, and the baby, that I have felt myself drifting from Patrick. We are connected by bone and love, I know. But there are other parts of a good marriage, I have now learned, that are built by words and time, not just lovemaking and laundry and hot meals.

It is delightful to know our love is not yet faded with weariness.

But it's impossible not to let the half-formed worries streak through my brain as I continue to clean his small wounds and check for any bruising along the line of kidneys and stomach. As I do, I cannot help but wonder if my own knowledge, gleaned from Esther's centuries of tradition, could help him in this new quest for an impossible cure.

And if I can use such herbs to heal, what are the risks if they succeed?

I understand enough what it means if I were to fail.

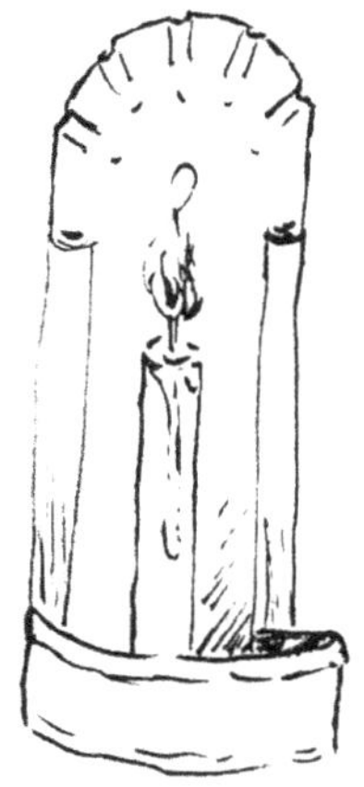

CHAPTER 7

April 14, 1884

I've no notion why half of Yves's posse is in my General. They came as a pack, looking as if they had nothing to do with their day but stare at Gil and Horeb's game of checkers, with Arnold pulling up a chair right in the middle. He sits with his forearms on his knees, leaning over so close I wonder if he needs spectacles.

"Ah's sayin', he'll capture the two in the cornah," he advises Horeb, his southern drawl sounding particularly drawn out as if he's talking to a young child instead of two old men.

Horeb spits into his tin, which he's not cleaned out in two weeks. I eye it up, considering how angry I'll be if it spills over my nice green and yellow new floorboards. The General is so very nearly put together just so. But as I've been organizing and putting up bolts of calico and striped ribbons and glass cannisters of buttons and lemon drops, the posse has been more and more frequenting the store, and it's high time they stop coming in only to loiter.

"You lot ought to clear out," I say, putting the giant cash register and the counter between myself and Patty as I do it. Patty bats her big blue eyes at me, and flounces both her hair and breasts at the same time in a pout.

"You kicking us out?" she asks loudly. The tip of her forefinger traces the handle of the short knife she keeps bolted to her belt.

Arnold turns from the checkers, just as Evan peers up from the tobacco bags, his mouth stuffed on both sides so full he can't even grunt. My fists ball into my newly sewn skirts, fresh from Helena's editing eye, and I only stare at Patty.

"You all heard me," I say. "I'm sure Yves is needing your help with your own storefront."

"Victoria's got it in hand with him and Natty," Patty says.

"And so now you're here spying on me?" I ask. "Thinking you can see how I set up shop and try and steal something more from me?"

"We ain't stealing nothing!" she says hotly, her hands on her hips.

I tilt my head at Evan, who slowly slouches over to Matthias, who has stood to the side with his arms crossed, staring at everyone and saying nothing to no one.

"That's just a bite," Patty says. She sniffs and glances about my very empty store. "'Sides, you ain't got no customers in anyhow."

"They're all afraid of you!"

Her rosy mouth curls. "Oh. I see, then."

"Get going, unless you want to buy something. I've a business to run," I say. As I speak it, I eye up the weapons dangling from each of the posse and wonder how exactly I could enforce my demands. For the first time, I think it's near time I'm getting myself a pistol to keep on the inside of my stockings.

"We's just checkin' tah make sure you're only stocking what you says you will, and you're not taking what's promised Yves," Arnold finally admits. He stands and stretches. I miss the glass of my big window, and can't wait for it to arrive. He seems a shadow in the dimness, his arms reaching sideways as the tendons in his back crackle.

"I've kept my word," I say. "Goods are divvied up as we decided." *For now,* I think. "Now go on and get back."

Arnold ambles out without a backward glance. Patty huffs at me, then spins around toward the door. Her bouncing also forces her buxom figure to catch Horeb's eye, which has him spinning right around to watch her come toward him and the door.

Except Patty notices his stare and she stops cold a few feet from him. "What you looking at, old timer?" she hisses. "I ain't no nasty whore—I kill whores when I can and I swore off menfolk, too. You keep looking and you'll wake to see you can't look no more." She unsheathes her knife.

"Only 'preciatin' the female form, is it?" Horeb asks, but his eyes are glued to the dagger. "No harm, madam, I hope?"

He turns back to the game in time to see Gil move illegally, and screeches. Patty rolls her eyes and departs, but Evan has disappeared behind the brown sugar bin. I close my eyes and steel myself for going after him—he's one of the quieter ones, but there's an emptiness in the quiet. I can't always tell if he means to be menacing, or simply doesn't understand that his dullness is fearsome. I've heard he kills without flinching, but maybe that's because he doesn't understand what he does. There's no way to know, anyway—it's not as if anyone in Flats Junction has gone out riding and raiding with Yves's posse.

When I open my eyes, Matthias has herded Evan to the door already, pressing the younger man out just by Matthias's sheer size. The two of them depart, and the sound of the door closing behind them makes me feel like floating. Or maybe melting. The day is mostly done, and I've business to do round town.

Heading over to Horeb and Gil, I stand over their half-finished game and land my fists on my hips.

"You just gonna stand there and watch, Kitty?" Horeb asks, moving one of his other red pieces. "A nice rest after watching over the posse folk, is it?"

"It's more I need you two to clear out as well. Can you finish tomorrow?"

"Nope." Gil's chair creaks under his bulk. He pushes his hat further off his head, so it looks like it might slide down his back, and shifts a black piece with a single poke of his thumb.

"What you needing us gone for?" Horeb asks, twisting to look up at me. "We ain't never caused trouble."

"I've got to meet Joe," I say, nodding over at Gil. "Your son and I are closing in on a deal at last about the Prime Inn."

Gil goes stiff in his chair, as if his rheumatism has locked up his legs and shoulders. Horeb glances between us and hunches his skeletal frame inside his faded shirt.

"Don't need to go doing that now, don't ya think?" Horeb ventures.

"Why not? No time like the present to make Flats Junction bigger and better."

"It's only …" Horeb pauses and shoots Gil a look. But Gil still doesn't change a hair, not even to grab the piece he's sure to win off Horeb in his next move.

I frown at him. "You can't possibly be upset about me coming in to work with Joe, Gil. You don't own the hotel anymore—you sold it to Joe years ago. He can do as he likes."

"It ain't that, Kitty, is it?" Horeb says slowly. "It's we've heard some of the thoughts you have for the Prime. Everyone's got notions on what you're meaning to do, and pretty soon it'll be too expensive for most folks to go for a bite, or have their relations stay, if you go fancying it up. That don't sit well, not least as you'll likely railroad Joe to do things what's too expensive for the business, ain't it?"

I stare at Horeb, then Gil. When neither seems inclined to say more, I cross my arms against the dull ache growing under my chest.

"You're saying you disapprove of me becoming part owner of the Prime Inn. Even though I'm clearly the best business owner in Flats Junction. Even though I brought in a seamstress business. Even though my father …" I choke down the last words. This now has nothing to do with Percy Davies. "Is it because I'm a woman? Or because of who my mother was?"

"It ain't that neither, you know?" Horeb now sounds like a wheedling child, trying to make me see reason in what is clearly something unreasonable. "It's Gil don't approve of the business terms. Joe showed him what you writ up, and seems to be you'll be cuckolding Joe at his own hotel."

My mouth drops open. Surely, they can see why my demands are what they are—I'm putting in money, fresh and clean, to better the hotel. Of course I should have a say on how it's improved, and whether electric lights go in or no. It's my funds! My idea!

"I'm not," I insist. "You're plumb foolish if you think so."

Gil suddenly stands, upsetting the checkers. The sound of two dozen pieces rattles across the floor, rolling under crates and bumping into piles of old boots.

"No," Gil says to me, looking at me all direct. Then he turns and walks straight out.

Horeb and I stare after him. I've never seen Gil leave when it's not mealtime, and we're hours shy of when Matt Winters or the Nail opens for victuals.

"I don't think he's coming back any time soon, ain't he?" Horeb says. His voice goes low on the end, and his face pinches. "I 'spose I'm supposed to choose sides, don't I? Well … maybe if I just settle down on the porch, like, that's halfway between you two?" He gathers up his threadbare coat and slowly exits. In another moment, the pop and creak of his thin body taking a seat on the bench out front filters through the walls.

I'm stuck looking at the overthrown checkers board and wonder if I'll ever find the pieces Gil knocked about before the Grand Opening. Does it matter if I do, if Gil's staging a walk-out on me? What in tarnation has gotten into him? I swear my deal with Joe is fair.

Or, fair enough.

Fine, it's near one-sided, but that's only as I'll be bringing in the fine foods and pretty lights.

It'll make a difference.

Folks'll come here specific for a fine dining experience.

I remind myself of this as I walk up Alley Road toward the Prime Inn, noting the lamps are already lit against the spring late afternoon, so it looks all inviting. Joe never used to think of such things, and I smile at knowing I'm making a difference already. My father ... I try not to think on it or the phrase itself, but I have an inkling that Percy would be proud.

He was always one to make a good deal, even if some called it blackmail. It got—he got—things done, and only myself and Widow Hawks knows how many of those things weren't entirely his ideas.

My mother can be very firm when she wants to be.

Joe's waiting for me behind the bar, his light hair shining with fresh water and his beard newly groomed. It's hard to believe someday he'll look just like Gil—round and punchy—but for now he's still strangely, strikingly handsome, with a broadness across the chest and thick arms that makes me wonder why he still hasn't found a wife since his childhood sweetheart died of the same diphtheria, the same year that took my brother. Most girls would be glad to wed him, I'd think. For me, I've just known Joe my whole life, and even thinking of kissing him puts me on edge. It'd be like romancing with my brother.

But such long old ties must come to something ... like our business partnership.

And as I look at him, waiting there for me and our meeting, his arms crossed, the old tell-tale tick of the vein on the right side of his jaw makes me pause a half-step.

Joe's never been unkind to me.

Neither has Gil.

So why am I so set on getting the bigger advantage over him? He's up for this, for creating the Prime Inn into something bolder and better ... but what's making me force the deal we wrote up last week?

Pride?

Greed?

Control?

He pulls out our little piece of paper, waiting only for our signatures and then a trip to see Tom Fawcett at the bank to make it official. I take the last two strides to the opposite side of the counter and place both my palms down on the slick surface. He's got it nice and cleaned off, too, and I can only wonder how many hours poor Lucy Brinkley scrubbed to make it so.

"Your father doesn't like this agreement," I say bluntly.

Joe's eyes jerk to mine. "He don't like a lot of things. Sides maybe Toot."

"I thought it was only her cooking."

Despite the seriousness of our meeting today, Joe's lips quiver. "Can't have one without the other."

"But he doesn't have her," I say.

"Yet."

We both snort a moment, and it leaves me feeling soft inside. I don't know. Less … uptight. When was the last time I laughed at all? What am I doing? Trying to run Joe out—away from his family business? Am I trying to push him out—it's not what I want, is it? I pull the paper toward my side of the counter to pick it up, scanning the familiar lines.

… proprietorship and profits of the Prime Inn to be split 50% between Katherine Davies and Joseph Greenman in perpetuity …

I'm not putting in fifty percent to ask for it out, and we both know it. I've done what I wanted at the first. Joe's finally convinced he needs the electric to keep up with the times … and I'm the only way he'll get it in his mind—both money and the contact with the electric company. So I've named my price, and it is one my father would not scoff at one bit.

But it's not fair.

Goddamn Gil for making me reconsider.

And damn Joe, too, for looking at me with those plain eyes, believing that he's doing what he must. Believing in *me*.

"You have a pencil?"

Joe stares at me. "What? For what?"

"I'm thinking we should make some changes."

"Now? I thought we was done finally. You aren't … you can't ask more from me, Kitty, I'm not sure the numbers work out already."

"Just give me one," I say, holding out my hand. "It's not going on in ink, so don't fret."

He slowly draws out one of the stubs from under the counter, bottles clinking as he rummages. I take it quick and strike out parts of sentences before I lose my nerve and start second guessing my own reasoning. Gone is the high percentage, and the ownership amount, too, and profit allocation.

When I hand it back to Joe, I get a strange swelling up inside my ribs as I watch his eyes dart and then go large as he understands what I'm offering without saying the words out loud.

"But … you're not getting even a third of what you was asking original," he says, setting down the paper gingerly, like he's afraid it's going to smudge or erase itself. "And you're putting in the fine food and the lights."

"You said weeks ago you'd never do a deal with me," I say, finding the words as I go, and hoping they don't sound plain foolish as I do. "And here you are, doing a deal anyway for the better of the town. You saw reason, and now I am. It's not reasonable for me to ask as much. This amount repays me back quick enough, and I'll still get the profits after for a good long while. It's all for Flats Junction, really, as we said. Building our place in the world up and all."

Joe looks winded, and then he reaches back under the counter for a pen and ink, followed by a cloudy bottle filled with a copper liquid.

"We'll sign now, and drink to it," he says, staring at me like I've lost my wits.

"Fine." I grab the metal nub and dunk it into the small ink bottle and quickly scratch my name on the line. He follows and then pours us a measure of the whisky.

When he raises his glass and clinks it to the lip of mine, I try not to think how Percy Davies would be shaking his head over my generousness, and how he maybe would say I've failed landing a profitable deal when I had it in hand. That I'd gone over soft.

But the way Joe's looking at the Prime Inn, as if he's never seen it before, and the way he grins at me, like we're in a secret, just the two of us? Well, it makes me feel like I've traded one choice for another, and while that might not be what my father would've done … it's better in other ways I might like better.

"I'll run this up to the bank, before Tom's gone for the day," Joe offers.

"Fine," I say. "I'm heading to see Marie about making the fine tin lanterns we saw in that catalogue, if she can fit them for electric once she's got them made." I wonder if I should bring the catalogue over, too—since Helena has ordered in one, others sometimes show up, too, as if the Dover Stamping Company has kept Flats Junction on their list for good."

"Good. I … this is good, Kitty." Joe comes from around the bar and grabs my right hand, pumping it twice and slapping me on the other arm, the way I see men do when they're pleased to see each other. It is a manly thing, and a bit rough, but I think I prefer it. It makes me feel like a real partner with Joe.

He and I leave together, but I go east and he goes southeast, so we agree to talk as we can, and I promise to let him know as soon as I hear from the Black Hills Corporation about when and how they'll be running wires to town.

As Joe heads to my father's old bank, Doctor Smith comes out. Even across the distance, he notices me and waves a hand in greeting. I return it, and lift my chin up higher to do it, and find my feet pausing as the doctor makes a line for me.

"Miss Davies," he greets as he nears, and tips his tall hat.

"A fine day," I return.

He looks up at the sky and then at me. When he smiles, there are happy looking lines around the patch of his missing eye. "It is indeed. Running errands?"

"Much to do, as always."

"Indeed. Would you like company?"

"I … guess so," I say, more because I don't know what else to tell him. And I've no good reason to put him off. "I'm to see the smiths now."

"I'll go with you," he says easily. "As I've not had the opportunity to meet them as of yet."

It feels strange to walk about town with a man at my side, and I'm only glad he doesn't offer his arm for the short distance.

At the combined blacksmith forge and tin shop, Thaddeus Salomon growls at his two sons out of the corner of his beard as they attempt to fix a wagon wheel.

"Kaspar!" he barks. "Pay attention to the heat. That repair looks like *gówno*."

"It doesn't look like shit," I hear Kaspar mutter as I walk through to Marie's side.

"Mine's better," Natan says, announcing it and poking his older brother at the same time.

"Boys!" Thaddeus sounds about ready to shout in earnest. "I'm not helping on this one—you've got to do it yourselves. There's no wheelwright for miles now, it's on you."

"Look, Pa," Natan insists. "My weld is smooth!"

"Who cares?" Kaspar scoffs.

"They will!"

"Will not, so long as it works."

Moments like this seem strange to me—is it natural for sons and brothers to be so riled with one another?

"Good day," Doctor Smith says, still at the door where I've left him. "I've heard much about your fine work around town."

Thaddeus's answer is a low syllable, lost in the wall between tinshop and forge.

"What can I do for you, Kate?" Marie asks, pulling me from her family. I take the last step over to her side to focus on her, where she's standing on the far side of the tinsmith shop. The big heavy square bench in the middle of her workspace is crowded with iron machines that look as though they'd be impossible to figure on how to use.

"Lanterns," I say. "Tin lanterns."

She approaches slowly, and as she does, I feel the unresolved words crumble between us further. We've no love lost between us, but I think we've come to a better understanding in the past year, since Kaspar was burned trying to put the fire out on my General. There's the other bits, too—my family's heirloom, a destroyed copper kettle brought from overseas, Helena's trip out east on my dime, the iodine I kept from Patrick which, according to Jane, is why Marie's young daughter died ... But I made it right, didn't I? I brought it later, for Kaspar.

I think we're better, now.

And I need her.

"There's these tin lanterns I've seen," I say. "They were in a catalogue."

"I know it," she says, sounding both resigned and amused. "Nancy gets it in for me, same as she sends a copy to the General."

"Oh. Then … you've a copy?"

Marie goes to her overlarge ledger and pulls out the floppy pages from the front. A small book falls out, too, which surprises me. I didn't think Marie was much of a reader, but the cover is long—*The Mechanic's Calculator and Tinman's Guide: Comprehending Principles, Rules and Tables* by a man called Quantrill.

"Lanterns?" she asks, flipping the pages of the Dover's illustrated pages. "You can order them whole from here, I think. Why do you need me to build them for you?"

"Is it cheaper for you to build, or for me to buy them, first off?" I ask. "Go back, not page fifty and a quarter—page forty-nine." I point at the design I want for the Prime Inn to match the glass and crystal chandelier I hope to place right dead in the center of the dining and bar room.

"I can't get in the mica for these," Marie shakes her head. "May as well order."

"What about glass instead of mica?"

Marie's lips press thin as she thinks, then shrugs. "Might be. I'd have to do the expense."

"It's not just that—I want this style with a glass shade, not mica, but it's more than that. They're not for oil, but for electricity. Can you make them so we can put them on the walls and hook them up?"

Marie swallows hard as her scarred hands pause over the soft paper of the page.

"I haven't put much stock in those rumors," she says at last. "People'll speculate all kinds of wild things, and I thought that was one of them. Is it certain, then?"

"Near enough, if I've anything to say on it. These would be up in the Prime Inn, and we'd connect them to the wires in town. Can you do it."

She shakes her head, the wild salt and pepper curls fraying on the knot of hair at the nape of her neck. But her fingers are already grabbing a piece of paper and she looks up at me with a wry small smile.

"You've turned my daughter's head, you know."

What's that got to do with it? I frown, not certain what she means, but she gives a little sound, like she's giving in on it, and sort of laughs.

"Helena is certain women have a place in this town," she says, "and a big one, and that it's possible to do anything. I suppose I might want to start listening to her about keeping up with the times or be lost to the past. I'll do what I can, Kate, and will let you know."

It's a victory for me—two in one day—and I leave with a small grin at Thaddeus as I go, which must look out of character, because I can hear him bellow to Marie even with the door closed.

"What could she possibly want? Did you say you'd do something impossible again?"

Doctor Smith has disappeared, maybe put off by Thaddeus's attitude, and I keep walking quick so I don't hear more, and I don't worry about Marie bowing to Thaddeus anyway. I'm going so fast back to the General that I don't see Moses Thompson until I near walk into him. He catches my shoulders so I don't tumble, and I shake him off at once.

"I was looking for you, as it were," he says, talking like we've been having a conversation for hours. "But the General was all wrapped up and the like."

"I'm busy," I say, making to pass him. He takes strides to match mine, turning his lithe frame toward the General. Does he mean to walk me back? "You don't need to come along. I know the way."

He bobs his head side to side and keeps on walking with me, but he doesn't do so quiet, and his words hit the air like pebbles.

"I'm gonna have to head out if the Svendsen ranch goes under. I thought you might … I wanted to let you know, as it were."

"What?"

He stops in the middle of General Street. Behind him, the lights on the Prime Inn porch glow a block away, and I'm so near the General itself that I know how many paces are between me and my back door. The smell of the

Lampton pig farm wanders in the late afternoon breeze, and behind it is the scent of the massive pot of broth the Yang brothers and their wives have made at Soup's Corner.

"You're saying the ranch might fail?" I ask him, trying to make sure I hear him right. "Danny and Oddvar lost some money?"

"Heads of cattle," Moses says. "There's whole bunches dropping, scores of them. Same at Brinkleys."

It comes to mind that he's telling me this because he's hoping I might miss him if he leaves. Will I? I don't know. I don't understand the way he looks at me, like he sees under my skin and into my heart. It makes me want to shove him, and tell him to take those eyes somewhere else, on some woman who would be glad for the attention and eagerness to help that he offers me instead. I don't know why he does, and what he expects in return. There's no currency between us, and it makes me feel full of unease.

"You're saying both big ranches are in danger of shutting down," I repeat. "Both. That … that's no good. Not for anyone … I …" I think of Doctor Thomas Smith, and his grand plans and confidence. "I need to go off. See Doc Smith."

"You feeling poorly?" Moses asks at once, leaning in. "Doc Kinney would fix you up right, and the like."

"No, no, I'm alright, I just … must go."

I pick up the ends of my skirts, careful of Helena's new stitches to make over the old skirt into lines that are a bit more in fashion, and move as quick as I might back toward the Prime Inn. If I'm lucky, Doctor Smith has gone back and I'll find him in.

And I am—he's just sitting down at one of the small tables and giving Lucy his order for dinner when I arrive.

"Miss Davies," he says, standing up quickly as I approach. "Are you … perhaps you are hungry. Would you care to join me? I have invited a few others to join me at my treat, but they have not yet arrived."

My eyes wander over the scuffed boards and bare tables, and for a half moment I think how lovely this place will look when I'm finished with it, not even thinking on how the menu will look and taste, but there's more pressing worries now than prettying up a dining room.

"There's trouble on the cattle ranches," I say, refusing to sit. "The cows are sick and dying. Loads of them."

"That's sorry news," he says, slowly taking his seat. He winces as he goes, and I see the yellowing on his jaw and neck, and that his cracked lip has still not quite healed. Doctor Smith's fight with Patrick has been spun at least a dozen ways the past week, and who knows which part is true. Rusty says they were fighting over Jane, which makes no sense. Alan told Harriet, who told everyone at Saint Diana's Lutheran that it was about something Helena Salomon was making, though no one knows exactly what it was. A shirt? A pair of pants?

"It's more than sorry," I tell him. "If the ranches go, there's less need for electricity. It'll be hard going convincing the Black Hills to come here. Flats Junction needs to be growing, not shrinking for me to make further headway."

Doctor Smith gives me a sidelong look, as if measuring how tall I am.

"You are not wrong," he says at last. "But I fail to see how my hospital can do more than what I've planned in aiding your bid for the electric company."

"Not the damn hospital!" I say, slapping my hand on the table between us. "Can't you go heal the cows? Get them to stop dying!"

"Oh," he says. His forehead goes smooth. "Well, I am afraid I can't help with that."

"Why not? You're a doc. Besides, if the Brinkleys go down, they won't help you with the hospital!"

Doctor Smith looks a bit put out at last, but only shakes his head. "I'm sorry, truly, but I don't touch animals. I'm too specialized to spend time worrying on beasts. People and their sickness are my sole concern."

He glances around the Prime Inn as if hoping someone important hears him and agrees with his way, but it's only Lucy behind the bar, and three other strange men who likely are just passing through. I'm guessing Joe's out celebrating our earlier partnership. I have a desire to go find him at the Nail and join in. It's my day, too. I'm officially owner of part of this place I'm standing in.

And yet … I have no one to go tell. No one to cheer me.

If I joined Joe and Gil and the rest, would they welcome me, or get all quiet?

Well, no matter. Something must be done, and my whole insides clench. There's only one other place to go.

"Very well," I say. "Enjoy your dinner." There's no time to waste if the cattle are dying as fast as Moses says.

"Miss Davies, I would hope you'd join me," he insists. As he half stands to press his case, Reverend Painter arrives, followed by Mikey O'Donnell still dusty from the lumberyard and Tim Bailey the farrier. "And my guests," Doc Smith finishes.

Each of the men nods at me as they take a seat at Doc Smith's table, looking a bit surprised they're all eating together.

"Having a meeting of your own I see," I say.

Doctor Smith smiles slightly. "If I am to stay in Flats Junction for the rest of my life, I should like to get to know the men who matter."

Reverend Painter and Tim both swell up like roosters at this, though Mikey just folds his arms and looks at the ceiling.

"Wise to know your neighbors," I agree. "But truly I must go."

It's closer to early dusk by the time I make it across town and stand in front of the Kinney house. The porch and roof are long done, thanks to the labors of Moses and Thaddeus and Patrick himself. I remember when he first built this place, with the extra help from my father and the support of the bank. It was before I started to learn the General's business under old Harry Turner, well after his wife May had passed. It was … it was back when I still thought there was a future for Patrick and me. It was before he met Jane.

It's Jane who answers the door, too. She looks at me like I'm some sort of spirit, and opens her mouth twice before speaking out loud.

"Come in," she says, sounding like a gracious hostess in a fine Boston parlor. It sets my teeth to grind, but I follow her in anyway. Inside, I can smell the lye and the spicy leather and medicine that's Patrick's surgery, mixed with a whiff of blends from my childhood—Widow Hawks must be baking her bean stew seasoned with sumac and juniper.

"Is Patrick in?" I ask, stopping right in the threshold.

"No," she says, her body tightening as she glances into the study. "Who's ill? I can go, though I don't—"

"It's just the cows," I say.

"Again?" Jane's voice sinks, dismay flashing across her cheeks. "How many? Which ranch?"

"I don't know, just Moses says it's getting so bad he's worried Svendsens might go out of business. We can't have that. It'll ruin the town if there's less jobs, less … everything." Can she understand it's like lighting the first match in a line of twenty? Once one goes, the rest will follow, a string of dominos and waterfalls. I'll be left here, stuck in Flats Junction.

Her nose flairs as she inhales sharply. "It would be bad for everyone's business," she says, and it's all I can do not to sigh loudly with relief. She does see the way of it, then.

Jane glances back toward the kitchen, and beckons. "Come along. I've got to nurse the baby."

I hesitate for a moment. Do I want to go sit at the table and watch my mother cook for another woman, acting like a grandmother who fits in so easily? Do I want to see a piece of the domesticity that might have been mine?

But today's been a day of ups and downs, and my feet follow Jane before I've made up my mind. Before I can speak, I'm sitting down on the bench, and Widow Hawks puts a tin cup of milk in my hands before going back to the stove. She moves the way she always does, like her steps are a dance to a song, and her fingers sprinkle in herbs to the soup pot with the same flick she did when my father watched her make food in the big house.

None of this comfort pulls the tension out of my neck and shoulders. I grip the tin cup so hard I can feel its walls start to bend inward.

"Kate is worried about the sick cattle, too," Jane says, picking up her baby and unbuttoning her bodice with one hand. "Apparently it's worse than Patrick says."

Widow Hawks glances over at us. The lines on her face are deep and the wrinkles seem longer than I remember. "Why does it matter?"

"If it gets real bad, the ranches will go under," I repeat. "We've got to stop them from dying. Does … does Patrick have any inkling on what it is?"

Jane exchanges a look with Widow Hawks. "He has a few notions. But they are only his hypothesis, and there's no evidence he's even on the right track."

"Is there nothing to be done?"

"Why don't you ask that fine new Doctor Smith to help?" Jane asks. Her voice is suddenly unnaturally sharp. "It sounds like you've had a hand in making him feel welcome."

"Of course," I say, disliking the heat rising in my cheeks even as I know it won't show. "And he's a grand plan to build a hospital if I can keep everyone floating and the electric company interested."

There's a moment of silence. I feel like I've offered a bit of myself with coming here, and put my feelings out on a platter. Can't they see this matters? And not just for me, but for everyone. This is for the good of everyone!

"You put too much on your own skin," my mother says, without turning to look at me. "One woman cannot build so much."

"Why not?" I challenge her. "You did."

She turns around and looks at Jane, and then me. "But I did not do so alone."

I stare at her, wishing I didn't see her point, but it's there, glaring and obvious. She had Percy, my father, to help her do anything she wished in Flats Junction. And he had her. And I … I don't have a husband. I don't even know if I have true friends.

"Kate."

I shift to meet Jane's gaze, which is direct and clean. For the first time in years, I'm looking at the woman who first walked off the train in 1881.

"I don't think you need to do things alone," she says, her voice soft but firm. "I'm learning that, myself."

For a short moment, I sense all the years of unhappiness and lies and loss slip off.

Should I stop doing so much without assistance? Will others help?

Wouldn't that be fine if it were true.

CHAPTER 8

Helena

April 18, 1884

Some days I swear I catch a whiff of the cow-scented leather and stale booze on the breeze. It's not true, of course, but it's like the memory of those three Army recruits is burned into my nose and makes my mouth feel parched and sticky. It helps I haven't had to walk much around town since, and I am grateful it stays lighter longer every day summer creeps closer. I try not to think about what will happen again when it shortens in the fall.

The only place I really feel tucked in and safe is here, at the table in my parents' home, where I've come for lunch again. I won't move back in—I won't!—but it just feels … better to be sitting across from my two little brothers, who are both taller and bigger than me now, and next to my giant of a father, who keeps shooting me suspicious looks out of the corner of his eyes.

It's not like anything happened. Mother arrived to get the story straight from me, as she says Father gets one if not three different versions of the gossip every week. She is surprised Moses Thompson is the one who saved me from damage, and Kate seems especially irritated, as if she's also beholden to the cowboy, too.

Either way, this whole mess has ruined everything, anyway.

How can I possibly go to the Fort now? I might run into those same men, and if they recognize me, won't they try to get under my skirts again? Can I even do business with the Fort, laundering and repairing uniforms and linen? Will I be set upon over and over once I start dealing with Army men? How can I ever really feel secure?

For that matter, how will I ever feel that way in Flats Junction now, too?

"You're quieter than usual," Mother comments as she brings over bread to match the stew. Babcia sits, then remembers the soup needs a ladle. She makes to get up, but Mother presses her hand into my grandmother's shoulder and gets it instead. She sits next to Kaspar and starts slicing the bread, though I feel her eyes constantly flicking at me.

"I'm just thinking," I say, and bite into a hot potato. It sizzles on my tongue and makes me wince, so I swallow it quick, which only scorches my throat.

Father shoves a tin cup already full of well water over and keeps pace with his eating. His black beard seems to have more grey in it every month, but he always manages to keep it from getting full of food. Natan, who only has a dusting of hair starting on his upper lip, has no skill, and already looks as if he's swallowed the meal without utensils.

"Do you have a ladle?" Babcia asks, as she stares at the bread on her plate.

"*Tak*, I just got … Yes. Right here," Mother says. She plunks a whole bit on Grandmother's bowl, and exchanges a quick look with Father.

"I'm going to go check on the coals," Natan announces. He grabs a huge hunk of bread and gets up from the table. He glances at Kaspar. "Coming?"

"Mm," Kaspar swallows the last of a spoonful of spongy carrots from last year's cellar and unfolds himself as well. He's almost as tall as Father, and his arm is nearly as good as new from his terrible burns, save the awful scarring he'll keep forever. "But I'll … Ma, I'll check your furnace and the coppers, yeah?"

Mother looks up from her own meal and nods, tilting her head as she watches my brothers go to the big oak door that separates the kitchen and living quarters from the forge and tin shop. I've always thought of Natan and Kaspar as nothing more than brothers, but as they go side by side, I notice how Natan's walk is the spitting same as how my father moves, the rawness of strength and muscle obvious. Kaspar no less powerful, but he seems to see the world with more sensitivity, less bullish. Well, what does it matter? They are my brothers and they will one day take over the forge, and I won't. Though I suppose I'll always get my nails done for free.

Thinking about Natan and Kaspar being successful business owners in the blacksmith shop makes my belly feel hot. I won't be left behind!

"Remember how we talked …" I try to gather myself under the dark eyes of Mother and the grey gaze of Father. "We discussed how I shouldn't be beholden to Kate so much? And without being hitched, I only have limited options?"

Mother only sits and waits. Father shifts, and helps himself to another helping. He lifts his eyebrows at my mother and mutters. "Remind her."

That's not for me—it's for Mother to elbow Babcia, who has been staring into space and letting her stew go cold.

"Berit—you want to eat?" Mother speaks quite loud. It jerks Babcia, who stares at her bowl as if shocked it has food steaming in it. She slowly begins to put tiny amounts of broth on her spoon and drinks it carefully, with a tiny slurping.

Mother shifts back in her seat to gaze at me again. "I remember discussing that your choices are limited, yes."

"And I thought about working with the Army," I say, more for Father's benefit to catch him up. I hadn't really thought about asking for his advice as well—more Mother's, as she had to build a business up all by her lonesome before she was married. If anyone had some ideas on how to do it, it would be her. "But now … now with having had some dealings with the Army …

I just don't know if it's right for me. I'm just stuck on what to do instead, to find other ways to make income outside of Kate's goodwill."

"Army's the fastest," Father says, his low voice rumbling into the table. He grabs another crust of bread and dabs it into his bowl. "You're smart on that notion."

"It just … I had even thought I'd maybe hitch onto David Fawcett's wagon next time he's in town and drum up business at the Fort. Caroline and his kids would keep me safe … but then what to do to get back? I just … I want to try, but I'm … I feel more …" *Afraid. Uncertain. Unsafe.*

"Fawcett's not too regular. He's got his routine. You'd be stuck riding about with them for weeks until they circle back to Flats," Mother reminds me. "Do you know exactly what you want to accomplish at the Fort? Maybe he can take a message."

"I … I think I'll do better if I'm there myself." Plus, I don't want to rely on someone else to make sure I get to speak to the commander, or someone right under him. Someone who's in charge of linens and bedding, and more than just individual soldier shirts and spare fixes.

"That's not unwise," Mother says. "They would be hard pressed to say no to a pretty face." She says the truth behind my words so bluntly, and I wish she wouldn't. No wonder she never did well socially in Chicago!

"I'll take her," Father says suddenly.

Mother and I both stare at him. Babcia just keeps on eating, the metal spoon clinking against the tin sides of the bowl.

"You?" Mother asks, looking at Father as if he has suddenly shrunk or turned blonde. "You hate the Army and anything to do with Fort Randall."

"I don't hate them," he counters, pushing back from his seat on the bench. "I just wish I didn't have to deal with them. But Helena's not wrong. They're a good source of income if you can get a proper large order. You know this, Marya."

Mother presses her mouth together, but she's not done yet. "And what— the two of you will just trek ten miles safely across the prairie and hope you drum up some solid business at Fort Randall and head back?"

"It's done all the time," Father says easily. He crosses his arms about his barrel chest, but I notice a few of the fingers in his hand tremble, as if he's feeling bad about forcing Mother to let us go on this risky journey. But he's not wrong—it's not that risky, not since Yves Gardnier's posse has kept to town instead of hurting travelers at random.

"What about the … Natives? Other posses?"

"Haven't been seen in a good long while and you know it. Posses neither, this is still Yves's territory. Stop fretting. It won't change anything."

"As if I could stop worrying," Mother mutters, and stabs a tiny piece of chicken with her knife. There's only a few of the old layers left who have stopped putting up eggs. They are stringy but good in a soak and soup.

"So it's settled," Father says, as if it is a calm and normal, everyday type of decision. "I'll go see about borrowing a wagon first thing this afternoon, and we'll be off as soon as I can find one." He stands, stretches, and clomps out.

Mother and I are left to watch Babcia chew a bit of bread and forgetting to swallow, and eventually Mother just sighs and shakes her head before getting up and moving dishes.

"I can help," I say.

She glances at Babcia and grimaces, and I notice for the first time that Mother looks harried and worn and worried. How old is she? I don't think I even know what year she was born. We've never celebrated birthdays in our house. And for that matter, how old is my grandmother?

"I don't like you heading off into the prairie," Mother says, pulling the always heating water from the edge of the hearth and grabbing a sliver of soap from the sideboard. "It sets my teeth on edge just thinking of you and your father in the wilderness."

"This will be nothing compared to heading east by myself," I say.

She pulls a face. "I don't like when you remind me."

"But it's something to remember—I've been on my own in the big cities. Father wasn't there to help me, and he will this time."

"Cities have policemen. There are protections in place. The Fort … out here, such places are a law onto themselves."

"I know, but you can't blame me for wanting—needing to try this."

She sighs and hands me the first of many dishes to dry. The water peels off the edge of the tinplate, a clear tear with a prism inside it. It reminds me of the colors cast by sunset on the mammoth buildings of Boston. The trip east feels like a dream, and I know I only really managed to stay safe because of the hints Hardy had offered and my own gut reactions, plus always finding a woman friend to walk about with. Once I met with the seamstresses at different shoppes, I was always surrounded and careful.

But this will be no different, I remind myself. It will just be muddier.

It only takes Father two days to settle up a wagon by borrowing Franklin Jones's. He's in a sour mood within two hours after securing it, because word gets around like fire on a dry summer day and Kate asks to go along to 'talk business' with the Army commander, though I don't know what exactly she could say to him. It's not like she can offer anything more that she already does with goods at her General. But Father can't say no—there's invisible politics always holding sway involved with who offends who outright, and no one wants to be obvious. I've gotten better at seeing all that now that I run my own shop, but I'm not near as good as Father and Mother in knowing how it all overlaps.

As soon as we have the wagon packed up with some of Mother's goods to try and sell—tin cups and small coffee pots, a few gentlemen's lanterns and cartridge boxes—as well as some examples of Father's better work on hinges and specialty tools he builds and my own samples of stitching and repairs, Kate arrives. She has her own small roll of sleeping blankets, and food for the trip there and back. We should only be gone a night, as it's a quick ten miles one way. Mother hands up bundles to Father and offers Kate a tight smile as she loads up the additional items.

"You think you'll find what you're looking for at the Fort?" she asks Kate.

Kate nods. "I would think so."

Mother's mouth stays in a line but, she doesn't argue. She's likely argued out after the past two days when she still tried to convince Father and me that a trip to the Fort was unnecessary, and we could just wait until the Fort commander arrives in town sometime and take it up with him then.

But it seems a fire's lit in Father, like he's hungry for a challenge or needs to prove something, and I'm just an excuse to get him out of the town. Kate coming along doesn't bother me any—I figure she's a businesswoman same as me, and she'll understand the merit of finding additional income. I just hope she doesn't realize I'm using it as insurance against her.

Word travels fast in Flats Junction on a typical type of day, and as we jump in, we're hailed by both Tim and Julie at the farrier's.

But we don't go more than twenty feet before the horses jerk to a stop.

Standing in the middle of First Street, looking very much like they might murder us, is Matthias Hummel and Natty Martin. Both have their arms hanging at their sides, looking useless and limp, but all that does is draw my attention down to the knives and guns glistening on their belts. Matthias doesn't move, like the great silent stone mountain he is, but Natty grins, showing off his jagged left canine. His gaze slides past us all, as if his eyes are filled with oil and can't look at anyone straight or for more than half an instant, and he adds more grease to his already slimy hair when he runs a hand through it and plunks his wide brimmed hat back on.

"Yves says we're t' come too," Natty says. He doesn't wait for Father to answer and makes his way to the bench spot, swinging himself up so fast that Father only has time to shift over his bulk just enough that not a speck of him will touch Natty, not even a piece of clothing. Father's back has gone rigid, his wide fingers on the reins are white against the pink and red scars. I curl my stomach in and try to make myself extra small as Matthias's giant frame clambers on. He sits in the middle of the wagon and looks at me, then Kate, and then out backward so all we see is the straining seam that runs down the middle of his coat and the golden back of his hair under the hat.

"Why?"

Kate's voice sounds like a crack. I look at her, and she's glaring daggers at Matthias's back. It's Natty who answers, though.

"Yves says we're to be the eyes on you, so's to make sure you don't have any plans to double cross him with the Fort."

Kate snorts. "And exactly how would I do that?"

"He says you already talked about him having the Fort as his territory."

"We did n—" Kate slaps her lips together and huffs. "I'm doing nothing of the sort."

"Then there's no trouble." Natty pulls out a knife and starts to slam it into the wood next to him. Oooh—Franklin's not going to like that damage, that's sure. "Go on then, Thad. We wanna get there around midday for a meal."

Father pauses an extra-long moment, as if he's making a point that he won't be completely cowed by these raiders, but he really doesn't have a choice. He only has his knife and a small gun, and what's that going to do? Start a gun fight on First Street between himself and the posse? He doesn't stand a chance against Natty's draw—everyone knows he's the best.

We head on out, with Mother's worried face watching from the forge doorway. Kate's fuming is so palpable I'm pretty sure there's a taste of it on the air, a tang of red-hot pepper and black smoke. I don't like it neither, but what are we to do?

"What's a pretty young thing like you doing and going all the way to the big Fort?" Natty asks. It takes me a minute to realize he's talking to me. I feel like all the street smarts that worked in Chicago fly out of my head, and I only stare at him with my tongue stuck to the top of my mouth.

"Don't talk to her," Father says. His voice is hard and sharp, like how he sounds when he's very angry but can't fix it. I've heard him shout like that occasionally, mostly with my brothers and me. It's different with Mother— more a fear than anger—when he shouts at her.

"I can talk to who I please," Natty says, his nasal voice going up. "Sides, how else we gonna pass the time."

"As you wish, as long as it doesn't involve my daughter."

It makes me feel all warm and full when Father says this, but then it slips away when Natty casts a glance over his shoulder at me anyway. It's silent, and maybe Father doesn't catch it, but it makes ice crackle in my gut, and then spider down my arms and hips. That look alone suddenly brings back the night the recruits grabbed me, and I almost tell Father to turn around and let me stay back. What am I doing, facing more Army men?!

"If you ain't going to cross Yves, what can you want with the Fort?" Natty turns his attention to Kate. Though he asks what I want to know myself, somehow him asking feels … vile. Kate only lifts her chin and turns her head to watch the land roll away from us. Her sleek black hair falls out of her pins bit by bit, until tendrils of it whip around her jaw and across her sight. She pushes it back with annoyance and glances at me. I feel like we share the same fright and worry, but maybe I'm only imagining she feels a kinship to me.

"You don't talk to the womenfolk," Father says to Natty. "And we'll all be just fine to and from the Fort."

"Who are you to say so, old man?" Natty hisses, pressing his face into Father's. "Ifen I ask Kate to share my bedroll, and she wants to, you gonna stop her and me?"

I shudder at the vulgarity, the casual way he talks about sex. It's part of life, I know, always simmering on the surface. I know my own parents didn't stop as they've aged—my new baby brother Garek is testament enough to that. But still … it makes me feel caked in dirt when he talks about it so obvious, and I glance again at Kate.

Father decides he won't pick a fight when he's driving the horses, and without anyone to spar words with, Natty eventually gives up poking at Kate and making side comments about her coloring, her bosom, and her height. She's not pale enough that her cheeks turn deep red, but she sits very still and her cheekbones turn a high rose until he stops. I wonder if she's dreading sleeping anywhere near Natty tonight.

The Fort itself is squat, sitting on the prairie like a beast trying to hide, except it's hiding in plain sight, with all the flat land surrounding it. The spire of a stone chapel rises next to all the halls and barracks. The smell of baking bread threads through the wind from the small bakery, and there's even a small building called a "hospital" but it doesn't look very grand at all, not like what Kate says Doctor Smith is planning to build in Flats Junction. But then again, the Fort doesn't have as many people living around as we do in town.

We're told the Fort commander, who Father says is called Lieutenant Colonel Peter Swaine, is already at his midday meal when we drive up. I notice two women watching from the doorway of one of the larger buildings, which Kate says is the Captain's quarters, and that must be Swaine's wife and a daughter. By the time we find a place for the wagon and get the horses some water, one of the women has disappeared into the blackness of the big house and the younger one waits to take us in. Kate leads the way, with Father trailing nervously and glancing at the wagon.

Natty grins at him. "Don't worry none, I'll watch the goods with Matthias. Ain't no fancy uniform gonna take your shit."

"It's not the Army I'm worried about," Father murmurs, but I'm the only one who hears him. I toss one look back at the wagon and the two posse members before the Captain's house envelops us.

There has to be at least two dozen rooms in this space, and it's all hallways and echoes until we get to the kitchen, which has two hearths and two trestle tables, and an uncountable number of pots, pans and dishes. My eyes dance over the battered tin and handful of copper, and the heavy irons hanging on hooks. I'm sure we can sell at least some of Mother's wares here, if not all.

There are a half-dozen men at the table, all served by the older woman, with her daughter soundlessly joining her over one of the fires. A few look at us briefly, but they're far too interested in their meal and drink, all eating with their elbows on the table and no linen on their laps to see.

The Lieutenant Colonel glances up at us as he saws away at a piece of salted pork. He is slope-shouldered, with a wiry, complicated mustache the color of wet sand and heavy-lidded eye sockets. He is in full uniform, but the collar is open and the brass buttons look tarnished. The presence of his wife and daughter give me a moment of doubt—surely they at least look after his clothes, and many others?

"Visitors," he greets, stuffing his cheek as he talks. Spittle and grease spray into his mug of watered down ale, which he then picks up and drinks to wash down the meat. "From Flats Junction, I'd assume."

"Where else?" Kate asks flippantly.

His eyes roll over her, and then meet my father's. "Where else, indeed?"

"We've all come with something to offer," Father says gruffly. He shifts his feet, and his thumbs ghost along his hips, where he often rests them in the copper rings he keeps on his leather apron. He's not wearing the apron now, and his wide hands look a bit lost, quivering a bit with nerves and lack of knowing what to do.

"And?" Swaine asks, taking another dripping mouthful of pork. "To sell or …?"

"Ideas," Kate jumps in. "At least, in my case."

His thick eyebrows shoot up, but the Lieutenant Colonel doesn't stop chopping at his gristle. "I'm listening, ain't I?"

Kate seems to go a little stiff next to me, but she holds her head straight and takes it upon herself to sit on the edge of the bench to the far right, which is empty of menfolk. She sits on it like a queen might, who is not impressed with her surroundings.

"Electricity," she states. "I propose electricity be run to the Fort."

Swaine snorts and guffaws, then chokes on the salt and has to chug his ale. He wipes his palm across his cheeks, leaving the shine of meat behind and hands his mug out to his wife. She takes it as if she can read his mind, and she measures out ale and water carefully.

"Electric? From where? All the way from Yankton?"

"Deadwood."

The answer seems to intrigue him, and he sips his new beer carefully as he stares at Kate. Father fidgets next to me, and I wish he wouldn't. They might remember we're here and we won't be able to hear what goes on. And Kate might not wish to tell us.

"What would I do with electric?" he wonders.

"Light your house, for starters," she says easily, as if she's been rehearsing it the whole way here. "And all the barracks and other quarters and offices."

"Gov'ment won't pay for such an expense when other forts don't have none," he scoffs.

"And your hospital," she continues. "With electric in the hospital, you can get better doctors and more. Our own new doc, Doc Smith, is putting in a large hospital in Flats Junction. He's fresh off from the east and knows everything about cures and disease, and he's going to hook up electric in our hospital."

This makes the Lieutenant Colonel pause completely. "You saying your hospital will be better than ours, then, eh."

"I'm only offering to share."

He sets down his mug and glances between his mates. Judging by the bands on their frayed uniforms, they're high ranking, or nearly. One, who looks fresh and too young to be out west at all, nods.

"We've got ourselves at least seven struck down by the dread black measles and two with the wasting runs," he informs Kate. "Our doc here can't do a thing for them."

"Electricity won't cure them, either," she says carefully. "But perhaps it would entice a doctor to come and … assist your physician." She's so perfectly political, I file away in my mind how she tilts her head and yet doesn't offer or overly promise or even offend the doctor here.

Swaine smiles slightly, though it doesn't fill his eyes with happy sparks. He sighs and puts his elbows on the table over his plate.

"I'm not opposed to it. You say you're truly getting a bona fide hospital, electric and all, eh?"

"And several other establishments."

"Hm. Well. It's only an idea," Swaine shrugs.

"It'll be more than that soon enough," Kate presses. "You might not want to wait, or else the lines will pass you by and the time for choosing electric or no will be gone."

I don't completely understand why it matters to Kate if the Army wants electric or not. With places like the Prime Inn getting it, and maybe Fortuna's and the General and even the bank, wouldn't that be good enough?

But there's no time to ponder more, because the Lieutenant Colonel pins me with his eyes next.

"And you, girl? We don't hold with whores here, mind. This is a family establishment."

Behind him, his wife flinches at his foul word, and Father shifts half in front of me. He crosses his arms and looks down his nose at Swaine.

"I'll ask you to speak respectable like in front of my daughter."

"Apologies," the commander says, waving a hand like he can make his cuss break apart in the air. "Well?"

I move slight away from Father, and suddenly I realize I'm standing right in the middle of the room, and all the pairs of eyeballs are staring right at me. Even when I was asking around finely dressed women where they got their gowns made out east, I wasn't this nervous. The lines on my palms turn hot and sweaty at once. I ball them up and look at each man particularly, then glance at the Lieutenant Colonel.

"I'm offering my services as a seamstress." I glance at the wife and daughter, who have paused and are looking at me now, too. It makes me feel like squirming. "I brought some samples of my stitching. Repairs, new shirts, sheets and whatever else is needed for linens."

"Laundry we do here," Swaine jerks his head at the two women near the hearth.

"Of course," I agree at once. "I've no plans to become a laundress. I'm simply here to take on any of the extra sewing for any and all. If anything, it might take some of the mending work off your women."

"Most of my men has got them an old soldier's wife box, and can do their own," Swaine states. "Why'd they pay for it, I don't know."

"Oh." My feet sweat through my socks. "Well, if they already do their own mending."

"You mean to tell me you prefer your men to spend the hours with their little boxes of needles and thread," Kate interrupts, spreading her arms out toward the whole room, "patching their own duds, when they could have a professional do it? I'd think you'd want them to have the extra time for drills against raids."

Swaine grunts, squints at me, and gives Kate a blank sort of look. "Bit rich talking about Indian raids coming from you, woman."

"I suppose you're a bit too green to remember my father, Percy Davies, the Welsh banker," she says calmly. "You likely know far more about the raids than I do."

It is beautifully done, the barbs and dance of reminders to one another. I don't know if I will ever be as savvy as Kate. But … *He'll say no.* I know he's going to say no to me, because Kate pushed … I don't know if I'm glad for her help or dismayed.

The wife steps closer to her husband. "Having a seamstress would be a gift, Peter," she says quietly, but her voice is rough and rich. "It would give me the time I need to keep up with this place. Twenty-seven rooms is enough for four women, and there's only the two of us. Please."

He cocks his head at her, and then twists back to me. "How'd you get it to and from Flats? A pretty thing like you can't be riding back and forth all the time."

"Fawcett, if that is amenable," I say, my heart suddenly banging in the middle of my stomach, as if I swallowed and ate it whole. "David can shuttle it safely."

The Lieutenant Colonel shrugs lightly. He looks up at his wife's eager face and then lets out a meaty sigh. "Very well, Dorothy. A gift." He pokes one of the younger men to his left. "Go shout out that anyone wanting some repairs or new duds to come see this gal before dinner." The young officer scurries out, leaving behind his messy dish for the daughter to clear.

It's done and settled all at once, and it makes me breathe out in rush. Why had I waited so long to do this? Was it because I always envisioned going alone? Because I could copy Kate, watch Kate negotiate?

My father's conversation is quick and terse, as he's no good at selling himself and always just sounds angry. It doesn't help that he learns, given the lack of official blacksmith, that the amount of work is large and the Lieutenant Colonel would prefer my father move up to the Fort itself to handle it.

"Can't," Father says shortly, his brow low. He crosses his arms tight. "Asking me to give up my trade in town is impossible. And my wife … my wife can't."

"If she's poorly, we just might have an electrified hospital soon enough," Swaine says, his glance sliding to Kate again.

"It's not that," Father says. The cheekbones above his beard turn pale pink. "She's a tradeswoman herself. She's not going to be a tinsmith in this small Fort. Not enough work."

Swaine leans forward. "Tinsmith—that's right. I heard tell of it."

"Yes. Has been for near twenty years now," Father says. I hear it at last. It's pride. He's proud of Mother!

"Oh, yeah, so you're the ones what made Bush's fancy sword all them years ago."

"We are. She is."

"Huh." He sits deeper in his chair. "That sword is the stuff of stories 'round here."

"We've brought some of her wares, if you'd like to see," Father remembers. He nods at me. "We can bring them in or—"

"No, no, let the boys pick over them first," Swaine waves his hand. "And if you refuse to move a forge up here, Salomon, I'll give you some of the smaller work."

It's not what Father was hoping for, but any additional work is always welcome. Most of Mother's tinware sells, and I have to beg paper and a pencil from one of the officers to write down how many shirts and some quick measurements I need to make. We also take a wool bag full of uniform pieces and other clothes for repair, and the stench of the unwashed cloth oozes out from the bag even after it's tied shut with a leather strap. Kate looks particularly pleased with her signed note from the Lieutenant Colonel, which she folds up and puts inside her satchel as Natty's glistening eyes watch.

We eat dinner and bunk at the Captain's house in one of the many stale rooms, and depart so early the sun has not risen the next morning. Father seems particularly itchy to get back home, and I wonder if it's because he's afraid the boys have ruined the forge or if he misses Mother that much.

"What's in the fancy paper you got, Kitty?" Natty asks. He sits next to Kate this time, his shoulder a bare centimeter from hers. Matthias sits opposite them both, and I try to keep my distance completely, and wonder if I should just go sit up with Father. The morning is filled with early birdsong and the barest hint of dew, and the sky is a pale eggshell that promises a cloudless spring day.

"Never you mind," she says crisp and tart. "Just know it'll help Flats Junction."

"Will it hurt Yves, then?" Natty presses. "Y'gotta tell me, or I'll tell him a lie." He leans forward, his hand reaching for Kate's leg.

Matthias shifts, readjusting his seat, and Natty pauses, glances at the mountain of a man, and slowly pulls his hand back, his eyes still cold and swallowing the last of the night.

"No need to lie," she says. "If he hasn't heard about my work already, then he's just plumb stupid."

This doesn't make Natty any happier, but he just chews on the inside of his cheeks and stares at her, as if trying to figure out how to torture the information out of her.

In a flash of realization, I get it.

If Kate's able to convince everyone to pay for electric, and then she's the one getting the electric company into town. And if she's holding the keys to something like that … well, then she's going to be just about the most important woman—person—in Flats Junction. And then I wonder about my own plans for the future. If Kate is going to be so powerful, do I really want to put distance between her and me?

"Woah," Father says, breaking into my epiphany. "Woah, boys."

The horses slow, then stop, and we all stand up from the wagon back to see why. Maybe wild horses, or Indians off the reservation, or …

Instead of any of those, it's six scraggly men on narrow horses, sunburned and lean and looking every bit as rough as they probably are. My whole insides slam against my skin, as if my body wants to force me to start running even before I've had the thought. But where would I go? They'd run me down in a half second.

And then I realize they are wearing faded Union uniforms, and it comes to me—deserters. There's always a couple, but these look like they've formed a regular group of raiders.

"Whatcha got in that here wagon?" one drawls. He fingers his gun, while others slowly put their hands on the holsters of their own.

"Nothing much. Dirty clothes from the Fort, a few vittles and bedrolls," Father answers. I think he's smart to say the truth, but then I think of my virginity, and the bit of cash for Mother's wares, and hope swiftly that they don't find out he's also lying.

"You mean to tell me you lot are just packin' laundry?" the leader cackles. "It's too early in the day for jokes. Come on, boys, let's check it out."

"Stop there," Natty says. His voice is oily and there's a new meanness to it. "Else you want to find out that it's not too early to kill a man."

"Oh, it's never too early to do that." The leader inches his horse two steps nearer. "But if you're willing to die on what's in that wagon, it's worth the chance."

It goes from cordial to gunfire in a half-second. I scream and dive down as the wood on the side of the wagon splinters into ash and fragments. Kate plasters herself next to me and covers her skull and mine with her hands.

There's a grunt from Father and the roar of his gun, and it's over in less than half a minute before the sounds of yips and a few squealing horses ring out as the last of the deserters fly away on their horses, getting far away from our guns. The smell of gunpowder floats overhead as I look up slightly, wondering why Natty and Matthias are both standing, unhurt, and double fisting their guns lazily as if nothing happened.

"I'm still the fastest draw around," Natty declares. "Damn fools don't know who I am anymore. It's Yves, keeping us living in a town. My reputation is fading and I don't like it."

"But that gave you the advantage," Kate says. Her voice is strong and steady, without a single tremor. "And we are grateful."

I never thought I'd be glad to know outlaws. The posse has always been scarier than anything else, but as I get to a kneel, I am shocked that she's right. Gratitude pummels through me, just as hard and swift as the handful of bullets that had shot out seconds ago.

"You alright, Thad?" Kate asks. I swing around to match her gaze, and see my Father holding his side. A small bloom of blood colors the dark grey of his shirt, and it's all I can do not to scream again.

"Scratch only," Father says. His voice is not very different, but he looks white, and green along the edges. "It just cut through the cloth is all. Missed me."

"How do you know?" I ask, reaching up to check the wound. He jerks away on instinct, and then glances down.

"It'd hurt more if it was a real shot," he reasons. "C'mon. Let's finish up before the wolves come and eat."

Wolves? I finally notice the three dead bodies. One is hanging from the saddle, stuck by stirrups or rope. Two are on the ground, with the riderless horses meandering close enough to their fellows, but already eating spring grass as if there hadn't just been a quick fight ending in death and blood.

Once again, shock and thankfulness rear up.

If it hadn't been for Matthias and Natty … Father and I would be dead, or at least hurt and robbed …

It will not help that Mother has been right about this trip.

"You go have Doc Kinney look at that when we get back, Thaddeus," Kate says, as she watches Matthias cut the horse free of the dead body. He does not even seem to notice the corpses, instead only worrying about taking off saddles and bridles, which he throws into the back of the wagon without a single sound.

"Docs," Father huffs. He winces as he moves, but the bloom of blood doesn't grow too much or very fast, so I hope he's right about it just being a nick. We leave the horses to roam free, and they head off at an easy pace toward the west, and we leave behind the dead. It feels sacrilegious not to bury them, though I know why we don't. Still, I make a promise to myself that I'll ask for forgiveness from Father Jonathan when I go to church again on Sunday.

"Well, if you have gone off Patrick, you could always see Doctor Smith. We've options, now," Kate says. She sounds very pleased about this.

She sounds pleased about everything as we continue on, like she's living on a high of joy after facing death. I'm not sure how I feel. I keep thinking on the dead Army deserters and the Army recruits, and how I'll have to depend on the Army for additional income, too. I'll even have to depend on David Fawcett for shuttling the linens back and forth. I'm still beholden to someone—menfolk—even as I try to build up a place for myself.

Listening to Kate makes me realize that even though she has plans and she's putting together the puzzle to build up Flats Junction, she's in the same position as me.

I don't like it, really, but what choice do I have? What choice do either of us have?

CHAPTER 9

Jane

April 24, 1884

The four slim notebooks are frayed along the spine, and one has coffee stains along the bottom of all its pages. Spaced along the center of the kitchen table, they are the compilation of an entire year learning from Esther and jotting down information she tells me, or that I strive to remember later when she speaks over laundry or dishes and I have no way to jot it down until later. Those are the entries I worry about the most as it relies on my memory, which became foggy in the last weeks of my pregnancy and sometimes is still just as muddled when I'm juggling Andrew, housework, and the occasional patient.

We sit opposite one another, staring at the covers as if they can read our minds and lift out the information that might be useful.

I pull one toward me and open the cover, and then the first page. My looping handwriting, which my mother always said was a bit too practical to be beautiful, covers the paper with as much organization as I could create. This has been difficult to do, what with getting knowledge from Esther's background as she recalls it, which is never with rhyme or reason, but as the flowers bloom each month, or as she suddenly has a thought.

"This journal is from the spring," I tell her. "Everything to do with April, May and June that you've offered."

"It is not complete," she says, sounding slightly dismayed. When I meet her dark gaze, sorrow and disappointment and resignation flit across the long planes of her cheeks. "I am not a woman who keeps medicine. I am not the keeper of anything in my family, and I only know what I saw in passing."

"Is there … anyone you can ask?" I dislike inquiring. It only serves to remind me how soon she will be leaving me forever. "Or send for?"

She shakes her head. "My ties are not so strong that I can go and beg a favor if only to take it away and give it to you."

"But it will save lives! The cattle are dying every week!"

Esther fixes me with a steady stare, unmoving and straight. "And do you not think many of my people will be glad of this? That it will mean the end of the ranches and farms, and everyone will leave? No, Jane," she shakes her head slightly. "It will not do."

Slipping a finger along the edge of the journal, which is softened by days banging in my apron pocket, I let the pages flutter and then close it.

"It's all I can do to help Patrick," I say, stating the obvious. "And to tell that damnable Doctor Smi—"

"Hello?"

I sling a leg over the bench in preparation to dash out. Few people walk straight in without knocking, as if it's the one piece of respect they can give in deference to Patrick as the doctor, whether they like him or no. How does Kate manage living where the door is always open and people can come in and out as they please?

My view is straight down the hall, but Helena Salomon does not move with haste, so it cannot be a health emergency, then. She closes the door behind her and walks in carefully, her eyes darting about as she cranes her neck in the study and surgery as she comes to the kitchen door threshold.

"I didn't want to wake the baby," she says.

"Very thoughtful of you," I tell her, as my eyes flit up to the ceiling. Andrew is sleeping in our bedroom for his long morning nap, which he has at last begun to take. Esther tells me that babes will often do this, though how they are so very tired mere hours after the night I do not understand.

"Is the doc in?" she asks.

"No—is anything needed?"

"Not really. Not like that. Only … I thought you might want to know. That is, I went to Fort Randall about a week ago, to take in some additional sewing, and my father went too, and Kate and some of the posse, but …" She pauses, and she seems to realize she's rambling. "There's some cases of the black measles at the Fort, too, and their doctor doesn't know how to cure it, but I thought maybe Doc Kinney might?"

"Oh, my dear," I say. "That is kind of you to come to ask." Does she know how much her confidence in my husband warms the pumping of my heart? Does she know the rumors that still swirl around Patrick—all manner of things, from him being an unethical sawbones to bringing disease to people due to his relationship with Esther? Perhaps she is too young to know or remember or even to care. Either way, the fact that she comes here, instead of to Doctor Smith, is something of a small victory. We will not be run out of town yet!

"Do you have a way to heal it?" she asks.

"Not … not especially, no." The slack face of little Perry Woodman flits across my mind, but I shove it away with little luck. The notion of battling that disease yet again makes my stomach revolt and my muscles go rigid, as if all the thoughts I've ever had flee, and I'm left a husk of nothing.

"Oh." She looks around the kitchen with eager, interested eyes, and I realize she has never been inside our house. It is not much to look at, though I am proud of my pantry, with its flat shelves and organized tins, and the oiled stove that gleams. Perhaps the best is the great counter where I manage the dishes or leave bread to rise, which has a window looking east that encompasses the prairie and, in the distance, the pale roofs of the Brinkley farm.

"Hardy is out with Doctor Kinney," I tell her. "But I shall mention you stopped by."

She flushes hard at that. "And about the black measles."

"That, especially. The doctor will indeed want to know. Truly, Helena."

With a last look about the room, she nods and heads out, closing the door with the same amount of care as when she entered. I suppose she is the eldest of several children and has been scolded enough on 'not bothering the babies'.

"It is a white man's disease," Esther says. "We do not have this trouble."

My eyebrows rise. "Never?"

"Not enough for it to be considered part of us, or our world." She pulls my springtime journal toward her and pages through it, pausing mostly at the illustrations. I don't know how well she reads English—or if she ever really wished to or bothered to learn. The Lakota do not write their stories and do not spell their words, as it is a language learned by speaking it. I suppose she had Percy Davies to help her navigate, and after he died, there was Patrick, so she never truly had a need, unless she was interested as a hobby.

"You've said before that we could use sweetgrass," I prod. "That the scent of it keeps any number of ills away."

"Bad spirits," she says. "But you don't believe in them."

She's not wrong, though I find myself more inclined to listen now that I've left my original Congregational denomination to join Patrick's Catholic church. True, it was partially for necessity of marriage and because Flats Junction does not have a Congregational church, but it seems once one makes a break from a long-used belief, one is far more open to continuing the exploration. Perhaps that is how scientists are, too—once they start learning more of the world, they are hungry to constantly keep adding wonders to their lives, to explore and learn.

"How do you use sweetgrass?" I ask.

Esther tilts her head, the long hair unmoving as today she has bound her braid around in a crown. She looks lost in thought, and if I did not know her well, I would think she had not heard me. But I only wait, tracing the patterns and whorls of grain in the pitted table. A few lost crumbs pile into one of the cracks, and I pull at it with the nail of my pinky.

"I recall we braided it, and let it dry," she starts, her low voice musical with memory. "We wove baskets with it, and necklaces, and it smoked constantly in our dwellings. It was the smell of our hair and our leather clothes, baked into our skin. It was done to keep us safe … that is how we say it … but does it work against all manner of illness? I cannot say. Maybe it did, because we did not suffer from this sickness. But does this matter, Jane? You will not use grass pots and burn it in this house every day. And if you will not … what woman in Flats Junction will?"

I open my mouth to argue with her, even though every point I have won't make a difference, when the both of us know she's correct.

This time, we are interrupted by Patrick, who comes straight into the kitchen without washing up in his surgery, leaving me no time to whisk the journals off the table before he sees them. Not that he will be angry I write, but the manner of the information in them will only serve to annoy him … to remind him that I continue to file away Esther's knowledge against his request and his preference.

This time is no different, and he stares at the four little books on the table with curiosity and then something close to a shadow of anger. The sound of Hardy tinkering in the surgery is the only sound for a moment.

"Still at it, are you?" he asks, his voice rough with the flash of irritation he tries to hide. His mouth trembles, but he holds his tongue, and I'm grateful we do not have another row that will only be a repetition of what we've shouted at one another in the past with no resolution to be seen.

"Why not?" I counter. "You never know if we might find something useful."

"You know how I feel about this," he says, dropping his medical bag by the entry and taking the few steps to the table. He stands over us, frowning at the journals as if they contain poison or lies. Perhaps to him, they do in some ways. It is everything he's been taught to disregard, and to see as false, and a barrier to teaching folks the true facts of medicine.

"I understand," I say, looking up at him. "I do. But I cannot help but wonder how medicine is discovered."

"What do you mean? You're talkin' about how a scientific breakthrough comes on, or a new theory is proven?"

"Yes. Take your favorite physicians … ones you quote often. Semmelweis, for instance. How did he learn anything new besides the dogma they taught in the medical schools?"

Esther meets my gaze, and the quick flash of warmth has me hiding a small curl of a smile. She sits and waits for Patrick, still as a pond in the late heat, her shoulders flat and unyielding.

His lips stop trembling, and his fists uncurl. After a moment, he shifts onto one foot, and he runs a hand through his hair.

"You're sayin' I'm ignorin' the fact that half of medicine is observin', watchin' others choose differently and seein' what they come up with?"

"Yes," I smile. "That's exactly it."

"Hm." He takes a seat next to me and stares at the journals. Slowly, he picks one up—the one from last summer, as it has mud stains on the back where I dropped it while harvesting beans and squashes. He pages through it, his eyes swiping back and forth quickly. I find myself edging to the corner of the bench, my breath tight inside my chest as if I'm waiting for the approval of a teacher or professor on an assignment.

"You must admit there's merit to that part of the profession," I press. "And it's an important part."

"But *you're* ignorin' the fact that most everyone who changes the norm, who insists they've discovered somethin' new, are met with ridicule. No one believes them. And it's not helpful if the source is disliked to start." He lifts his head to look at Esther with apology.

"You only speak the truth," she says. There is no blame in her voice, or even sorrow.

"And you speak of Semmelweis," he continues, glancing at me. "You know he spent his career tryin' to get folks to agree with him, to see he'd discovered the source of infection, to believe him and do what he said to stave it off.

Until he compiled data, usin' that observin' and watchin' you speak of, doctors believed women died of childbed fever because of putrid air or seasonal changes or even livin' an amoral life. Now we're sure it's not that, and Semmelweis had the answers from the start. But back when he'd figured it out, no one listened, and it drove him mad, it's said. It's only now, years after his death, that we know he was right."

"I won't be driven mad by the quest for knowledge," I say, "or to compile what Esther tells me."

"You're missin' the point, Jane," he says, shaking his head and sitting up tall.

"I'm not. I was only being a bit flippant. But truly, Patrick, if we even just keep it here, between us—"

"Is there a secret?" Hardy asks, coming into the kitchen with the usual lean look of hunger around the corners of his eyes. "A doctoring one?"

We share a long look between the three of us before Esther soundlessly stands to get food for the boy, and Patrick sighs.

"I suppose you ought to learn how to hold your tongue soon enough."

"I can keep a secret!" he says, his eyes going wide and blown with earnestness. "I really can. Honest!"

"It's more than that," Patrick explains. "There are times when you don't need—or shouldn't—tell the whole of something to a patient or their loved ones. Or times you know if you force an issue, it'll only make things worse. Or if you're onto an experiment but don't want folks to know too soon, in case you fail."

"I see, doc, I do," Hardy says, taking the spot Esther just left. He wiggles his bottom on the bench and rubs his arms. "We sure do a lot of riding, don't we?"

"It's part of the job, aye," Patrick says wryly. "Until they start comin' to us."

I swallow the reminder that if Doctor Smith gets his hospital, patients will indeed come to a place instead of the physician traveling all over. And yet, I have to hope that there will always be a place for home care as Patrick offers, especially if the gloomy reality is that we might have to go somewhere else to find a place if there isn't one here. I certainly cannot envision my husband working with—or under!—Thomas Smith!

Oh, how I wish he had not arrived!

What will come of it?

I do not like that he has singled out Patrick, stalked him to the western territories. Of all places to choose for a hospital, he'd be better off building something closer to Yankton and Vermillion … but here? It is an odd choice, and reeks of little more than spite. Yet what can we do? What can we say? And perhaps worse … how do we draw a line and wait to see who in Flats Junction would come to Patrick's side of any such disagreement?

The knock on the door is loud this time, startling all of us. It's not the usual staccato of urgency, or the quick tap of a friend stopping by. This is a pound, three strikes like a hammer blow. Patrick heads straight to it, Hardy a shadow behind him even as Esther brings over warmed crisp made from last year's dried apples and sass.

"Thad. Come in," Patrick's voice carries down the hallway, and the heavy steps of the blacksmith follow my husband back into the kitchen. Patrick re-enters and heads over to put the kettle on for hot water, the movement old and practiced. There are times he forgets still he has women to do such things, but I've never resented his casual familiarity in the kitchen.

Thaddeus Salomon takes up a bit too much room, and not for the first time do I wonder how Marie manages to never be intimidated by her giant of a husband—I think I'd constantly be jumping about at his low and loud voice and his height. But today he looks peaked under the beard, his skin a waxy yellow-pink along the cheekbones, and sweat stands out on his temples.

"My wife won't leave it be," he states. "So I've come."

"And what can we assist with, Thaddeus?" I ask, hoping against hope that for once the Salomons will have come to us long before it is too late.

"This." He shoves his leather apron to the side and lifts up the cotton shirt to expose an ugly laceration along the bottom of his ribs.

"What—did one of the boys swing a rod of hot iron too close?" I ask, taking in the pucker of the skin, and the angry purple and rose all along the slice of unhealed flesh.

"My boys know how to handle themselves in a metal shop," he growls, and shoots Hardy a pointed glance. Patrick's apprentice shifts from one foot to the other and colors his usual light red, but he doesn't look at his shoes.

"The heat would have seared the skin different, too," Patrick adds softly, mostly for my benefit. In that, relief melts into me like just-made butter. If he's still offering medical knowledge, it means he is at least not too angry about my journals on Lakota herbal remedies.

"Why didn't you bind it up?" I ask. My eyes run along the curl of putrid flesh.

"Marie is many things, but she's no healer," Thaddeus shrugs, putting his shirt back down and glaring around the room. "It stopped bleeding, anyway."

"Because it's fillin' with pus. Infection. It'll poison your blood soon enough," Patrick says. "To the surgery then." He nods at Esther. "Bring the water when it boils, aye?"

She nods and the rest of us all file down the hall, Thaddeus leading the way, and I marvel that he does so without argument or even speculation that Patrick will saw him in half. That alone must mean he is worried about his wound.

Thaddeus puts himself gingerly on the table in the middle of the room, rumpling the linen and looking very uncertain. I won't be surprised if he decides in the end to bolt, but then again, if he's come this far, Marie must have been after him without end.

"How did Marie convince you?" I ask, as I pull out a few clean pieces of cotton for rags.

"She swore she'd not come to our bed until I do," he says gruffly.

"That can't always be too much a chore," Patrick says. "Sometimes a man might sleep just as well in the quiet of a spare room."

"I haven't slept alone since sixty-seven, and I'm not starting now." The yellow color in Thaddeus's skin gives way to a pale flush for an instant.

I bend my head back over the linen cabinet to hide my smile, and Hardy clears his throat, then makes a quick and transparent excuse to go check on the water.

"What's it from?" Patrick asks as he selects a few tools, soap, and our precious iodine. I want to peel back the shirt, which has spots of fluid seeping through, but the idea of stripping Thaddeus Salomon feels strange and intimate and something only for Marie. That said, I'm supposed to play nurse and not be squeamish about such things. It's just … Thaddeus. He might bite my head off for even touching the hem.

He saves me by ripping it off, hissing through his teeth as he lifts the shirt over his head himself. The skin stretches and looks like it might tear, so I must assume it's full of fluid, and when I dare to put my hand to the area around the laceration, it's too warm.

A notion falls into my head, a drop of water that sends out ripples of ideas.

"I'll be right back," I say quickly, and step out before Patrick can ask why.

Hardy's already coming in with the copper kettle, though, and I wave him through. Upstairs, the whimper of Andrew's early wakening makes me quicken my pace. If he can hold off, I might have a chance to do something with Patrick … if he and Thaddeus will allow me. Thaddeus is prickly at the best of times but perhaps if he feels woozy and feverish, he will be less likely to protest and do anything to heal up fast. The only reason I even think it possible is because I used herbs on Kaspar's arm with success.

Esther says nothing as I go into the pantry to retrieve the leather roll I keep behind the crock of brown sugar. It's grown fatter as the months fly past, crackling and snapping with dried plants in wax paper and vials of oil and tinctures carefully placed so I remember which is beggartick and which is goldenseal.

"Don't use the comfrey," she says as I come back out. It's what she often says, as if I will forget her warnings even after all these months. "It's too far gone for that."

"And I'd lock in the infection," I finish. "I think I will see if they'll let me use the arrowroot balsamroot resin."

"*Hutkáŋ tȟáŋka*. Yes, that will help very much. Make sure it is sticky enough to stay."

"I don't want to do too much." I glance at my collection, which is only a fraction of what I have stored away elsewhere in the pantry, or must wait for the next season to find. "Patrick will say it is unorthodox, and Thaddeus …"

"You might wish to make a poultice instead. Poultices are less worrisome. You still have some *čhaŋ wíziye*—the old man's beard?"

"Yes." I squeeze the leather between my hands, but not so hard I'll shred the dried flowers in their cloth packets or break the little glass vials rolled inside.

She nods. "I will make more hot water."

Upstairs, the soft sounds of Andrew continue, but I hope he does not wail – not when I'm so close to trying some of the Lakota medicine Esther has offered me. I want to try—I want to do right by her. I want to show that it's worthwhile to learn something like this. Perhaps this is where all my many years of curiosity have led me at last.

There's a half-strangled shout from the surgery, and I bolt back down the hall. Patrick has Thaddeus on his back on the surgery table, the blacksmith's legs dangling down from the knee as Patrick and Hardy peer and poke at the wound, and Patrick has poured the first of near scalding water over it.

"Trying to make it worse?" Thaddeus growls. "I don't need a burn to go with."

"I have to clean it, and then will see how far the infection has spread," Patrick says. "If we don't do our best now, aye, I'd carve off your flesh, Thad, but by then it'd be in your blood and you'd be mostly dead anyway."

Thaddeus turns his head away and stares at the ceiling. Patrick nods at Hardy, who does another pour of the hot water, which I notice has soapy suds swirling in the middle. The patient jerks a bit, but he seems to have given up any further argument.

"See there, how the flesh is bright red, with the flesh peelin' back a bit and pink puffy skin around it?" Patrick points at part of the wound. "That's the worst part."

"What do we put on it?"

"Some iodine. I might have cleaned it up properly and you'd not be dealin' with this had you come straight away," Patrick mentions to Thaddeus.

"I'm no stranger to injuries," the blacksmith reminds.

"Burns are one thing, if they're shallow enough, but this … you were shot!"

"Shot?" I stare at the men. "What happened?"

For a short while, I distract Thaddeus by asking him questions about his journey to the Fort, and am only mildly surprised Helena didn't mention this injury when she visited earlier. Perhaps she didn't realize how serious it was, or believed it was not her business to tell on her father's health. Either way, I'm glad he's come and hope we can heal him—I cannot imagine the devastation Marie would feel if she lost her husband too early in life. I have a vision of her turning black and brittle, and then shattering. Irreparable.

Thaddeus jerks as Patrick inserts his curved needle. "What are you doing now?"

"Seein' if it'll take a stitch, now that it's as clean as I can make it." Patrick frowns at the single insertion. The wound is already covered in iodine, and I'm surprised Patrick used so much. He also must be quite worried. *As clean as he can make it?* I look over the injury again, too, and realize he's right. The infection is already quite deep. Hot water and iodine are likely not enough.

"Well, it's better than carving it off," Thaddeus grouses. "Go on, finish it."

But when Patrick makes another stitch and pulls, the soft, infected skin stretches, creating more damage to the outer layer of flesh instead of pulling the laceration together.

"Why won't it close up?" Hardy asks.

Patrick shakes his head and takes out the scissors, undoing the two stitches he just made. "It's too far gone for stitchin'."

"Well, then. Is that bad?" Thaddeus wonders.

Patrick ignores him, and flashes me a quick look. There's early panic in it, and a bit of resignation. My hands ache to hold up the leather roll of herbs, and offer the idea. But …

"If you aren't sewing it up, what will you do?" Hardy asked Patrick, as my husband dabs even more iodine onto the entire area, turning the skin and the angry gash a strange orange-red with a purple tint. The smell of it, metal and chalk combined, fills my mouth with saliva.

"A bandage. It'll just have to stay clean, which is the tricky part," Patrick says, staring and frowning at the rip in Thaddeus's side. "If you've still got iodine from Kaspar's burn, Thad, that would work. Maybe once it's healin' and not infected anymore, I could try to stitch, but by then it won't be worth it. You're just going to have a big scar."

"No stranger to those, neither," he says, waving his many-scarred hands and forearms.

So that's it, then? Keep it clean and just hope?

"I … I have a thought," I say, my heart picking up speed as I speak up. "If you're worried about it staying clean, and to fight the infection already in there…there are some options."

Patrick turns his frown on me. "Not now, Jane."

"It's just an antiseptic," I start, glancing at Patrick for some sign he will let me do this, but he's just standing there, tensed. "A…a way to kill the infection in the wound. And it could cover the area so it stays clean. And…and we could cover it in a poultice that is specifically for open sores like this."

"A poultice," Patrick says at last. "Of what?"

"Old man's beard. It's just a plant, a … lichen. I've got some dried I can send and if Marie can be given instructions? You'll need her help to apply it and re-bandage."

Thaddeus doesn't look half as nervous as I expect. He only sags slightly, his chest curling inwards. "So it's all fixable, then, *tak*?"

"Yes." I hope so, anyway.

"Maybe," Patrick says, his word tumbling on top of mine.

I widen my eyes at him. "It's better than not trying."

"Hm." He turns back to his instruments and picks up the hook splinter forceps. "Or perhaps I should puncture the skin a bit more, let the pus drain out. Then come back tomorrow, Thad, and I might be able to stitch it up."

"Patrick—" I begin.

"Not now, Jane."

The curt dismissiveness sends chills across my body, as if he left me to be swallowed by the ice on the Missouri river. I tell myself it is because he is nervous, because he doesn't know what to do. He does not want to destroy the newly minted, still-fragile friendship with the Salomons. He needs them— their acceptance.

Patrick shows Hardy how to carefully insert sterilized needles into the obvious pockets of pus, and the yellowy-white oozing of it soon mixes with the iodine.

To be perfectly honest, it looks even worse by the time they are done. My hands are soaked with hot water and soap and rubbing alcohol, and we've gone through most of the clean towels in the surgery.

Hardy stares at it, and then at Patrick, and even he seems to realize it's not done a bit of good at all.

"Patrick," I start quietly.

He shakes his head, but when he looks up at me, it's with a different sort of frustration. "You still think the plants, don't you?"

Thaddeus, who has kept himself quite aloof during all the pokes, pulls himself to his elbows.

"Marie would want to do everything," he admits. "And we know what you did for Kaspar. Well, then, doc?"

Patrick glances between Thaddeus and me, and lets out his breath.

"We'll put together a receipt," Patrick says. "Wait here with Hardy."

I follow him, when he tilts his head into his study, and he closes the door part of the way as soon as I enter. Behind it, he grips my chin with one of his wide, bunchy hands and his blue eyes search mine. I can't detect anger or even interest. It's a calculating look—clinical. It makes me feel as if this moment, this injury, might make or break us—or at least, how our marriage works.

"This is the answer, then?" he asks. "You think?"

"It's better than what you're attempting. Even Hardy can tell you're at the end of your ideas."

"Can he?"

Perhaps the true question is - *Can we truly work together?*

"You are sure of what you're doing?" Patrick presses. "What you've offered?"

"I am," I gaze at him. "I trust Esther, and her ways have healed others."

"Every patient is different."

"And in that, all kinds of medicine are the same, aren't they?"

He suddenly leans in and kisses me, hard and full, surprising the words sitting on my tongue and banishing them. When he pulls back, his hand moves from my chin to my waist, as he draws me into a quick embrace before letting me go and moving to his desk for a piece of paper and a pen.

"Very well. Hot water to wash. Place iodine everywhere, and then?"

"In the mornings, warm the arrowroot balsamroot resin so it's sticky and place all over the wound. It really is an antiseptic, Patrick. It's supposed to be—" He waves a hand for me to continue dictating. "And then in the evening—after another wash, yes? … Take the old man's beard and reconstitute it in warm water and place it over the wound for the night."

"And always bind with clean cotton cloths," he finishes, speaking out loud as he scribbles. His handwriting is strangely neat, as if it's something he focuses on more than the next person, but I suppose illegible medical instructions are useless.

He straightens and reads it over silently before handing it to me to do the same. As soon as I do, I look up at him, to where he watches me, and at last his eyes have gone soft. He looks at me as if I'm his newlywed bride, as if he still feels he's the most fortunate man. This is proven further when he smiles at me and takes back the receipt and nods.

"I did indeed choose the right woman for me," he says. "We will make a fine team in this, too, Janie." His voice turns lower, grudgingly rueful. "And yes. I can see some merit in usin' medicine from the earth. In this case, for instance, it is the best choice for the injury."

His admittance makes me feel like I am soaring, jittery and excited at the same time. We return to the surgery and the three men watch me work when the new hot water is ready. It feels strange for the audience as I'm guessing exactly how the poultice should look—but I don't want to ask Esther, either.

None of us hear the door scrape open, or the tapping knock as it does.

"Hallo?" Susan Brinkley's white hair appears, and then the rest of her, as she steps into the near over-crowded surgery. "Oh—Thad! What … you're

…” Her soft eyes widen as she takes in the drippy green plant I'm pressing gently into place, packing it into the open sore.

“Got shot, didn't you hear?” Thaddeus says, speaking lightly, and likely trying not to feel odd sitting on a surgery table, shirtless, with wet lichen pouring water down his side.

“No—I haven't been to town until today,” she says, holding her post at the entry.

“What is it, Susan?” Patrick asks, shifting to look at her. “The cows? Or—”

“It's my Henry, though the cows ain't any better, either,” she says at once. “His gout is getting worse. The expensive waters the other doc had us pay for aren't doing a lick of good, and I think it was only snake oil instead of anything else. They stink of sulphur.”

“Wh—what did Doctor Smith have you do?” Patrick asks. His voice strangles on the name of his nemesis, but he keeps his body relaxed, and his hands only twitch instead of bunch. I nod at Hardy to start winding the clean linen around Thaddeus's middle, capturing the plants in place against the skin.

“Some place out west near Bozeman's got some fancy springs, where there's people what go and take in the waters to heal. He said it would help, but I can't help wondering if he just wanted to take our coin and have my husband drink something nasty. Suppose it kills him?” Susan's voice goes higher as she speaks. “He's taken to his bed after only two days of drinking it!”

“The gout hurts that much?”

“And his gut, now, too.”

“Lay off the water, then, and let me know if he gets worse or the runs. There's little to be done for gout, as you know,” Patrick says. “Though … Jane?” He looks at me and opens his hands.

I don't understand at first.

And then, at his small smile, I do.

“Would he be up for trying something a little untraditional?” I ask.

“Like what you did for Mitch's Alice when she was sad, and her milk was poorly? Yes, certainly. Henry will try anything at this point, and so will I.”

I glance down at the roll of leather, which is open on the side table, and try to recall everything and anything. It's rough and homespun next to the gleaming silver tools of Patrick's trade. Perhaps I should get my journals. They're not memorized, but I'm sure I can jog my memory when I start to page through them. My hope is that someday, it will all be second nature, as easy to remember and pull from my mind as Patrick does with his knowledge and cures and diagnosis.

Thaddeus gets up as soon as Hardy finishes tying off the bandage, and picks up his shirt, but he seems in no hurry to leave. Perhaps he means to pay—with cash!—and then I realize he's also just as interested in the gossip. I suppose if anyone gives him trouble for putting natural medicine on his wound, he can point to Old Henry and say it has become in fashion. Before medicine and doctors became part of the world, did not many a great-grandmother do something similar if she had the know-how?

"I … I think we could use mint, to sooth his swelling," I say.

"We have some of that in the garden. Can't get rid of it if we wanted," Susan says dryly. She clasps her hands together in front of her apron. "Surely that's not all?"

How, in one day, have I gone from arguing with Patrick on the merits of Esther's medicine, of using 'women's ways' to him offering me a place at his side, and a voice? I recognize the enormity of it while in the middle of it, and wishing I didn't have to make such decisions with everyone hanging and waiting on my word. It feels like a performance, yet with strings attached. Expectations. Hope.

I'm not sure if I like it. Perhaps I will get used to it.

"Um, if I might get my journals. I just want to double check—excuse me." I brush past Susan and hurry into the kitchen.

Esther is there with Andrew, keeping him quiet on her hip with a clean bit of rag soaked in milk.

"He'll do for a bit, but he's hungry," she says.

I nod, and begin to flip frantically through the journals. Perhaps I will rewrite them as I can, and arrange things somehow by ailment and alphabetically.

"We—you told me about a root—for a tea. For pain in feet and hands and other aches."

"There are many like that," she says, and shifts Andrew to her other hip. "None are right for a gash like Thaddeus has."

"It's for Old Henry," I say. "Susan's here looking for something to relieve him."

"Oh, then you mean the black cohosh. Yes. A tea for that."

"Twice a day. But—it's very dear. You gave me some of yours, and I don't know how much to offer the Brinkleys." When will I be confident? Why does she have to leave so soon? I need her yet—and yet also know with her here, I will never truly learn by necessity.

"It does not grow here," she says. "You must go down the Missouri, past Vermillion and further south."

"Iowa."

She suddenly smiles. "You do remember."

"I try." I inhale and catch up the journal, even though I haven't found the right note. "And just think—if Old Henry uses this and it works … think of what that will say about you. People will … they will want your knowledge."

"They will want it, but they'd prefer to hear it from you," she reminds gently. "I am glad to leave this piece of myself behind when I go."

I want to say more, but I feel the pull of the waiting Susan, and hurry out with the journal clutched to my bosom.

They are all discussing the cows again when I step back in, and I go to find the long scraggly dark brown roots of the black cohosh, keeping an ear on the conversation.

"If we don't get the sickness under control, all the head will be gone, and we'll be out of business," Susan says darkly. "Danny Svendsen's heading south sooner with his herds, like he can outrun whatever ails them. Foolish if you ask me. Liable to kill them all, going now."

"All the herds?" Thaddeus asks. He's back clothed, with his packet of medicine and instructions on the surgery table beside him. His arms are crossed, and he looks as if he'll be right as rain soon enough, now that he has a 'cure'. I wonder what Marie will say.

"Yes. All, and all now," Susan says again. "I don't know. It's strange, like the cows are cursed."

"Curses aren't real," Patrick says quickly. "But it will be an experiment."

I jot down the instructions for the cohosh—tea twice a day and how long to use the pieces of root before discarding them—and hand it to Susan. She gives her thanks, and parts with a coin, though she looks at it as if it is very dear to part with. How much did Doctor Smith swindle out of them? Or is it truly that their farm is on hard times now, with the cows dying so frequently? I don't like to consider what that means for the Brinkleys … or for Flats Junction.

We send them off together—Susan toward the General, and Thaddeus back to his forge. Hardy goes into the kitchen, already hungry again, and Andrew's quiet fussing grows steadily louder in the kitchen as Patrick and I stand on the porch.

"Black measles, cow sickness," I murmur. "It feels like it's all falling apart by mysterious diseases."

"I'd trade either of those for something easier, like diphtheria," Patrick says, his voice tight with frustration at his lack of ability to fight what ails the cows and people. "Maybe Danny's got the way of it, takin' the cows away. But I don't know if that will fix the missin' link."

"You think the real problem is something else. Something we don't know."

"It's the only thing that makes sense."

"Oh, I hope we can figure it out," I say to him, as we turn back to the house and our infant's noises. "Not only to show that Doctor Smith he can't win … but to save Flats Junction."

It feels as if it could become that existential.

As if the crumbling edges of our town are tied up with the wealth of our farms and the health of all the people. I find my hands itch, as if I could grab my teas and tinctures and oils and find a cure for it all. Or perhaps that is simply my nature. Is it unique to me—to wish to heal and help and save?

Or are all women able to see how everything is connected, and how to sew together those connections to build a community or fix a problem?

Either way, it becomes ever clearer that something must be done—and for the first time, I feel as though Patrick and I are facing it together.

CHAPTER 10

Kate

April 26, 1884

"We're on our way, and the like."

I pause rummaging on the lowest shelf behind the counter and close my eyes. Part of me wants to be that young girl working for Harry Turner once more, who is small enough and unimportant enough to curl in unsuspecting places around the General and listen in to all sorts and manner of conversation. It's how I saw my first naughty postcard, and heard about what men prefer from Fortuna's girls. It came in handy, and I used those same moves later when I wanted to beguile Bern. It's how I learned lots of things.

But I'm not that girl anymore, and Harry is long dead.

Yanking a dusty tin toward me, I slowly stand up and shove the traitorous pins back toward my scalp, where they itch and poke like the devil.

"Where?"

Moses Thompson looks at me with that steady, patient eye and sets his hat on the counter between us. For the first time, I'm sure glad Gil and Horeb don't sit in the window anymore. It's still only Horeb sitting out front, not close enough to hear and tease me later.

"South Kansas way with Danny and the rest of the boys."

"No one's staying back this year, then?" I ask. This is news, but I don't like that I'm beholden to Moses for it. "That's something to know."

"Can't spare anyone, with taking all the remaining head, and not knowing if any'll get sick, as it were."

"It's early."

He nods, and wipes a finger along the glittering top of the lemon drop jar. It comes back perfect and clean. I stand and watch, and hug the tin in front of me, tapping my foot loud enough that he can hear it.

"I'm here to ask if you'll wait for me," he says. His voice is staunch and matter-of-fact, but there's a glimmer of some emotion under it. When he swallows, it's so loud I can hear it clear across the counter and in the air between us, and I don't know if he's nervous or anxious or just plumb blind where I'm concerned.

He can't be asking this. He doesn't mean it. It's just sentiment on the eve of his departure, I'm sure. Just some hare-brained thought that because I'm a single woman, I could use a man like him. Never mind that he's a fine cook, that he's handy.

"Why on earth would I?" I blurt. The sides of the tin can from Harry and Mae's time, rusty from the many forgotten years sitting on that low shelf, bite into my palm.

He just goes on looking at me, as if I can read his mind. And I can, sort of. I can re-hear the echoes of the words he's said to me, the gentle nudging, the help, the calmness … and that damn surety that we're connected.

"You don't even know me," I continue. "Besides, you're a cowman."

"I've been many things, and the like," he says easily. "But in the end it comes down to something simple. We're the same, you and me."

"The last time you said something like that, I believe I slapped you," I say, the fire of that moment rising up in my fists, as if waiting to snap out again. "I don't understand why you're so interested. Why you keep … We are *nothing* like the same."

"That's true, in some respects, as it were," he agrees. "I'm a man, and you're a woman."

"No," I interrupt. "My answer is no. I won't marry you."

He nods, once, and picks up his hat. Back straight and shoulders square, he ambles out in that long, certain stride, and the door closes way too slow behind him. So slow I can hear him greet Horeb and say something uninteresting about the weather and the mud, and then he's gone and …

And I don't suppose I'll ever see much of him again.

After a long moment, I realize my arms are aching something fierce, and it's because I'm hugging the tin can so tight against my bosom it's leaving marks in my bodice and shirt waist, and this is one of the new ones Helena brought over to test the pattern on me. She says I'm tall enough for some of the patterns, and I'm happy to oblige if only because it makes Sadie and Elaine a bit green with envy when they come in and see it.

Why—*why* did Moses have to ask me such a question, so early in the day? Now that'll nag on me all day! As if I'd ever say yes to him, no matter how generous he's been in the past, helping me out … He … he can leave Flats Junction. I cannot. Where would I go? Who would have someone with my nose, my skin, my cheeks, my hair? Flats Junction is the only seat of power for me, and I can't imagine going somewhere else. Trying somewhere else …

And if he stayed, what? He could help me take control of Flats Junction? Barter with the electric company and the Army commander? Be … a helpmeet? How?

We're two misfits, that's the real truth, him and I. That's how we're alike.

And that's no way to go about building something bigger here.

I won't go trading my freedom for a marriage that isn't advantageous.

If I ever marry at all, that is.

His off-hand, casual proposal makes me feel all scratchy, and I shove the rusty can back on one of the counter shelves without really reading what it is. It's a relic from Harry's time, maybe even back when Mae was alive, and I … I just can't sit still now.

Might as well keep working on that legacy. How else will I make Flats Junction bigger and better than when Percy was running it with Widow Hawks?

Father and Mother.

What would he say if he was here, watching me? For that matter, will my mother ever speak up about my plots and plans? I'm sure she'd figure on them. It's half her handwork on this town. At least a quarter of the buildings exist because she saw … she planned … she told my father what would be good for everyone. What would give him power.

I march out of the General and slam the door behind me so hard it makes the hinges squeak. Horeb twists in his seat with his mouth puckered, ready to spit into his can, and his right cheek looks swollen with a sore tooth because of it.

"I'm off. General's closed."

He spits and wipes his mouth with the back of his hand, which is permanently stained brownish yellow.

"You just opened, didn't ya?"

I shoot him a look that is half pleading and half annoyed, and take the steps down two at a time.

Something … anything to make me feel …

To shake Moses's marriage proposal.

Why does it bother me so much?

Is it because it's the first I've ever received? Or because it was him doing the asking?

I try not to overly chew on the thoughts as I make my way up to the Prime Inn. When I enter, Sadie Fawcett, with her youngest boy clinging to her skirts, turns from the bar, where she's spread out lists in very careful order in her neat handwriting, the long loopy capital letters taking up more paper than is proper.

Joe gives me a half-hearted smile, which quickly turns to something more desperate. In the far corner, Gil makes a very huffy noise, stands, and clumps out without looking at me.

I swing back to Joe. "Didn't you tell him we worked it out square?"

"It's the principle of it, he says," Joe explains, looking even more miserable. He gestures to Sadie's overeager lists. "There's … decisions to be made. Fancy and fine things, and I'm …" He looks around the bar room, which is probably as clean as it's been in ages. Only the gouges and scuffs remain, waiting for their new paint. That'll come soon. Joe promised, and the paint is ordered. I would know—I sent out for it. The General can get anything, for anyone.

"I'll look at the lists," I say, sidling up to Sadie. "What're these for?"

"Well, if Joe means to make this truly the prime stop on the rails, there should be new furnishings, don't you think? Better chairs, finer bedposts upstairs, and all the best foodstuffs we can bring in."

"We've already talked about that," I say, trying not to sound too testy. "What does it matter to you?"

"Well, I thought … if you needed a loan, I could get money from my Tom," Sadie says, looking wide-eyed at me.

I try not to roll my eyes. She may be a few years older, and much longer wed, but she's still the same Sadie as she was when I was young and watching her flirt with every other man before she fell for Tom.

"I don't need money from Tom," I say. "But I do appreciate the offer."

"Oh." She looks around and deflates, absently patting her little boy's head. "I … see. It's only Doc Smith says he thought it might be grand, if you had the cash to do even more with the place than you'd planned."

"Did he now? When?"

"Last night, when we had him over for dinner," she says, too quickly.

I glance at Joe. He just shrugs.

"I thought you had Doc Kinney at your beck and call," I say, very bland on purpose. "He knows your family and your needs the best."

It's the kindest way I can skirt the common knowledge that Sadie is mortally afraid of sickness and has kept Doc Kinney well busy with her and her children's every nick and pain.

"But a fine new doc from out east isn't anything to ignore," she insists. "And he healed my son's toothache! The one Doc Kinney hasn't been able to fix, now. I've told everyone—it's a near miracle is what."

"A miracle." I glance at Joe, who just shrugs.

Sadie lifts her chin. "We're just being friendly-like anyway. And he got me thinking on what else is needed here." She waves her paper.

The shopkeeper in me pokes my spine, and I gather up a smile for her. "I'd like seeing your lists. I'm sure you've got grand ideas Joe and I can see about doing."

"I do!" she insists. "Here. Start on the fine dining list—wouldn't it just be the ticket to keep champagne on ice, with oysters and maybe even … strawberries?"

I pull the crispy sheet of paper close, just as the door swings open so fast it hits the wall and makes a bang, the sound like a smack of a shotgun butt on a hardwood floor.

Joe and I turn together just as three dusty men swagger in, looking for all the world like they own the joint. In another second, it's clear they think they do, as the front man starts waving a pistol at the ceiling.

"'Round o' beers and whiskeys both, and then a full meal. Two meals. For me an' my fine companions."

The voice does it, more than the face.

It's the last of the three Army deserters, in town after Natty, Matthias and Thad ran them off.

I want to duck down, in hopes they won't remember me, but they seem intent mostly on the bar. One leers at Sadie, but she grabs up her boy and holds him to her, as if she can defend herself and him by the move.

Joe glances at me, like I would know how to handle this, but he grabs the whiskey as soon as all three have their bellies up to the bar.

"Two rounds first," the leader says, placing his pistol on the bar like an omen. The way everyone stiffens and I know what is hidden under the ask. They won't be paying.

Joe pours three shots, quick and messy, as the golden liquor spills out across the tops of the glasses.

They down them at once, as Sadie and I don't move. I try to think how many other patrons are in the bar room, and sneak glances out of the corner of my eye. A few … most I don't know … but would they report the ruckus? Would they say we aren't safe place? Will this ruin the electric company's interest in our town, once word gets back that all alliances are spun on a breakable thread? All spun by me?

They will see through me. They will recognize I hold power without a true grasp on it.

When will it no longer be the echo of my father's name, but the statement of mine that makes men mind?

"Well, what else ya got here for our likes?" one drawls. His eyes are stuck on me, and I know he recognizes my skin, my hair, my nose just by the way his own turns up at the full square look he takes of my closeness. "Surely not just the leftovers of some fool what likes 'em halfway."

"Don't reckon I know what you mean," Joe says, calm and cool, except for the tremors in his hands. "There's no more brothel turning in this here establishment. We runned that off when we made it fancy fine and prime. You want some lovin', head over to The Powdered Rose."

"Too rich for the likes of us, Marty," one of the deserters whispers to the leader.

"I'll take what I can free," Marty agrees. "Which one of these … wimmen-folk are better?"

"I never!" Sadie lets go of her voice, and it's a screech and a shriek and a scream all rolled together, and makes everyone in the room wince and duck, as if the sound is a physical thing that can bite. "I've never been called—never in my life!" She pulls her youngest out from the sheets of her skirt and pats his shoulder like it's evidence. "I'm a married woman, I tell you, and if you touch me, Tom will … he'll …"

"Fine—maybe not you, but the other, then?" Marty's arm snakes around the edge of the empty shot glasses, sending one to the ground in a brassy tinkle of broken shards. "I remember you. You're another one what got away."

For the first time, I wish I had a powerful gun hidden in my stockings.

I've never had need for one—the position of my father and then my own too big and bold for folks in Flats Junction to make a mistake.

But these men … they do not care one whit about Flats Junction.

Or me.

Or my place in it.

"Let her be!" Joe roars. He inches down the line of the bar, and I realize that while I might not have a weapon hidden away, he most certainly does.

But the deserters know this, can tell by how he's tiptoeing along the way, and one whips out a pistol at the same time another does and actually fires, smashing a round into the large mirror behind the booze.

Sadie screams, as does her son.

The other deserter lets go a bullet too, just for fun, into the one lantern Marie has managed to make so far as a prototype, its shiny tin an obvious, blinking target. I hunch down low as he chortles as the round tears a hole through her careful patching, allowing the oil to leak down the wall in an oily river.

"You touch 'em, you answer to us, it ezz clear?"

Never in my wildest dreams would I expect to be happy to hear Yves' nasal French accent. I glance around Sadie to watch Yves, Matthias, Natty, Arnold and Evan walk in very casually, except for the weapons they each hold, one per fist. Every one of them looks far too thrilled for the excuse to wield them, and I don't want to know how Yves forced Patty and Victoria to stay back and miss the potential shoot out.

Because shoot out it looks to be.

Yves levels his decorative pistol at Marty's face and grins. "That be my business partner, you think to call a whore," he says, very casually. "She has zee big plans for this place and you will ruin them?"

"What's it to you?" Marty spits. I give him some credit, to be so unaffected by ten guns staring him down.

"Her business and mine are tied, it ezz in my interests." Yves smiles. It is the kind of smile meant to be a leer and a promise, and the sickness in it makes me want to gag.

He glances at Joe, then me, and then, briefly, at Sadie, as if her position as the bank president's wife means little. Arnold begins to clean his teeth with the edge of one of his guns, and Natty offers an evil grin and a snort, finally recognizing the gang that had accosted us on the plains.

"You wish to die?" Yves asks into the silence. "Very well."

He lowers both of his pistols to Marty's chest, just as the other four members of the Gardinier posse double down on the other two nameless recruits.

"Not now," I say suddenly. The power of the words jumps in my veins. I'm the one in charge, not Yves—not even Joe. "Not here. I just had the floors polished clear and I won't have you all staining them with blood. Send them off. They should know not to come back 'round."

"It's a plumb fool idea, letting them off so easy, Kitty," Joe says.

Yves's eyes flash, all leaky red and weepy, and the shine of his bald head rivals that of the lamps and candles. "I say zee man is right. Kill them now. No trouble later."

"But that is not civilized," I protest.

If I had my way, these three would be shot full of lead and shrapnel in a second. But now is a perfect time to put myself in a place of unquestionable power. If everyone bows to me … if they all listen … the illusion is worth as much as the reality.

Yves considers for a half-second, and then suddenly lowers his guns. The others follow his lead, and he nods at me, and then the Army deserters.

"Go, then. You've cut it close to zee law, but not enough to die for it," he says, sounding very pompous and as if he's read such a line from a book. I raise my eyebrows at him, and he ignores me, which I find both frustrating and proper given the show we're putting on for these awful men. Besides, if we go shooting down deserters, eventually the Army won't take too kindly to us in Flats Junction, and that bit of promise from the commander might go away, and suddenly there's no government money to help bring in the electric …

Sometimes I think I ought to draw myself out a map of all the pieces on my own chess board.

The deserters crawl out, and I'm guessing they'll make a line for Matt

Winter's or even the Golden Nail to drown out their sorrows and loss of masculinity. I'm glad they're not so stupid that they can't count the number of guns they'd be up against, and how fast they'd lose.

"That was done very nice," Yves says, watching the door shut behind the last of them. He holsters his gun and lifts a finger to Joe, who immediately brings out more shot glasses and the bottle of whiskey.

"I'm impressed you came so quick," I say.

"It is not every day we hear zee shot of guns in Flats Junction, it is so quiet," Yves points out. "We are always very ready, are we not, boys?"

Natty and Evan say nothing but chug back the booze, and slam the glasses down in unison. Arnold inspects his under the golden light of the saloon, and I want to snap at him that there's no impurities that'll bother anyone, but he also tips it back. It's only Matthias who doesn't reach for his, and Yves, without blinking, shoves me the giant's serving.

"Come, Kitty. For saving your hide."

As I tip back the gulp of spirits, I sense Sadie making a line for the door, herding her son out faster than he can walk, and they're gone by the time I set my own glass on the bar next to Joe. Joe himself looks pale and waxy, and I wonder if this is the most action he's seen in months.

"Well, then, the drinks are on the house," I say. "Your service is noted."

Joe starts to nod and clear off the smudged glassware, but a hand up from Yves freezes Joe in his tracks. For a brief moment, I wonder why Joe's so lily-livered, and then I realize it's not Yves or even his men, but all the weapons still bristling and ready for firing that has Joe overthinking his every move.

"Service is zee word," Yves says quietly. "I have been thinking zee same thing."

I don't know where he's going with this, and I will myself not to jump into the conversation. Yves just continues to speak very conversationally, like I've been talking to him about this for months.

"And so I think I will declare myself zee Mayor of Flats Junction," he says. "There is still not one, and if I am going to stay here—"

"Won't you miss your … roaming ways?" I blurt. "Don't you want to see how … how the Fort might be profitable for you? It'll be more than being a mayor."

"Maybe it ezz time I retire," Yves says smoothly. He places his most decorative gun on the counter. It's set with brass edges and unnecessarily filigree, and I can't help but wonder what corpse he plucked it from in years prior. "Maybe it ezz the right time to do something bigger. I could … run Flats Junction. No more of this …" He waves his hand across the room, and then out toward the door. "If I am in zee charge, that is."

"You think you can manage such things, then? Domesticate yourself? Win an election?" I'm baiting him, but I don't know how else to ask the question. I never went to a finishing school, or learned how to be fine and fancy with my manners while getting my point across. Jane's better for things like that. Maybe I should ask her for some notions on how to be all feminine and shine. Maybe that's how she snared Patrick Kinney those years ago.

"With you by my side, Kate, there ezz no need for an election, ezz there?"

And that's the veiled question, after all.

I want to laugh at the irony, the ridiculousness, the utter lovelessness of the proposal. If I must give Moses some credit, he at least gave some hint at affection.

But Yves says we will stand as equals—and he has more power, a part of me argues, and I try to find my way around the statement. I can't. Not this fast.

And I despise that I'm even considering the merits of Yves's marriage proposal.

That's what it is. I am no fool.

Two.

In one day!

No matter how covered up Yves's words are, they are still the same as Moses's. And worse for it, because I can't so easily refuse the posse leader. Not when so much of our delicate agreements hang on his goodwill and my attempts at flattery and generosity to keep him in check.

"I—I have to consider the Grand Opening," I hedge. Do I sound like I'm pleading him? Begging? I decide no, and straighten my spine and pretend I'm not cowering because of the number of guns facing me. I'm *not*.

"What of it?" Yves inches toward me, like a dog scenting blood. I wish someone—any of the menfolk in the Prime Inn would have the balls to stand up to Yves. Who among them would? Who would dare to tell him no, thank you and—.

"If you want to partner with me on everything, then the General's success is an undeniable part of it." It's my voice cutting through the room, sheer and smooth as new silk. Where I find the gall, I don't know. Maybe it's something left over from Percy's side, or my mother's people. A bravery I refuse to admit, or something just as rough.

"So you are saying after your great event, then you and I will be zee couple about town?"

"I am certain with the General in full operation, all manner of possibilities are open," I say, firm-like and without a shred of tremor in my tone. I don't dare glance at any member of the posse, in case breaking my eye contact with Yves will make him strike out. Or notice I'm a lying woman on my very word.

"That ezz something then. We shall be very fine, Miss … Katherine." He thinks to butter me up, giving me that old name, but all it does is remind me of a childhood I detest.

"Flats Junction is getting bigger every week, and yes, we're all part of it," I agree, hoping no one keeps him talking. Let this moment be done, even though he was a hero. Even though I can tell he's swollen with it, preening under the swagger.

Everyone will know what went down by this evening, if not morning.

Yves slips his guns back into their holsters, and they tinkle against the bits of metal embedded in his belt. I note the others do so on his action, all rehearsed and in time with one another. Like they're some sort of beast, lots of arms and eyes but one brain. I spare a glance so fast and fleet it's not meant to register on each of the men. Vacant Evan, greasy Natty, aloof and vicious

Arnold, and the mountain of silence that is Matthias—against Yves's cold-blooded maneuvering. None of them will stop him from claiming me as a bride, but none of them will shoot about the Prime Inn without his say-so, either. There's power in him, whether or not I want to recognize it.

And when I follow them out of the Prime Inn, looking like I'm shooing them out but without a broom, I stand for a minute on the steps and watch them all amble in their own way back to the old cooperage, where their goods spill out from the door in no order. Patty and Victoria are waiting for them, identical frowns on their faces and arms crossed. For a moment, I wonder exactly how much sway Yves has—he has to convince a bunch of killers and roamers that it's in their best interest to stay put for good.

Not my trouble, I remind myself.

No, instead I'd rather feel better about my place and my importance after such a shaky day, where everything feels all shifty below my feet, like the prairie has turned to dusty sand and isn't hard packed mud and ruts any longer.

So I stop in at Nancy's to send a wire to the electric company, reminding them of how Flats Junction is waiting for them, and how there's money and then some to pay for it, wondering when I might entertain their fine gentlemen in Flats Junction with the finest rooms of the Prime Inn as their base. I throw in a second hint of the Army hoping and wishing on their service, and the big hospital that'll be built, too, just as soon as they arrive and start digging lines.

Nancy sniffs at the cost of the wire, but I put down my good hard cash and she shoves away her judgement and promises to send it before the day is done.

Then it's to Helena's, to see how the newest patterns in from Boston and Chicago-way have come along, and she surprises me when she says she's gotten in a few from New York as well, courtesy of one of her better friends at a Chicago hatter's. I don't dwell on how Helena could make such friends so fast, and chalk it up to her wide-eyed youth and not her coloring or her personality. How could she learn to be all sparkling, anyway, with Marie for a mother? It puts a balm to my soul to have the time and space to make these inquiries and to remind everyone of my place, my necessity, my importance.

I don't need a man like Moses and I certainly don't need Yves to do all this!

"And I'll be sure to use the latest fabrics on the skirt!" Helena calls after me, as I shut the door.

I stick my head back in, hair falling everywhere. "I'd expect so."

She flushes, but nods, and I let the latch catch as I head back toward my store.

By the time I circle round to the General, the sun is starting to turn down, though it'll be a bit yet till true dusk.

Well, I've got to do something big and fierce now, don't I, as I've put Yves off on account of needing to do something just so for the Grand Opening! I've been … putting it off bit by bit, I suppose. Letting folks fester on excitement, maybe. Or because I just don't know how I can juggle that on top of everything else I'm supposed to be managing.

How should I do it all? What woman is meant to?

No one, that's who.

We're all trading one task for another, without any pause to consider which one we'd prefer to really undertake! Shop owner, mother, daughter, wife, it makes no difference. We're all trying to do it all in a dozen ways. And I … I'm doing the biggest things, aren't I? And because of that, I'm over my head, if I stop to admit to myself. I'm drowning in it all, and I've no notion which way to swim for a shore.

I'm so lost in my own swirling, twirling thoughts that I near run right into Jane as she comes round the other side of the General. We both stop at the foot of the stairs just in time.

"You wanting something?" I ask her, my voice crispy.

"No—no, not today."

"Good. 'Cause I'm closing up."

She glances up at the door, then the sun, and clearly decides not to call me out on the timing of my decision. Her lips go thin, and then her shoulders square up, though nothing will make her as tall as me, and I relish it by glowing down at her.

"Have you … heard any more on the hospital?" she asks. Her voice is cool and meek, but there's something else in it, and I can't catch it. I know Jane less and less since she married Pat, and I find I don't care if she's hiding something.

"Nothing in particular," I tell her. It's the truth, though I don't know how much Jane knows other than whispers and rumors.

"Are you … helping him? Th—Doctor Smith?" she presses. "Getting him … support? Funding?"

"What if I am?" I cross my arms, taking satisfaction that the fabric still has a little crinkle left in the starch. "How does it matter?"

"Because he's … what do you even know of him?" she asks. "How do you know he's not some joke, a phony? A snake oil salesman and nothing—"

I hold up a palm. "Don't make this about jealousy, Jane. I can see what you're playing at, and it won't work. Just because Doc Smith came into town with a big idea, and most folks are behind it, including the Electric Company and the Fort commander … well, it's too bad Patrick was too … distracted to come up with the notion first."

Her eyes narrow. "Are you blaming marriage and a child?"

"What else could it be?"

Tension quivers down her arms, and it makes me take a tiny step back, then chide myself for the moment of weakness. Jane … mousy, small Jane … would never strike anyone or anything. It's not in her to lash out.

"He's not a good doc, Kate," Jane says. Her voice goes lower, quieter, like she thinks the clouds have ears. "He's … if you don't want to believe me, ask. Paddy'll tell you all about it."

"What does Pat have to do with Doc Smith?"

"Ask … about how Patrick took his eye. And why."

The words jolt me. Hard. I'd been too busy being a fine lady to inquire about Doc Smith's missing eye—I assumed some sort of riding injury or trouble with a patient.

But Patrick? Maiming a man?

It does not fit within my world. Patrick is not violent. He's never been so. He's shunned it, in fact, and made a point of always welcoming anyone, of any color or creed, into his home. Almost like … like he had something to prove.

Something begging forgiveness …

I glare at Jane. "I don't see what this has to do with me."

"You're spending an awful lot of time with all these folks," she says, her words catching. "I just thought you might like to know all the sides. Facts." I notice stains on the front of her bodice, blooming and wet. She's been waiting for me—to talk to me on this, while her infant waits for his meal.

I don't want to believe that Thomas Smith is a bad egg. He's brought too much promise, too many grand ideas, for me to let him go. I could, I know. One word from me … I have done such a thing before.

But I don't want that to be my secret legacy—burnings and hangings and arson and death.

I want something bigger. Long lasting.

Electricity. A hospital.

My father brought the railroad, and I … I will do more.

"Suppose I tell him to head out of town," I say slowly, playing the game with Jane anyway. There's good that comes from trying to catch all the sides. "What then? All my hopes and dreams for the next decade for this place die, too."

Jane shakes her head. "There's other ways to build a hospital, if that's what your heart is set on. Not saying Patrick is the answer, but he could help you. Bring in other docs who he knows won't steer you false, if you won't have u—him. Just … be careful."

"You and your husband have not left any reason for me to trust you," I tell her. My heel grinds into the stones at the bottom of the stairwell, a mix of granite and mud and muck. "I'll do as I see fit for this town, as that's all that's left to me."

I march up the stairs, pounding so hard the nails vibrate. Horeb watches me, his face strained and intent in that I know he's heard every word, but he doesn't speak as I let myself into the shop and lock the door with a thick click.

I don't want to think about Thomas as a liar and a cheat and a charlatan. He's too … refined for that. And he treats me too well to be some half-baked doctor looking for a quick place to make a dollar.

Still … *Patrick* took Thomas Smith's eye? *My* Pat?

It has to be something serious, then. Must be. Had been …

And he won't tell me himself. Even after all we've been through, Patrick has never offered me up this piece of the past. Instead, it's Jane. Jane, going out of her way to warn …

It hits me like a strike of flame, so bright it's white instead of blue, a color that comes with understanding and sits, burning, in my chest.

If there is something to be uncovered, I am now a step ahead of Thomas Smith. And how? Because of … other women. There may indeed be some small wealth in a network of others who can make things happen. Speak truths. Send word across town, quiet and stealthy and without men who will ask and subdue.

Maybe … I do not have to do it alone, after all.

CHAPTER 11

Helena

April 26, 1884

The minute Kate lets the door completely shut behind her, I hide the couture fabrics and patterns under the machine in a wicker bin and go back to dashing fast, tight seams along the trim of a wool uniform bottom. I'm almost done and ready, which is saying something as I didn't think I'd have to be ready so fast, but Sadie told me just this morning on the way to the Prime Inn that her brother-in-law is in town and could pick up the shirts before he left.

And maybe I don't need to be ready quite this fast, but I sure do want to show all those Army boys and that commander's wife that I'm worth the bit of trouble to send out for mending. Fast and well done. That's the ticket.

I bite off the navy thread, and go to the machine for the last work on the long stitch sewing together the back of a shirt. It's clean now, thanks to me pulling a load of wash water at my parents' house, but the cotton is still so stained the fabric's a soft pale yellow from untold months of sweat. I'd been too afraid to drench it with vinegar or even lye in case the whole thing just fell apart in the wash, which would leave me unable to replace the shirt itself and would cause a whole mess of trouble on my first order.

"Greetings!" David Fawcett says, entering first, but then holding the door open for his wife and one of their adopted children. I'm grateful at once that they didn't bring their entire brood of four into my tiny sewing space.

"How goes your day?" I ask, not looking up from the seam I'm almost finished with, and then … then I just need to bag it all up. Sweat, even on this spring day, pebbles down my backbone. I wiggle in my seat, wishing the tickling would stop.

"Well enough. It's always a fine day when we have a wagon plumb full of supplies and goods again," David says. His English accent isn't as clipped as his brother Tom's, though I suppose given how much time he spends with wilder folks makes it softer.

"You've seen your brother?"

"Have. And Sadie, too. What's this about a new doc, all fine and fancy and fixing my nephew's incurable toothache?"

"Oh, yes," I nod quick. "That'd be the new Doctor Smith."

"A real miracle worker, by the sound of things."

I shrug, not knowing if there's something political behind the words. Maybe I'm just partial to Doc Kinney because he was here first, or maybe because Hardy works for him. Or maybe I just am learning how to do town politics themselves.

Caroline stands near enough to watch my fingers fly along the edges of the sewing needle and sways a bit to the rhythm of my feet on the machine's treadle. She's almost too tall for a woman, her height bolder given the broad curves of her whole body. Even with uncountable months in the sun on the prairie and harsh weather, she's still copper-haired and bright-eyed, with thick hands used to cooking over an open fire and hauling great weights. I wonder if they mourn still that they have no children of their own, with their own coloring. But the way their eldest girl sidles up to Caroline's side and presses into the warm curl of her hip seems to be all Caroline needs to feel motherly. She presses the dark head to her and smiles at me.

"You work that machine like it's an extension of your arms," she says. "I've never seen a contraption move so well, so fast."

"It takes practice," I say, then whip the garment off and clip the trailing raw thread with a tiny gilt scissors.

David, in all his mountain man leathers and furs, fills my space near the door, the great bearish hulk of him looking every bit out of place amid my dainty laces and delicate silks. He looks like a grizzled monster, but there's a kindness in the eyes above the thick, long beard, and it's that what I think makes him a successful trader between the Lakota tribes, the Army, and the folks in places like Flats Junction.

He turns that kindness on his daughter when he lifts a strand of ribbon an inch thick and the color of late summer grass, a fine velvet like that of a spring antler.

"What of this, Oyewakanwin? *Tȟózi?*"

"*Wašte ye,*" she says, her small round face brightening up, a great shine lifting the brown of her irises.

"We will take a yard of it," David declares.

"Tell me where your bags are," Caroline says, "and I will start packing what is needed to return to the Fort. Do you have a way for the men to know which is their own goods?". She looks about for a place to start folding, and assumes rightly that it will be the bed or nothing.

But her words make me feel foolish. Stupid and young. It had all happened so fast, and I didn't really think the men would need help recognizing their own items, but her idea has so much logic. Suppose some of them fight now, over goods, and no way to prove it? Now I've brought more trouble to the

Fort than help—what will the women there say? They'll blame arguments over mended shirts on me—and I won't get more work. All of it, even Father's injury, would be for nothing.

I wordlessly pull the wicker basket out and begin taking out the shirts, trousers and a few uniform jackets that were ripped near unwearable. Everything is mended, sewn and fixed, but I can only be upset with myself for forgetting this last piece.

Caroline glances at me briefly, and my worry and consternation must show some, because she gives me a little smile and shakes her head.

"We will tell the Fort commander that we expect the men to have some identification—initials stitched in, or a mark on the hem—and if there is none, then to have them see who fits best in the cloth."

"That still doesn't fix it," I say, admitting my fault.

She shakes her head. "Can't always be on the womenfolk to remember these things and manage them all."

David brings over the ribbon as we pack up the last shirt and vest, and nods at me to measure out the yardage.

I do, being a bit generous as I cut the velvet. It's good business, Mother would say, though David Fawcett is known for being fair and honest, else he wouldn't have lasted so long as he has. That's what Father says, anyway.

When I make to hand it to the little girl, David plunges his hand into his weathered possibles bag and the clink of coin and bone makes me shake my head.

"Please, no need to pay. It's the least I can do—you adding my bundles to your wagon."

"I'm going that way anyway," David shrugs. He pulls out a few bits of old coins cut in pieces, tiny cones of rolled tin half-rusted to bits and threads of old calico mixed with grease. "Caroline says too, we should help a young lady out. It's the right and proper thing to do." The word 'proper,' in David's accent, makes him suddenly sound very British.

"I mean, it. I know you'll take a bit of my pay for your trouble—."

"A single percent is all. Tom told me how to run the figures," David says quickly.

"But let me do this then, for your daughter," I say, handing the roll of ribbon to the young girl. "What does her name mean?"

"Mysterious Track," Caroline smiles at me, then her adopted daughter. "It is the name her family gave her, before."

Before. Before they'd died. Or been killed. Or whatever other horrors this young girl and her brothers had seen ... Sometimes I saw things in Chicago and Boston and New York. Ugly things. Drunken stupors and women wearing too few clothes and too much rouge on their knees, and heard offers no lady or unmarried girl would ever want to have poured into her ear if she had a choice. But I didn't see slaughter or watch my family disappear.

"We'll bring the money back as soon as we come back through," Caroline says, echoing the promise of her husband. She brushes her hands down the sides of her own mix of hides and leathers—all practical clothes for the rough living out of doors—and glances around my little shop once more. "It would be something to need a dress made of stuff so fine." She flashes one last smile at me, and then beckons for her daughter to walk out. "*Waŋná.* Now."

"*Pilámaya ye ksto,*" the young girl whispers, and it takes me a good moment after she leaves to join her brothers outside to realize she'd been speaking to me. Thanking me.

With the Fawcetts gone, I have the rest of the afternoon to get serious about that skirt for Kate I've promised, now that she's seen and approved of the patterns for the Grand Opening, and the fabric is in from the east. I turn to the letters that came with some of the patterns. Each one is a jewel, a memory encased in my mind, even though I know enough of my city girlfriends that they likely have changed their hair, hats and bustles thrice since I last saw them. I read their letters and smile to myself, tucking the remembering more securely in my heart. Kate does not realize what a gift she gave me—a chance to leave. I could have disappeared, and never returned. But I'd just have been one more shop girl, in the end. In Flats Junction, I had my family. And a chance to make something bigger, to be my own woman about town, just like my mother. The biggest gift of all was that I had the choice.

I don't think many of the women in Flats Junction have the choice of it.

One pattern is for a particularly tight and long bodice, which Miriam Petersen says is all the rage coming out of Europe. *It is what I will cut for my own wedding dress*, she writes. *Because yes, at last, Paul Young has asked Father for my hand! No more shop hours for me come winter! Do you think you will be in New York for the wedding?*

And then there's Gert Albine's opinion of the latest bustle: *Mark my words, Helena, it's coming back but with drapery you think is outrageous, and that's because it is. The amount of fabric will be enough to tear a woman's hips to bits—I don't think it will be a trend that lasts. Lucky for you, you may not have to manage it ever, out in that romantically wild western land …*

I'm placing the first piece of the carefully cut out papers on my bed when the door opens and blows those not yet pinned down about on my coverlet. I snatch at them, catching them just in time, and clutch them to my chest. They make a soft crinkling sound, like tired crinoline, and I turn to see Doctor Thomas Smith standing in my shop door.

It's hard to describe how I feel seeing him now. He's my elder, and I'm supposed to defer to him as a potential customer. But I've heard the talk about how he and Doc Kinney fought from Hardy, and I just don't know what to believe anymore.

So I plaster on my carefully practiced city girl smile on my face and gesture around my seamstresses lair. "What can I do for you, sir?"

"Doc Smith will do," he says, and takes off the top hat. "I've come to order in hospital gowns and drapery, linens and such."

My mouth drops open, and it's all I can do not to drop the patterns to the ground. "You mean to tell me you want me to provide the hospital—the one you've yet to build—with everything?"

"Bed clothes and sickroom clothes, nappies and the rest, yes," he says, and leans against the door jamb with a careful elegance. "I suppose I could send out east for them, but the expense of ready-made goods traveling this far on unreliable rails … I might do that, in the beginning, but I think folks will find the hospital itself a bit more welcoming if they knew all the soft goods were created by one of their own. Don't you think?"

He's not wrong. Everyone will be thrilled—especially those who have had some help with my business, like Elaine Warren and Sadie Fawcett. And Kate, who will see her investment grow tremendously. I wonder if he knows—if he's figured out how connected she and I are. Is that why he's offering this work to me?

"How do you know I'd do a good job?" I ask. "Do you want any recommendation?"

"Do you think you need to provide any?"

"No—only it's a big order on no one's word," I say. Finally remembering myself, I put the patterns down carefully under a pile of empty spools.

"I presume because you're still in business and quite busy that you do fine enough work," he says. "That is recommendation enough for me."

"But—" I cut myself off, and bite my lips close. No need to tell him my opinions. It's not my place. Even if I think his ordering of linens feels more than a little premature.

Yet he seems to be able to read my mind. A small grin slides across his mouth, and he straightens from my door and brushes any bits of dust from his shoulder.

"You think it's a bit early for me to do this," he says. "I can't say I blame you, though you must agree that it makes sense for me to get ahead of such things. Give you time to sew and order in the cotton you'll need. Wouldn't you say?"

I nod, but then can't help adding, "You're sure it's not too soon?"

"I've got Kate Davies's blessing," Doctor Smith says. "She's the one with the say-so around here, isn't she? What with the electric company, and all?"

"Guess so," I say. It falls flat, and sounds shocked even to my own ears. Is Kate the most powerful person in Flats Junction? He's not … wrong. I just never heard anyone say it out loud. It feels strange to say a woman is running it, like it might be known but never said, because it'll make all the menfolk feel strange and unnatural.

"Well, you make your orders. Get in the bolts of whatever it is you need, and I'm sure you'll still be stitching by the time the thing's built and I come to collect and pay." He smiles at me, breezy and sure. "Now. To see that Yves fellow. He's quite the man about town, isn't he?"

"He's new. Like you," I say, surprising myself by speaking up.

Doctor Smith pauses. "And yet Miss Davies has partnered with him."

My mouth opens and closes. I feel as if I should say more, but I don't know how or what. And the pause seems to reaffirm what the Doctor believes—that Yves is important, and not just a highwayman playing at civil life.

"Good day," he says.

"Is it true?" I blurt. He pauses his departure, hat in hand. "Is it true you cured the incurable toothache of Freddy Fawcett?"

"Of course I did," he says, looking surprised I'm mentioning it. "It was quite easy. I don't understand why Doctor Kinney couldn't manage it all these years."

"Folks say it's some sort of a miracle."

He smiles gently. "That's kind of them to think so." Doctor Smith pushes off from the threshold and ambles northwards, and my gaze follows him as if I'm half asleep. Did he really just come in and order ungodly amounts of linen from me? How … how should I pay for all that raw cotton and linen? Suppose … he doesn't pay up? And if he's thinking Yves is someone important … well, firstly, that'll go straight to Yves's head which doesn't bode well for anyone, and secondly … what does that say about the doctor's ability to read people and see them for what they are? Anyone with eyes can tell that Yves and his posse aren't exactly clean-cut members of society.

But Kate's propped him up, just like she's propping up Thomas Smith.

Like she's done me, too.

Maybe I shouldn't be so much a judge of her methods, seeing as I'm benefiting.

Still … what's she doing, making deals with all sorts of folk? Is that really what it takes, to run a town? If so, I'm glad to leave it to her.

Feeling a bit lost yet, and not sure if I should be celebrating my huge order or feeling scared and nervous, I wander out toward Sadie's big house, thinking I could ask her about some tea or something, just to wear off the shock.

As I turn around the front, I notice Hardy walking across the street, looking both ways, before he lands on me and his face lights up.

"I was just coming to say … hello," he says. "Doc's home for a short bit, so I thought I'd see if you were busy or …" He takes in my face and pauses on the edge of the street. "What's wrong? You feeling poorly or so?"

"No, no," I say. I didn't realize I was wearing my feelings so obvious, or maybe just that Hardy can read my eyes better than most, as he has almost from the first time he walked into my father's blacksmith shop and picked up the apprentice hammers.

"What is it, then?" He glances up and down the road. "You need to get in? Out of the sun?"

It's not too hot a day, but I let him steer me back around and into the pale shadows of Sadie's house. She's back from the Prime Inn, her face peering between the lace curtains of her sitting parlor, watching every touch of Hardy's fingers on my elbow. When she catches me noticing, she only smiles and nods vigorously, wiggling her fingers.

Well, now I can't bring him into my little seamstress shop with her witnessing it. I don't think Sadie would say I'm … acting improperly, but I'd bet she'll speculate if the occasion calls for it.

So I keep us on the patchy lawn outside the window and let her listen in as best she can through the leaded glass.

"Just had a big order," I tell Hardy. "Maybe too big."

"You think you can't fill it?" he asks.

"Or maybe it's too good to be true … but if I fill it, it'll make me."

"Can you manage it? Or just do half, if it's too dear to do the whole thing?"

I sound like Mother, I realize. And he sounds just like my father, when she looks at him with something like panic in her cheeks.

I straighten up and will my hands to my sides, so I look very much in control of myself and my situation.

"I just think it's too big … too much … too soon … to celebrate making linens for the hospital when they haven't even broke ground for it," I say.

Hardy's pale eyebrows go up. "As far as I know, there's no land set aside for it yet, neither, so maybe hold off on buying that cotton bulk."

"But suppose it gets going, and then I'll be behind!" I say, and my voice goes up even against my will.

"Can you clear paying for a bit, and just make the sheets? And if nothing happens, folks will always take a new pair of machine-made sheets, I'd bet. Prime Inn would, or maybe even … um … Fortuna. Not that I'd know her sheet quality," he says quickly at the end, the deep pink climbing his cheeks.

"I suppose I could do that," I say. "It's not ideal but … and then wait for them to break ground or something and then buy it up and go?"

It feels better, talking it out like this. It's less lonely, and I can see my thoughts laid out bold and plain, like it's so obvious I don't know how I didn't settle my mind and think of it from the start.

"There, then. Settled," Hardy says. He smiles at me briefly. "I'm sorry I can't walk you places this evening, but Doc Kinney wants to go see the Brinkley cows again, and there's a new patient out north who's got the black measles and refused any fancy care so it's likely they're goners … so doc wants to see if any more are struck sick."

He glows when he talks about this, his whole body filling with energy and something like awe. But his hands don't tremble, and there's nothing nervous about the way he holds his head now, or how his movements aren't the clumsy movements I remember from when he was the apprentice under my father. I can imagine him holding a knife to skin and stitching with easy and calmness, and I stare at him like I'm seeing him for the first time, the sunlight falling slowly down the horizon and the side of his body, so he's part glow and part shadow.

"How does it feel?" I blurt out. "To have a true vocation?"

His head moves to the side as he considers the word. "It's not that, is it?"

"Sure it is," I say. "It's something you're so sure about, doing the work with the doc."

"I don't know. It's just the one thing I'm good at," he says, shifting a shoulder up. "It makes me happy, knowing I'm doing well. I've never had something I understand like this."

"Well, consider yourself lucky," I tell him. "Not everyone gets such a life path."

"Your parents do," he counters. "And you, too. Don't you think?"

Do I want to be a seamstress the rest of my days? I don't know—I have always enjoyed the art of it, the math of it, and the way it has nothing to do with metal and fire. But do I see myself poking tiny holes in my thumb and forming gowns as quick as they come into fashion? I suppose part of me will always like it, and enjoy it, or I wouldn't be trying to build something more … but that's just it. I'd rather be seeing over a hundred seamstresses myself instead of minding the treadles, having them make what I've created out of the recesses of my brain, using the colors I dictate, the ribbons I demand.

"I guess … I do," I say slowly. "But where I'm at now is just the start."

"Me, too," he says, and grins at me.

The kinship stretching in the space between us is warm and strong, and it's something like our friendship but also more. We feel … similarly. We have the same hopes and dreams and desires, even if they're in completely different fields. What kind of contentment is this, to know I have someone who sees and understands this?

Does Mother have this kind of companionship? Mrs. Kinney? Does Kate ever plan to allow someone to share her own ambitions?

Hardy glances around the edge of Sadie's house, and then up to see her eye in the lace. He waves slightly, which sends her backing up into the gloom, and then looks at me with his pale blue eyes like he wants to keep on talking. And I'd let him.

"Better go," he says. "Doc Kinney's gonna be ready soon enough, and I don't like having him wait on me."

He turns, but I grab his wrist quickly to halt him.

"Thank you," I say, feeling a little shy suddenly, like I'm some quiet girl who never talks to strangers or boys in general. "I'm glad you were here to speak on this."

"Well, now you have some notion on what to do, right?" he says.

I start to shrug, but then change it into a quick nod, and try to keep the smile from blooming on my face. He reads it anyway, and smiles at me, like we've both landed on some sort of grand life secret.

"That's good. I'm glad," he tells me earnestly. I let him go, and he heads back across the street, hailing at old Mrs. Molhurst next to the Kinney's, who sweeps the corner of her porch with diligence that borders on insanity, even though most people know it's only because she's a widow and what else should she do with her time?

I turn back to my own place, renewed with something like my own vocation, indeed. If Hardy is all set to live his life as a doctor, and feels it in his blood and bones, then it's high time I stop wallowing and going back and forth, too. Time to stop being so … nervous about the possibilities. I didn't want to work under my mother because I wanted to do something I knew would give me a bigger path, an easier one, and one I could grow far bigger than a tinsmith's shop.

This is it, but only if I pour it with just as much joyful energy as Hardy does working with Doctor Kinney. So, then, I've already managed the Fort, and while I made a mistake on identifying clothes, I'll take Caroline Fawcett's advice to heart and learn. And I'll get more orders from the Fort, too, I'll warrant. And maybe I can order some cotton, and have it on hand for the hospital, but in the meantime, sheets and curtains for the Prime Inn. Kate will like that—she'll be especially pleased if I use fine prints and edge them with ribbon or a bit of lace. I'm guessing she and Joe Greenman will pay top dollar for that, too.

And Kate—she's planning that Grand Opening!

The ideas zoom through my head now, and I can see them like pictures frozen in my memory of things to be—I'll make bright bunting for the Grand Opening, and let it hang from all the windows and rail and roof of the General, swagged up and flapping and colorful. And between that and the Prime Inn, the Fort and the hospital, and how many folks will come to Flats Junction, I can maybe ask Tom Fawcett for a bit of a loan, and build something bigger, so I have dress forms in the window. I'll write to Miriam and Gert, and even Laura in New York, who told me I'd never need high fashion in a backward territory, and have them send out their leftover scraps to get me started on some of the newer trimmings.

I grab my hat and put it on properly, even though I'm only going across town to the General to talk straight away to Kate. I'll look professional when I make my case for her extra business support. It's late afternoon, now, nearer dusk than before, but I don't want to wait—I want to ask her what color she wants for banners for her Grand Opening, and when I need to have it done by.

I'm going to be very busy, building something grand myself, if I have anything to say about it!

I'm so busy thinking, in fact, that the whiff of too-ripe booze is the only warning I have before rough hands pinch my face and muffle my scream and pin my arms. And all I see before my vision explodes into black starlight is the notion of bunting in the wind, all red and pink and yellow.

CHAPTER 12

Jane

April 26, 1884

It is too early for the delicate seeds. There's no point in attempting flowers, either. Marie grows geraniums every year, and roses, too. I think she has some sort of old-world magic in her blood to do so.

But I'm plunging ahead with the beans and lettuce at least, and the squash. The tomatoes need to get in if I'm going to stand a chance to get a crop before the winter closes back in, but they tend not to like the less sunny weeks. It's a risk I'll take. Same with the carrots and the potatoes and turnips.

The gardening is a fine distraction, reminding me that even with the loss of our most prominent patients – Sadie and her children – we will still have food to eat. An incurable toothache cured by the fantastic Doctor Smith!

"Pure luck," Patrick had said, when we'd been told by David Fawcett not to come round. "Just like I was unlucky to be the doc to deliver Sadie of her premature daughter."

"I didn't even know Freddy had an incurable toothache."

"He didn't. Was a back molar, taking its sweet time to erupt. I could've cut it open months ago, but infection would've set in. I'm guessin' Thomas turned up just as it broke at last, curin' the boy … or so he's callin' it that."

There is nothing to be done to change things, now. The Fawcetts have made their choice.

Esther sits next to me, poking holes in the new-soft dirt. Andrew lays nearby under my one umbrella, which has seen very little use out in the Territories. It feels frivolous to go about town with it, when a bonnet will do and my hands are always needed for something else. He coos and sleeps, and seems content to stare at the shapes in clouds—rabbits and dragons and bears—though of course he is too young even for bedtime stories about such things.

I open my mouth to ask whether we should put the onions next to last year's garlic bulbs, which shoot up green and tall already this spring, but I'm cut off by a scream, which carries across the houses and bounces in yards before being cut off mid-sound. There's a muted shout, and then nothing.

The silence afterward is what catches me even more.

It is as if in the dead air, there's a balance of life and death. Change. It reminds me at once of the time I stood in the same backyard with washing dripping from my fingertips getting the first whiff of smoke tendrils. It was the day Esther's home burned, when I still called her Widow Hawks, when I was green and new in Flats Junction and did not realize the events leading up to such an act of terror and ugly hate, nor what would follow afterward.

I scramble up, grab up the baby, and swing to Esther. She is already on her own feet, silent and elegant in her leather and calico, and moves as one with me toward the front of the house and into the street, as if we are made of the same mind.

Pausing on the edge of the road, I look both ways, trying to see if anyone else is running about, or even if someone heard the scream.

It's only Emma Molhurst on the porch next to me, her broom tilted in her left hand as she stares toward the corner of East and Main. She's squinting, her wrinkled mouth pursed, but she catches my stare and jerks her narrow chin toward Fawcett's.

"Came from that way," she says.

"Sadie?" I ask.

"Didn't sound like her."

I don't bother to wonder how Mrs. Molhurst had a read on the different screams and yells of her neighbors, or even if she's right. I move in that direction, gripping Andrew to my bosom, and every hair on my arms standing up straight, frizzing at the ends, and a chill racing up and down my spine.

As we near Sadie and Tom's, another half-garbled scream, ending in a sob, is again cut short, as if the person is only partially able to think of calling out, or is hushed. It just sounds so … terrified. It doesn't sound like children at play, or a fight in a yard, or even someone having a yell at their man. It sounds like … horror.

I turn the wide arc of the corner in front of Sadie's house with Esther at my side, glancing up at the lace curtains as I go. There's no sign of Sadie, or her boys. For a moment, I think I might have imagined it all. Or maybe it's nothing. Even if Emma Molhurst says she heard it, too.

But then, before I can finish going around Sadie's wide white house, the scream comes one more time. It's a brutal sound, and close, and it makes me stop short and clutch my baby near. The shout that follows, the wet sound of flesh slamming into bones and muscle, sends an answering quiver in my gut. There is no doubt something is wrong, and I cannot believe others did not hear it this time. It is too wide and loud and awful.

Esther moves before me, her sure stride halting again as she turns the last bend in Sadie's yard, drawing up so tight I bump into her back and jostle Andrew against her shoulder blades.

On the ground before us, just outside the open door of her seamstress shop, is Helena Salomon. Her sweet sprigged dress—made in the same fabric as my new bodice from Patrick—is muddy, the lace edges of her petticoats torn, and one stocking ripped down to her boot top. She's clearly thrashed and put up some sort of a fight, but based on the blooming red and black on her face, she's been beaten as she did. And badly.

The three men who surround her are shadowy grey in the early evening light, which sweeps in great swathes of lavender and rose above us. One has his trousers undone, the wide edges of his shirt poking out along the darker red of old, soiled undergarments.

Movement catches my eye, and I glance up to see Sadie watching behind the lace of her parlor curtains, her face the same milky cream as the fabric. I want to shake my fist at her—why did she not dash out at once with a skillet or a poker?—but then I realize I am also unarmed, and these men do not look pleased to be interrupted.

"Well, lookee boys," one slurs. "Now we each ca' 'ave one."

"I ain't touchin' no red woman," another spits, and then aims a kick at Helena's side. His boot connects, even though he stumbles backward after he makes contact. The other two chortle at him, which only makes him angry. He swings another time at Helena, who can barely curl herself away to protect her stomach, she's so battered. It makes me snap.

"Stop! Stop this at once!" I shout, throwing all my strength into my voice. "Enough!"

The man pauses, which sends him teetering into his partner, who falls to a knee in the mud and curses. His friend eyes us, slits of black in the gloaming glare up at us.

"Now lookee what you done made 'im do," he snarls. As he gets up, he takes a step toward Esther and me, and I take one back without thinking how weak it makes me look until after it's done and he's begun to leer. "I kin make ya pay for my dirty pants."

"Stay back!" I say, stupidly loudly. Where is everyone?

"No, I don't think I'm gonna," he says. Behind him, the largest of the men has picked up Helena, who flops in his arms. Dread spills into me at her limp body, and my throat is coated with sand, my mouth sticky with dry spit. "I think I'm gonna take my sweet time with you, and the girl, and make sport of the old Injun."

"My husband will be home shortly," I say. "And Mrs. Fawcett can see this—she will report you."

I point up at Sadie. She starts, and starts to back away from the window, her curls shaking. When the man follows my finger, he only smirks up at her as he sways toward me.

"She ain't gon'tell."

"You don't know her—she'll tell everyone."

"Naw. She's too lily-livered. 'Sides, there's no law here. I know it."

He lunges for me, but misses as I step behind Esther, who has not moved an inch since she stopped at the scene. His misstep makes him fall again, this time splatting the entire front of his clothes into the April mud and new grass of the Fawcett yard. It takes me a moment in the soft light to realize he wears an Army uniform, and I wonder if these are the same deserters who have caused trouble all month, or if there are just more and more of them.

"You get up," said a cold voice behind me. "And you two, step away from my business partner."

I swing around to see Kate, cradling a shotgun at her elbow, looking very confident about how easy it will be to pull the trigger.

The first deserter at my feet looks up, his mouth spitting dirt, and he blanches the color of clouds and chalk when he sees the barrel of the gun not four feet from his face. Kate spares a quick look over at the other two.

"Drop her, gentle like," she repeats. "And step away." She speaks slowly, almost like she expects these vile men to not speak her language, but then I realize it's because she can tell even better than me how absolutely drunk they are.

Both of them clumsily take a few woozy steps away from Helena, who lays unnaturally still. I want to run to her, but don't want to ruin Kate's moment or the power she has over these three in this moment.

There's heavy breathing on Main Street just as Fortuna comes hustling up the road, all in peach and pink satin and trailing blue garters and pearled shoes half-buttoned over black striped stockings. Worst, her famous breasts are not quite contained in a corset only partially put on, as if she came out of The Powdered Rose in the middle of getting dressed for the evening. She's carrying her enormous cast iron skillet, swinging it with casual strength. Behind her, Del sprints to catch up, huffing from the Powdered Pig with only a broom to fight.

Rusty comes hustling between the livery and the post office with Alan Lampton, and Harriet hustles behind Alan with their blind child on her hip, except both Rusty and Alan have dangerously sharpened farm equipment in their fists. All these folks, arriving and primed for a fight … and then I realize it has been perhaps a minute since Esther and I saw this unfolding. Only a minute, and yet it feels like five. My heart pounds as if I've sprinted all the way across town to St. Diana's. When I look closely, I can see Kate's chest rises just as quickly as mine and her nose flares. Perhaps she is appalled by what she sees, just the same as how I feel, too.

"Heard enough of this from the General's porch," she says, shooting a hard look at the other town folk who close in on the three troublemakers. "And Horeb was able to see clear through the buildings to note what was going on."

"Same trouble as what Thad said he seen out the Fort way," Rusty mentions. "I'd bet my livery on it."

"And they're the ones we just ran out of the Prime Inn not six hours ago," Kate agrees.

"You suppose they're the men who made passes at Helena earlier this season?" Fortuna wonders. She quivers in the chill of the spring night, but perhaps it's fear, too. Del seems to take it at that, as he sidles up and slips an arm slowly and lightly around her rounded shoulders. For once, she doesn't glide away and take a whack at his head.

The three men stand, surrounded, their sausage hands hanging from their arms. Their eyes dart to each person and pitchfork, Kate's gun, and then one another. One makes a run for it suddenly, his arms and legs wheeling. He moves too slow for Alan, who makes a fast jab at the back of the man's thigh.

It stabs the flesh of the hamstring, causing him to go down hard with a howl so loud it makes the closest dogs join into the lament.

"Where you think you're going?" Rusty says, taking a stand next to Alan.

Kate hoists the gun up to her bicep, her finger dancing on the trigger. "That's right. A trial might be too good for this scum, but I suppose it's that or shoot them here in cold blood."

Her voice is so calm, and the way she holds the gun makes me finally feel sturdy enough to take tiny steps toward Helena. Handing Andrew off wordlessly to Esther, I'm able to get to the younger woman's side as the rest are stuck in a stalemate. *Please let her be well—let her be breathing.*

I kneel in the churned ground, which somehow feels chillier here than in my own garden, and turn Helena carefully onto her back. Her breath comes in short, hard pants, as if her lungs revolt against anything deeper. Her face is a mess of cuts, bruises, and a broken nose which has spread purple and black toward her right eye. I don't think they violated her—I don't think they'd had time. But even so …

"She going to be alright?" Kate asks.

"I don't know yet," I answer truthfully. "We can only hope so."

One of the Army deserters makes a snort, muttering a word that sounds suspiciously like "little bitch", as his buddy helps the injured one to limp upright. Kate swings her gun around and fires it right at the man's foot. Blood and bone and mud spray into the air as the man screams and drops to his knees.

"That's about enough, I should think," Kate says. She's still dead calm.

I swallow at the gore leaking out of the man's foot. He is babbling quietly and sobbing, and his two buddies have frozen in place. Do I offer to help him? Patrick might. But I can't … Helena must come first, and there's only so much I can do out here in the open without compromising her virtue any further. Her right arm shows signs of bruising and twisting, with a clear pattern of a thumb and four fingers. There's likely far worse injuries in the flesh of her stomach and ribs, and I'm quite sure some of them are fractured if her short tight breaths are any indicator. But I won't be able to see if there's anything worse—or if she's bleeding in her organs—here. Before I even ask the menfolk to help move her, though, I feel I must wait until everything is less volatile. Perhaps if I make one small movement, Kate will shoot at me too, and claim it not out of spite, but a mistake in the heat of the situation.

With the additional shouts and gunshots, more figures move in from further streets—Elaine Warren, Trusty Willy and his mother Toot, with Gil in tow along with several other patrons of The Golden Nail—Orville and Anna Pavlock and the Horowitzes. Matt Winters pokes his head out from the mess hall, and the Baileys have come out of the farrier, and even the Brewers arrive looking mostly curious. Father Jonathon shows up, harried, with an annoyed looking Lara O'Donnell, who takes one glance at the three Army deserters and announces she's off to get Mikey and his long gun. Nancy's come out of the post office at last, her elderly father-in-law George trailing her, looking confused. Horeb wanders over and is joined by a harried looking Tom Fawcett out of the bank's front doors, with Nels Anderssen behind him. The only folks we're missing are those who are out on their farms—the Henderssens and Brinkleys and Zalenskis and the Wu brothers.

And … where are Marie and Thad?

"We'll run them out for you, Kitty," Alan offers.

Del nods, and steps away from Fortuna to heft his broom higher. Without looking at him, she hands him her skillet. His arm drops with the weight of it, but he rallies and hoists it to his shoulder and glares at the men. No one seems to care one bit that one is bleeding profusely from his foot, and the other has fluid oozing from the back of his leg.

Tom Fawcett exits his back door—he must have run straight in to check on Sadie—and she follows him after a moment herself. Tom's carrying his own rifle, the brass gleaming like it's never been used.

"Yes, indeed," he interjects into the conversation. "I shall help you remove them."

For a moment, I have to wonder where these men have left their own weapons—did they think they could survive on the prairie, let alone misbehaving in town, without them? But perhaps they've left their guns with their horses. This idea does not just occur to me, as I cradle Helena's lolling head, because

Lara arrives with Mikey, both of them looking like they might keel over after hustling their great bodies to and from the lumbermill, but Mikey also has Joe Greenman with him, and between them they're leading what must be the men's three horses.

"These are yours," Mikey says, still holding the reins of two. "But the guns sure ain't."

"Yes they is!" the only uninjured man says, making his chest puff out. In the growing dark, he still looks pale and slick and green along the edges of his jaw, where his motley beard sprouts in tufts.

"Nope," Joe says, pushing his hair back from his clear brow. "That's government property. Says so stamped right on it, and seeing as you boys ain't working for the government no more, they ain't yours."

The argument holds, even though the one man still standing and not weeping or whimpering like his comrades looks livid about it. Nels hobbles over on his crutch and starts to rifle through the packs on the animals, tossing out an additional gun and large knife.

"You can't go takin' all our gear!" the deserter says plainly. "How's we suppose to hunt and get our meals?"

"Not our problem, sounds like," Elaine Warren says. Lara, standing near her, nods vigorously.

Toot simply stares at the three of them, her skinny arms crossed tight across her flat bosom.

"Them are the ones what ran out without paying their full tab," she says to no one, but Gil nods, and Trusty Willy scowls.

"And the ones who caused trouble earlier in the Prime," Joe says, repeating Kate's earlier accusation.

"We're all in agreement these men are no good," Father Jonathon finally finds his voice, which sounds ghostly coming from the dark corner where he stands in his black garb, the shadows swirling around his feet. "But we should not harm them any further."

"They're lucky we're not killing them on sight," Kate says evenly. She lowers her gun anyway, though perhaps a bit slower than she ought.

At last, Marie's face appears between Harriet and Sadie, her eyes wide and her mouth pressed together hard and tight. Thaddeus is a hulking shadow behind her, and everyone makes way silently for Helena's parents.

To Marie's credit, she doesn't wail and shriek with sorrow or shock. Instead, she only gets down to her knees across from me in one fluid movement, the dampness seeping into the stained leather apron she wears over her dark green calico work dress. She grasps Helena's hand between her scarred palms, the slim, needle-pierced fingers hanging limp from the wrist. For a moment, she only stares at her daughter's face. Perhaps she sees her as a babe or child, or looks for some sign of life. For a moment, Helena's eyelids flutter, the shine of them cutting to Marie, and then the whites roll upward and under once again.

Thaddeus stands over us like a great beast, bristling with anger and fear, his arms crossed tightly across his own work leathers, and glowers at everyone under his thick brows and beard.

"*Co do cholery*," he says, the Polish sounding gravelly in his straining emotion. His voice settles over everyone, grounding us to the scene, to his daughter's battered body. "What in hell is going on?" He turns slightly toward the groaning men on the ground, to the other standing a bit apart from his friends, and his eyes widen in understanding. "You! Again? *Zabiję cię*! I will kill you!"

Thaddeus dives for the Army deserters, his size making the movement look far too violent. Several of the women cry out, and Kate picks her gun back up. With a sickening crunch, Thaddeus's knuckles connect with the bottom of the leader's eye socket. It takes Mikey O'Donnell, Tim Bailey and Robert Brewer combined to leap onto Thaddeus and hold him back before he can do more damage.

"No more fighting!" Mikey says, yanking on Thaddeus's arm.

"Says who?" Thaddeus thunders. His eyes do not fall on Helena, as if he cannot bear it.

"I do," Father Jonathon pipes up. "They have been hurt enough, and we are sending them on their way without a weapon to come back to do further harm."

Thaddeus shakes off the other men, but he bristles with poorly concealed frustration at his inability to strike further.

"These are the same men who came at us," he says, glancing at Kate. "When we were coming from the Fort."

"I know," she says. Her voice is grim at last, as if she's allowing herself to react. "I recognized the leader—the one who got away."

Tom Fawcett, Joe Greenman, and a few of the other men force the three deserters onto their horses, ignoring the cries of pain and distress of the two who continue to bleed out. I want to stop them, to say the wounds should be cleaned and bound or they'll fester. But perhaps that is the point—it is a slow death and awful, but the actual blood of it is on no one's hands. I glance about to see if anyone else is concerned about sending these three out into the wild hurt and surely likely to die, but faces are hard and slack with a wide array of feelings—none of them kind.

As soon as the deserters have been forced out of town, with several of the men following to be sure they head out, everyone breathes outward. Kaspar Salomon arrives with his brother Natan, Berit in tow, who looks pasty and perhaps more confused than old George Ofsberger, and they have tin lanterns already lit. Sadie disappears to get a few from inside her house, and Rusty opens the livery doors so the thick gold light from inside spills like rectangles on the deep grey of the land and buildings around us.

"That settles that, then, ain't it?" Horeb says, as if it's done and dusted and Helena does not still lay prone on the ground.

As Horeb spits to the side, she gives a small groan. Marie leans over her, then looks up at me. "What ails her, Jane?" she asks quietly. "Is it mendable?"

Thaddeus finally bends close as well. "Marya—is she …?" He can't seem to finish, the words choking him. He braces a wide hand on Marie's shoulder, and she tangles one of her fingers with his but doesn't answer. It takes a moment for me to realize she's still waiting on me, on my diagnosis. The trouble is, I cannot—will not answer. I don't have one. Not yet. And it tears at my heart and bleeds sorrow into every fiber in my arms and neck to hold in words, to do as Patrick trained me and to never over promise.

Through all of this, Esther has not moved, nor spoken. She stands to the side, holding my child, but her eyes are only for Kate, who looks as if she's a princess towering above everyone else for how she carries herself.

In the gentle silence, she looks around at all the familiar faces, a fraction of whom I have grown to know and like over the years, yet so many who hold this town on their shoulders. And Kate … she knows them even better than I do.

"There will be more like that," Kate says into the circle of flickering lantern light. "That's not the last time we deal with this. The Army's been sending more and more green recruits on the trains west, and some of them will come here."

"If our womenfolk ain't safe, what kind of place is this?" Del asks.

"You ain't got no womenfolk," Fortuna scolds, crossing her meaty arms over her chest.

Del gives her a sort of incredulous once over and frowns. "Sure I do."

Fortuna opens her mouth, then closes it, and grabs back her skillet, but she doesn't move from Del's side even as she doesn't spare him another glance.

"He's not wrong," she says. "If I have to watch for such scum, my girls won't be able to work."

"It's high time there's some real law and order in Flats Junction," Mikey states. Lara nods vigorously next to him, and there's an immediate murmur in agreement.

"We got Old Henry," Julie Bailey mentions. "He's been like a mayor all these years."

"But he ain't elected. Nothing's official, like," Tim says to his wife. He looks around at everyone and raises his hands, where old scars from nails and horse kicks pepper his skin. "Not saying he ain't done a fine job."

"Is it a mayor or a sheriff what's needed?" Robert Brewer wonders, ruffling his blonde beard. "Or both?"

I stand up, though I don't move from Helena. Next to me, Marie's head—black and sprinkled with white—bows over her daughter, pressing a hand to Helena's cheek and leaving dusty fingerprints in her wake.

"Old Henry Brinkley's getting too sick and old to be de facto mayor," I say. It's not a loud statement, for all it's laced with truth, and I feel the weight of dozens of eyes on me as soon as people realize I'm speaking. I wish I didn't have to—I feel foolish and still not certain I have a place or a voice among them—but if there's anyone to speak for the older man, it must be me. He is … like a patient. Or enough of one, through Susan, that I can speak to this, at least. And I feel I must do something or say some words after doing nothing— after being unable to immediately help Helena. The helplessness of my hands has given way to my tongue.

"There will need to be a vote," I say, straightening further. In for a penny, in for a pound, as Patrick says. "And I'll personally put down Kate's name to run."

The muted uproar is quieter than the bark of a gun firing, but it still bites into me as if I've been thrown into the midst of a hundred tiny pebbles, or perhaps the ice of a winter storm. It is not anger or hate or even rage, but the blast of a collective exhale and the immediate reaction of men and women at the notion of Kate in an elected position.

And why do I even do this? It is not a premeditated notion—not ten minutes ago I had the thought that she might shoot me if I moved wrong— no, it's not that. Is it guilt? A way to make up for the fact that I married the man she wanted? Or is it something truer and real? Do I know, deep down, that she will do a wonderful job?

"A woman can't be no mayor, I don't think," Rusty says, scratching the side of his head. He checks under his fingernails after he does and then shrugs. "Or I never heard of such a thing, anyhow."

"Not saying you ain't done well with Harry's General, Kate," Alan adds, glancing at Harriet and their child.

"Suppose we do elect a woman mayor," Nancy says slowly from the edge of the group. She folds her arms over her plump middle. "It could happen. Kate would do a fine enough job of it, I'd warrant."

"A woman's place is beside her man," Trusty Willy says, then cringes at the look he receives from both Elaine and Toot, who whacks him wetly with a dishrag to add her point.

But Kate has no man, and no one wishes to offend her enough to point it out. I realize it's up to me to press the idea, given I started it. Gulping down my bubbling insecurity at continuing to be at the center of attention, I begin to tick off the names of those that will support my reason.

"There's merit in working with your husband," I say. "And many of us do—Elaine and Sadie and Sally Painter, Lara and Julie. Myself. But there's many of us who don't, and carry all the work without a man's help and are doing fine work and could see running this town just as well as a man. Nancy runs the post ever since her Douglas passed." I nod at her, and she returns it. "Fortuna runs the Rose alone, and Marie has the tinshop." I pause just short of mentioning Helena, and reminding everyone what happened to a young woman working alone and unescorted. So I pin Kate, who stares at me as if I have changed the color of my eyes in front of her, and offer a small, humorless smile. "Kate runs the General and the town better than any man. I would vote for her."

Perhaps this is indeed a peace offering between us, as the sentences leave me and wash over her, something between us seems to wither and settle. Anger and hurt and past awfulness that sits in my mouth like a bitter tea every time she and I interact—it disappears a bit as she inhales and smiles wider.

The crowd, led by most of the women, contracts, and begins to circle around Kate, even many of the men. Isaac Horowitz's nasal voice carries over the layered darkness about how he once saw a woman running a town down in Missouri, elected or no, and she ran it with an iron fist. Others speculate and chime in their opinion, but I can tell much of it is favorable. Perhaps I've started something too big—now there will be a race for elected seats or arguments of politics around porches. But is that not what growing is? It's too late for me to take it back, and maybe … even if no one remembers what I've said tonight, I will know I was a catalyst for change, even if it meant speaking up and against my natural quietness.

Across the Fawcett's yard, I meet Esther's eyes. She is not glowing with pride at Kate, but she does not seem bothered by the notion that I've offered up her daughter for the position her late husband once held in his own de facto way. She finally—finally—moves and finds a place to stand over Helena's head. Thaddeus doesn't make space for her, his bulk crowding over the young woman's bruised body.

"She should be woken, if we can," I say to Marie. "We should get her in bed, and sit up with her all night. I will gather my supplies and leave a note for Doctor Kinney."

"Tadeusz," Marie says, looking at her husband with eyes full of emotions so dark and warring I must look away. "Let's get our little girl home."

The big blacksmith picks up his daughter with a tenderness that makes my heart ache. It is as if he is staring down at his brand-new baby instead of a woman grown enough to wed. He and Marie disappear into the mingling crowd, their silent sons and Thad's mother-in-law trailing behind.

I watch them go, and then make my way to Esther and Andrew and explain my plan for caring for Helena tonight to start. Together, we turn back toward home, though I glance behind once as we go, where the lanterns dance oily ochre on the churned-up mud, and the townspeople of Flats Junction begin the ageless debate of who will rule them, and what they will trade for it.

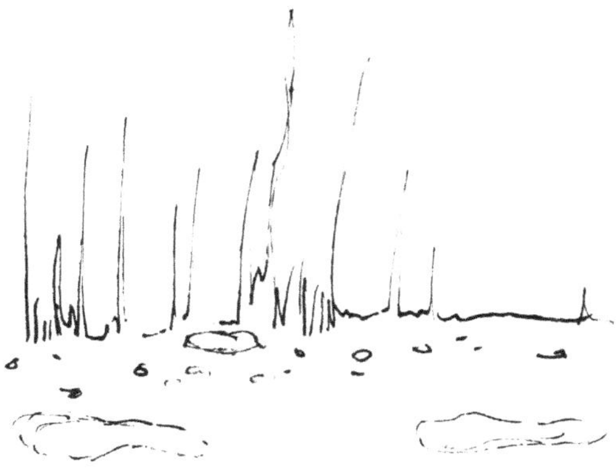

CHAPTER 13

Kate

May 21, 1884

There's no point in holding the Grand Opening party at my store while I'm busy every extra minute officially campaigning for mayor. And surely there's a silver lining to this, because it means I don't have to answer Yves's veiled marriage proposal, seeing as how I told him I won't even consider it until after the Grand Opening. And I've got a prime excuse on why I'm not hosting it. Even he can't complain, as he can see the merit in me being even more powerful. As much as I hate to dwell on the thought, I'm sometimes affected by the notion that of all men I've met, maybe Yves is the only one to see me, and my ambition, and to want more of it for me alone, as if he can see the hunger always gnawing at me and wants me to find an end of it. It's only too bad I've no interest in marrying him. If things were different—if he were less disgusting—maybe I'd consider it and call it a well-made alliance of the mind if not a delight in the bedroom. I've sold my body for lesser purposes.

Parts of this campaign trail are less savory than others, though, including this moment when I stand on Patrick and Jane's freshly minted new porch and wait for someone to come to the door. Please let it not be only Pat. I haven't been alone with him now in years, and I don't know what it'd do to me—to us—if I am again.

A speck of relief and something a bit softer hits me when Jane opens the door and pushes the screen wide.

"Kate," she says, her eyes flitting over me quick and fleeting. A nurse's look if ever there was one. "Is everything alright?"

"I'm not sick, if that's what you're asking." I step into the hallway without waiting for her to invite me in. The house smells different than when Pat lived here with his Aunt Bonnie. It's spicier, the crumbly bits of herbs and sweetgrass and dried flowers mixing with roasting corn and sumac—scents of my childhood—and now there's some new layer, a cloying sweetness of soiled nappies and sour milk and baby skin.

"Do you want to come back to the kitchen?" she asks. "Esther is kneading new bread, and I'm—"

"No, I've come to see you."

"Oh." She glances at the surgery to the left and Patrick's office to her right, and settles on the office. As I follow her in, I note the smoothness of her dark brown hair, tucked into a thick roll at the nape of her neck, and marvel at how she's still without a bit of grey in her crown.

She turns at the side of the desk, but doesn't take a seat, so I don't, neither, but that's fine as the straight-backed chair Pat keeps for guests is uncomfortable at the best of times, as if he doesn't like meetings or wants to keep the patients from staying overlong and listing too many of their ailments.

Jane doesn't speak, she just stands there looking at me. I try to read her in between the fine lines along the edges of her chocolate eyes, so very near the same color as mine, even though that's the only thing we have in common.

She's short and extremely curvy, and I'm tall and long in all the places that shouldn't be straight. And she's a proper woman in more ways than she's not, and I'm … I don't fit anywhere, even here in Flats Junction, which is the only place I'll ever be able to live and matter.

But more than what I see, is what I try to feel—that lost inkling of friendship we once shared, and the reason she threw my name into the ring of contenders for mayor, to be the official leader of the town. Why? Why did she offer it? Does she think it will erase everything else between us? Or make up for her marrying Pat? Or even as a way to show she … still wants to be friends, even after everything she's done, and I've done, that festers in the air whenever we're in the same room.

"I've come to ask you to get my mother gone," I say at last, going straight to the point. "It's high time she returns to her folks, and the weather's fine enough for her to go."

"You were with us when we went to fetch her back," Jane counters. "You said you wanted her to live here."

"I never said that."

She bites her bottom lip, and I can fair see her mind racing backward, and then can see when she realizes I'm right. I never wanted my mother back, but I sure knew how awful it'd look if I didn't go along with Pat and Jane's plan to bring her back, as if she was family and blood to them. I know how to pick my moments and what games to play more than most, and if Jane doesn't understand that by now, then she's dense.

"Anyway, you've made your point having her here all this time," I continue. "She knows you care for her, she's helped you with your firstborn. But now it's time she goes back."

"Why?"

I look everywhere but at Jane instead of answering. Saying the truth will be ugly—too ugly. I don't want reminders, is all. I want people to think of me and not my father when they cast their vote. I don't want his widow here reminding them of what she did to help him build Flats Junction out of the prairie. I don't want them making comparisons on the cut of our noses and cheekbones, either.

"Has Patrick made any progress on the sick cows? The black measles?" I ask instead. "It'd be good to get that under control sooner than later."

"No one wishes for that more than the doctor," Jane says stiffly. "We—he's working on it, but it's like asking one man to fix a problem that has been here long before he was born, and has eluded many doctors and veterinarians. You're asking for a miracle."

"I've no doubt he can figure it out if he puts his mind to it," I tell her. "Besides, aren't you dabbling in my mother's ways, too? Between the two of you—"

"Why this?" She cuts me off hard. "Why do you care—why now?"

"I care about this town getting righted," I say. "And if there's some disease creeping in on our livestock or children, it's my duty to make sure everything's being done to fight it."

She stares at me for a long moment, long enough that it sets my fingers fidgeting along the folds of my skirt.

"You're not elected yet, Kate," she says at last. "Don't make me regret my nomination."

It's a hollow warning and we both know it. Her words are done and spent and she can't take them back—they were said in front of too many folks. I'm the front runner, and so far running uncontested, but I'll see this done right so no one can question my authority.

Maybe … it grates me to grind out the next words and they catch on my teeth. "I never did thank you for that. So—you have it. My thanks."

She nods briefly, but there's doubt writing itself across her forehead now, and I quickly make my apologies for disturbing her day and see myself out before she can shove deeper into my motives or rip me apart with a few keen observations. I don't like that she can do that so well—see things, as if her mind's turning over a hundred questions at all times, her brain working out problems with information she's stored away somehow by over-reading. It's plain unnerving, for a woman to have such a mind. How does Pat manage it, and not want to keep his books locked away from her?

I borrow one of the spare horses from Rusty's livery to ride out to the

Svendsen house, going the long way on the east side of Flats Junction between St. Aloysius and the old buffalo jump hill instead of going past the Salomon house and the old Davies place. I don't like looking at those colorful windows and the scalloped edges to the roofline. It brings back snippets of the old days, when I'd walk home from school or run, depending on who was chasing me and whether they had fists of pebbles or sticks. My only comfort is knowing how much my father would turn on his deathbed to see how it's become an unofficial brothel and inn, and how chipped the pastel pink and peach paint is on the sideboards.

As for Marie and Thad … I try not to think about how Helena looked after those Army deserters had finished with her, how she looked near death. She's not—Thad says she's recovering fine enough back in their home, and even itching to get back to work as it is, but Marie has doubts, and I guess Helena's hands tremble too much to thread a needle.

I wonder if a hospital stay would have been better for her than going back home, with Marie hovering and Thad frowning in the corners. Maybe Helena would have been better off with Thomas seeing to her busted nose and the cracked ribs instead of Patrick. Though I guess I shouldn't be thinking unkindly—Patrick did a fine enough job and she's recovering—maybe it's just habit.

I've already gotten the Brinkleys, weeks ago now when I was there with Thomas, to agree to support the idea of his hospital, along with the electricity that'd go with it. I haven't spoken to Old Henry or Susan since—and I'm guessing I should keep my distance now that I'm on the way to take over from Old Henry in his position as unofficial leader. And anyway, Oddvar Svendsen is the last one I need to get behind all my ideas. Anette Zalenski did the convincing to her Jacob and the rest of his folks out at their joint farms. Once I have all the wealthiest behind all my notions, then I'll write once more to the Black Hills Corporation—an official invitation for them to come down from Deadwood way, stay at Joe and my Prime Inn, take some meetings with the ranchers and farmers, talk to Lieutenant Colonel Swaine about how the government and Army will take part in paying for the electricity, and talk to Thomas about the hospital. They'll have to see how much they can make if they string their wires this way, and I'll be known for my work bringing electricity to Flats Junction at last. It'll be grander even than the railroad my father brought back in the 60s.

The Svendsen ranch has needed a woman's touch for near twenty years or more. Oddvar's wife Margit stopped taking care of the finer things back when her older son Davie left for California and wrote back that he'd be making his living running multiple brothels and gold mining what was left since the original rush, and he wouldn't be sending a cent or himself home ever again. Davie never had any love for ranching or his own folks, but the way Nancy tells it, his first letter home, laying it out cold, shut Margit down hard. I sometimes think that's why Danny is so kind and so generous and gentle to a fault. It's like he's making up for Davie, like he's hoping he'll break his momma out of the prison she's built in her heart and mind. And likely there's some other wound there, cut so deep it won't heal. Something that keeps Davie from thawing his own feelings.

Danny's not home—he's south yet with Moses and the rest of his cowboys and their herd, trying to stay clear of the fever that drops their cattle dead. But Oddvar is home, and he's the one who answers the door. For being in his mid-sixties, he's aged well. Maybe it's the Norwegian blood, or maybe it's just luck. He's bent near in half with age and wear, even though he must have once been as tall as me—or as tall as Danny. Like Danny, he has no beard, as if it just won't grow, and I try to remember everything my father once complained about regarding Oddvar. That he doesn't like spending his pennies, even when he has a million of them. And if he does spend it, it's only to buy even more land.

"Morning, Oddvar," I say. Behind him, in the airy wide room, Margit stirs a pot on the overlarge iron stove. She doesn't turn when I speak, so I focus instead on just the old man. "I've come to talk business."

"I not sell da land," he says at once, firm and crisp and precise even around his rounded accent. "It not for da sale."

"I don't want your land," I tell him. "Not even a half-acre."

He chews on his inner cheek for a moment, then nods and opens his door wider, an unspoken invitation to the heat of his home.

It's a spartan house compared to others with his same level of wealth. Everything has finely sanded lines and clean cuts, stained a bright golden color with blue and red horses painted on the cabinets and patterns that remind me of snowflakes except these are yellow not white. Each chair has a heart cut out in the center of its back, an odd romantic type of design if I would say so, but I don't and just take the chair he points to as he takes the one at the head of the table.

"I've come to see if you'll get behind the idea of electricity." He only looks at me, and I hope to high heaven he understands what I mean. I try again. "You know, for electric lights. And if you like it, maybe we could get some of the wires out to your house, your barn. No more candles or worries of fires …"

He tilts his wiry body back in his chair, reminding me of Horeb, and bites the flesh of his thumb as he stares at me with those pale blue eyes.

"Who else likes dis? Da electric?"

He keeps his tone even, but I can see the spark of competition in his jaw, and I'll play right to that and then some. I lean forward toward him, and rap the table.

"Brinkleys are in, and Zalenskis and most everyone in town."

He waves a bunchy, grizzled hand at that. "I not care for da town, what dey like."

"Well, you should. We're even putting in a hospital—a new doc is in town and he's grand plans for one, along with the electricity. This is going to put Flats Junction on the map in a big way."

"Do I care, if my cows all die?"

I try not to cringe at the doom in his words. "Well, I don't know about that, but maybe the new doctor can fix it, if the old one can't."

Oddvar's pale yellow and greying eyebrows go up a tiny bit at that, but he shakes his head further. "What else thinks dis be a good idea?"

I don't know what he's fishing for now, but I dive further in. If I can just get him to agree, then I've covered all my corners.

"Well, the Army's doing it. They're using good money from Washington to pay for the electric to come to them, too."

The chair legs thump down as Oddvar flattens them onto the worn planks of his kitchen. He wrinkles his nose. "How much cost is it?"

"Not too much. And everyone will share it, anyway."

"Da Army does dis, you say?"

"I've got the promise for it, in person, from the commander at the Fort himself."

He breathes in once, then twice, a slow wheezing that sounds wet and clunky. Margit doesn't move from her ongoing stirring of a pot, and whatever's in there has no scent at all. Maybe it's just water and she's forgot to add pork and beans.

"If da Army does dis, then I will."

Oddvar reaches across the table, hand to the side, and it takes a moment for me to realize he wants me—*me!*—to shake on it. I do, even though I wish I didn't have to make such promises yet. A handshake is near as good as a contract, as my father always said, but what can I do?

I take the same long way back into town, but then cut round to see how Joe's doing with the ongoing updates to the Prime Inn. The curtains are still not there, given Helena isn't sewing things yet, and there's still no silver lanterns from Marie screwed to the walls. But he's painted the boards along the wall and has shined up the mirror, so there's progress, and I try not to look annoyed at how slow it's going. Some things just can't be rushed, and I should know it firsthand.

So I walk Rusty's horse down the street to Yves's place, which smells of old meat that hasn't been kept salted in the barrels and rotting sugar, but at the same time, I haven't been able to shut him down, so I guess it's on him if folks slowly start bringing their business back to me if he won't keep his place clean. It's Yves that gives me the most sleepless hours – not knowing what he'll do or when, or whether he'll take me up on my plans or leave Flats Junction for good. Will he make a deal with the Fort, and leave me and my General? Or will he ask for more than I'm willing to give?

When I slip in past Arnold and Evan drinking on the front porch, it takes me a good half minute to adjust to the gloom. I keep thinking they'll cut a window to let in more light, but none of them do, and I'm not inclined to help their business succeed. It helps me, actually, for it to slowly die on its own, especially since Yves is sticking it out much longer than I expected. I have to give him credit—he didn't get bored like I'd hoped, but at the same time, it means he's had to shift his lifestyle and keep his posse together while he forced it. It takes a strong will to do that, and I can at least admire that about the man, sleazy as he might be.

Matthias is in there, wordlessly cleaning out the pickle barrels, while Patty and Victoria perch on stools by the counter and do nothing other than whisper to one another and giggle. Just as Patty puts her hand on Victoria's knee, I clear my voice. Loud.

They jerk apart, and Matthias stands and turns. I put my hands on my hips and make a sort of impatient movement with my chin.

"Where's Yves?"

"I'll get him," Victoria says, hopping down. Patty only gives me a sneer and a leer and follows Victoria out, her hand snaking back to Victoria's waist as they head into the back room.

Matthias looks at me square on, his gaze just on my face and nothing else, and then he goes back to moving barrels. The ease with which he moves a hundred pounds is unnerving, like it is nothing to him, and I wonder if he's ever met an obstacle too much to handle.

"Yezz? Kitty?" Yves wanders in from the back room, buckling his belt along his hips and buttoning his fly. I don't want to know why he was lounging about without pants on in the middle of the day and keep my face from grimacing as best I can.

"I'm just seeing if you've thought any further about what we've been discussing all these months," I say. "You've had plenty of time to consider."

"And you've been so busy too," he says, his pink-lined eyes trembling with unshed fluid, and the black tooth on the bottom of his gums visible as he flashes me a smile. "Zee chatter about zee hospital, zee electric company … it eez impressive."

I shake off the compliment, not sure if I can speak to any sort of praise, and just stare down at him. "What about you working with the Fort to build up your standing here? Have you thought about that?"

He studies me for a minute, and I think he's trying to figure out exactly my play, and why I keep pushing and prodding him along certain ideas. And then he cracks a wide grin, filled with loose teeth and bumpy gums.

"I think I'd rather just wear zee lawman's star and do as I please while you do zee real running of zee town. How does that sound, Kitty?"

I cross my arms and frown at him. "I wouldn't have any authority to just run the town if you were sheriff and I was mayor."

"Sure you would. I would make it so."

"That's the whole point of elected officials. There's rules and laws and protocols."

"And I can make it zee rule that everyone has to do as you say."

"What would you be doing in all that free time? Making more trouble?" I demand.

"No, no, just living zee easy life while you do what you like, what you do best."

I shove down the sudden image of me, running all of Flats Junction with no one to stand in my way, everyone bowing to my ideas, no matter how big, and anyone who stands between me and my plans would have to deal with Yves.

But then I'd be beholden to him—as his wife at the very least. And if I displeased him … if I didn't play my part just as he hopes, then it could all come crashing down. He could make my work and my power disappear.

"You'd have to be elected as Sheriff anyhow," I remind him. "And the lawman and mayor work together. It's a business arrangement."

Yves waves aside the issue of needing to be voted into the role, as if he has no concerns about his ability to win on a ballot. "So then marry me, and as your husband, I can give you all zee power you need if I am sheriff."

My mouth opens, then snaps shut as I notice Matthias standing along the wall, unmoving and staring at us. It makes me feel as if I've been stripped and laid bare, to have such a conversation so baldly in front of him—in front of anyone. There's no privacy in this place, so even a sloppy marriage discussion is ripe for listening. I press my lips together and turn back to Yves, who stares up at me with some sort of strange combination of awfulness and respect, and I only find the faded argument, which sounds thin even to me.

"I told you, I'm not thinking of any wedding until after my Grand Opening."

I turn around and leave before he can come up with some other angle to argue, and walk the horse back to Rusty's livery with anger curling in my blood.

Who does he think he is, countering my plans? He's not smart—he's here and having some legitimate work because I gave it to him on a silver platter! He's not on the wrong side of the Fort commander or getting arrested from sabotaging trains. He's thriving—all because of me! And at the same time, I want to be rid of him. I want him gone. His usefulness isn't completely worth the trouble anymore. It may be I need to make another call on Lieutenant Colonel Peter Swaine to talk to him not only about keeping deserters away from Flats Junction—which would be my plan when I am mayor anyway, to work with the Fort on security—but to neutralize Yves. Maybe there's a way to arrest him on trumped up past charges, proven or no. Maybe I can find a way to break up his posse, giving him less power. Get rid of them, their constant malignant presence. Ask them to patrol the outskirts of town, or the Fort, or both. Get them gone. Maybe …

"Kate!"

I stop a few yards from the livery and turn west, where Marie hurries toward me. She's not wearing her working leathers, but she looks just as harried and busy as usual.

"How's Helena?" I ask at once, worry spiraling up my chest. "Is she well?"

"Healing, and fine enough, all things considered," Marie says. She stops in front of me, and presses her mouth together, then lets out a breath. "I've a favor to ask." My surprise must show at once, because she hurries on. "Not for me—for Helena."

"What's she need?"

"She needs a guard."

It's not at all what I was expecting. Maybe money for medicine, or more lace and fabric, or some sort of nerve tonic sent out for from out east. But a guard? Protection?

"How am I supposed to do that? I can't stand outside her seamstress shop with a gun all day," I say testily. "Why you even asking such a thing?"

"Not you," Marie scoffs. "I wouldn't expect that from you. I'm thinking one of the posse men."

This is the opposite of what I'd just been musing—how to run them all out of town. And now to purposefully give them a job? Something to ground them further in town? My whole body rebels against the notion, but I can't tell Marie any of it. It'll expose me … my mind. My plans and how much I've privately controlled …

"Why're you asking me?" I ask. "Go talk to Yves."

"But you have sway over them," she presses. "You've cooked for them, convinced them to clean up their thieving ways, got them to stop extorting everyone, even yourself. You … you can ask it. They'd say yes to you."

"And what, you just want one of them to sit outside Helena's place forever? She'll hate it, and it'll drive away business."

"Until there's some plan to be sure no more Army deserters or other riff-raff come into town, this is how it must be. Or I'm shutting it down. Her dress shop. It's over, and your investment is gone." She crosses her arms, then loosens them to drop. "This is not up for negotiation, Kate."

"You'll what, lock Helena up so she can't come to our—her business? You're taking away everything she's built. How would you like it if it happened to you?"

"It nearly did," Marie says tightly. "You are too young to remember it, but I had choices too. Marriage without a trade. Trade and no marriage. I got lucky, I know, to end up with both at the end, but Helena needs some sort of protection. She's tried it on her own, without a man, and no matter what we want for ourselves, until the world changes this is how it is. Without someone watching over her, I don't want her sewing dresses and making plans until she's wed."

"She has plans," I remind Marie. "Big plans. A storefront, seamstresses, and more—enough to draw people from all over the territory to order gowns and more."

"And I'm sure you're not upset about that—it'll double your investment in her little budding business. I'm no fool—I may not know my letters well, but I can do math, and even the little I know I can see how her dreams benefit you. Don't let them die, if not for her sake, then for your own hopes."

I want to smack her for her tone, but my hand only twitches. She's older than me, and something about whacking my elders is still buried in my bones. And the trouble is, she's not wrong. Not about any of it.

"So you're saying these are your terms for your daughter to continue working on our joint venture."

"It's what I'm saying."

I know in the end Marie won't have the last say—Thaddeus might, or even Helena's future husband, whoever that might be. But buried in her defiant words and tensed muscles I sense what she's trying to do. She's trying to salvage Helena's business, same as what I'd want. She's not saying no to the dream, just trying to find a way to make it safer. Possible. To stave off a repeat of the attack, because she knows what it is to be a single woman without protection. I know this, too. We've both of us been lucky in that regard—building our businesses without feeling as if we can't. Helena's not so fortunate. In the end, Marie wants the same thing as me—success. She wants this town to stay strong, too, and her daughter as one of the future pillars.

"Have you talked to Helena?" I ask quietly, the last thought filtering down just like the late spring sunbeams do on my shoulders. "What does she want?"

Marie has the grace to look a bit nervous. "I … I actually haven't asked her."

"Let's do that, then," I say, and then offer Marie a real smile. One that reaches into my eyes. She checks at it, and I guess I have never really smiled at her, with real feeling. "Together."

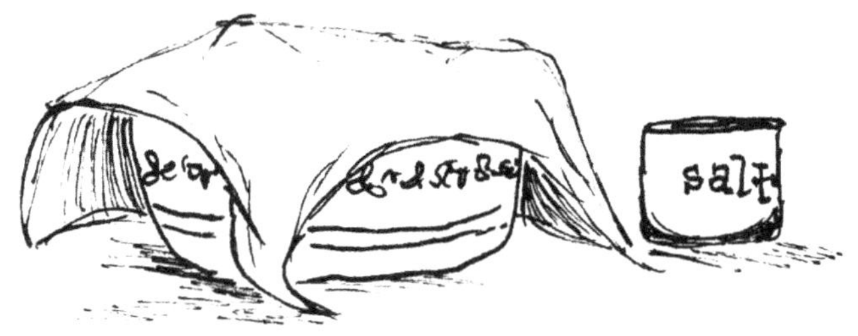

CHAPTER 14

Helena

May 21, 1884

Grandma adds one too many handfuls of flour to the bowl, so I quickly pour in a bit of water when she's not looking so the bread won't be too dry and not rise.

When she turns back, she frowns, and reaches again for the flour jar.

"It's ready for kneading, *Babcia*," I tell her.

"Is it?" she asks, sounding very confused.

"Perfectly sure," I tell her. "You can do the first round, if you want."

She stares at it, and for a moment I consider the notion that she might have forgotten how to make bread. But then she dips the tips of her long hands, and memory takes over as she starts to smash the ingredients together.

As I set the water pitcher back down on the table, my first two fingers twitch, but the entire hand doesn't tremble, nor does my wrist or arm or elbow. If I twist too fast, there's a hot pain under the right side of my rib cage, and if I laugh it makes the bruises buried in my liver ache. The patches of blue and purple on my face have faded to yellow pale enough that if Mother kept cosmetics, I'd be able to hide them completely, and only a small bump on my nose remains of the break. I'm only glad I was still not entirely awake when Doc Kinney cracked it back in place.

It grates on me to be home, under Mother and Father's roof, after spending time on my own in the seamstress shop. I'm more well-traveled than they'll ever be. I've seen taller buildings and glorious dressmaking shops and dined in glittering cafes in Chicago and New York, and bartered for pre-made tin goods directly from the manufacturer.

Mother won't let me go back to work. She says it's too soon, that she wants to keep an eye on me, but it's really because she's afraid. She's always been afraid of losing her family, the way other people are afraid of death itself. Instead, she's afraid she'll fail to keep us together, and my injuries are one more excuse, one more way she can prove that it's important to keep me nearby and not striking out on my own. Part of me wishes Kate needs to send me back east again for something—anything.

And yet … I don't know if I could ever walk outside alone without feeling my heart jump into my mouth, or be out after dark alone in the prairie. It's like the comfort of this town and all the stretching grasses and pine forests have been stripped away. My childhood has been gone for years, but this is a different kind of stealing.

I hide the salt from Grandma as she's already used it and will forget she has, and check the baking oven's heat. The old chores come back easily. Feed the chickens, grab a fistful of herbs for the stew, churn the butter. I can only hope after weeks away from the needle, I'll still remember the size of a hem by looks alone, and how to string up the sewing machine.

I haven't been back since those men …

It could've been so much worse. This I know. But sometimes it feels like it *was* as worse as it could have been. Violent things like that just don't happen in Flats Junction. At least, not in my memory.

The back door opens. It's Mother ... and Kate. I cringe a bit inside when I see them together, as if all my guilt about leaving home without explaining myself—or fighting with my parents, more likely—combines at the notion that they speak without me. It doesn't matter that I came back, I know. It matters that I left on my own, without a blessing to do so.

"Berit—it looks delicious," Mother says, glancing at Grandma. Kate doesn't say anything as she glances around our kitchen, her eyes settling on the bouncing flames in the hearth, and then on the many tin mugs lined up on the mantle.

But when her eyes finally land on me, they are not hard or cold, and my body melts back away from the tension that strung through my muscles when they appeared.

"We thought we'd ask you about returning to work," Mother starts.

I close my mouth against the immediate comment at this, even though it goes against everything she's been saying for weeks.

"Live back at the seamstress house, or stay here, or ..." I don't know what all my options are, or why Kate's even here. Maybe she's put pressure on Mother, saying she requires me back at work, that she doesn't want her investment lost.

"I suppose it's up to you," Mother says, her voice raw and honest. "You're old enough to travel, old enough to wed, but ... This is different. I know you've been itching to go back to it."

I start to shake my head, but she holds up a scarred palm, and I swallow my words at once, the reaction engrained.

"And maybe you're ready," she says, and slides a look at Kate. "And I'm sure Miss Davies doesn't want too much time to run past before you're back at it, with whatever her plans are for it."

"And mine," I remind. "I have plans, too."

Mother shifts inside her corset, inhaling quietly as if holding in her temper and crankiness inside of it. "If you want to leave this house, then I've asked Kate to request a member of Yves' posse to watch over you."

My eyes feel like they're overlarge. "Wh—who?"

"I don't know, though … maybe not Natty. Or Evan," Mother says, looking at Kate thinly now, as if daring Kate to object. "Or Arnold."

"That's getting a bit particular," Kate says, speaking at last. They've discussed this then—my future, my return to work. I set my back molars together so I don't glare, the tightening in my jaw causing saliva to pool in the valleys of my mouth. They've been talking like I have no say, like I don't get to decide—.

"We thought we'd ask you," Mother says, slashing my thoughts in half. "Do you want to just stay home? Or go back to the dress shop?"

"And if I choose the shop, I have to do so with some outlaw staring at me?"

"It won't be so bad, to have a guard," Mother says. "We don't know if … those men are still … and there could be others."

"I survived the wilds of city streets," I say, repeating the old argument, even though it no longer holds an ounce of weight, given how terribly those men, how they beat …

"Just until we can get the town more organized," Kate says smoothly, too quickly, her smile too easy. "Until there's an elected mayor and sheriff, until I—until the Fort can maybe spare a few official guards if we need them, too. Whatever it takes. It won't be forever."

"But I can get back to work?" Hope sears me, filling me with something foreign, until I realize it's a smile trying to break through. "And I'll be … safe?"

Have I smiled at all these past weeks?

"That's the plan," Mother says, though she doesn't look as happy as I feel, and Kate's frowning now, as if I've given the wrong answer.

"Then I choose the posse, the guard. And getting back to working and living alone," I say at once, quickly and as firm as I can muster before either of them tries to come up with some other reason why it's the wrong choice. I ignore the flutter in my chest as I think about going back to the seamstress shop, exiting that door without flinching. The ache in my gut and a phantom of the pain in my nose feels like a jolt of heat, and I push that away, too.

What is it Father always says? *Death is the way of it out here. You know this.*

Well, I didn't die. And I don't plan to let this stop me. I can't. I have too much to lose.

Mother nods at Kate then, once, as if some pact has been settled. Kate looks even more surly, and I wonder if she's not wanting to beg a favor of Yves. But wouldn't he be glad for it? He's always going on about legitimacy, business, and making a life in town. This will make him even more engrained. She will make his day, won't she?

"I'll let you know," Kate says curtly, and leaves without saying goodbye to any of us.

Mother turns back to me, putting her hands on her hips, and then her eyes fall on Grandmother, who has been staring off to space and left half the dough unmixed.

"Let me help you finish up," Mother says, reaching across the planks and edging the bowl out. "Berit. I've got it, thank you."

"Oh." Grandma glances at her hands absently and rubs them on her apron slowly. "Should I make the bread?"

Mother and I exchange looks, and I fold my arm around Babcia's elbow. "Why don't you watch the fire, and make sure it doesn't go out?" I say.

Grandma does as I ask, wilting into a chair near the hearth, and stares at it with intent for only a moment before her pale blue eyes go all dreamy again.

"While we wait to hear from Kate, do you suppose you could help me in the tinshop?" Mother asks. She's careful with the ask, like it's a delicate question.

My eyebrows go up at it anyway. "You know I'm no good in there. I'll make it worse, whatever you set me to make." Between us, Urszula was better at tinsmithing, like the knowledge of it lived in her veins and hands. And even my brothers have a knack for it, compared to me. It's yet another reason I wanted to find something else—so I wasn't stuck helping mother or only a goodwife.

"Well, then. I'm not going to set you up with hammers," Mother says, shoving her fists into the bread dough. She's so forceful the bowl partially lifts up as she raises her arm, then clatters back down as she punches once again. "I need you to order more fancy things from the Dover people."

I might choke on this second surprise. "You—you're wanting to continue working with them? With ordering things instead of making them?"

"I'm no fool, Helena," she says, looking up at me from a lowered forehead.

"You weren't wrong to say I needed to move with the times if I'm to stay afloat. Even your father knows he has to watch for industry changes as best he might. No—I'd like you to order pretty finials."

"For what?"

"Lanterns. For the Prime Inn."

"Did you keep the catalogue that came with the crate I brought back?" I ask, a little testy. "Or did you destroy it?"

Mother's mouth goes thin again, but she doesn't back down. "I kept it. It's in the shop."

"I'll help you," I promise, feeling strange in my own skin suddenly. It's a peace offering, maybe, or something more. Bigger. "You'll have to tell me how many and how much."

"I … I would be happy to assist you as well however I might." Now her voice is stiff, growing harder just like the dough she kneads. "Perhaps display some of your smaller goods on my shelves. If that would be … amenable."

Now I let my mouth drop open. This entire day—all these sentences from my mother are foreign. Is it because she's giving me back my freedom? Supporting me? Seeing me not just as a child, but at last as something more. A friend? A fellow business owner?

"You don't need to look so shocked," she says, turning wry and testy at the same time. "It cannot be that strange for me to wish to work with my own daughter."

"No…no. But it is … unexpected," I tell her, going for honesty. It's like she suddenly has seen me. Or accepted me? I don't know what it is. It's like testing the ice on the Flats Basin River right after a recent hard freeze. Is it real? Ready for weight? Or will I go crashing through?

"You've survived much," she says. "More than most. And yet … you still choose to go ahead with your life. You are not afraid."

"Not too much," I say, continuing the track of honest talk. "And if I don't face life again, I'll be stu—frozen forever, afraid to do anything."

She smiles slightly. "I think sometimes we are nothing alike, and then I realize we have some things where we are exactly the same."

"I'm not you."

"No," she says simply. "Thankfully, you're not."

Mother lifts the dough out of the bowl, testing its weight and solidness in her palms, and then lets it drop heavily into the stoneware bowl. "Is the bread oven ready for proofing?"

"Should be," I say, scooping up the bowl and throwing a wet rag over the top before shoving it into the pre-heating cave next to the hearth. As I do, I can't help feeling as if my heart is breaking apart a little, but also revealing something beautiful under the old layer. This conversation with my mother feels like being reborn, or finally coming into adulthood. Or learning that someone sees my true face.

It feels disjointed and wonderful and thrilling all at the same time.

Because unlike Kate, who sometimes befuddles me or is too intimidating to understand, my mother must love me even if I do things differently than she might. She has proven it now, with her words and her decision and her offering of a choice for my future.

So I turn away from the bread oven and give her something in exchange, a confidence and a confession and a peek into who I am. If it doesn't go well, I can go back to being a daughter and not a woman. But if she understands …

"How did you know you wanted to marry Father?" I blurt. "Was it your decision or did your families make you?"

The question, always burning deep inside and always too precious to ask, bursts out of me. If we are sharing kindness, and she's in a giving mood, or at least willing to treat me like an adult, maybe I can learn a few life lessons that she's always been too tight lipped to answer.

Or, I realize, maybe I've never really had a quiet chance to ask her. She'd never speak of certain things in front of the younger children, or even with Father in the room.

It takes an entire half minute of her staring at me, her hands dusted in flour and salt, before she clears her throat or even twitches.

"It was my choice," Mother says quietly. Her dark brown eyes go soft inside, wet and dim. "And his. No one forced it, or even really expected it."

"Was it love? Or just … convenience?" I wave my hand at the front of the building, where, behind the great oak door, their combined metal shops live and heave with industry as Father, Kaspar and Natan bang away on the anvils.

"I might say a little of both," she says. "But … no. There was affection. Love, though I didn't call it that until after we were married."

"Does Father love you?" I ask. This question feels even worse to ask, like a peeling back of something precious. But I think about how Doctor Kinney looks at his wife, and how some of the other couples share obvious desire, and I think about … *him.*

"He has never said so," Mother admits. "But he does."

"Even though it's not obvious?"

"It's obvious to me," she says, and a secret sort of smile pulls at the corners of her mouth. "And sometimes it's not flowery words or sugar promises. It's someone who sees you. Supports what you wish to do with the hours of life you're given. Who is steadfast for you, always. Romance is all very well, but it does not last a lifetime. Not in the way you might expect."

I want to ask specifics, about love and marriage and bedding, but it sticks in the back of my tongue. "So it's like … friendship and affection and … more … rolled up together?" I can't say *desire.* Not in front of her.

"Yes. Like that," she says. Red splotches rise on her cheeks, but she doesn't back down or look away from me. "And you realize you are no longer alone."

I nod, and fidget. I'm grateful she seems just as eager to stop the line of our conversation, even if it's the best one we've had—or maybe the most honest and womanly we've had ever. It feels as though we see more eye to eye. We are family and we are friends. There's a thread, steadfast and sturdy between us. It feels … good.

She hates the chickens, just marginally more than me, so I take the task of checking for the next round of eggs. I want to be alone with the revelations and thoughts she's scattered in my mind just like the scratch feed I throw to the birds. Love is … steadfastness. Support. *Someone who sees you, and will help you with what you wish to accomplish.*

I know who my person is. It has been since before I ever left for the east, and it has not changed with my return.

And yet, Hardy has no trade. No job that provides an income. He might support my dreams, but he cannot support me. Us. A life.

Besides, for all he's always been kind and friendly, there's never been an ounce of … obvious romantic overtures from him. Even I haven't fully expressed interest he could see as encouragement.

But maybe it's alright if I have to wait. I don't want to fall into a marriage. I still feel … strung tight after the attack. I want to get my life back to what it was before I dive into a marriage, or even hint at one. I want to find my footing again, and stop being afraid of the dark. Having a guard at the shop will help. Having the needs in my shivering fingers will steady them. I still will make curtains for the Prime Inn, sew bunting for the Grand Opening, and mend shirts for the Army men.

Mother has dealt with her own struggles. She lost her family, her daughter, and even me for a little while. She rips her own flesh, even though she lives as if none of us notice. She fights against a darkness that lives inside her like a black dragon, circling always. I can certainly face the world again. I refuse to wallow in being a helpless victim, a woman without strength. Before I face Hardy, I will still make a mark on my own little corner of the world. Maybe even build that boutique shop.

Those Army deserters are nothing. I will not let them rule my life. I refuse it.

I must find a way to smile again, to shove down the fear and pain and memories.

I *will* find joy in my work. I *will* look toward building something bigger and better.

Why else did I survive if not to do so?

CHAPTER 15

Jane

May 27, 1884

The sound of steps following me is unfamiliar. It's a slow gait, but the strike of each boot sole slams down on the hardening mud with a crack. All I know is it's not the step of another woman and it's not Patrick, either. I manage to look straight ahead for only another twenty paces before I finally give in and turn to look.

Doctor Thomas Smith is much closer than I had realized. He halts with me, only a few feet away, so near that I can smell his cologne, a too-sweet cloying weave of cloves and musk.

"May I help you, or would you like to pass?" I ask, gesturing ahead.

"I'm on my way to the Brinkley farm," he says, his voice clipped on the ends of the words in the hard-to-place accent he uses. "If you're heading along that way, perhaps I might join you?"

"I'm going to the same place," I tell him, and my voice is too hard. "I can't imagine my husband would like me strolling with his … competition."

He comes up alongside me regardless of my frostiness but has the sense not to offer me his arm. I stay rooted to the side of the churned road and stare up at him, daring him to admit the truth, to reveal anything of his intentions.

"I don't know if we are truly competition," he says. "I'm set to be a hospital man, while Patrick is sure to be a simple country doctor all his days."

Fury radiates from my skin, making it feel prickly like when there's pins and needles poking along a limb. I swallow, hard, and continue to glare at Doctor Smith.

"And what is wrong with being a country doctor?" I ask.

"I didn't say there was."

I hold nasty words behind my teeth, where they fight to burst out. But I won't make this worse for Patrick—for us.

"Hm." I turn to walk again, and he keeps up with me, even as I march ever faster. That he can do so without looking like he's hurrying only bothers me slightly less than the fact that he has chosen to indeed walk beside me, even when I have told him not to do so. It feels as if I have been violated, that my space has been eaten up by a man I loathe. And yet he has not even touched me with his sleeve.

"I do hope Henry has fared well with the tonic I've ordered," he muses. "I'm sure if not, he will be the first patient I bring into the hospital, which of course he has agreed to help pay for, just like the others in Flats Junction. Kate has been so very helpful. Do you know her well, Jane?"

"Mrs. Kinney," I correct. "I have not given you leave."

He slices a glance at me, sharp under that shiny top hat. "Do such formalities still exist out here?"

"I'm a proper Boston woman, Doctor. I have expectations. And you cannot think after your vulgar display with my husband that I would give you such casual allowances."

"He started it."

I hold in a gust of air, full of fury and outrage. There's no real purpose in me sparring words with this man, and I am sure to give up more than I will gain in doing so.

"And in the end, I will finish it," he continues, as the Brinkley homes inch closer, their matching whitewashed boards gleaming in the warm morning light. "Soon enough people in Flats Junction and the Fort and beyond will trade home care for hospital. It is worth me trading the east for the west, to have such opportunity. It would not be possible in the city, as the hospital doctors and the positions themselves are inheritance more than anything else. But here … yes."

"There are many other towns that could benefit from a hospital," I say. "Why not set up one in Yankton or Vermillion or even Deadwood?"

"Perhaps. A city comes with so much bureaucracy," he muses. "Out here there is a chance to write my own rules. You must be able to see the merit in this."

Having a civil conversation with this man leaves me feeling as if I am covered in a thin coat of dirt. Perhaps it is shame. Would Patrick be appalled to see this? To know I am fraternalizing with this doctor, who has caused him so much trouble? Who is surely here to continue to do so, for some strange petty vendetta?

As we near Susan and Old Henry's place, I slow down, and he follows out of habit.

"You're wrong about hospital care," I tell him. "People here are slow to change. And I've seen the statistics—hospitals often have a much higher rate of mortality. Folks go into them and never come out, even when they'd have healed just fine at home. They are not the modern wonder you are selling."

His lip curls upward around his left front tooth, a look that makes him suddenly look very much like an evil pirate out of a dime novel.

"What do you know?" he snarls softly, quietly, so his tone does not bounce and echo through the homes nearby. "You're only an uneducated woman."

"I know enough to read, and I know what I've read," I counter, just as lowly. "But what I don't know is why you're really here. You chose this for more than opportunity. You've come to torment Patrick."

"And why shouldn't I?" he says. His voice even lower and darker and menacing. "He's cost me an eye, a wife, and a practice in Boston."

I can't imagine Patrick being so bold, nor so powerful that he could do all that.

"You're lying."

"Ask him," Doctor Smith says, darkness creeping into his eye, a frown lowering his brow as he dips his head at me. "See if he dares to tell you the entire truth."

The barb pins me, striking deeper than the doctor realizes. *Truth?* Piecing together Patrick's past has always been like putting a puzzle together, without knowing the shapes or colors or subject of it. And if I asked, would he tell me the truth? Or only parts of it, omitting others, as he has done many times in the past?

"Yoohoo! Good morning!"

The shout comes from above and slightly to the right. I peer over Doc Smith's shoulder to spot Susan Brinkley waving with a dishrag. I smile and wave back, and note how her face dims when she sees who I'm walking with.

"Everything alright?" she calls, concern thickening her shout. It is for me, I know, and I wonder if it looks as if Doctor Smith is threatening me. I suppose it might, and I admit to myself that I'm relieved to be interrupted. It is a blessing to have the doctor step away from me, bowing slightly and opening his palm to allow me to approach the house first. It's impossible not to see the caustic intent or the sarcasm buried inside the gentlemanly movement.

"All is fine," I tell Susan, as I hike up the stairs with my skirts bunched in a hand, so I can carry my basket with the other. "I've just come to see how your husband is doing."

"As have I," Doctor Smith says behind me. "I'm certain by now the tonic has arrived?"

"That it did. A while back," Susan says. She catches my gaze and blocks the door to the house with her wide, curvy bulk. The barring is not meant for me, and I duck inside under her arm, but step just to the side so I might listen unseen. I tell myself it is so that I might assist Susan if needed, but in truth I only am immensely curious, as always.

"Mrs. Brinkley—"

"Leave. We've no interest in your doctoring," Susan says, her voice mild enough. "Your tonic did no good for my man's gout and made him take to his bed with a bad stomach. Jane's herbs and teas did more for him than your fancy waters."

"I'm certain, ma'am, that—"

"Get off my porch." Her voice rises. Outside, a front door creaks and slams shut. I wonder which of the daughters or daughters-in-law are now watching it. I do hope they're holding a nice heavy rolling pin or skillet, too.

"Really, I don't—" Doctor Smith's voice still sounds reasonable, but there's an edge to it now, a frantic, dangerous tone.

"And there'll be no support for you for your hospital from any of us Brinkleys," Susan continues. "Not if you can't even handle a simple bit of gout."

"It is very advanced gout."

"And yet Jane's cures worked fine enough. Enough that, for a bit, he could manage the pain and walk decent half the time, not take to his bed with the chamber pot. And after we gave you that money, had it ordered in … I suppose we can't ask for that tidy sum back, either. Now, I won't say it again, doc. Get gone, or I'll holler for the rest of them."

"If I could just see the patient—"

"Alice, Marta, Cora!" The shout is practiced and powerful, a burst from Susan's strong farm-trained chest. This is a woman who is used to bringing in her men from the fields for dinner and getting them all to mind.

Tina must already be the one watching—her and George live next to Susan and Old Henry, so she likely has heard the entire exchange.

Seeing Thomas get run off the farm by a half-dozen angry women wielding cooking implements will be a vision I'll share in careful detail to Patrick, and I'm happy to add my body to the intimidation, even though I don't have a weapon to brandish.

I turn into the doorway just as Susan advances, and follow her down the stairs to join the other wives. Alice has little Freddy on her hip, but holds her vast bread paddle. Marta has both of her daughters with her, red-haired just like her. Cora's brought both of her sons, both who look scrappy enough to attempt a fight if given the leeway by their mother. And Tina has a meat fork.

At first I don't think even this display of female defiance will be enough, but Doctor Smith seems stuck on Tina's fork.

He walks backward down the ruts running past each home's front door for a few steps, and I wish it was mucky enough that he'd slip and fall backward.

But instead he simply stares with his one eye, narrowing it slightly, before spinning on a heel and walking slowly, precisely down the middle of the road back toward Flats Junction. The Brinkley women grin at each other, exchanging a few small words, but I can only watch Doctor Smith's back for a long moment. It is tight and hard and square, and I'm certain we have solved nothing, and only raised the ire of a sleeping dragon. He'll reach town in no time at that pace—already he's halfway there. I wonder what he will do … what he will say …

When I enter, I find Henry not in bed, but in a chair with his feet propped up. This is good—it means she's been using the herbs I gave her, and consistently, too. Susan goes to hover behind Henry's chair. Her cheeks are still somehow youthful and plump and round though her neck sags with age and her eyes are nearly lost in the creases of her skin. When she smiles, she looks jolly, but when she is angry, her face falls into lines of disdain, as she did when she walked Doctor Smith off her property.

"I see you're better," I say. "I'm very glad."

"Will you have us continue the … plants?" Susan asks.

I've come prepared for this visit, and feel all the better for it. "Let's try the peppermint," I say. "Do you happen to have some already up in the gardens?"

"I do."

I follow Susan down the short steps toward the backyard, where a gigantic garden sprawls out under the afternoon sunlight. It must be utterly glorious in the height of summer. This early in the season there's only the winter garlic and early onions, lettuces and curling pea vines. On the far end three of Susan's granddaughters, in various ranges of age and wearing a mix of colors and aprons weed so close that I cannot completely tell which arm belongs to which girl.

"Here's the herbs," Susan gestures to the left. "Will you want a lot or a little?"

Would Esther make a tea or a poultice? Perhaps both. I did not ask in advance, wanting to prove to myself that I can do this without her aid. I know peppermint—and lavender—will work, but suddenly feel helpless and illiterate. Is this what Patrick battles each time he enters a house and tries to figure out the puzzle of the illness within it? I kneel into the well-tilled dirt and finger the soft, floating petals of the early mint. The leaves are still small, the new rhizomes poking out moon-white and lavender. Susan stands over me, hands on hips but with an open face, waiting. She believes me, I realize. She wants to try anything, and she believes I know what I'm doing!

Pulling the leaves off a stem, I grab the lavender too and then stumble to my feet. Susan steadies me as I straighten, and her hand is firm and sure under my elbow. I smile my thanks at her. This close, I can finally see her eyes are brown, like mine.

When we go in, I ask for hot water for a poultice, determined to try that first, and settle next to Old Henry on faded embroidered pillows to unwrap his aching, swollen feet. I only hope there are no ulcers or burst sores, or the mint will sting.

Susan bustles past with a huge iron kettle, and nods to the mortar and pestle, which sits, cracked and rather large, on the edge of the sideboard. "There for crushing as you wish."

I smash the leaves together and the spice and softness of the herb lifts into my nose at once, creating a stiff, bright green paste. As I wrap it up in a piece of cloth that Susan provides, men's voices jumble on the porch and soon enough, all of the Brinkley sons tumble into the house, on break from the fields for lunch.

In a matter of moments, Old Henry is a king holding court, his broad, red joints still bared and throbbing, but his eyes are bright as he swivels between his sons: Young Henry, John, George and Mitch.

"So it is – you think?" Old Henry asks. "There's no question?"

John sighs. "No question. Nearly all the cattle who were still sick yesterday are gone."

"Gone?"

"They're dead, Pa," George says angrily. "And it's the damn bloody murrain for sure."

"Christ Almighty," Old Henry settles into the chair back and winces as I come over and fold the first of the poultice over the bright red swells.

Susan appears next to me with a fat plate, heaped with a steaming cup of the peppermint mixed with her hot water.

"Here you be, my dear," she settles the plate on the top of Henry's belly and his hands catch it clumsily. I notice he has a glob of red around the knuckle of his thumb as well.

"What is this, woman?" He stares at the tea and sniffs with disapproval. "Looks horrible."

"Tea," she says primly. "And you'll drink it if you know what's good for you. Jane says it might work."

I ignore the warm flush of pride, unnecessary and unhelpful, and continue to smear the poultice over the fat bubbles of pain on his feet.

"That's a fifty gone in two days," John Brinkley complains tightly. "And Doc Kinney says it likely there'll be more before it's out of the damn system. Beg pardon, Mrs. Kinney."

I nod, ignoring the cuss, and move to re-wrap Old Henry's ankles.

"It's the damn Svendsen cattle, still since they came back from Texas last season," Young Henry says. "It has to be. Their steers are close enough to our fences. In fact, I saw Hank and Moses riding them right next to the rails the other week."

"I'll talk to Oddvar," Old Henry says, but his face is drawn into tight lines. Is it worry or the taste of the tea? He sips again and his lips, thin and dry already, go thinner. "He and I decided back in the late 70s when our herds were growing and when the first news of the fever started to come up from

Kansas and Nebraska about making a corridor. His men have to go back to sticking to it. Now, Mrs. Kinney, will this concoction work, then?"

"I am sure it won't hurt," I tell him. "But it'll help even more if you stay off your feet."

Susan promises to force Old Henry to keep resting, and I leave as the other women show up with their contribution to the midday meal. With children and babies and dogs, the entire house suddenly feels crushing, the noise and shouts and chatter outlandishly loud compared to my mild household.

As I walk back toward home, alone this time thankfully, I reflect that this might be the first time I've been welcomed into a home where my notion of home care and medicine was expected and accepted and believed. What a wonderful, outrageous moment, and it has passed me by, so that now I can only look backward at it and marvel. I suppose the best of it is to realize I have traded my role of housekeeper for fully fledged nurse at last.

When I get home, I nurse Andrew and write up my report on Old Henry for Patrick, so we might combine our information and keep his medical files up to date. Esther is slow roasting a slab of bacon and pork from Alan's pig farm, and I think I might look to how much lye we have and wonder if I can render some soap from the leftover fat, when Patrick and Hardy rattle in from the porch and Patrick walks into the kitchen without setting down his medical bag or taking off his hat. Hardy is behind him, an overeager shadow eyeing up the morning's half-stale bread.

"I've a question for you," Patrick says, looking straight at me. "We have a patient out at the Grady farm, and I'd like you to come with us."

I tilt my head at him. "That doesn't sound very much like a question."

"Oh." He has the presence of mind to look a bit abashed, but plunges ahead anyway. "That is, you should come. It'll do you good."

"Should I take the baby?" I ask, rising while burping Andrew at the same time.

He hesitates, and in that moment, I realize he is nervous. It sends a skittering down the planes of muscles in my back and across my neck.

"What is it?" I press.

He runs a hand through his dark hair, pressing his trembling lips together, and I can fairly guess at the thoughts rumbling across his mind.

"It's the black measles," he admits at last, finding my eyes. "But the young man is not too far gone—enough that I must have hope."

The quiver starts deep in my stomach, where the core of my heat begins, and spreads outward, turning into chills along the way. By the time it hits my fingers, they feel like ice, even in the mild spring weather that seeps into the house from the hall and the back windows.

"No," I say. I grip Andrew tighter than I mean, and he makes a tiny squeak. "I think I will stay here. You've Hardy to help you, anyway."

He stares at me, and I feel as though he is measuring me against some unknowable notion. I think I might fail this test, whatever it is, and brace myself for his disappointment.

"You want to be a nurse. To help me."

"You know I do, in my own way."

"Then you must face your fears. And failures. You know I myself have failed every time with this illness. Let's face it together this time."

It feels cowardly to do otherwise in the face of this argument, and I glance at Hardy and Esther before I nod so tightly it makes the back of my head hurt. Yes, I will go, even knowing there's next to no chance of success. Putting Andrew in a sling, and picking up the roll of medicines, I follow Patrick out to his waiting horse. He walks with his usual loose gait, his lunch bundle from Esther and me swinging in the hand opposite that of his medical bag. Hardy has his own horse borrowed from Rusty's livery today, and I wonder how many miles they already put on this morning. And then I realize it must be a fresh horse. Patrick would not have spared the extra expense for Hardy just for patient rounds. Hardy would have ridden with Patrick all day … until now. Patrick did this for me, so I might ride with him.

As much as trepidation fills me to see yet another black measles patient die in front of my eyes, I also am filled with quiet amazement. That he should go through the expense and trouble…that he should wish for me to succeed …

That thought keeps me from descending into panic as we head north and west out of Flats Junction, past the Wu brothers and their homestead, and along the lines of Svendsen lands. The Gradys are in the brushy edge of another pine forest, where field and prairie battle with low bushes and towering trees, not too far from the Woodman homestead. Old brittle needles from last year crunch under the horse hooves, and Andrew sleeps in the well-fed slumber of a newborn even with the occasional cry of a hawk or snort of the horse. I will cover his face again when we enter, in hopes he does not get the dreaded black measles. It would kill him, this I know—if we cannot save an older child, how can we hope to save an infant?

Inside the home, the fire has overheated the single room and loft above, and there is no one indoors except Orla and her eldest son, Michael, who looks better than I had anticipated. He's even sitting up in bed next to the fire, his hair the same carrot-red as his father's, if I recall Lugh correctly. Orla herself has coppery hair, and her accent sounds like Patrick's only thicker.

"Good of you to come, doc," she tells us, as she pulls over chairs from the kitchen table. "He's been feelin' poorly for a wee bit, so when the spots showed, we thought to send f'you, 'specially after what happened to the Woodman boy." The trust in her eyes feels like hope and belief and something like kinship. I wonder if it has anything to do with Patrick's heritage matching theirs.

"So how long have you been feelin' bad, young Michael?" Patrick asks conversationally. He pulls out his stethoscope and his curvy tongue depressor, the nickel of it a soft silver in the glowing hearth light.

"About three days," he says, leaning back on the pillow. His brow shimmers with sweat, even as he tremors with fever. "Spots just came last night."

Patrick does his typical initial observations, and I only take notes with the hand not cradling Andrew. Hardy stands behind me, listening and watching, and I notice he tries to hold his breath without seeming to do so, as if he fears the air inside the house itself. Or maybe he's just trying not to be too nervous.

Michael has been in the brush, clearing more land, and he says the worst of it was the bugs, which were everywhere even this early in the season. He does not have purple fingers or blackening gums, and his toes are only mildly swollen, pink not red. Patrick's movements are unhurried and almost languid, and within the first fifteen minutes, both Orla and Michael have relaxed, the tension in their shoulders and in her quick movements settling to something like hope. And I realize I am harboring hope, too.

Please, please let us win this one.

Patrick needs it.

And I know I do, too.

After Patrick finishes the first set of examinations, he turns to me, picking up my notes, though I can tell he's not really reading them. He doesn't need to. Instead, his lips move without sound, and I think he's reciting all the medicine he can offer, trying to figure out some new combination. Hardy only stands mutely, and I wonder how many such patients he's already watched wither and die a terrible death from this mysterious, inescapable illness.

"What do you have, Janie?" Patrick asks quietly. "What have you brought this time?"

I don't look at Orla as I unravel the leather of medicine, the vials clinking and the packets of seeds and dried leaves crinkling like dried rattlesnake tails.

"Viral or bacterial, that is the question I cannot answer," Patrick murmurs, looking at the medicine I have, his eyes now glazed with incomprehension. I wonder what this must look like to him—unlikely help, a woman's attempt to stave off death, perhaps.

"Does anyone know?" I ask. "We do not know how it starts, but are there any papers?"

"Nothing. Not from anyone I know, or anything that has been published that I've been able to get my hands on," Patrick says, looking frustrated. "I used to have access to so many medical journals, in many languages and from all over the world, but here … here we are lucky for last month's newspapers to arrive sometimes."

I nod, and let my fingers brush over the strands of dried flower heads, and pause at the prickly tops of the purple coneflower, echinacea, or, if I recall

Esther's word for it—*uŋglákčapi*. She says it is best if a tea is made every day, and I wonder if it is too late to make a difference even though we have caught the sickness early. Perhaps if we have him drink three cups a day instead of one? And then there's the fetid marigold, for too much bleeding, like under the skin that Michael will have soon enough, if the early spotting is anything to go by. And for the pain, the fever, the headaches?

"Peachtree willow bark," I say, mostly to myself. "And the coneflower. Each five times a day, three at the least. It is better than nothing." I glance over at Michael, who is pretending not to listen. "He's young and healthy. Maybe there's a chance."

"Orla," Patrick says, turning around to the mother without consulting further. "Would you like to try a few things? There is no modern medicine for this yet, but there's the old herbs, the woman's way."

"Like in the old country, aye?" she says, sounding very comfortable. "Like me mam and aunties would do?"

"Somethin' like that, but more from around here," Patrick amends.

"Oh, aye, then. If it's the best way, you say."

"There's no guarantee," he warns. "It may still not work."

"That's the way it's always been, doc," Orla says. Sorrow rises in her wide pale face, but she hides it well. I suddenly wonder how many other children she's lost over the years. And this Michael, so close to manhood! It would be a terrible, awful shame. It fills me with deeper determination, and I begin to pull out more plants, lining them up on the top of the scuffed table.

"Then we will do it all," I say. Hardy leans in as I choose, and so for his sake, I list out the ingredients. "Dandelion for any germs that might be living in him, mouse ear everlasting for a poultice for his swollen toes and hands, and yarrow to stop the bleeding in his skin."

I don't know if any of it will work. Neither does Patrick, but he does not stop from speaking to Orla as if this is a grand plan and certainly has some chance of success. I spend my time writing careful instructions, then letting Patrick take the lead, so it is as if he has the final say. He seems inclined to do it, and it's only halfway through the evening, after we've eaten a light soup with tiny spring beans and early onions and bread that snaps, that I begin to suspect that it's because he either doesn't want the wrath of the family to fall on me, or because he truly believes there's a chance my cobbling together of Esther's knowledge might work. And, I suppose, in light of the fact that he has nothing to offer, it is indeed better than nothing.

Hardy dives in, as if used to grinding dried plants in Orla's wooden mortar, and watches as Patrick measures out a teaspoon of each, creating potent, powerful teas and forcing them down over Michael's sore tongue so often the poor boy has to use the chamber pot more and more as the night wears on.

It's nearing ten o'clock, when Lugh and the other children are already asleep in their beds and Orla has nodded off next to Michael, who dozes without tossing and turning in his hot bed by the fireplace, that Patrick stirs from where he's been staring at the patient.

Hardy has fallen asleep sitting up too, while Andrew sleeps in my aching arms, which wish to put him down if only I could make myself not to be afraid to do so. Patrick has taken some brief turns with him, but the infant is fussy and seems to wish to be mostly with me in an unfamiliar place. Or perhaps Andrew senses my own unease and is glad to be near me as I am with him.

"Well," Patrick says, so quiet it's near a whisper. "It's not worse, which is something. We should know in another day."

"Another day?" I rasp. "Are we to stay that long?"

"At least until noon," Patrick says. He drags a hand down his face and then through his hair, smoothing it back before tugging on the back of his shoulder, easing out the strain from lack of movement these last two hours. "If he stays the same, there's hope. Real hope, Janie."

That same hope swirls inside of me, a cacophony of what-ifs and perhaps, maybe and might've. Suppose I've guessed it right, or we caught it early enough, or the boy is strong enough, or the teas are the proper ones, or it's some unknown combination of all of these or some of them, some luck, some providence, some simply the way it is to be …

I hang onto that thread of hope as if I ought to be able to will it into truth, and it keeps me awake with strange energy so that Patrick does not worry alone. Andrew settles down in my arms and slumbers away, blissful of the tensions racing up and down my entire body. One moment I think that all will end as it should, no matter the result. Other times I throw all my emotions behind begging, forcing, requiring my teas and herbs to work. Is it possible to think something into being? To force an action against the impossible?

As the morning creeps by, and the lunch hour builds, I pour yet another cup of the echinacea tea, from the purple coneflower, extra strong and heady, and hand it to Patrick. Michael drinks it himself, and though he still seems feverish, he does not seem worse.

It all comes down to the rash—and I find myself holding my breath, just like Hardy, when Patrick peels back the blankets to see how it is. It is something he has waited to do since last night's supper, so that he might be able to see a difference instead of checking every other hour. I understand why he did so, but at the same time, it is like asking a child not to sneak a piece of toffee as it cools on the sideboard. I have wanted to look every hour myself!

"The spots are … Jane, come look," Patrick says. His voice is utterly neutral. Faced with the results, I find myself choking on bile, on air, and hand Hardy the baby without asking so I might be able to focus without distraction.

So I might be able to see my failure.

The spots are muted. Pale pink against skin that looks more yellow than purple, as if there is bruising beneath it starting to heal.

"And how are you feelin' this mornin'?" Patrick asks Michael as he peers closer at the rash. I stare at it, my hands feeling loose and empty. I don't want to believe it's possible and yet cannot help the tremors of my mouth. It would be too soon to smile. Too soon to call it victory.

"About the same, doc. Maybe not so wrecked all over," Michael says. He hands the empty tea to his mother and shifts a bit on the straw mattress. "Could use the pot again, though."

"Yes, yes," Patrick says. He puts the blanket up to give Michael the bit of privacy allowed in such a small room, though it does not hide the sound of the boy's urine hitting the empty clay.

With the blanket hiding the patient, Patrick's eyes go wide as they meet mine, and then flash to Hardy's.

Together, we hold in our gush of air, our muted whoop of shock.

The rash is not worse … and it seems better. And the patient should be worse. Not the same. Not slightly feeling a bit less awful …

"You sayin' my boy will do?" Orla says. I turn, having clean forgotten she is in the room with us. "That it won't kill him, the way it did young Perry?"

"There's nothin' for sure," Patrick says. His voice even quivers, as if he's unable to believe, same as me. "He might still take a turn for the worse, but you keep givin' him all the herbs and teas, five times a day each as Mrs. Kinney and I have said, and I'll come back tonight if I can—tomorrow mornin' at the latest."

"He's not worse," I can't help adding. "That … it is enough to be ho … pleased." I refrain from saying 'hopeful'. As Patrick always says—it is best not to give hope, especially not too soon or too early or when it is all still too uncertain.

But I do hope. I pour all myself into hoping.

And when we're riding back home, I allow myself to feel the ache of the hard chairs and the many hours of vigil at Michael's bedside, and also give myself over to that hope as I tighten my hold on Patrick's waist.

"Did it work, Pat?" I ask when we are out of earshot from the house and even from Hardy. "Is it worth considering for others?"

"It may have worked, aye," he says. "And if it does, truly, it's a fair miracle."

"It's a cure, then. Something that's been here all the time, in the prairie around us." I don't press for more—for vindication for me or Esther or her people or the months of learning I've put in. I don't ask for recognition or praise, either. It is enough that we might have saved a life at last and beaten the black measles for the first time.

"It's somethin' to consider as a cure," Patrick amends, but his voice is the lightest I've heard in years, perhaps even since our wedding. "It's a start. And I vow to … I promise you we'll work on it. We'll try it again, and see if we can figure on what works best, and what must be done for the best chance at success. If Michael survives … Janie … it changes everything."

I think about the day before, when snide Doctor Smith spoke down and so dismissive of my husband, and I lay my head on Patrick's back.

"It'll make you better than Thomas Smith," I say. His stomach tenses under my palm, but I hold on just as tight and continue. "People will come to you, not him, and it won't matter he has a fancy hospital, or whatever ugly rumors he says of you, when he tries to destroy you."

Patrick goes still. "What do you mean?"

So I tell him about my encounter with the other doctor, of the veiled accusations, and after a long moment of silence, my husband unravels the twisted paths of the two physicians—their apprenticeship, Thomas's treatment of Patrick and his use of rumor and lies, how women died under Thomas and important patients, too, and how much he blamed Patrick enough to run him out of Boston, and how Patrick got back at Thomas, even though some of the violence was not planned.

"I do not know if I completely regret stealin' his eye," he says at the end, as our house comes up at last. "I think sometimes I had the better trainin' in the end, what with Doc Stassen and Chilling, learnin' the horse and animal healin', and then bein' able to get Tara and Bobby together … I think sometimes I was luckier."

"But now he's here, trying to do the same thing again!" I say. "We can't let him."

"We won't," he says, and takes my hand in his. "Besides, now I'm not facin' him alone. It's not the same this time. This time he's comin' at me in my home, my town. And we might have a secret cure for the black measles, thanks to you."

Hardy turns his horse right to return it to Rusty, and Patrick guides his mount to our fence line to let me off. As he helps me down carefully, so Andrew isn't jostled, he smiles at me, the blue eyes crinkling deep in the corners, and then he kisses me right there in the front yard where anyone can see.

There are words hidden in the kiss, and as I watch him go to board his horse at the livery for the afternoon, I realize I've found a new space within our marriage, as if the place I've been trying to clear and find between us has been built at last, so I might forge my calling with his.

It is a different hope, but a hope for the future just the same.

CHAPTER 16

Kate

June 1, 1884

The weather is perfect, and I'm making every reason to be outside instead of stuck in the General's dim room. Two steps from the post office, where old George nods off in the early summer warmth. Inside, vicious swipes of a flat butter knife indicate that Nancy is in the middle of her usual morning routine to open everyone's mail, which she'll then hand over innocently and act surprised and mildly offended if anyone speaks about the cracked seals.

"Kate!" she calls, spotting me from the dim inside of the postmaster's. She comes out, her hands free of mail, looking for all the world like she's been sitting inside bored instead of gathering town gossip. "Your ostrich feathers are in."

She hands me a package, which might have been thin had it not been for all the wrapping re-stuffed inside, the seal broken and the feathers poking out.

I'm not going to ruffle her today, that wouldn't be good campaigning.

"Good—I'm just to Helena's now," I say, taking the package. "She's putting together a fine hat for the Grand Opening and voting."

"You still thinking of the mayor job?"

"Yes. Why?"

"Only thought I should mention that old Simon Zalenski is thinking he'd run."

"How do you know that? He never comes to town," I say, shoving down the scattered worry that rises up at her words. "I'd have heard if it was serious."

Nancy shakes her head. "Only that Veronika wrote her youngest sister back east about it, speculating that her husband might throw in his name."

He can't. He's too old, and he doesn't know a thing about how Flats Junction works. He's a farmer, a father, and doesn't ever come in unless there's a gathering. Who would want an absent mayor?

But Simon's been round a long time. The Zalenski name is large, his children and grandchildren, and people who married into the family, and *their* families …

"He better not," I mutter.

Nancy smiles at me, but it's not sympathetic. She crosses her arms and leans on the railing of her little side porch.

"I'm not saying don't run, Kate. Just giving you a fair warning is all. Mayor or no, it ain't going to be easy for you."

"You are truly planning to run for it, Kate?" Hannah Horowitz, the shoemaker's wife, comes around, two letters clutched in her hand, and plops herself right in the center of our conversation so fast I'm sure she's been eavesdropping on the other side of the wall.

"Sure. Sounds like folks want it," I say. "Least they did when the idea was floated."

"But you're not married."

I wiggle my thumb at Nancy. "Neither is she."

Hannah glances over at Nancy's dozing father-in-law. "She's widowed. There's a difference. Everyone knows that."

"What about Marie Salomon?"

"That was before my time here," Hannah sniffs. "And I'm sure there was just the same questions then. A woman ought to be married."

"But a man can run for mayor without being so?" I challenge her. Between the news about Simon and yet another poke at my marital status, I'm feeling prickly all over.

"It'd be less questioned, if it was a man," she says. Her shoulders sink a little. "I'm not trying to be cruel here, girl, just reminding you what you already know. There's expectations."

"Don't you think if I was thinking of getting hitched, I'd have done it by now?" I ask.

"Not for lack of trying, Kitty." Nancy means well, I think, but all it does is rip open the old wound of Patrick choosing Jane, even after he'd told me otherwise. After our past, living in my parents' house. After what we'd been to each other, all those years ago.

Never mind that I don't want him anymore.

I don't want *any*one anymore.

I just want to have enough, so I never have to worry about not.

"Well, I'm sure folks are used to me running things without a man to meddle," I tell Hannah. "And I can put all my attention on the town, instead of the kitchen. As it should be."

There, that feels like a proper campaign pitch. It works, too, because Hannah just inhales and shakes her head, and then takes the step up toward the post office door.

"I've one for Vermillion and one for Yankton-way," she says to Nancy.

"I'll handle it." Nancy puts out her palm, but Hannah clutches the sealed envelopes to her chest with both hands.

"And I'll stand and watch you stamp them and get them into those sacks, if you please."

"There's no need to wait. It's my job."

I leave them to bicker and continue on toward Helena's. As I round the building, garish green skirts whip around the corner of Helena's dress shop, and I stop cold. I've no desire to run into Patty or Victoria today, and don't have the energy to face off with anyone today. There's too much to do, now that I've settled on the notion that I'll combine my Grand Opening with the same week that the vote for mayor is set to be late this summer, and I've put off all the details till now. And now I'm near out of time to get it all done. Helena said she has the first of the bunting ready at least, and I'm fair pleased she's been quick to go back to the needle. There's hope she will not fall into some sort of darkness after what … after all she's been through.

Patty and Victoria's voices, high and demanding, bounce around the houses, getting higher with each half-word. I strain to listen without actually going to the front of Helena's dressmaking shop, and soon enough I don't even have to work hard to hear.

"You let us in right now, you big lug!" Victoria demands.

"Or we'll tell Yves, we will," Patty adds.

There's a bit of silence, as if the air is inhaling their words and not bothering to answer, and I realize that heavy quiet is just Matthias, standing there as Yves told him to do. An immovable mountain of shape and bulk and bone, standing right in front of Helena's door. He's been there every day, without fail, as silent as a snake that sits unmoving under a shady porch, until Helena gets back to Marie and Thad's place. She hasn't slept alone again yet—I think it's the only bit of weakness she'll let on.

"We just wanna shop a bit, buy a bit of lace, maybe, or a spool of silk," Patty tries again. "Order me a new frock or something."

I wait, holding my breath, wondering if they'll pull their too-quick knives on him, or threaten something worse than Yves's anger. But it's still nothing from Matthias, and I let a grin chase itself briefly along my mouth, mostly because I like seeing Patty and Victoria not get their way. Yves is too soft, letting them always work around him, and he gives them what they ask for always—that bit of lace or candy. I remember all too well from when they'd come into my General, demanding all sorts of bits of luxury.

They get tired of pestering after another minute and flounce off back north toward Yves's store. I can hear their boots flapping on the hard packed dirt, smacking in a huff. I suddenly imagine Yves needing to deal with his whiny women, and wonder if he'll bother to force Matthias to do his bidding. What'll Yves do? Wave around his knife and pistol and say please? Matthias generally does what Yves says, though. And then I remember that Matthias has stood up to Yves before. Once. And I'm not speculating on why.

Marie's request went against my plans for what to do with the posse and how to run Yves out soon—he swelled up like a bullfrog at the notion he was in charge of protecting Helena—and I'm thinking I made the right choice to keep the dressmaking shop for now. Once Helena grows it up, my investment will be paid off and I'll just make my percent of her profits, and by then Yves will either be bored staying in town, or will have come up with some other mischief and I won't need him, anyway. For now, though, I like that people think I have such sway over Yves and his gang. Even if it's always hanging just by a thread, and any quick disaster'll snap it.

When I know Patty and Victoria are well and good gone, I walk up at last. Matthias is just about to sit on the wide stool that is positioned directly in front of the screen door, so he has to move it just to allow folks in and out. He straightens when he sees me, but just stands there, arms hanging, and looks at me as if I'm something other than myself.

Oh, I want to ask him why he was chosen to guard her. Or if he somehow silently volunteered. And if he minds standing out under the narrow bit of shade, perched on that spindly stool.

But Matthias doesn't speak. Everyone knows this. Or at least, if he does, it's been to me and on his own terms. Unexpected-like and rare.

"I'd like to speak to Helena," I say.

He waits, unmoving, but my voice has carried into the shop and Helena's carries right back out. "Kate's fine, thank you."

My eyebrows go up as he drags the stool and then even bothers to open the screen door for me. I walk in without thanking him, and he goes back to sitting and staring at nothing.

I walk all the way into the back of the shop, where Helena is busily hemming what look like long strips of fabric—too long for stockings or a sleeve—and when I stop in front of her machine, she pauses the treadle and lifts up the bright yellow tube.

"It's streamers—to go with the bunting!" she says, sounding very pleased with herself. "They can be wound around the porch beams or hanging under the bunting in the same swoops …" She leans down, inspecting her handiwork.

"I didn't order those," I remind her.

"I know," she said. "But it'll look even better with them. And you said you wanted it grand—more than grand."

She's not wrong. I did say that. I just don't know why she cares so much to help me—maybe it's obligation? Her head bobs at her bed, which is piled high with more of the bunting she showed me earlier. There's plenty more of it now. Enough to plumb go around the entire porch roof.

"It looks mighty fine," I tell her, lifting up the finished half-circles just for something to do with my hands. I trust her work. "It'll be done much sooner than I was thinking." I pull out the ostrich feathers from the package Nancy handed me, and lay them out flat on the small space of wood next to the machine. "And here's these."

"Oh, that's dandy. I wanted to make sure it was finished on time," she says, and goes back to using the machine with her feet, running the needle and cloth together with such ease I am distracted for a minute. "And with the ostrich feathers from Nancy in, your dress and hat will be done, too."

Inching closer, I bend and lower my voice, so it doesn't reach Matthias. "How's it with …" I toss back my head, so she can catch my meaning.

"It's been really good," she says, whispering back. "People call in what they're here for, and if I don't say anything, he won't let them in. If I say for them to enter, he does."

"How did you figure on that?"

"Learned by error, mainly," she says, then leans in. "He doesn't say anything, ever. Do you think his tongue's been cut out by Yves?"

"Who says that?" The rumors always swirling around the posse are larger than real life, but I sometimes think Yves himself starts them, just to keep people guessing.

Helena shrugs. "I don't remember. Maybe Kaspar or Natan."

"Your brothers put too much stock in gossip."

"It makes sense," she insists. "Otherwise why would such a strong man do anything little old Yves says?"

I have wondered that, too, but it's no good asking and expecting an answer.

"Well, I can tell you he's got his tongue. I've heard him speak a few times," I reveal. "But he doesn't answer questions, so it's not worth trying."

Her eyes go wide, and I hurry to add, "I wouldn't go telling anyone, in case it makes him mad."

"Right, of course," she says, her voice going lower and thicker.

"Anyway, I was also going to see how you fared," I say, pitching my voice back to normal. "See how your work is going now that you're back in it."

"Fine enough," she says. "I wrote to my friends for more patterns. Spring styles will be coming out of Paris soon enough, and they'll show up in Boston and New York right after. I'm thinking, maybe …" She pauses and looks around the tiny, converted building. "It's quick, and maybe too soon, but I could … we could expand."

I lower my chin. "You got extra funds to invest on that?"

"Some," she says, a peachy pink flush rising on the tops of her cheeks. "I take in the mending for the Army, and it's a lot of work. And the curtains for the Prime Inn'll bring in money. Joe's paying for that, he said," she says quickly. "He said he doesn't need you to foot every bill, as the place is still half his."

"Mm." She's becoming independent of me, sooner than I would have expected. "Well, suppose you wanted to buy the old cooperage and set up a bigger dress shop, a fancy place like you saw out east?"

"Yves and his posse have a store there," she says, her eyes flicking to Matthias's back. "I was thinking of building up a new place, with clean wood and two rooms in the back—one for storage and one for living."

"That's a lot of space for one woman," I say, wondering what Mikey would charge for so much fresh lumber. Houses go up all the time in Flats Junction, but they're not usually very fine.

"It's not much different than the General," she counters. "And besides, someday I might get married."

"No man will go work for his wife," I say.

She looks at me evenly. "I wouldn't ask that. My father and mother work side by side, so I know it can be done. But my husband might have a completely different trade, so it'll work. Can we—Kate? I'll pay you back a good quarter of what you've already spent, and then we can pool the rest to see what we can build. Please ... please let me."

I don't answer at first, my mind too busy with figures and lines, adding and dividing. We'll want Tom Fawcett to draw up some paperwork for us, on top of a loan we'll likely need to do it right. How thin do I want to stretch myself and my money? And even as I'm asking this, I know I like it. I like having my fingers on the pulse of lots of places. My father would say it's wise to spread risk like this, but mostly he'd be proud I'm gathering power to me. I touch so much I'm untouchable.

But when I spin back around to look at Helena, where she sits frozen by her sewing machine, she's watching me with unguarded hope. Wishing. And something else shines in her face—something like awe.

Is that how she sees me?

She doesn't know what I've done to get here, and how.

But that's what clears my head, this obvious adoration.

"I see how it'll be profitable, if you can work hard and maybe do a hire," I say. "Or two."

"Yes?" She stands, the streamer tumbling to the floor. She snatches it back up and holds it tightly between her palms. "I'm glad. I'd hoped ... I wasn't sure you'd say yes, and then I'd have to figure out how to manage my plans alone."

"You've got plans?"

"To be just like you," she says, and looks me straight.

Be like me? Who on this earth would want to be like me? Some half-white, half-Lakota spinster? Doesn't she realize that the cost of the power I hold in town, the cost of being *me*, comes with the price of loneliness.

"You don't want to be like me," I say.

"Well, enough like you that I have my own way in the world," she amends. "Thank you, Kate." Setting down the streamer, she comes around with her hand stretched. When we shake hands on the deal, her eyes do not leave mine, and I wonder what this is. Friendship? Kinship? Family? It feels like more than just business, and something like elation fills me up so quick I pull away before the sharp stab in my eye becomes more than a hint of a tear.

When I go to the door, I'm still trying to figure out what I feel inside. Elation? Sisterhood? It feels wide and strange inside my stomach, as if I cannot hold it inside me, even if I don't have a single way to name it.

Matthias is already up and moving the stool. He opens the screen again, holding it until I'm clear of it, and doesn't let it bang shut, either.

I'm five steps back toward the General when I realize he's one behind me. The blue eyes meet mine with strange clearness, as if he's only looking at me and thinking nothing more. No strategy, no consideration on how to use me, just looking straight at me because I'm … Kate.

"You are goot?" he asks, the German accent still thick as I remember.

I stare up at him, tongue stuck on top of my mouth. "Not so well, but I'll manage." It's maybe the most honest I've ever been, the pure words pouring out before I can stop them. But why not? Who will he tell? "I always do."

He frowns a little. If there are more words building inside him, they don't bubble up, or at least not very fast.

"Thank you, by the way," I say, to clear the strange air hanging between us. "For watching over her. It … we're really grateful."

Matthias goes still, and I turn away from him, sensing the invisible string tying him to Helena's shop door. A hand grasps my forearm—his—stopping me from walking off. But when I look up, there's still only silence across his wide brow.

"What?" My voice is hard and sharp and snaps. He does not flinch, an unflappableness that reminds me of Moses, though it is without the sparkle in the eye or the flash of a grin. He is immovable, and without a tremor of feeling.

"If you haf a need," he says. The vowels broken and rusty. He releases my arm, and then returns to his post on the stool in front of Helena's without looking backward at me, and I'm left hanging in the middle of Sadie's yard as if I've been cut loose from a cord.

A need? Does he think I ever *need* for anything anyone can give? He does not know me.

No one knows anything about me.

Maybe … I don't even know me …

As I take Main Street back, my mind lost, I near run into Esther—my mother. *Widow Hawks.* I never know what to call her. As a daughter, of course, she is my *Iná.* But it has been years since I've given her the title, and it still scratches to call her Esther, the name my father gave her. I'd never asked him—or her—why that name. Or if she liked being called Esther Davies, which she was called long before the short time they were officially hitched.

She only looks at me, her arms folded over the thick handle of a woven basket, which sags in the middle, all soggy and caked with clumps of mud.

I stare back at her, wondering what she sees when she looks at me. The only thing I've got from Percy Davies is that my coloring is paler than hers. And maybe my mouth is thinner. But otherwise I look mostly like her, and her family. It was my little brother Murdoc who was a chip off Percy. Would he have been like him in character? We'll never know, and maybe I'm not too upset that I don't have sibling competition. What if he'd been easier than me, a better businessman? Or worse, more loving … a better child?

The silence eats at my throat, and buzzes my ears. I can't stand the way she gazes at me with such calmness. Like she *knows* me.

"What weeds are you pulling now?" I ask, putting all the derision I can into the words.

She lifts the basket up slightly, even though it's clearly heavy enough. "I'm harvesting herbs from the garden."

"The gard—" I realize she's coming from the southwest, back where her old burned house is all but ash and sand and black charcoal giving way to grass.

In the back, she kept her garden, half of them with plants she'd dug up from the cake-house before she left it for that old, unused long house. It's still there, filling up with the deep emerald plants and wide leaves and budding colors in those delicate shades of May and June—white and pink, mostly—showing me that even with her house and things gone, she's still unchangeable.

I haven't beat her.

I haven't made her go away.

She keeps coming up like the weeds I thought would have choked that garden out by now. Instead, it's like everything I've done has only made her put down tighter roots.

"Jane could use the slender milkvetch, too," she says, tracing a lavender flower. "For nursing, to help, as the infant grows."

I frown at it all, not caring the names or what any of it does. But my quiet must bother her now, because she jumps into it this time, and I feel a little triumphant when she does.

"I am glad to see you, Katherine," she says. "So you know from me, that I will be gone before your Grand Opening."

This surprises me so much, I leave my mouth hanging open and forget to swallow for a moment, long enough that I'm sure a fly will find its way in and lay eggs. Closing it up real quick, I shake my head, thinking I heard her wrong.

After all I've done to keep us separate, now she's just … going?

"Now?" I ask. I know I'm sounding as strangled as I feel.

"Soon. Before your great event," she says, still all calm-like and simple.

"You coming back?"

"I don't think so. It's time I stop trying to live on both sides of the path. There has been time spent here, and now I will go there. You do not need me."

"Doesn't Jane?" I wonder. My forehead hurts for all the pinching of the frown. I rub a hand on it so hard the calluses on the tips of my fingers are sure to leave lines.

"Yes. And I am glad to have spent time with her. Teach her the ways of the *wapiyekiya* medicine. Meet her first child. But one cannot always live life for another. My heart says I should return to my family. It is time." Her glance shifts, a flat quick movement that puts me on edge. "I think this would please you."

"I …"

The notion of Esther finally leaving for good, for keeping away and not reminding anyone of my bastard birth. Without her around, all the folks who still remember Percy, and how this town was before the rails even, well … they might forget that she was only a lover for decades. They might forget my illegitimacy.

But if she goes, she won't see what I've done. I'll be unveiling more than the General Store in all its official new glory. She might not see me become mayor. Or see me run multiple businesses—more than Percy ever did.

She won't be able to realize I've done more, and built something bigger than she or my father could have dreamed for me.

So maybe it's pride that makes my tongue loose. Or maybe because I want the one last piece of my family to be there when I come out of all these years with power and strength and a name that will last longer in Flats Junction than my parents'.

I guess it's probably pride.

"Oh, stay," I say, all careless and shrugging. "Don't go too quick."

Her eyebrows rise up slowly. "Stay."

"Yes. Why not? At least watch what legacy I'm building."

Those eyebrows stay up, and she only looks at me again. I feel hot under the neckline of my bright plaid dress from Helena, which I've taken to wearing often so I look city-fine and important enough that I really can be a lady mayor.

Without answering, Esther Flies-with-Hawks walks off toward the Kinney house, leaving me feeling stupid and empty, and not knowing if she'll be there or not.

I try to shrug it off. She's never been one for emotion, and I won't give her the satisfaction of me running after her, begging her to watch me become successful, to be proud. I don't need her approval. I'm not doing any of this building for her. I'm doing it for … me. And for Flats Junction. So, there.

My Grand Opening will be more than a party, though. It'll be the official voting day, too. Father Jonathon and Reverend Painter had folks agree in the two separate churches that doing both on the same day made sense, as most folks will be in town for the celebrations and the farmers don't want to have to come in twice if it can be helped. If I'm lucky, half the folks will be liquored up and will vote for me because they don't think too hard about a woman ruling them. Besides, who else will they vote for? No one else is working so hard to talk about the idea, and if anyone's putting themselves forward, they're not making much noise about it. Who else would do as good a job, besides me? And everyone knows it, deep down. I'm sure of it, by now. I've made it clear and clear again that they *need* me.

I just hope in the end it won't come down to something that looms over me all the time—the fact that I'm unmarried. Today only reminded me about that issue. Hannah is most certainly not the first, and likely won't be the last, to point out that it's not done to have an unwed woman running things. But then if I was married, wouldn't they say my place is in the kitchen, silent behind my husband? If I knew Marie well enough, I'd ask her how she managed it, the whole running a business alone and without a husband, and then landing one that let her keep on her trade instead of pushing her to the hearth. She makes it look as though that's the way it should be, all seamless and easy. It's not anything like easy.

Just as I near the General, another shadow falls over me. I look up, thinking it's Horeb, off for his midday meal, but his spot on the bench is empty, and the place looks abandoned. Is that how it looks, when I'm not inside it? All cold and barren? Or does the General always look like that?

"How have you been, Miss Davies?"

Only one person calls me that.

I smile a little at Doctor Smith, feeling pulled out of a taffy dream, stretched thin and pale on the edges with the unknowns and the stress of … of everything. I haven't even stopped into the Prime Inn yet, to see how Marie's lanterns fare, and whether we should match the curtains Helena's making to all the new linens and blankets in the guest rooms.

"I've been busy," I say to Doctor Smith, and move past him up the stairs to the General's porch. "How's your hospital planning coming?"

"Well enough," he says. He follows me up, his eye bright under the brim of the fine hat. He pauses on the top step, so I'm still above him, looking down at waiting on him to finish his point for needing to talk. "Do you recall you were wearing this gown the first time we met?"

The romance throws me off. "I … I suppose it would be."

"You looked like you'd stepped off a fashion plate," he says, smiling a bit more, as if he's very pleased with what he sees. It takes all my effort not to check my hair pins, and I hold my hands stiff at my sides.

"Well, that'd be Helena. She knows the patterns."

"You do not give yourself, and your beauty, enough credit," he says.

I hold my ground as he takes the last step, and don't let him see how fast and hard my heart is thumping, or why the ground seems to teeter and tilt under the soles of my shoes.

"And you understand the mechanics of business, of seeing the future's possibilities," he continues, then takes off his hat. He's got very dark hair, nearer to black, but there's that gray, too, right round the corners of his ears and along the cowlick just off to the side.

"You flattering me to make some request on your hospital?" I ask, a bit more testy than I am normally with him. "Just spit it out."

His eye crinkles, but his smile doesn't get any wider, like I'm amusing or playing coquette.

"I'm not requesting anything for the hospital," he says. "But for myself. Do me the honor of marriage, and together we can both have what we want."

The baldness of the proposal sends me reeling, even though I don't even blink as he waits for my answer.

How many proposals is that, just this spring? I've gone from none to three in a matter of weeks, and I can't say I'm wanting any of them. Not Moses or Yves or even Doctor Thomas Smith. There's nothing in my blood singing, no stirring to have them in my bed, and I think I'm right sick of using sex to get what I want, anyway.

But what did he say? *We can both have what we want.*

Does he know what I want?

Do I, really?

"I understand you're running for mayor," he says, pressing his case in my silence. "And I'm sure you've heard the … questions about a woman with your status doing so alone. Married, you'd have no barriers to your goals. And as mayor, you can quickly approve anything I might need for the hospital—what land to use, for instance. The electric can come to the hospital first, perhaps—or your Prime Inn, of course. Whatever is needed to put Flats Junction further on the map."

He's saying all the right things. As if he can read my soul and drink my deepest hopes. Am I so obvious? Or only to him? I don't know this man, this doctor from the east. He doesn't know me. Nobody knows me. Or understands me. Not really.

But will anyone just see me? Not the daughter of a banker or a bastard-born half-Lakota woman or a general store owner or a businesswoman … but me? All the pieces and layers and broken bits that I don't even know about myself? Does anyone have the chance to pick up those busted pieces and make themselves a whole person, or is that impossible?

And what's he offering me, really? Exactly what I've always told myself I want: a strong white man to legitimize me, to give me the extra backing I need, what I might require if I'm going to be successful forever. With such a man behind me, one with some power, no one can push me off. No one can stop me.

Doctor Smith isn't Bern—the cowboy turned lover who did my bidding for a tumble in my bed, but who would have never married me. He never said so to my face, but I knew. My heritage was beneath him, even as he spilled himself on my stomach. Doctor Smith isn't Patrick, either, promising love and then changing his mind. And he's not Moses, who might be helpful in the kitchen and come with his own scars, who only sees how similar we are and never that binding myself to him does not give me the strength I need from a husband.

Time feels like it's flowing out of me, but it's been only seconds since Doctor Smith put his proposal, and I find my tongue dry and my throat coarse and painful. I clear it, willing saliva to fill it all back up.

"There's not love or affection in your request," I tell him, when I find my voice.

"Of course not," he says. "It would be incorrect to say there is, when we know so little of one another personally. But that can come with time, don't you think?"

"Yes," I tell him.

He goes still, and it's only the white around the edges of his knuckles that give me an inkling that he's feeling nervous at all. "That love will come?"

"Yes is what I mean," I say, willing myself to look a little bit content and pleased, even though I feel heavier than I did a moment ago. "Yes. I'll marry you."

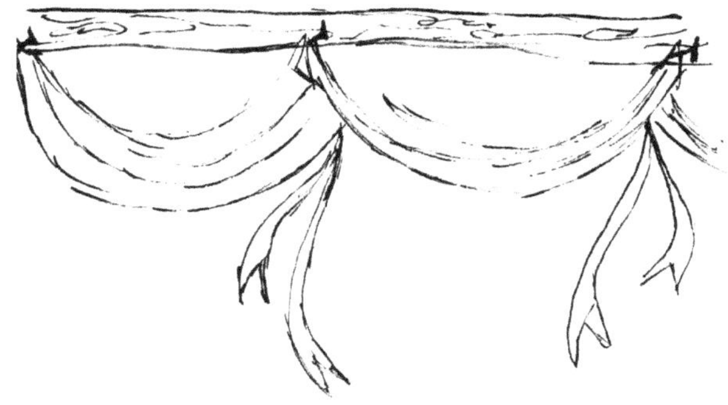

CHAPTER 17

Helena

June 30, 1884

Tying the yellow silk streamers is easy, but tacking up the bunting has required nails and a hammer borrowed from Father, and I leave the forge with Natan and Kaspar's teases ringing in my ears. In Mother's tinshop, little Garek's babbling is a full octave higher than that of the big boys, and the loss of my sister Urszula hits me so hard that I have to pause in the shade of the schoolhouse and frown away the sudden tears.

I blink very fast. Tears will unleash more than nostalgia, and I've done a fine job of pushing everything down so well that my family doesn't even think to ask me how I'm feeling anymore. Smiles and a chipper face can do wonders, both inside and out, and I'm determined not to let anything stop me or slow me down. Not even the shuddering nightmares that haunt my sleep, or the way shadows lurch to catch my skirts in the evenings, leaving me tense as I walk through town, even if I'm never alone to do it. That quiet posse man, Matthias Hummel, never leaves me to myself unless I'm obviously in the presence of someone else, like my parents or Kate. Sometimes I think that's part of it – I'm not truly ever able to be afraid, because I'm not given the space to do so. It's best this way, I think. Surely.

Even now, his wide, slightly stooped shoulders block part of the sun slanting from around the dry boards of the school. Inside, it's silent, as there are no lessons in the summer, but the bees that live in the roof thrum as if there's still recitations going on.

Ignoring Matthias, I straighten up and continue walking with my hammer and nails around to the General's front, where my yellow streamers flutter just so, with the light catching their edges and tips and making them look like they're coated in silver and diamonds. I gaze up at the porch roof, and for a moment I wonder what it had looked like when the old one was up in flames. It had to have been like watching a dragon devour the wood, and hot too, given how bad Kaspar's burn had been. He's lucky it healed, I know, but I've noticed he swings the hammers carefully now, and with detailed care. Sometimes he is in with Mother instead, and I wonder if he still has pain, even now. I suppose I could ask Hardy. He'd know.

Matthias disappears into the General, and I can't guess why, so I just stand and squint up at that porch roof and consider how ladylike it would or wouldn't be to climb on the railing and start tacking it up.

"Going to look nice, is it?" Horeb Harvey asks. He sits alone on the porch now, while Gil makes do between the Prime Inn and the Golden Nail. I wonder if they've had a big fight, or if Gil's just that sweet on Toot Warren that he'd leave his longtime friend to his lonesome.

"It should look very lovely," I say. "Silk and everything."

"Hope it don't burn down this time, don't we?" he says, lowering his voice before spitting into his tin. "Shame to see."

I don't know how to answer that, but I'm saved when Matthias comes out, looking as if nothing in the world will ruffle him, with a ladder tucked under an arm. It's the one Kate keeps in order to get to the top shelves where the finest fabrics are, and where she stores extra dry goods. He plants it in the dirt and holds it steady with one huge hand, and simply looks at me.

"Right," I say, hoping he's nothing like Natty or Evan or Arnold, who would look up my skirts as I climb. I would expect Patty and Victoria to do the same. But as I take each rung, he doesn't even bother to glance at me, let alone stare up my petticoats, and I will my fingers to stop trembling, otherwise I'll be sure to slam my finger with the hammer instead of the tacks.

It's slow going to wrap the bunting around the entire porch especially since it seems like everyone who is into the General for goods has to comment or stop to chat.

"Oh, how marvelous," Grete Fawcett says, poking her husband, Larry. "We have to come back into town for this!"

"We got cows ready to give birth any time, I should stay on the farm," he says. His accent is the same as his brothers, but he's a mix between Tom and David—a gentleman farmer, Mother would say.

"But it's to be a *grand* opening, a *grand* party," Grete says. "We'll bring the boys."

"All seven?"

Grete shades her eyes to look up at me. "It looks perfect, Helena!"

I nod back, my feet swaying and my mouth full of the small nails.

It's like that without pause for the better part of an hour. By the time I'm halfway, Kate exits the General to see my progress.

"Looking fine, Helena, very fine," Kate says. She smiles at me, a tight sort of smile that barely creases the corners of her eyes. She pushes pins up into her raven hair, and then does it thrice more, even though there's no more to be done. Her hands flutter and twitch, then go back up to her hair.

"I'll have extra." I pull the last tack from my lips and gesture at the cloud of silk and cotton on the bench opposite Horeb with the hammer. "Do you want it over the windows?"

Kate looks around, like she has forgotten she has windows, her eyes cloudy.

"Hm. Yes. Over the windows. That would be fine."

"Good." I wait for something else from her, watching as she shifts her feet, ignoring Horeb as the wheels churn in her head. She glances up again, and her gaze sweeps over Matthias, then me on the ladder. "Don't let your ma see you up there, she'll be none too pleased."

I shrug, sure by now Father has told Mother about me borrowing the hammer and tacks and for what. Kate doesn't seem like she could deal with many more distractions, and I don't blame her, what with the Grand Opening and the voting for mayor coming up soon enough. She looks thinner, the color bleeding out of her cheeks, and I would ask her if she was feeling poorly if I thought it my place to do so.

But we're not friends. Business partners, yes, and I still feel … I think she's something different from me still. Experience? Do I put her on a pedestal, even as we're working together to build things in Flats Junction?

So I don't ask her right away, and the moment is lost because Doctor Smith arrives and climbs the steps as if he owns the General himself.

"Good day, Horeb," he says, and is only rewarded with a curt nod and another zinging spit. Doctor Smith glances at Kate, but doesn't say anything more. He just comes to stand just behind her and watches me with a very placid sort of gaze, as if he's not truly interested in the grand opening or decorations. And I suppose he must not. What man likes to consider all the trimmings?

Kate doesn't look at Doctor Smith as she surveys the bunting and then gives a sort of nod and shrug, like she's reminding herself of all that must still be done.

"Let's hope the weather holds, then," she says at last.

"We'll hope," I echo.

Horeb and I watch her enter the General with Doctor Smith trailing her, and neither of us miss his hand hovering right at her low back, where her bodice meets the full gathers of the skirt. When the door closes, Horeb meets my eyes and shakes his head before spitting again.

After putting in the last tack in my hand, I descend for more while Matthias moves the ladder a few feet over. Horeb watches without moving his body, and it feels so odd to have him there alone that I can't stop blurting out my thoughts.

"What kind of fight did you and Gil have?" I ask him.

"That what you heared, that we had us a fight?"

I glance at Matthias, but he doesn't even look from the ground where he's digging the ladder feet in, as if he's not interested in town gossip one tiny bit.

"Just what I guessed," I say. "Why else would he stop playing checkers with you? You two are like … well, you're like an institution in Flats Junction."

A twinkle appears in Horeb's faded eyes. "That so?" He sighs and unfolds his gangly arms, slapping his long, gnarled fingers on the knobs of his knees. "Just so happens I'm the victim here, Miss Helena. Stuck in between as it were, a-twix Kitty and Gil. See, he been none too pleased about how Kate's muscled Joe about, but I see what she's doing and why, and I don't got no quarrel with her anyhow. So I'm supposed to choose between the two, but can I?" He leans back and crosses his arms again. "This way I'm not *in* the General, see, but I'm not abandoning her, neither, you hear?"

"What's wrong with how Kate's working with Joe? Gil sold the Prime to his son, and he can do as he pleases. Does he just not want a woman in charge, making it fancy?"

"'S not about bigger or better, sometimes it's the principle of it, and Kate went about too hard-handed," Horeb says. He doesn't bother to lower his nasal tone, and I wonder how much Kate can hear inside.

"She and Joe are business partners, making the place fine enough. They're hiring my mother, me, working with Sadie—Kate's making it better, a little woman's touch," I argue. "She didn't barge in hard-handed, I don't think." I don't know for certain, but surely Joe would be upset if he'd been treated unfairly.

But I suppose that's not common knowledge, a business contract. I don't even know, and I am the closest thing Kate has to something like a partner. Why is it the older folks are so close mouthed about money and finances and dance around each other so much instead of being a bit more forthright? It seems to cause all sorts of trouble.

"She compromised," I finish.

"Didn't offer enough of one, maybe," Horeb says, and lets his skinny shoulders rise and fall. "Or hasn't bothered to tell Gil about it." He clamps his lips together and looks away, the conversation clearly finished, leaving me feeling all prickly inside, as if needles are sliding around inside my blood— slick but not painful.

It must be time for dinner soon enough, but I want to finish this instead of leaving half the bunting to wind and twist. Matthias has not moved, waiting yet by the ladder, so I pop a few flat tack heads in the seam of my lips and head back up to continue.

Horeb's words eat at the back of my mind as I aim and hammer round the rest of the porch. If Kate hasn't been bothered to make things right with Gil of all people, does that mean her deal with Joe is less than ideal? Is she cheating or has she just not cared to fix an old friendship? Does that mean she doesn't care, or that the distraction of the General store's grand opening, the hospital talk, the electricity and the upcoming vote is too much for her?

What *would* a good leader—a proper mayor—really do to make Flats Junction better?

Do you trade friendships for alliances? Blackmail and force things through for the better good? How does anyone make such decisions, alone? I try to imagine Kate in charge, wearing a bright sash across her finest dress, directing folks right and left, and the image is not too far-fetched. She cares about the town, that's for certain, but I know, having worked with her, that she cares something fierce for her own self, too. I suppose that's true of most folks—I'm the same, in my way. Is being in charge of everything trading your life for service, even if the best decision for most will hurt you? Can anyone do that, or are people too selfish for it?

Will Kate make Flats Junction better? And, as Horeb said … is bigger always better?

What will I do, when my tiny seamstress shop goes from Sadie's summer kitchen house to a large building, full of bustling machines and shop girls and dress forms with unspooling bobbins underfoot and the hum of voices and customers without end? Will I make choices best for the shop, for staff or will I choose to rise myself up, even if it's on their sweat?

I suddenly feel very dizzy, and grasp the top rung of the ladder to steady myself. The ground below swings back and forward, and I suck in my breath and close my eyes for a long moment. There's only two tacks to go, and I try to put them in with care, but one goes in crooked and the other I miss and the hammer nicks the corner of my fingernail.

"*Cholera!* Damn it!" I hiss, sucking on the thumb. The climb down is slow and woozy, and my heel slips as I step off. A palm catches my elbow, the callouses making a rasping sound on my sleeve. Looking up at Matthias's stoic face, I wince and smile at the same time. "Thank you, Mr. Hummel."

He doesn't even grunt, just steps aside, picks up the ladder, and barges right into the General store with it without looking back at me, or even how nice the bunting looks now that we've spent the better part of a day hanging it together. With the last of the tacks, I put the remaining bunting over the big window, going on tiptoe to finish the job at last.

"Looks real good, Helena."

I turn around as Hardy and Doc Kinney pause their horses on Main Street to take note of the streamers. Hardy gazes at the bunting with a shine to his eyes, as if he's completed the work himself. Doc Kinney seems to take the whole thing in, from the new parts of the store to the decorations and the fine glass Kate has put in, replacing the front one that had shattered during the fire.

"I think it'll hold up nicely for the grand opening," I say to Hardy.

"And it'll have folks for miles talking about your fine skill." He grins at me, and there's something like delight or understanding or contentment filling him up, and there's something in my stomach that releases.

"Where you two off to?" I ask, twirling Father's hammer with a flick of my wrist.

"Brinkley farm," Doc Kinney supplies. "Seein' how the cows are doin'."

"Doc Kinney thinks it's something seasonal killing them, maybe," Hardy explains.

"Oh." I think about the Brinkley farm and Svendsen ranch, and how they're the biggest in the area, followed closely by the Zalenski family's holdings. If the cows keep dying, the jobs will disappear … so will the town, and any chance I have of building the dressmaking shop. A swelling of hope fills me up, and I look at Doc Kinney with respect filling my muscles. "I do hope you figure what ails the cattle, doc. I'm so glad you're trying to fix it!"

He smiles at the earnestness in my voice. "It would be a shame to see these farms fail," he agrees. "And all other businesses with it." Doc prods his horse with his heels and walks the animal off slow with a nod at Hardy.

Instead of following the doctor immediately, Hardy gives me another smile, as private a look can be with Horeb still on the porch listening and watching.

"How are you doing, Helena?" he asks. There's so much gentleness—*knowing*—in his voice, that it washes over me like a swell of water, or like a blast of winter wind full of ice. A sob, broken and stiff, climbs my throat, and I want to drag him off his horse and tell him all the half-sentences and uncertain feelings I've crowded out under a thick layer of determination and ambition.

"I'm … alright," I say instead, and manage to sound very normal.

The smile falters on his wide-open face, and it's clear I've not fooled him one bit. But Matthias exits, and Horeb stirs, and Hardy just nods and follows Doc Kinney.

I wish he'd turn around and come back and shake the words out of me, so that I could feel free of them. There's no diary for me to write how I've compacted my world so I don't lose everything I've built, and how I've written my narrative so I don't freeze up and let those scum ruin my life.

But I haven't cleaned myself from the inside, and it's starting to devour me in tiny bites.

Horeb makes a sound like a dying bull, spits, and stands, his eyes glued to Hardy and Doc Kinney's back. His face collapses into tight wrinkles.

"That there doc is lucky he ain't been runned out of town, ain't he?" Horeb mutters, but loud enough I hear him clearly.

"What?" I swing around. "What's happened?"

"Nothing lately," Horeb says. He crosses his arms around his rib cage tighter. "But now we got options, don't we?" His chin juts toward the General's door, where Doctor Smith is still in with Kate.

"Do you know if Doctor Smith is a better doctor?" I ask, feeling strangely protective. And then I consider if I'm feeling that way because of Hardy, or for the physician himself. "At least Doc Kinney has been here a while and knows how the west works." And my parents have finally given in and started using him, which to me says more than anything.

But Horeb just glowers. "Comes down to what we said afore, young Helena. Who's gonna do right by us, by the town? Doc Smith's been here for months and no one's had a limb sawed off or been sick under his watch that I've heared of. Back in my day, that was enough to run one doc out of town in favor of another."

My mouth falls open, but I slam it shut before I can argue. Especially because I don't know why exactly I'd be arguing. Would it be to save Hardy's reputation, or because I really think Doc Kinney's the right choice for Flats Junction? I don't know.

"Well, I think we shouldn't be hasty," I say to Horeb, and pick up the bag of tacks to return to my father along with the hammer.

The General store door opens as I comment, revealing Doctor Smith with Kate seeing him out formally.

They stand next to one another, almost awkwardly, and Kate's gaze slides to Horeb, then me, and then at last on Matthias. She shivers, even though the midday heat is full force, and gives Doctor Smith a smile that doesn't show her teeth. Everything about her screams tightness and something insincere, like she's a wound-up toy that explodes.

"I'll let you know what I hear, when I hear it," she says to Doctor Smith. "And we'll make further plans from there. After the election."

"Yes, of course, my dear. After that, we can finalize all our other plans." Doctor Smith swoops down and captures Kate's hand and brings the back of it to his lips, lingering overlong. So long I shift my feet, and the scuffle makes him stand back up, tip his hat, and walk down the stairs with a springy sort of step.

Kate meets my stare and lifts her chin, ignoring Matthias now completely.

"What?" she says testily. "That's proper courting, that is, especially after talk of marriage. You'll see, someday, Helena, when it's your turn."

"A wedding at long last, is it, Kitty?" Horeb says. Something like shock and wonder fly across his forehead, and then he stands, clamps a wrinkled hat on his head, and ambles to the stairs, too. "I think I'll pop on over to the Nail, see if Gil's there."

"Horeb Harvey." Kate's voice is slick and cold, and stiff enough that Horeb pauses with a leg partially raised. She glares at him. "Don't you dare be making wagers on my future."

"That what you think of me, is it?" Horeb asks, the feigned innocence completely plastered. "Would never."

"If folks start talking tall tales about it—me—I'll know it was you." She spares me and Matthias a quicksilver glance. "I know it won't be Helena. Or … Matthias." Kate raises her eyebrows at Horeb and taps her foot.

He sighs, suffering and long. "Fine. No wagers on your future." Horeb walks the rest of the way, then pauses along the side of the building and looks up, a devilish gleam in his eye. "But that don't mean I won't gamble on Doc Smith's future!" He disappears before Kate can say another word, and I hide the hysterical laugh rising up my throat as she swings back to me.

"And if I do get married to Doctor Smith, what of it?" she says. "About time I did tie the knot, and why not with a fine city man like him?"

"You do as you please," I tell her. "It's what I always marvel about, with you."

She seems mollified, and I leave her to sweep the General's porch while she keeps an eye on Clara Henderssen and a few of her children making their way with a wagon to the store, likely to trade.

As I walk back to the forge, the notion of Kate actually getting married and changing her entire situation starts to gnaw on me. Matthias, a step to my left, does not seem at all bothered by this news. But for me, it tangles inside like yet another knot in a long line of them. If Kate weds, and her husband takes over everything, does that mean Doctor Smith could shut me down if he thinks the investment too slow or frivolous? Does that mean he could take her money and pour it all on his hospital, and take it away from the Prime Inn, from my mother so the lanterns she builds will not be used?

Is becoming an adult like this, with all the questions pouring in at all times, as I try to muddle through each day and find my place? I don't know if I like this, and wonder if I have traded womanhood with my childhood too soon, becoming a businesswoman before I am ready to face all the challenges of it, in all the terrible shapes and dangers and trials it entails.

Or is this how it always is, all of life? Not knowing, merely guessing and hoping and planning for a future that is never fully controllable?

CHAPTER 18

Jane

July 3, 1884

Tonight is Kate's Grand Opening, and I can't help feeling frazzled. Maybe it's the worry of crimping the edges of the early squash pie just so, or how I will manage holding Andrew the entire time, and hoping Patrick will not treat this like a typical July fourth party and pour too much whiskey down his throat. Already my hip stiffens as I shift my infant son to the other side and pinch the last of the dough with my left hand, which is clumsily done, cracking the tender dough in such a way that I know it will be ruined as it bakes.

It's quite foolish of me to wish Patrick were here to help. Perhaps I truly have been spoiled to have a husband who helps in the kitchen whenever he is home. Hardy does too, as if the good doctor's influence permeates every piece of the boy's existence.

As I think of my husband and his apprentice, the front door shifts and the stamp of boots and low manly chatter fills the hallway. Patrick enters just as I slide the pie into the belly of the iron oven one handedly. He swoops in to grab Andrew with a flourish, juggling the baby with an ease I envy.

"You smell like you spent the night sleeping with hundreds of cows," I say, turning to face him. My nose tightens on its own. Hardy looks as if he slept *under* the cows.

"We're no closer to figurin' out the source of the sickness with the Brinkley cows," Patrick says. He speaks absently, with a thicker lilt than usual. He gazes at Andrew like the boy is brand new, or perhaps with the ongoing wonder that at last he's a father. "But we've figured on some of the symptoms and spent most of the night rearrangin' them into different pastures – the ones we think are sick or know are, and the ones lookin' right as rain."

"It's the law to do so now, Mrs. Kinney," Hardy says, sitting on the table and rubbing his forehead. The skin is pink where the brim of his hat doesn't completely cover him in sun. "Doc Kinney says the government says we have to keep things separate when we see sick cows."

I look to Patrick, who just nods, and sits himself down as well. "Brand new law, Jane. End of May. Doc Daniel Salmon is investigatin' the reasons for the fevers in the cows, and I can't help thinkin' he's onto some theories that we could use ourselves. For the black measles."

"Can we?" I ask, feeling the familiar swell of eagerness rise up at the promise of something new to research. "Could we write to him?"

"We don't have a lab, or even a microscope," Patrick says.

Neither of us says what the other must be thinking—that if Thomas Smith gets his hospital, he'd likely have the lab and microscope. And what would we give, or trade, or beg to have access to it? My whole chest lurches against the idea that Patrick would have to grovel to get what is needed to make headway in science and medical care.

But I think he would do it, if it came to it.

And I would not think lesser of him.

"Why don't you two draw baths," I say. "Hardy, you can use the tub out back."

With the heat of July beating down on us, the swollen air of the kitchen makes it hard to breathe, and I envy the men their cool well water and time to wash, but there's no time for that luxury this morning. Not if I'm to bring the pies to the Grand Opening tonight. And the voting, I remember. The whole of Flats Junction will vote on a mayor at last.

Patrick hands me Andrew and goes out to pull in buckets of water for himself and Hardy. The boy, with a glance at the unfinished second pie, follows to help without a word.

I go back to rolling pie dough one handed, and wishing I could somehow invent straps to put the baby on my back to leave both my hands free. I just cannot envision how that might work so the infant doesn't slip through and his head does not loll about and break.

A creak on the stairs along the kitchen wall announces Esther's appearance, but when I glance to look at her, I stop moving as ice sweeps across my shoulder blades and down my back. She is dressed in her leather moccasins, a long tunic belted with a colorfully worked pattern in beads and paint, and carries a large satchel in her hand.

"N … now?" I force myself to ask that, instead of saying "no!" but the feeling rises up, stale and unnerving.

"Today is a good day for walking," she says simply. "I feel it is time to go."

"What about Kate? Her Grand Opening?" It has nothing to do with Kate, I know, this feeling of fear and sorrow that washes through me in great waves. How is the baby so calm? I place him down on the mat in the far side of the room away from the stove, where he immediately rolls onto his stomach and looks about the world with wide and unhurried eyes.

I grab Esther's hands, willing her to hold tight to the planks of the kitchen floor, to stay static and unchanging. Her eyes drink in my face, and a smile pulls at the corner of her mouth.

"You will be fine, Jane," she says. "*Tókša akhé waŋčhíyaŋkiŋ kte*. Surely, I will see you again." Her fingers, enclosed in mine, are dry and firm and warm. They are longer and stronger than mine, and can do much more.

"I wish you would stay," I say, not caring that I sound desperate and small. "You have been here … I have known you since my first day in Flats Junction. I don't know … I want more time."

"We always want more than we have, if it is a good thing," she says. Her palms inch out of mine. "I have told you all I know of the plants of each season, which is my gift to you, for taking me under your roof and letting me live as if I am your mother. For giving me a little grandson." She crouches down with her usual ease, fluid and smooth and graceful, and cups her hand around Andrew's head. "*Taŋyáŋ yahí*," she says to him softly. "It is good you have come."

A clattering at the back kitchen door reveals Patrick, attempting to haul in our two big buckets for his bath upstairs. Sloshing in the backyard confirms that Hardy is already in the barrel out in the garden.

Esther stands at Patrick's entrance, her eyes soft around the corners, with a brightness I don't expect. It is the most emotion she has ever shown, even when facing terrible crimes against her. My husband, always observing, notices the bag and her clothing and drops the buckets. They slosh, overfull, and cover the threshold with clear water, as if it's the culmination of all our unshed tears combined.

"*Tákuwe hwo?*" he asks, using the bit of Lakota he knows. "Why? Why now?"

Esther shrugs once, with a single lift of one shoulder, and walks up to him. "You were the right choice," she says, looking at him full in the face. The words strike a chord of memory buried deep inside, words spoken at yet another farewell to another woman I do not expect to see again. Shaking my head, I watch her take Patrick's hands in hers and squeeze them.

"I'll always be beholden to you, to Percy, for takin' me in, givin' me a place to build a practice, have a home. For takin' in Janie, and for comin' back with us when we did not want to let you go … We won't follow you this time, even if we want to," he adds, glancing at me without humor. I feel as if my boots are glued to the ground, and I think if I get unstuck I will fly to Esther and fall on my knees and beg her not to go, as if I am some girl in a novel.

She picks up her leather satchel, filled with so few things. Even since her house fire, she has not accumulated much of anything. It looks meager and yet she is perfectly contented, as if no item in the world is worth harboring with jealousy.

As one, we follow her to the hallway, my shoulder touching Patrick's arm as we go. At the front door, she pauses to look at us. A line appears in the middle of her forehead.

"I do not know what ails your cows, Pat," she says, the comment completely surprising me. "Or how to fix the black measles. But sometimes it is not possible to fix everything, even if we know how to do it. And sometimes the answers come where we have never looked. You do not need to save the town to prove yourself a good doctor."

She glances at me one more time, and the smile she gives me is full of a little bit of everything. It is the silence of our first days together in her old house. The stench of rotting animal corpses on her front door and the crinkle of broken windows. It is her cool hand on my neck as I retch, and her sure hands on my thighs as I miscarry and bleed out. It is spools of thread and the flash of a needle, the unfurling clouds of smoke from her house fire and the thick nuttiness of her cornbread. In her smile is the secret to pressing oil from plants and the names of all the flowers in her garden.

I am crying. She lets the smile drift, and turns and walks away from us without looking back, without twitching her shoulders. Turning right onto East Avenue, she passes the Molhurst home without a glance, and does not stay on the road, but instead takes a lesser path up toward the old wagon stop on the ancient buffalo jump hill. In a few moments, she is lost to the shadows of the pines, which swallow her as if she is part of their darkness and her limbs are their branches.

My sniffle breaks the utter quiet of our porch.

"Where is my handkerchief?" I murmur, hunting blindly in my pockets and feeling every inch the sentimental fool. I knew she was going to leave.

It was not a surprise. And while it came so swiftly, I could not imagine how much differently she would take her leave.

"Here, my love," Patrick says. He hands me his massive kerchief, still folded with the iron as it is when I launder it. I wipe at my eyes and hand it back to him absently. There's an instinct to stay at the door, because to go back into the house without Esther is to make her absence permanent. It makes me feel itchy and irrational and full of an emptiness that screams.

"Jane," he says. His fingers touch my waist, and I move toward him instinctively. "She wanted to go. We have no hold over her."

"I know all this," I say. I sound testy and flatten my tongue against the sharp barbs I want to hurl at him—at anyone. "Just until it happened, I'd held onto hope that I'd somehow convince her ... that she'd change her mind, perhaps."

He gently closes the screen door so it doesn't bang, and then pulls me into a light embrace. His hair and clothes still reek of cow manure and barn, but he seems to know even more than me how much touch will soothe. I melt into him, letting my brow hit his chest, and will myself not to be angry. I knew she would go. She had said so. She'd promised to go.

"You'll be alright," he says, trailing a hand down the center of my back. "We will be. Esther will be happy with her family, and I expect they will be glad to have her back. Change is as change does."

"It doesn't mean I have to like it," I say, and pull away from him to look up into his eyes, which are brilliant and blue even in the darker hallway. The gentleness of the moment breaks when he cracks a yawn, which he quickly covers.

"Sorry, Janie," he says. "It was a long night."

"You should wash up, and then take a rest. Hardy, too," I say, forcing briskness into my tone. "The baby and I will keep an eye on the pies. And ... I suppose Hardy can sleep upstairs now, in the spare bedroom, now that ..." Now that Esther's gone for good. But I can't say those words. It will make me feel far too bereft, and today is to end in celebration, not sorrow.

Patrick does not protest, and I help him haul up two more buckets of water before leaving him to clean himself in the washroom. The sound of his knees hitting the sides of the tin tub echo down to the kitchen, and when Hardy comes in, I send him up to make himself comfortable in a bed at last—no more need for him to bunk on the kitchen floor. He's too tired to do much more than thank me and drag himself up.

Soon enough, there's no sound from upstairs, and Andrew dozes on his mat as I pull out the first pie, the second ready to go in as soon as I refill the stove belly.

The activity is barely enough to keep my mind from careening in twenty directions. I can't seem to settle on any one thing. The Grand Opening, the voting, Hardy's apprenticeship, our needs and our lack of funds, the cow disease, and Esther's departure all clatter around like a maelstrom in my head, each bumping into the other and yet none of them settling.

When the knock comes at the screen, I barely hear it, as my own thoughts shout. It is not a very insistent knock, either, but it comes again, and I wipe my hands on my apron as I go to answer.

It's Carl Henderssen, the younger son of widowed Kjersti—Nels's sister-in-law. He's closer to Hardy's age, but is undersized, his face thin between cheekbones and jaw. In his smudged hands, he spins his raw wool cap, and he looks into the house with anxious eyes.

"Doc Kinney?" he asks.

"I'm the nurse," I say. "What is it?"

"My big brother. El. Elbert, ma'am."

"Is he hurt?" I debate bringing in the boy, but Patrick has only been laying down a matter of minutes. If it isn't surgery … the notion of getting out of the quiet house fills me with purpose, quieting all those other swirling worries and thoughts and questions. It is a center I can focus on, something to give me something to *do*!

"No, just fierce poorly." Young Carl looks up at our new porch roof, then over at Emma Molhurst's house. She's not visible, but that doesn't mean she's not eavesdropping on the other side of her elderberry bushes.

It takes all of a half second for me to make a decision, and I tell him to wait while I gather up my medical supplies and Andrew and scratch out a quick note that I'm off to check on Kjersti's son. For a fraction of a moment, I consider grabbing up Patrick's medical bag, too, but decide against it. He might need it himself while I'm gone.

Cradling Andrew in one arm, with my hat slapped on, both notebooks of Esther's knowledge in my apron pocket, and my leather roll of herbs and oils under my armpit, I'm sweating in the July heat within a minute as we head south and west toward the far end of town. Kjersti's husband Terje died before I arrived in town, though I don't know from what. The off-color joke Horeb tells is that perhaps he was smothered by Kjersti's buxomness. As it was all before Patrick's time, and the old Doc Gunnarsen didn't keep patient files, there's no way to know unless one asks directly. And that would be improper even out in the west, I believe.

When we arrive, there's a horse tied up outside, and I recognize it as one Hardy rented out the other week from Rusty's livery.

The door slams open, just barely missing my nose, and Kjersti towers over me, blond hair falling behind her and her green eyes wide.

"What are you doing?" she says to Carl, ignoring me.

"I got the nurse," he tells her. "Two is better than one, yah, *mor*?"

She takes me in, with the sweat swelling under my arms, the sleeping infant, and my haphazard medical items and sniffs. "He tell you my big boy is suffering? After all I've been through, losing my Terry too soon, too young, raising these boys alone, the only two I have left, and now my Elbert is wasting away … it's more than any woman can bear, Mrs. Kinney."

"Might I see him?" I ask. "Perhaps I can help."

She steps aside. Carl darts in first, and I take a moment to adjust my sight against the glare of the late morning sunlight. As Kjersti shuts her screen door behind me, she sighs loudly—so loudly I'm sure it can be heard clear across the front yard—and says mournfully, "I don't know what else you can do, Mrs. Kinney. The doctor has been using all his newfangled tools and still can't figure what ails my Elbert."

Doctor? I spin and finally notice Thomas Smith in the gloom of the far corner, where he sits on the bed in the great room. The whole house is one huge square, with kitchen, dining room, and bed dancing together in the tight space.

Doctor Smith stands when my eyes land on him, as if he has been waiting to take control of my arrival, and steps forward, wiping his hands.

"It's only a fever," he says calmly. "A terrible one, to be sure and it can always take a turn for the worse if he is not tended properly by his mother, but nothing to worry on." He smiles at me and Kjersti together. "I shall leave the receipt for my fee here, or would you wish to pay it at once so you are not in debt?" His one eye fairly winks at me, as if we are in on the treatment plan, and I have agreed to it already. "I'm terribly sorry to pull you away from your day, madam. Is your husband unable to attend to the sick these days?"

I raise my chin. "Doctor Kinney has been out all night, actually, tending to the sick." I make a point of omitting *what* was sick. "Carl asked for help, so I came."

"He was right as rain until a few days ago," Kjersti explains to me. "Went out to see his friend, Michael Grady, now that he's well again and about. Helped the family for a day and a night clearing some more land for farming and came home. And then took to his bed. Such is my lot, that my own son spends time with his friend, instead of home, helping me!"

My mind pauses, then backtracks, reeling at the name and implication. We'd known Michael had pulled through, and Patrick made a point of checking on the Grady family. None of the others came down with the black measles. And it's been a month since Michael was ill! How could the disease sit so quietly, hurting none of the others, only to land on Elbert now?

I move to the bed, but Thomas Smith grabs my arm, hard and fast, so I cannot go the last three feet to Elbert.

"I've done what can be done, Mrs. Kinney," he says.

Yanking out of his grip without dropping Andrew or my kit is tricky, but I manage it without more than a glare at the doctor. At Elbert's side, I see all the same signs that had crept on Michael Grady, too—the same discoloring, the same black spots mottling the skin.

Strangely enough, this does not force a sinking ball of despair in my stomach. Instead, I feel inflated, full of relief. It may not work, but we have caught it early again, and now at least I have some plan, and I know how it should be. Everything I know to do falls into my head with a calm certainty, brushing away the fragments of sorrow from Esther's departure. I am both inside my body and out of it.

"You could perhaps put on a pot of water to boil," I say to Kjersti. "And we'll make some soup."

"Tea and soup?" scoffs Doctor Smith. "I assure you, Mrs. Henderssen, the blood-letting I just gave your son should suffice. If he gets too uncomfortable, call me again, and I will do it once more to let the humors release."

"And I assure you, doctor, that the remedies I bring have been proven to work on cases like this, so long as we start now and do not let up," I say crisply. Quickly settling Andrew on his blanket on another bed, I turn to unwrap my medical kit on the table. Against the brass latches of Doctor Smith's city fine case, my own leather and vials look scratched and smudged.

His lips curl into some sort of smile and sneer mixed together. "Snake oil, at its finest. I have seen charlatans and quacks do this in my travels. I would have thought it beneath you, a woman and a physician's wife at that."

If I could find the words to fling at him, stop him from speaking, I would, but I find them stopped under my tongue. Kjersti doesn't tell me to quit, so I just take out the herbs and check the labels, hoping by ignoring the man, he will leave in a huff.

"If you must do something more, a good dose of castor oil will help expel the fever," he says. He does not move from his position between the table and the bed, and I suddenly worry he will physically block me from the patient.

"Tea," I say again, trying for prim. "If you please, Kjersti."

She moves, but slowly, as if the drama between Thomas Smith and me is something out of a high adventure novel. Doctor Smith, seeing she is moving at my direction, grabs a bottle out of his medical bag and shakes it hard.

"Castor oil it is, then," he threatens.

"It won't work," I say. Clearing my throat takes another moment, and it feels as if I have swallowed thistles. "You haven't spent any seasons here to know this disease. With all … *respect* … you don't know how it manifests and how it is treated. I do. Now, stop with these ridiculous ideas and let me get on with it."

He stares at me, his one eye glittering in the low light of the room. Without a warning, without a single flicker in his face, he swings the bottle of castor oil at me. The sound of the glass hitting my cheek makes a dull *thunk*, and a lightning rod of pain jolts under my cheek and something hot pours out of my left nostril.

"Shut up, woman," he says, so very mildly. "You have no place here and don't know a thing about medicine."

The salty tang of blood on my lips makes me blink, and I bring up my hand to check if there's worse damage to my jaw and teeth. Unable to tell for sure, I find myself mute at last, afraid to open my mouth lest blood pour in or pour out.

When I find Kjersti's eyes, they are wide and the color of emeralds, but she has stopped putting water in the kettle. In the corner, Carl gives a soft sound, like a whimper, but choked. Even Elbert has paused his tossing to stare at me.

Forcing sound from my mouth is like talking through wax. "What harm is there in letting me try what I know has worked in the past?"

Doctor Smith's countenance changes slightly at that, flattening and hardening while looking almost gleeful.

"Do you have a medical license?" he asks softly. "Do you need me to expose you and yours as a fraud?"

"I—we are no such thing. Patrick went to college. And we have proof this works. Speak to Orla Grady yourself," I say, looking now only at Kjersti, ignoring the growing sting along the left side of my face, where it tingles and pulses and swells. "She will tell you that the teas and herbs did—"

"Enough!" The bottle rises again, and I cringe in spite of myself. Doctor Smith leaves it up, but acts as if it is there on its own accord. He only shakes his head. "I was called to doctor a patient. You're getting in the way."

I feel foolish and frightened and angry. Saliva builds in the valleys of my gums, but I only re-roll my medicine, and pick up my child. Without Kjersti to eject Doctor Smith—and now likely too scared to do so—there is nothing for me but to go or risk further harm to me. Or worse, to Andrew. If Thomas Smith will strike me in front of witnesses, thinking he is above reprimanding … what else might he do?

Still dazed, I step back out into the street, too shocked to cry or speak.

It feels odd that the world has continued these past minutes, as if nothing is different. Is this how Helena feels? Surprised the sun still shines and folks laugh and joke, and the bunting she made swings merrily in the bit of breeze picking up on the prairie?

How does she bear it?

How will I?

Hoping the hat hides the damage of my face, I hurry home taking Second Street to the north, in hopes most folks are already starting to mill in front of the General and post office, setting up tables and helping prepare for Kate's big night. Perhaps I can use enough pressed powder to hide my injury. Perhaps it's not too bad. Perhaps it will be dark enough, and no one—

"What the hell happened to you?"

I stop to see Marie Salomon standing in the center of the road outside her tinshop, holding a large basket of fresh bread, her elbow interlocked with Berit Salomon, who in turn has a grip on the toddling little Garek. Berit stares ahead at the festivities, toes tapping, but Marie has latched onto my face and the way she stares at me confirms my fears. I must surely look terrible.

I don't answer, but I don't brush past her. How can I speak of this? And it is so trivial, compared to the horrors Helena went through. I will never forget the way the bruises bloomed across her ribs and the cave of her young belly.

"Does it look as bad as it feels?" I manage. My voice sounds fluffy.

"Do—it's your nose and your mouth. Did you get kicked by a horse? Lose any teeth?" She comes closer, dragging Berit with her.

As they near, Berit notices at last, too, and her pale eyes clear with distress. "Oh no! Jane Weber! You're injured, *honning!*"

Neither Marie nor I correct Berit's lapse with my old name, as Marie squints at me and gently cups my chin.

"You're going to be black and blue for a good while," she says quietly, and her dark eyes stare into mine. "Tell me it wasn't the doc."

"It was," I say, the words a gasp. "It was, and he's—"

"Oh *gówno*," Thaddeus swears, seeing the whole thing as he steps out of the forge with his two sons in tow. "Who did this?" He looks murderous, and for a moment I can see the merit in having such an overwhelming man about. Marie never must worry about being harmed with him as her husband.

Now that protective glare roves over me, as if he is trying to see where else the blows might have landed.

"She says the doc," Marie says, her voice tinged with anguish. "I wouldn't have—"

"Doctor Smith," I grind out, holding my mouth tight so the fresh wound doesn't bite further up my cheek. "Not my husband. Never Patrick. Never."

Marie's body sags slightly, color running across her face and then retreating. "Of course, I didn't … that is …" She draws herself up and relinquishes Berit to her son Natan. "You say the new doc did this?"

"Why?" Thaddeus's question sounds like thunder, quiet and rolling and dangerous.

"I tried to help a patient—Kjersti Henderssen's boy is sick with the black measles—and he didn't … like being questioned," I say.

Marie and Thaddeus exchange glances, then Marie nods at her sons to go on toward the General and the growing mix of activity near the center of town. Kaspar glances back once and gives me a worried nod of greeting, and even in the middle of my shock and my terror, I attempt a small smile in return.

"I don't like this," Marie says. "It's not done, not even out here."

"He thinks he can do as he pleases, with talk of this fancy hospital and other rumors," Thaddeus says. He looks at Andrew for a moment, the hard lines around his nose lightening briefly, as if he remembers when the infant was born in his home with something like affection.

"What other rumors?" Marie asks sharply.

Thaddeus looks uncomfortable for a minute, and I wonder if some of the awful things about Kate are finally out in the open—notions I've speculated on but have decided to let go, as what good comes of dragging up sorrows of the past if all others have left them behind? Would people connect her to the lack of iodine and the surgical deaths that followed? The fire at her mother's house and her own General? The hanging of Bern Masson?

"Well, it seems Kate and Doc Smith are thinking of tying the knot," he says. "Anyway, it's what I overheard Helena and Hardy discussing the other week."

"I heard it was Yves who proposed to her," Marie counters. "Anette said so."

I switch Andrew to the other arm and jostle the medical items as I do. The glass vials clatter lightly inside the rolled leather. "Either way, I should be home. What is there to do now?"

"Tell people what happened," Marie insists.

"It'll be Jane's word against Doc Smith," Thaddeus says quietly. "Folks won't think it's true, some will say Jane is saying so because Doc Smith is bringing competition to her husband."

I stare at Thaddeus as if he's gone mad, but he raises a palm. The fingers on it shiver lightly, and I wonder if he wishes he could punch Thomas for me.

"You know I'm only saying what others will consider, not what I believe myself," he says solemnly. "What you do need is Kjersti and her boys to speak up."

"Do you think it'll come to that?" Marie says, her gaze still roving my face, as if she could clean up the wounds just by willing away the blood. "That we'll need witnesses and a judge?"

"Otherwise they'll think Patrick did it," I say, realizing at last what Thaddeus is getting to. His cool grey eyes meet mine squarely, honestly, and I shiver. "And they'll stop using him ... they'll all go to Doc Smith, even though he's ..." I think of that poor Henderssen boy suffering from the black measles, likely wasting away even now, precious time slipping by without the right herbs, without the echinacea.

I could march back to Kjersti's house and force my way in and beg her to try the herbal remedies, braving whatever violence Thomas Smith swings my way. I could go home and ask Patrick to come with me, but the two men will likely only brawl again. Maybe I could beg Thaddeus to come and force the issue, but that is dragging in a man to a fight that is not really his. And I do not want anyone to think I cannot lean on my own husband anyway.

Marie and Thaddeus watch me churn through my thoughts, and I inhale sharply, realizing I've been standing in the center of the street in a daze.

"I'll go clean up," I say, at last remembering the unbaked pie. Well, Kate will only get one from me, then. So be it. "Maybe it is really not as bad as it looks."

Marie gives me the kind of look that makes me realize the hope is rather fruitless, but she and Thaddeus let me go on my way without stopping me further. I can feel their gazes, and their speculation, on my shoulder blades as I walk east.

When I walk in the house, Patrick is awake, pulling the second pie, perfectly browned, from the oven. The house smells like brown sugar and buttery squash and sweet raisins. And when he turns to look at me, his body looks as if it has been yanked by a string, he draws up so tight and so stiffly.

"Jesus, Mary and Joseph," he breathes. He is before me in two wide paces, my face in both of his palms. "What happened, wife?"

"I failed a patient," I say first, and the tears come at last, hot and acid on my bruised cheeks. "Thomas was there first, and he … there's nothing to be done, Patrick. Nothing. The boy will die."

"Where is he?" Patrick growls, and he doesn't mean the patient. He lets go to take Andrew for his blanket and to go to the small pitcher of well water I keep boiled and sterile on the sideboard. "After I clean you up, I'll go take his other eye."

"I … I almost wonder if that's his plan," I say, sinking to the bench. How has this day held so much, and yet it is not even evening yet? "To get people to think we are incompetent. That you beat me. That you are a violent, unpredictable Irishman. That they should all trust him. He's not won the people here one way. He'll do this next. He wants to ruin us. You."

Patrick's wide fingers are as gentle and sure as I remember as he strokes the drying blood from the corner of my lips. His face blazes with ambition, with certainty.

"He won't. He can't. You forget, even with Esther gone, we are not alone here. I have given many good years to many families, and you have lately, too. That will matter."

"I hope you're right," I whisper.

And then I am silent as he fixes my face and presses cold cloths to my swollen cheek. He thinks we have sway, that we can change the course Thomas has begun to write for the narrative of this town. Perhaps. But in this moment, as pain throbs along my jaw and into my forehead, I do not know who in Flats Junction has the power to rid ourselves of the latest and worse disease of them all.

CHAPTER 19

Kate

July 3, 1884

The Grand Opening is in full swing by late afternoon, and without any official beginning. It's only when I realize most everyone is mingling and someone's playing a banjo that it's started. There's no time for a speech. I'm not sure if I'm right glad about that or not. Relief and nerves struggle inside my stomach, tangling up with one another so I feel I might lose my breakfast all over the fine new gown Helena made.

Sometimes it seems we all pull on toward these festivities, but beyond this, there's no true way to mingle together, not with the different churches and the scattering of all newer sorts of folks who have trickled into town over the years. Events like this bond us, I think. They're a place for courting and for sharing and making memories. And don't memories bind a community? I'd think it so. The bright streamers on the General add something like frosting to the whole thing.

It's not a July Fourth event, but a body would think it were, considering the vittles spread out on makeshift trestles, the barrels of sweet water, and the preparation for a dance floor in the center of town. Folks who rarely come in more than once a month are there, from Simon and Veronika Zalenski and all their family to all the Wu brothers who start looking for easy work. The Yang brothers and their wives have their big soup pot set up nearby instead of at Soup's Corner, and are selling cheap, while old Shen gives rides to the little ones on his pig. Alan and Harriet have one of their own pigs on a spit, while Tina Brinkley and Lara O'Donnell oversee an alarming array of baked goods.

"We'll just see which one of ours has the least left at the end of the day, and it'll settle things between us once and for all," Lara says to Tina.

"Sure thing," Tina says, all amiable like. She winks at me as I pass. I have to turn my head so Lara won't see my smirk.

Isaac and Hannah Horowitz have half-price shoes out on a table, most of them boots for the coming fall season, which is hard to think on in the heat of July. Toot and Gil walk arm in arm around the tables, with her pointing out what she baked. Gil catches my eye, and gives a slow nod, catching me mid-step. I'm supposing Joe might have told him how our arrangement changed, but I don't like how he won't come back and play checkers like he did. Horeb is getting grouchy, and besides, it would let folks know all is well.

"He's spending time at the Nail now."

Elaine Warren stands just behind me, her massive bosom keeping her from getting too close without getting too intimate.

"What for? He think he'll win her?" I jerk my chin up at the couple.

"Oh, he's already won her," she says. "But Willy's mother won't let on."

"She should. She's not getting younger."

Elaine shrugs, then twists to face me directly. "So you want to be mayor, they say. Think you can manage that and run the General, on top of you taking over half the Prime Inn?"

"Joe's still in charge of it," I say quickly. "Just investing to make the town better, myself. Not unlike you buying Helena's sewing machine."

Her face loses its fine creases as a smile flickers. "Fair point, Kate." Then she gets a little less pleased. "I suppose it was too much to ask that they'd not show."

Yves and his entire posse cross the street and stare at the tables of food ready for the eating. From the distance, even Evan's vacant stare has a spark to it at the view, and I cringe at the thought of all of them diving into the well-made, prettily frosted goodies. Making my way to Yves, who stands between Matthias and Arnold looking too mighty and pleased with himself, I get right before him and cross my arms tight.

"You tell your boys to behave nice. This is for everyone," I say. "I mean it. Don't go ruining things from the start."

Yves wipes his hand across his bald head and blinks those pink rimmed eyes at me like he's trying to sweeten me up. "This eez your party, Kate. Matthias will keep zee boys well, but I cannot speak for zee girls."

I spin to see Victoria and Patty all giggly over a platter of very small cakes, as Lara tries to point them in the direction of her own vittles. Shrugging, I turn back to Yves and fix him a direct glare.

"I mean it, Yves."

The little man only tips his head and strolls off, trying for the gentlemanly gait that only looks loose on him, and Arnold grins that blue-white smile to follow. Matthias stations himself on the end of the table with his arms crossed, and even though Natty and Evan look like they'd launch themselves clear across and flop on every pie they could, they slide a glance at the German and don't budge.

If Matthias is here, though, then Helena must be safe with her folks. I glance around for Marie and Thaddeus and find them setting out an excessive amount of bread—the only thing Marie can do without ruining. Helena's not with them, but she's talking to Hardy off a ways instead. She catches my eye and waves slightly, but doesn't move from Hardy's chatter. What can those two have to talk about, anyway?

There's more distraction when Lieutenant Colonel Peter Swaine and his wife Dorothy arrive along with several of the Army men and their daughter. A thick flicker of triumph licks my bones and I shove it down, reminding myself there's no sense in calling it that until the votes are counted and all is done and dusted tonight.

The Fort commander waits for me to approach, and I do right off.

"You came, and I'm right pleased," I say by way of greeting, and bend one knee just a bit at the wife. "Ma'am."

The missus gives me an unreadable look, and holds her daughter tight to her side by a hooked elbow. The girl, who must be close to Helena's age, gives a little tug on her mother.

"Oh, is that lemonade?" she asks, almost breathless. "And—new boots? Half price? Oh, *Mother*! It's like a circus!"

"The lemonade is sweetened, a little treat out of my General for all to try, no charge," I say. "And Helena—you know her—she might be happy to show you some of her ribbons in from out east."

"A grand party you give," Dorothy Swaine says, and lets her daughter lead her off.

And it is a grand thing, to be sure, this festival. It's mine and for me, but … it is for everyone, too. It is. I can see it and feel it, and I'm glad of it.

"I'm mostly here to speak to you personally," Swaine says, even as his eyes rest on the beer barrel Dell has rolled out of the Powdered Keg. "About that electricity you promised."

"These things take time," I say evenly.

"Not that," he says, pouring his attention back on me. "I mean the Natives."

That happy heat in my belly goes out like someone tossed cold ash and soaked sand on a new fire. "What of them? They're at their reservations."

He gives me the kind of stare that makes me want to wiggle away, like he's judging whether I'm playing stupid on purpose or don't know that some leave their reservations and go hunting and shooting and killing on their whim and desire.

"I need assurances that the electric lines from here to the Fort will be secure, if I'm investing gov'ment monies on it. Can't have no fancy man in Washington say it were a bad investment on my part, relieving me of my post, see." His eyes narrow and sidle to his wife and daughter. "They'll send me further west at the best of it, and Dorothy and my Mable … well, that's no place for 'em."

"And what do you propose I do?"

"Was your idea, weren't it, woman?" he asks, tetchy now, and looking a bit more churlish than I'd like. I try not to look to see who's watching us.

I think about my mother, about her ability to speak to her family. Maybe … well, it'll be something I'll have to swallow and ask, and if I know my mother, she'll help. If not for me, then for Flats Junction, and for what she built here with my father.

"I've some plans and connections on that front, don't worry," I say, putting all my confidence in the words. Where *are* Pat and Jane and my mother anyway? They're late.

They aren't even around as the light goes from butter to rose and then at last to lavender. The vittles get snapped up quick as can be. Soon it's just quiet enough that I'm feeling compelled to make the speech I'd planned to do to start the whole thing off earlier.

At the top of my porch steps, I raise my hands half to my chest, but no one pays me any mind. Toot, Gil and Horeb are all squeezed tight like fish on the bench outside my door, and Toot leans forward.

"Want a whistle?"

"How so?" I ask.

She pokes Gil in his ribs, and the two of them stick their fingers between their lips and blow in unison, resulting in a double loud pierce of high-pitched nonsense that sets half the dogs to howling in town and a few people drop their food. Cusses follow in the dying noise, before everyone takes note of me in my fine new dress and the pretty bunting fluttering all around me like I'm going to be in a photograph for all time.

"I'm just up here to thank you all for coming in to enjoy the vittles—and for supplying them, too—and to say the General is open in full at last, from top to bottom with more goods than before, and plans for even more city items than ever. And—just so I can clear up some things too. You may have all heard that Joe Greenman and I have gone into business together, and that's so. He's still the main owner, I'm just a small investor so he can shine the place up for more folks to visit and bulk up all our business. I mean to make Flats Junction a place that stays on the map forever, see, and the only way to do it is to make us bigger and better than the other places on the rail line."

I sneak a little glance at Gil to see if he's taken note on my place with his son, and if he has figured it out, he sure hasn't blinked or shifted. When I turn back to the crowd, I find Joe standing with Rusty and Mikey. He raises his beer to me in salute.

"I'm also happy to announce that it's not just rumors. We *are* indeed getting that hospital—and with it, electricity."

The rise of noise swells with a mix of cheers and wonderment, questions scattering between the joyful chatter and whoops. A few faces jump out at me—the bright freshness of Helena's, the shrewd dollar calculations in Fortuna's eyes, the gleam of interest in Tim and Julie Bailey's and the mild surprise in Bianca Brewer's. Children jump without knowing why the adults are bending and swaying with the news. I finally spy Patrick, who is bent slightly to hear Thaddeus over the roar of delight. Jane and my mother are nowhere to be seen, until I spy Jane's gleaming chestnut hair nearby, speaking to Marie, her face in the dusky shadows.

My view is blocked by black, but it's only Thomas's tall hat, coming toward me from the mix of faded calico and plaids in the slow evening falling over us. He's wearing a suit—the only man here to do so—and I find myself satisfied with his appearance more than I expect. So much so that I give him a nice big smile when he climbs the stairs. It makes him pause, and his one eye goes a bit wide.

The hubbub doesn't go down at first with Thomas Smith at my side. There's whispers and comments passed between folks, rippling from one ear to the next. I can't imagine what it might be, other than speculation on how they each might get a taste of that electricity. But the quiet trickles through bit by bit. At the end of it, there's only the argument between Tina and Lara left, loud enough that everyone can hear the entire bit.

"Of course you won!" Lara's soprano, familiar to everyone who goes to St. Aloysius, rings out. "You got your whole family to shovel in your vittles!"

"It's not a secret I'm the best baker," Tina says, but a laugh hides in her voice.

"In your family, not in the whole of Flats …" Lara suddenly notices the silence, and looks about desperately. She latches on Father Jonathon, who immediately hunches his shoulders. "Father. It's a sin, to be prideful of a talent, isn't it?"

"It is, if one uses it unwisely or unkindly," he attempts.

It's too weak a case for Lara given the color rising on her neck, but Tina quickly pats the taller woman on the shoulder. "Never mind that, Kate's got more words."

Lara shakes off Tina's hand, and it's obvious to everyone in town that the feud is far from over. I suppose it'll mean even fancier things at the fall harvest gathering, and I notice Dell smacking his lips, likely in the same anticipation. Fortuna notices and he quickly lowers his chin.

"Right," I say, feeling the weight of a thousand eyes on my chest. I want to fidget and adjust my bodice, but Horeb would leer too much and besides, I know Helena's sewn it so it won't move an inch. "Ah. One more announcement for now, before we get to the seriousness of voting on mayor and all. I should like you to know I'll be marrying Doctor Smith."

This is not met with the cheer I expect, and I keep the slight smile on my face out of shop habit only. It's flat cheeks and furrow between brows more than anything.

"Just so you know," I try, pushing harder now. "In case you're worrying on a single woman trying to manage it all alone."

The looks go darker and harder and narrow. It crushes the bit of desire I felt growing for Thomas as he walked up to me in his tailored suit, and I tell my feet to stay put instead of stepping away from him. It's just new, is all. They're surprised, those who didn't get an inkling from any of Horeb's gambling.

"He's an outsider, Kitty," Joe Greenman calls up. "It's awful quick like."

"You holding out for her, Joe?" Nancy yodels.

He turns bright red and buries himself in his beer. Others shift on their feet, and I think maybe I spoke too brash. But … wasn't that the worry? That I was unwed and running for mayor?

A stir in the back, near the crumbs of the food tables, causes a few folks to move away, until Yves, flanked by his posse, stands in a small circle. He's too far for me to see his face well, but I think he's trying very hard to look calm.

"What about me, Kate?" he asks. "What about our … understanding?"

"Our business and partnership in that regard remains, though I still recommend you consider other options, as I mentioned to you this spring. If only for your men," I say. I sound like I can sometimes, all confident, even as my heart feels like it might shoot out of my mouth.

"Yah, Yves. My reputation …" Natty complains. "It's going soft."

"We don't want to be no shopkeeper's servant all our days," Patty adds.

The disagreement among them all disappears amidst the rise in discussion among everyone, which goes in too many directions to count. I try to shout across the heads, but there's no use.

"Excuse me," I say to Thomas. My body feels all itchy near him, but that's just the leftover prickles from my announcements. "I've to settle something."

He just nods, and stares out like a lord over everyone, watching with his hands behind his back, that one eye watching and noting. He's a scientist, so I suppose some are already his patients.

I fight to Yves, nodding at those saying congratulations and ignoring those who look at me like I've lost all sense. When I arrive, he's standing with his arms crossed and grinning. He catches me behind Matthias's bulk and smiles wider, showing his watery gums.

"I have missed zee lively chats we have," he says to me.

"That's 'cause we're stuck playing shop girl!" Victoria says. Patty puts her arm around Victoria's curvy waist and nods tartly.

"Ah's just sayin' it's a safe bet on the money," Arnold drawls.

"I do have a solution," I say quickly, ducking between him and Matthias. "If you would consider it as an option."

They all pause, but barely. There are words flickering in the spit on Natty's lips, and they're not likely kind ones.

"You could be busy protecting big things. The Fort, for instance."

"They got their own Army for that job," Patty snorts.

"No, no, something else. They want help protecting the electric lines from the … the tribes." Never mind that I'm sure my mother will keep her people away. It'll at least get most of the posse away from Flats Junction.

"That ezz not the whole of it, Kitty," Yves says. "I had offered you zee marriage, too."

"You … you won't want a wife," I say quickly. The phrases stumble all over themselves trying to get out. "You won't want one waiting on you at home, pestering on where you've been and what you're doing."

Yves's eyebrows rise very slowly. "I won't? I think I have been seen, as you say, zee trick. Trapped, eh?"

"No, no, the opposite," I say. "I'm giving you choices, see, instead of being locked with me."

His nose flares. "But zen if I am going to be out doing zee roaming to ehh … 'protect' the Fort and zee electric … one never knows what might happen out there. Zee lines might … fail?"

I close my eyes for a fraction of a minute and try not to scream, or come up with some sort of story that will make everyone turn on Yves at once. It won't work, I know. It won't work a second time. There's not enough steam behind it, and folks have gotten used to him and his posse around town. It doesn't help that they all look kindly on Matthias for acting as a guard on their Helena.

It's just … impossible. There's no way around it.

I want to control it all, but I just …

What else can I give? What else can I trade? What dreams, what expectations, what hopes and plans? I've put them all out and put my money out there, too. It's been my bed, my body … I can see what I'd build, and how it would all come together, but it depends too much on what I can't see or fix. Even with my future marriage, now I've lost Yves, even as I give his posse what they've been begging for. I thought, I'd calculated and hoped and gambled …

Does it always come to this?

Giving up one thing in exchange for something else?

Is having it all together an impossible ask?

Is it only women who must balance that line, or men as well?

Yves's threat hangs in the night sky above me, now puckering with bits of flame from countless lanterns and the song of a fiddle. For a short moment, I miss Moses's jaw harp. But the notion flies off quickly when I watch Yves whisper to Arnold, who in turn mutters in Natty's ear. The sound of talk, of speculation and music and gossip makes my ears go ringing, like the dirt under my boots has turned to clay and muck and will yank me down into darkness.

I can't breathe.

But I should be very pleased. I've got near enough what I want. Now I just need to find my mother and convince her to instead of keeping her people away, to have them watch those lines between us and Fort Randall for Yves and his mischief.

If only I could keep him occupied …

Matthias blocks my way out of the posse's loose circle, and when I try to move past, he's at first like stone. His eyes glitter down at me before he takes a small step to the side, and I shiver with something that feels like silver and gold down my spine.

I hunt for my mother, my nerves feeling hot on the ends, as if my fingertips might explode. There's too many moving pieces. Every time I try, everything I do …

My heel grinds into someone's toe, and I whirl with an apology on my tongue. It dies when I come face to face with Jane. It's not so much that it's her, and all the anger and ugly things between us cloud the space, but it's her cheek and mouth and the swell on the side of her nose. It's too puffy, though I can tell she's trying to hide it with a new swoop of her hair and the way she keeps her face tilted way from the lanterns.

It's so fresh that there's still a bit of bright red blood in the corner of her lip, and it colors one of her teeth when she tries to smile at me, as if there's nothing wrong.

"I … where's Widow Hawks?" I ask. "I told her she should come."

Jane's face goes from pale to grey in an instant, the lantern light making her look like near melted wax. "Wi … Esther is gone."

"What? Gone?" What is this feeling pounding into my skull? An ache? Is there medicine for the way my heart jumps from throat to hip, the way my lungs cannot rise and fall? "Where? When will she be back?"

The strange look running across Jane's injured face is distracting, near enough that I almost want to ask her what happened. Did she run into a door? There's something hard but pitying in her eyes, like she's sorrowful. She switches her babe to her other shoulder to keep on patting his back, which only gives me a better view of her battered face.

"She won't. She's gone back to her people."

My mouth falls open and I have to push my teeth together so hard they jar my cheeks. "What … *now*?" After I'd been kind, offering her to come to my party? After I'd been … like a daughter? I try not to growl at Jane, holding onto the last of my official front. "What did you say to her, to run her off?"

Her hands pause in their tapping. "Me? Nothing. She wanted to go. She told me months before that she would."

"But … but she—"

"Everybody shut it! *Zamknąć się!*" Thaddeus's voice is a boom and a shout and a terrible thunder. It's a yell everyone recognizes, maybe even more than my own, and the whole group stops their dancing and chatting and drinking to turn. Thunder, the only cowboy still in town manning the bit left on the Svendsen ranch for old Oddvar, burps very loudly at the end of the echo.

Thad is now standing two steps down from the top of my General's porch. Next to him is Marie, of course, but it's Patrick beside her. The visual is like a jab with a hard spoon to the underside of my ribcage. He is not wearing his Stetson and by the looks of his cheeks, he hasn't touched the whiskey. Marie keeps glancing at him while shadows shift behind them both as Horeb, Gil and Toot come to the railing. Thomas Smith stands to the far side of the porch, more in shadow, but looking every bit like he's amused with our small town antics.

"I have something to say," Marie announces.

If I knew better, I'd say she's nervous. Marie has never liked being in front of folks, the center of attention. I suppose she and I are similar that way. I frown up at her between the shoulders of Tim Bailey and Reverend Painter. What's she doing, changing the tone of the night? We haven't even got to the voting part yet.

The trouble is, because Marie never speaks out in public, everyone's all concerned in what she wants to say. It's unusual and unnatural for her to be there like some great dame, her wild black hair with the grey streaks all blowing out of her knot, her face creased with fine lines and her dark eyes burying in their sockets.

"I'm saying that Doc Smith is no good for Flats," she says without frills. "He's not welcome, and I say he needs to be run out of town, same as we did those Army deserters who hurt my Helena."

Doctor Smith jerks away from his lean on the rail, his body tense. I want to go up to him, but my way up to the porch is blocked by Marie and Thaddeus, and Thomas's way down is just as blocked. For a moment, I wonder if he'll leap over and dash away from everything.

"Why?" Elaine Warren calls. "What's he done, other than make Doc Kinney feel all shaky in his standing?"

"You know we don't take much stock in docs," Thad says quickly.

My throat goes sticky and then dry like it's been scorched with rough leather. What's going on?

"If you don't take much stock in doctors, I suppose your word doesn't matter much," Doctor Smith mentions. "I'm sure this is all just a friendly haze, isn't it? For the new man in town."

What about me? I'm tied to him now. I'm half with him … doesn't he think to look to me to help him?

"I'm saying he's no good. And he has to be gone," Marie says firmly. "You know us. Thad and me … we were here before there was a rail. Back when this was only Flats Town and there wasn't St. Diana's and Percy Davies still ran the bank. We've weathered the hard winters and the Crow raids and the lean times with you all. And I say if we have to have this fancy hospital and a doc, then Doc Kinney's the man. Doc Smith … he's the real quack. He's the liar. He's the one cheating you all."

Marie doesn't use elegant words, and the simplicity is worse. Folks start their muttering and murmuring again, and their awful chatter and gossiping tales. The churning in my head is the crashing of my own hopes. My skin feels overly tight, and I want to burst out of it.

But I can't.

It's not Yves who's all trapped up.

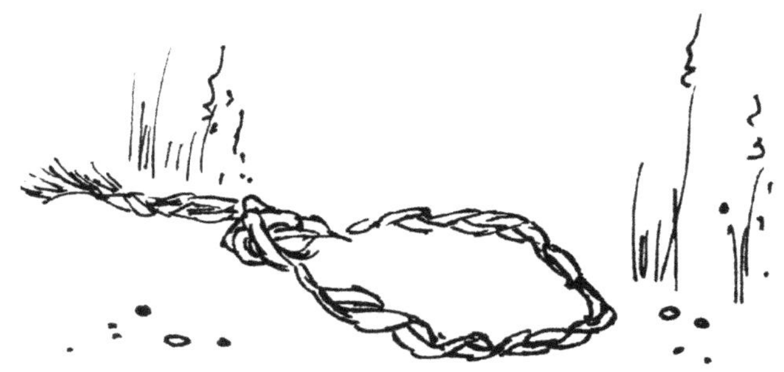

CHAPTER 20

Helena

July 3, 1884

My father, standing on the General's porch, is tall enough that my streamers get stuck in his beard. He bats at them as my mother speaks, speaking to the town like she knows just how to manage a slow boil. Next to me, Hardy hasn't taken a single breath since seeing Doc Kinney up there next to my folks.

"Do you think I should go on up there and be next to the doctor?" he whispers to me lowly.

"Too late now, I think," I tell him. "Everyone knows you're on his side of this, anyway."

Just like everyone in Flats Junction now knows my parents have pitted themselves against Kate. And what about who Kate has on her side? Yves and his whole scary posse … well, except Matthias. The Army and the Fort commander, and all her electric contacts. Even Doc Smith himself. Do mother and father really think they have enough sway against all that?

"Looks to me like Doc Kinney has too much to gain with the other feller leaving." The pinched voice is Sally Painters, still in mourning black, standing off to the side. No one listens to her, and her mouth squeezes into a hundred tiny lines when she has no audience.

"I think I gotta go up there, Helena," Hardy says again. He moves to go up, and I grab his arm to hold him back.

"Why? What good will it do?" It's worry I feel, I realize. I don't want him getting on the wrong side of this, and it's too early to know which way it'll fall. I'm scared it will all come to fist fights and kicks to ribs, and …

And I think my days of traveling so brashly alone to the east coast are over.

"I have to show I stand by Doc Kinney. And Mrs. Kinney, for what happened. We can't have that Doctor Smith here."

"What's wrong with him?" When I stand on tiptoe, I still can't see above the crowd, and there's no hint of the city doctor's tall hat. "He wants to build a hospital—I'll get business. Maybe you can even work there."

"He just hit Mrs. Kinney today, Helena. 'Cross the face with a bottle."

Chills spill across my chest, down my arms, and pool like ice in my stomach. Flashes of my own beatings, as hazy as they are, spin across my eyes. And through it all, Mrs. Kinney, curved over me, seeing to my blackening eyes and aching stomach …

I stare at Hardy for a moment before something like an iron weight curdles in my stomach.

"Doctor Smith whacked Mrs. Kinney on the face?" I say. Too loud. A dozen faces swing to listen, but they're just blurs. I'm still only able to revisit the glimpses of the attack outside my shop, the rough hands and hard leather boots, the raking of dirty nails under my skirts and inside my knee …

"I gotta help him," Hardy mutters again.

"Come on," I say suddenly. "We have to find Old Henry."

"He's not here," Hardy says. "We just been to see him. Susan's got him resting at home, Doc Kinney's orders."

"Because he's sick and his gout's no better," I say, reciting the gossip my father told us around the dinner table. He'd gone to see Doc Kinney about the bullet graze, and came back with more than just a cure. "He'll vouch for Doctor Smith being no good!"

Hardy's eyes meet mine. "I don't got a horse."

"We'll run," I decide, already inching toward the back. "And hope nothing bad happens while we're at it."

A glint of boyish joy rises in Hardy's face, and a hint of challenge that I feel matches mine. Here's something I can do! I can't fix my own past, or change the tremors still living in my bones, but I can help.

We start off with a quick walk. Soon enough, we jog as one.

Knowing he won't judge me for being too unladylike, I raise my skirts above my knees to go faster. By the time we reach the cowboy bunkhouse, we're both near sprinting. The sound of his breathing next to me matches my own, a slight burn and hitch in the lungs as we go faster. Brinkley land stretches out far to the north and a bit east, but the houses themselves aren't more than a leisurely conversation's distance from Doc Kinney's to Old Henry's porch. Behind us, the lanterns and little house lights look like overlarge fireflies plastered to the darker prairie. The sky is not full dark, but a deep periwinkle blue, the first stars burning already, bright and pure and white.

We slow as we get closer, and I suddenly find myself feeling wide and free, the strange tightness I've held ever since being accosted loosening up my bones and my tongue for the first time. It's like this might be one of the few times I can be … open. Anything might be possible, out here in the wide land, under the starlight.

Before I can overthink it, I fling the words at Hardy. "You … you like me. Don't you?"

He doesn't stumble, but his breath changes a bit. The cadence is now opposite mine.

"You're bold," he says, but hurries before I get defensive. "I like that. You.

I like that you're bold and you're you." He slows suddenly, forcing me to walk fast now instead with him. I think it helps we don't have to stare at each other, the summer night giving us a bit of intimate privacy. "I've held a candle for you from the first day I ever saw you."

I start to grin, but he's only shaking his head.

"But I have no family, Helena. Your own didn't even want me."

"That's not—"

"True. Yes, it is," he insists. "Now I'm learning under Doc Kinney, who half the town doesn't like, and I've no way to make money."

Our future together is implied in everything he says. I see it in my mind, a pale possibility if only given the time to solidify.

"I can make money," I remind him. "A woman can help. Look at my mother. Look at Kate. Look at ... at half of Flats Junction."

"And what if I'm having to be a traveling doc, in order to make a living?" he argues, but it's a tired sort of argument, like he's already gone through this whole thing in his head. The idea makes me feel hot and buttery inside, that he's been dreaming of me. Of us.

"I like that you'd go off and do things. Help people. You've always done that—helping my mother when she had Garek, fixing Kaspar's arm, and even this." I wave my hand at the nearing houses. Only one has lantern lights in the main room. "Getting Old Henry. I'll have the dress shop, you go and save folks, and we'll be just fine."

"But I won't be home every night always," he says. "It won't be regular."

I nod, and dare to reach and grab his hand. His wide palm and thick fingers, so clumsy over the forge but so very sure over an open wound, latch and lace with mine. "That's fine by me. I ... no matter what I've done and seen and been through ... I've never wanted to trade my independence for marriage. It'll suit me fine, Hardy."

"Gerhardt."

A tickle of something makes my mouth quiver. Laughter, I think, or maybe a giggle. "Gerhardt."

"Alright," he says, squeezing my hand. If it weren't so dark, I'm sure I'd see his cheeks stained tomato. There's a small quaver in his voice, but he sounds serious anyway. "I'll talk to your father."

Just like that, then. Excitement and nerves jangle in my throat.

Just like that I've landed myself my future, exactly as I would hope it, marriage or no, and yet I won't be alone again.

Comfort and jubilation override the seriousness of our trek to the Brinkleys. I might not be that brash girl who went to Boston and made friends from nothing, sneaking around the dress shops until friends were made and alliances built. I might not have a traditional life, but it will be on my own terms, no matter what I've seen and suffered. I'm still doing as I said I would.

I'm building a life. My way.

Hardy knocks on Old Henry's door very loudly, and we both hear Susan's voice muddled on the other side. She opens it a moment later.

"What is it?" she asks.

Behind her, Old Henry calls out at the same time. "Another fire?"

"Glad to see you're not on your back, sir," Hardy says steadily, peering into the warm gold of the front room. "We … that is, Helena and I have come to ask for your help. There's trouble, and you're likely the only one most everyone will listen to."

"That so?" Old Henry sounds extremely pleased.

Susan glances at me, then down, and I realize Hardy and I still hold hands. I give a small shrug to my shoulder and offer her a small grin. She returns it, and then spins on her husband.

"You are to rest. Doc Kinney's orders."

"That's just it, ma'am," Hardy jumps in, easy as buttered bread. "It's about Doc Kinney. And Doctor Smith, too."

"Easily settled, isn't it?" Susan says. "Doctor Kinney is better, of course."

"I don't know if half the town would agree with you," I say, glancing at Hardy, who just nods, looking miserable.

"I thought it was going to be a night talking about who'll be mayor," Old Henry says. "Has little to do with me."

"Why aren't you running for mayor?" I ask him. "Folks expected it."

"Why, girlie, I've been mayor of a sorts for years now. High time to retire, don't you think?" he says.

"But … but everyone really listens to you," I say. I think of Kate and her plot and plans, and still feel undecided about how it's all come to this. "Like tonight. They have to listen to you!"

"Change and time go hand in hand. A body can't live forever," he says, and gestures to his swollen feet, the toes purple and bulbous.

"Kate's running for it," I say.

"I heard that," he muses. "The town could do worse than Percy Davies' daughter."

I want to ask him if he thinks she'll do a good job or end up selling out. I want to know what it takes to be a leader, whether that be a business person about town or an elected official. I want to know how he did it, playing judge and sheriff all these years. Maybe then I can make a decision of my own. But every question makes me feel disloyal to Kate. She's given me so much. How can I question her motives?

And I want to make him come to town, but he won't budge. *Doc Kinney's orders.* I want to argue, to plead with him to come, but I can see there's no moving him.

I look at Hardy. Well then, it's up to us.

Hardy and I run back to town without speaking, and without the Brinkley patriarch in tow. I don't know what we plan to do on our own, but my pulse matches my breathing, so fast and pounding the constellations wink instead of stay still, adding to my dizziness.

When Hardy and I arrive, the argument is still going so strong there's invisible lines drawn in the dirt. Groups of folks stand in clusters, some clearly on one side of the argument instead of the other. Kate stands near the General's stairs, but hasn't climbed them. Near her is Matthias, Yves, and the rest of the posse. The Fort commander and his men stand to the side looking extremely amused. Some of the younger Army men have their sleeves already rolled up in anticipation. Mrs. Kinney has joined her husband on the porch next to my parents, and her face, turned in the light, is stained black and blue and mauve and her mouth sparkles with fresh blood.

By the sound of it, things have degraded into insults instead of results.

"I ain't got to do anything I don't wants to!" Franklin Jones barks across to Nels Henderssen. "An' just cause you're happy with what the sawbones did, don't mean I gotta be!"

"I never said was happy about it!" Nels roars back, waving a crutch. "I just didn't turn into a senseless, wife-beating dru—"

"Ja, you to stop calling my man so!" Bess Jones shakes her fist. "He's nutting like, no more!"

"This is not about injuries from near ten years ago!" Even my father's shout is ignored. He glances at my mother with frustration rolling off his crossed arms and she just shakes her head.

"Look, folks," the Lieutenant Colonel Swaine steps out, hands raised. "I understand you're debating doctors, but I just want to be sure at the end there's a hospital."

"You just want it for zee electric lines," Yves sneers at him. His nasal voice is so grating it cuts above the constant chatter. "You do not care for else."

"Oh, and you are?" the Fort commander snarls back. "First electric line cut, I'm sending the boys out for you."

"It will be the Lakota to do that. That ezz who we fight," Yves dismisses.

"Ha! I know who you and your ilk are."

"So my reputation is still known?" Natty calls hopefully. Patty smacks him across the chest, but he still looks pleased in a very oily way. I shudder, and remind myself if it weren't for the posse, I'd likely be bones in the prairie by now.

"Doctor Smith cured my Freddy," Sadie reminds. "That is a miracle not to be ignored."

"It was not a mir—!"

"Shall we go patient to patient?" Doc Smith calls from the porch, where he's trapped to the side and aiming his words at Doctor Kinney. "We can go back to our apprenticeship days if you like, Paddy."

"This is easily settled!" Fortuna calls out. "Who else was witness to what was done to Jane?"

"Kjersti Henderssen," Mrs. Kinney says. "But I don't think she'll leave her sick son."

"Well, and who cares if Doc Smith hit a woman," Tim Bailey says loudly. "Maybe she had it coming. Womenfolk do sometimes."

The comment explodes between the two sides of the discussion, with phrases along the lines of 'what does a woman know anyhow? She was out of line to be doctorin'!' to 'Doc Smith oughta be held accountable, he's new!'

"Now hold on!" Mitch Brinkley says. "I got something to say on this. You all know my Alice has had her sickness, and my Pa has the gout something fierce. Doc Kinney had the right of it, not Doc Smith. So there you have it."

If the Brinkley patriarch can't be here, his son is as good as it gets, I reckon. Until another luminary of the town decides to speak.

"Doc Smith cured my boy!" Sadie reminds us all.

At the bottom of the General's stairs, Kate is a pillar of stone, her dark eyes not leaving my parents and the doctors on opposite sides of the porch. I'm glad she hasn't looked at me. I won't be able to hold her stare. Hardy has sidled away from me, to a spot just behind Doc Kinney, and I suddenly feel very much like a raft left to float down the Missouri river right after a spring melt.

"Doctor Smith told my ma and pa he'd send out for some fine waters west-way, made special," Mitch counters. "They paid dear for it, more than I'll say here as it'll sound like bragging. Well, it didn't work." Mitch makes eye contact with most of the people closest to the front—Sadie and Tom Fawcett, the Baileys and two of Fortuna's girls—EvaRose and Tilly, unashamed of their bright pink silk and feathers. They all look at him straight, and then at Doc Kinney.

"He got worse taking them waters," Mitch finishes staunchly. "Got him the runs, as my brothers'll tell you."

"He sure did!" George Brinkley hollers from somewhere in the back.

"We was taking bets on when the outhouse would overflow!" John Brinkley adds.

"And then Doc Kinney showed up, and now Old Henry's not losing his insides," Hardy adds, then looks very nervous about speaking up. His eyes find mine and he makes a small motion with his hand. I smile at him, feeling pride pick at the corners of my eyes.

"Where's Old Henry to vouch for this, then?" Reverend Painter asks. "Let him speak for himself."

"What, and you saying I'm a liar?" Mitch grinds out.

"You certainly prefer Doctor Kinney, I know."

"And you think Doc Smith's better?"

"What, exactly, do you mean to say?" Kate asks evenly against the quiet. Her eyes are glued on Doc Smith, and his on her.

Mitch looks over. "What I'm saying, Kate, is Pa was worse under Doc Smith. I would expect a number of folks to feel the same. He's new, he's untried, and I had my eyes seeing candy with all his fine talk of hospitals."

"Flats *does* need a hospital for the town to grow!" Kate cries out. Her cheeks take on a bright color, high on the bones, and her black hair falls like spilled ink down her back. "It's Pat who's against it—he's angry he'll be shoved out, I'm sure. Who wouldn't be?"

"I'm not against a hospital, or even the electric," Doctor Kinney says. He sounds calm enough, though Doc Smith still looks like he might like to bolt if my father wasn't in his way.

But at last I can sense it. What I'd hoped for—that folks are calm enough to listen, really listen, to reason. It's a leaning, as they all wait to hear the next words, to weigh them against their own hopes and thoughts.

"What I am saying is the Brinkleys won't be funding any hospital if the likes of Doc Smith is going to run it," Mitch says, then claps his hat on his head and steps back to Alice's side.

"Ayup. Pa says so," John Brinkley adds. "You all are welcome to go on and ask him yourself. He'll like the visits."

Wild hope rises in me—there! Maybe people will rise for Doc Kinney at last! My Hardy will be a doctor in a hospital here, and won't need to travel or work as hard as Doc Kinney for his livelihood, just like I chose an easier but similar path to my mother's.

A thought trickles into my mind as I listen, and I slip away from the crowd and dash through the greasy shadows across town. My skin itches from sweat, and I wish I still wore the soft loose clothes of my childhood. But when Kjersti Henderssen calls through the door asking who's there, I'm glad I look like a respectable shop woman when she opens it.

"What?" she snaps. "I've sickness in the house."

"I know," I say quickly, catching my breath. "But I … there's debate in town."

Her face closes. "I'm sure. Bodies can't help but fight anytime there's a gathering."

"It's to do with you—with what happened today."

"I'm no gossip," Mrs. Henderssen says, fear clipping the end of her sentence. "Don't want no more trouble—there's enough for my family, and I—"

"I just need to know—did he hit Mrs. Kinney? Doc Smith?"

"What's it matter?" she asks. "Who'll take a woman's word against a man's? Half the town thinks he's some miracle worker, anyway."

"Mrs. Henderssen—"

"So what if he did? What's done is done, and my boy's dying," she half-sobs and slams the door in my face.

It's all I need, though. I can be another voice, though I don't know if it'll still be enough. It's better than nothing.

When I sneak back, there's still the debate on which doctor will be better, and no one seems to think the town will be big enough for both.

I sidle past Kate and creep up the stairs. My father shifts to make room for me, but I shake my head slightly and take my place just behind Hardy. When I put a hand on his shoulder, he shifts to make sure I have a view. No need to see it, but I know my mother's dark eyes watch every movement.

"It's no difference to me if the locals aren't part of the hospital." Peter Swaine steps up next to Kate. His meaty shoulders half block her from view as he turns to the town folks. "The Army's got interest and the funds enough in the end."

"But which doc'll run it?" calls Mikey O'Donnell. "There's what matters!"

"To you all, but not to me," Swaine says. "And if we're shouldering a good share of the cost, we'll determine which doc runs it. But it's clear to me Flats Junction itself needs to be a bit more civilized before any of these plans can come to light."

"Doc Smith will be best," Reverend Painter's deep voice booms. "I think that's clear."

"Doc Smith beat Mrs. Kinney!"

It's my own voice, sounding frail in the night. The crush of a thousand eyes makes me want to shrink back behind Hardy. I hadn't meant to shout it, though how else would folks know?

"We don't got proof," Dell Johnston says. "Got to have proof."

I want to mention how this same group hung Bern Masson without anything but Kate's word, but I'm glad the mind of a mob hasn't taken over. Swallowing my nerves, I stand up straighter.

"I just went there to ask her myself."

Out of the corner of my eye, Doc Smith makes a swift movement, but then seems to think better of it.

"Kjersti Henderssen said so, eh?"

"You calling my sister-in-law a liar?" Jarle Henderssen challenges.

Everything sounds like it's going to go back to fighting in a moment, but Doc Smith steps into the light on the railing. He smiles at Kate, then at the town. She doesn't smile back.

"What's a woman's word against a man's, after all?" Doctor Smith says, turning and opening his arms. I notice Tim Bailey and the Reverend nodding. Larry Fawcett starts to nod too, notices his wife Grete glaring, and stops. Even Father Jonathan looks uncertain.

"Well, that's true enough," Swaine says, nodding at Doc Smith. "Civilized it is, then. I'm pleased at least some of you can see sense. Maybe we need to keep some Army folks stationed 'round town, make sure it's all tidy without brawls like this near breaking out over a little disagreement from now on."

Grumbling starts at once, and my throat feels tight.

Army men? Recruits, deserters, men in uniform, lounging around every corner?

I can't! I won't see it—it'll … I won't be able to breathe!

Before I choke on my own fear-filled spit, I bend around Hardy and call down. It's not something I plan. Maybe because I know the Fort commander already, or because I like the way his daughter and I share the same hairstyle, or because … because I will say anything to keep the streets free of those unruly men—

"I'm expanding my seamstress business!" I call down. "It'll be a proper dress shop, with the finest fashions sent in special just for me from Boston and New York. If that's not civilized, what is?"

"That's true," my mother adds. "The Prime Inn, too, is all fancied up soon enough with electric lights and silk drapes."

"Yeah!" Joe shouts from his position by the beer barrel. "Is!"

"I own two businesses, and as you can see, they are quite popular," Kate says, sounding more than a little offended. She crosses her arms and gives the Fort commander an even stare. He completely ignores her.

"I'm bringing in a new stamping machine!" Nancy Ofsberger announces. "And a new telegraph that works even faster."

"And I bought Helena a sewing machine!" Elaine Warren reminds everyone, loudly. Her husband, Trusty Willy, adds quickly, "Plus we're ordering in a cherry pitter! Brand new machine, I tell you all!"

"We are *not* getting that," Elaine whispers fiercely to him.

"I just told everyone though."

Peter Swaine just raises his hands lazily. "The Army doesn't care about a fancy inn or a dress shop. Besides, this is all women's notions. What can a woman do to—."

I don't know why I can't hold my tongue. Maybe it was the failed race to get Old Henry, or the way my mother spoke in public for the first time in my memory. Or the letting go of the tight fear in my gut or getting Hardy to agree he wants to marry me. Maybe … maybe I'm tired of playing the role of the girl, who must always be second and play by more rules than the men.

The words burst out, ripe and juicy and full of frustrated truth.

"A woman—any of us—we build more than most anyone at all!"

CHAPTER 21

Jane

July 3, 1884

Helena's shouted words echo across the street for a long moment. "And that," I say suddenly, my voice crackling as if full of dry sand, "is precisely why I'm voting for Kate Davies to be mayor."

It is the first I've spoken since this entire fiasco with Marie and Thaddeus taking a stance on the General's porch. Marie had insisted they speak up, and Thaddeus didn't object, which is as good as his approval.

"It has to come from us," she'd said, *"not you or the doc."*

And now it's all sideways and muddled, and we've gone from trying to get Doctor Smith out of town to whether Flats Junction is worth electricity and whether women can be successful.

No one hears my call. Everyone's still taking stock of who does what.

"My parlor is as fine as the ones in Deadwood!" Fortuna calls.

"Sure is," Dell agrees, and then looks like his head might swell and pop when Fortuna rewards him with a massive smile and a tweak to her bosom.

"And I'm still the best cook in the whole town!" Toot states. Everyone nods and mutters with agreement.

The Fort commander finally starts to look as if he's a bit out of his element. I glance down at my sleeping son, the stinging side of my face sending shivers down my neck. It's all still so fresh, the blood throbs right below the surface of my skin, aching with each pulse. The wetness of blood at the corner of my mouth tastes like a thick stew, tangy with iron and salt. I'd hoped to make it through the night without anyone noticing, showing up when the shadows would be long enough that polite conversation would keep people from outright commenting on the new bruising.

"All this talk of the women managing things," I call out. "Tonight's for a vote. I vote for Kate."

Those nearest the stairs hear me, including Kate herself. She turns her liquid black eyes—so much like Esther's—on me, questions racing across them. I still don't know exactly why this is important to me, that she should have this. Do I think that when she's busy running the town, she will stop any last secret pining for my husband? Do I think it is a way for me to atone at last for somehow winning his heart—and if it is, will she think it enough? Or do I truly think she is the best for the job?

"I do, too. It's Kate Davies for mayor for me."

The voice is Mikey O'Donnell, and more townsfolk start to pay attention when they realize the conversation has turned. Heads bob, necks twist, and I watch the ripple from the higher vantage and think perhaps tonight we might see something monumental occur. It's a heady feeling, to realize I am part of it. Is this what it is, to watch history unfold in front of one, to feel the way the air crystalizes and every sound feels overly sharp?

"I vote for Kate," Helena says from behind me.

Marie throws Helena an exasperated glance, and then looks up at Thaddeus.

He stares at her before giving the slightest of nods and turns to the town people.

"The same for my wife and me," he says simply, crossing his arms tighter.

"Aye," Patrick says. His single word bounces across hats and bonnets, and soon enough there's all the yeses and of courses and nodding without an argument raised. I'm hopeful, I realize, that this will distract everyone from the discussion of whether Patrick is fit to be the doctor or whether Doctor Smith should replace him.

And with Kate in charge … she could just run Doctor Smith right out of town to protect Patrick. That's what she would do, how she has always operated. Even if … even if he's no longer able to marry her. A seed of doubt curdles in my stomach, and I push down the tendril of concern that perhaps I have overshot or misread Kate. It would not be the first time … but where Patrick is concerned, she's always been steadfast.

Amid the mutters of agreement for Kate, who has turned a triumphant face to the crowd, the Lieutenant Colonel still shakes his head.

"Not enough," he says. "It's not enough to call yourself citified and get yourselves a mayor. You need the law. A sheriff at the very least."

"Well, that will be Yves," Kate announces. She's so swift and smooth about it that it catches even the Commander off guard. His mouth snaps shut. Nearby, Yves looks both surprised and terribly pleased before his eyes narrow a little bit. Perhaps, like me, he is always trying to solve the enigma of Kate.

Kate doesn't even turn to look to see what affect she's had on the posse leader. "He knows the land better than most," she says, sounding very reasonable. "And he has the manpower and the cunning to protect the electricity."

This is not such a popular decision, as the clouds pass across many faces. The Commander, though, looks very intrigued. Perhaps because Kate was able to solve his question so seamlessly. Perhaps it was a test, and she passed it at once.

Something feels off to me, like the shade of a color that has too much of another shade in it. I frown to myself, trying to understand the edge that slides down the inside of my chest.

"What will happen to Yves's store?" someone shouts from the back.

"He can keep it if he wishes, but otherwise, I will absorb and pay for the goods and sell them in the General," she says, and nods at Yves. He crosses his arms, but still says nothing, as if delighting in watching his future be handled by Kate.

"How do we know he'll do the job right? You vouching for him, Kate?" another asks.

"How do we know any sheriff will do the job right?" she asks back.

As the questions come, Kate answers them with an efficiency that reminds me of the first time I saw her in her store—all grace and elegance and sure-footed movement. This is like a dance to her, this haggling, and she is winning.

At last the feeling solidifies in my stomach, and I turn slightly to Patrick. He bends to my mouth, so I can speak lowly.

"It is as if … she is already acting as mayor. Without an official vote," I say. Annoyance twists my voice.

Patrick shakes his head slightly. "Percy never held an election either, Jane. We aren't a state—there are no rules or constitution to follow."

This does nothing to soothe the growing ruffling I feel as I watch Kate grow into a role she has not actually won yet. And still … no one seems to think anything more be done or said. It's as if my voice catapulted the decision, even though there has been no final count.

It does not feel *civilized* at all.

The chatter ebbs and swells, side conversations breaking apart the attention of many, and someone starts tuning up a banjo again. The Commander muscles his way to where Yves and his posse stand and starts to ask questions about his history on the prairie and how well he knows the local tribes and rail systems. Thomas Smith joins them, pushing past Thaddeus at last. The three of them look like an unholy trio, hatching a plan that will grind Flats Junction into the dust.

It's likely just the pain in my face, forcing me to think such sorrowful things.

Yves looks as if he's been handed a gift, and my stomach turns over at last.

"Can we go home?" I ask Patrick quietly.

He hesitates for a moment, but he puts a hand on my waist and guides me back down the stairs.

Kate pauses in her vivid discussion with Tim Bailey about importing tacks for reshoeing horses to reach out for my forearm.

"Jane." Her face is lit from inside, as if she is filled with the glow of the sun. Have I ever seen her so radiant? Is this what she wanted, then, this power? This prestige?

"Congratulations, I think," I say to her, unable to fully meet her bright gaze.

The joy fades a little in her cheekbones, and she does not let go of my arm. "I … I appreciate what you did, speaking for me. I … thank you."

I didn't realize that I'd wanted to hear the words—to gain her thanks and recognition. Perhaps it is something I've been craving since I met her. And yet now … the words feel hollow when they hit my ears, and are without the warmth I'd hoped. Perhaps I had wished overmuch, that something like this could make us fast friends at last.

"I will only ask one thing in return for your gratitude," I say quietly. "That you keep Thomas Smith out of town. Please."

Her gaze hardens and turns glossy, and she refuses to glance at Patrick behind me.

"As mayor, I'll be taking into consideration everything on what's best for Flats Junction. Maybe it's just electricity. Maybe it's that and the hospital both. Maybe it's two docs, or maybe just the one. Never you worry, Jane. I'll do what's right."

It's a political answer if ever there was one, and stirs the spinning of unease I feel as I watch her turn back to Tim to discuss the merits of steel over traditional iron for his business. Others stand behind Tim, brimming with excitement and fresh inspiration, likely, in the hopes that they too can find success in the tailwind of Kate's.

Just like this, then, and she is mayor.

Resentment spears my bones, and I try to shake it off. Perhaps I'm just tired. I never wanted such power for myself. I should not begrudge it of her. Besides, I was the one who started it all.

I do not think I have made a monster of my attempt at kindness.

I hope I have not.

Patrick takes Andrew from my tired arms, and then steers us off to the side. I look for Hardy out of habit, and see him still on the General's porch, speaking earnestly to Helena, Marie and Thaddeus. Thad looks as if he might start spitting fire, but Marie's face is clear and perhaps a bit elated. A fleeting speculation has me turning to my husband as we leave behind the crowd.

"We ought to consider how we might soon start to pay Hardy for his time."

Patrick frowns. "An apprentice doesn't earn anything but experience."

"Perhaps times are changing."

"Our finances are not," he counters.

"I'm only thinking that he might want to consider a life beyond just medicine. He cannot want to live in our spare room for the next ten years."

"It takes a lifetime to learn to be a doctor."

"Not all men wait as long as you to marry, Patrick," I remind. "And I gather you were too busy to look for a wife until I forced your hand."

"No one has ever forced me to do anything I didn't want," he says strongly. In the dark on the way to our house, his face is unreadable. After a moment, he sighs and moves Andrew to his other shoulder. "Except, maybe Thomas."

"Jealousy," I say.

"Just that."

I suppose that is something of what festers between Kate and me—and has since the minute I arrived in Flats Junction on that blustery March day in 1881. Perhaps we both were jealous of the other, but in gaining Patrick in marriage, she perceives I have won. She does not like that I am happy.

When I think of her, glowing like a bride with all the attention tonight, I wonder if she is happy. Truly, contentedly happy.

For I am so. I am filled with such feelings when I hold Andrew's soggy bottom to my shoulder, when I see Patrick standing near me, ready to hold me in his arms for sake of nothing but feeling our limbs twined. There is loss, to be sure, with Esther gone. That is the way of life—change and loss and death. But I *am* happy—happier than I have been my entire life.

The only marring of that happiness is the uncertainty of the future here, in Flats Junction. Kate's answer on Thomas was unsatisfactory, but how can we force anything? What can we do to change the possibility of Thomas still gaining a foothold here? For all Marie and Thaddeus's words, it is unresolved. Even with Old Henry pulling back from the hospital, the Army will still vouch for it, if only for the electricity.

"How can we get Doctor Smith out of town?" I murmur. "We have to get him out of town. Not only for us, but … for the people. They are not safe with him. When I think of poor Kjersti and her sick son …" I close my eyes, remembering the cool way Thomas smacked me with the bottle without a flinch or a glint of emotion. What kind of man is that, to be so violent to a woman? He is dangerous, in a way I cannot name but know deep inside.

"You are right," Patrick says. "He must be forced out. It helps that Thaddeus and Marie spoke, but it will take more than that."

"What can be done? What can we do?" I wonder.

Patrick looks up at the sky again, then out over the prairie, which is the color of washed navy, tipped with silver and white. The grass rustles with the evening breeze, and in the distance, the sounds of the Brinkley herd waft to us on the same wind.

"We'll get serious about narrowin' down the cause of the black measles. And the cow sickness. If we can figure out one of them—how it starts or how it spreads … maybe that will be enough."

"A scientific breakthrough," I say. Despite my worries and the vertigo of change I feel under my shoes, I can't help the rise of anticipation bubbling up. It is as if I've devoured an entire sugar cake. The giddiness comes from the fact that he said *we*. *We'll* do this. Together. "Do you think something like that will be enough to get Thomas out of town? Can we do it soon enough?"

He turns to me, and the moon washes the right side of his face and cuts shadows along his ears and under his jaw. But even in the half light, I can sense the intensity radiating off him, into me, bonding with my own ambition.

"It will have to be enough," he says. "Or else there is nothin' for us here."

"Then we ought to get to work, husband."

I open the screen door and enter the hallway. Instead of going to the bedroom or kitchen, as I have countless times before, I turn left and into the study, where the medical books wait. But Patrick doesn't follow me.

I turn, to see him standing in the hallway, staring at his medical bag. "What is it?"

He finds my eyes, and the tremble of his mouth makes me know what he wants, even though he is afraid to ask me to go back.

"You want to try," I say, stepping out of the study. "I'll come with you."

We walk south toward Kjersti Henderssen's house, avoiding the remainder of the night's party. Music trips on the air, and the slap and clip of boots dancing is almost as loud as the singing and dull roar of chatter.

We don't use a lantern, and Andrew stays quiet, so that no one notices us arrive and knock, or when Kjersti opens it a crack and then wider when she sees us.

"You've come back," she says, relief coloring her voice with unshed tears. "Do you think—is there a chance?"

Patrick walks in directly toward Elbert and begins examining him at once. I lay Andrew back where he had lain only a few hours ago, and turn to Kjersti.

"Let's start that water to boil," I tell her. "If we are lucky, there is indeed a chance."

The vigil begins again, now a familiar dance, and goes through the smallest hours of the night. It feels dreamy and slow, as if we walk through air as thick as molasses together. Patrick understands the methods now, and we take turns pouring tea and herbs down Elbert's throat. Kjersti watches, hardly breathing, and soon understands the rhythm enough to help.

By breakfast, I notice the flush of fresh color in Elbert's cheek, and his fever seems less. I'm afraid to say anything, and Patrick won't, either, but when I meet his gaze over the boy's head, I know we feel the same.

The boy will live.

We are not beaten, yet.

CHAPTER 22

Kate

July 4, 1884

Before Peter Swaine departs for the Fort in the morning, I meet him in the Prime Inn. Joe has outdone himself with a full swell of breakfast, which includes eggs with an orange sauce and thick slabs of sourdough. I almost suspect him of paying Toot on the side for the vittles. Dorothy and Mable Swaine have yet to come down from their room, but the commander is not standing on ceremony waiting on his women and is halfway through his meal when I step in.

"Glad to catch you," I say, putting all sorts of jovialness in my voice. I make sure not to catch Joe's eye, in case he gives us away. He'd sent Lucy round the back to let me know Swaine was down and eating in good spirits, but it is better if it looks like it was just chance and luck.

"Miss Davies," he says, then pauses. Egg bits clutter his mustache as he offers a small smile that doesn't light up his face fully. "Or should I say Mayor Davies?"

"Miss is fine for now," I say, and shove away thoughts of Thomas Smith and his proposal. I sit across from him without waiting on his invitation and place a paper on the table where his elbow and the coffee won't get it smeared. I've only just had Tom Fawcett put together this contract an hour ago, and the ink still looks wobbly.

"What's all this?" he says. "Too early in the day for legalities." He stuffs half a piece of toast in his mouth and chews with it open.

"It's only a formality of what we've already discussed many times," I say. I make it sound like it's a simple thing. "It'll be necessary for the bank, and the electric company, to see it's official."

He pulls the paper close, leaving grease stains where the pads of his fingers touch. I stare at them, and how the pattern of his fingertips looks like swirling worms.

"You said you'd spend government money on the electric. So now it's just signing to say you're planning on putting cash toward the whole plan, so it's not just my word." I think I should say that it would help having a man's signature on the idea, that what can just a woman do to convince businessmen to invest in lines out here, but that would not sound very good at all after last night.

"Right." He squints at the paper, but the sound of heels interrupts his reading. Dorothy and Mable, looking scrubbed pink and wearing fresh dresses, march into the room. Dorothy holds her head up, and I catch a view of what she must have been like, back living in the city before she followed her man west.

Swaine notices them too and stands suddenly.

"Why Missus Swaine," he bows a bit. "And the Miss Swaine. Do join me, ladies, please."

High color rises on Dorothy's nose, and Mable is young enough that she grins outright at her father's posturing.

"Thank you, sir," Dorothy says, and sits at her husband's right side. Swaine casts a long look at his wife, an old gleam in his eye, and gestures for Joe to bring more food. Lucy scuttles over with plates and clattering silverware. As Swaine fusses over Dorothy and Mable, getting them settled, I suddenly wonder if I will ever have such a moment. I've agreed to marry Thomas Smith, but can I imagine him behaving so, if I were to come down in the latest fashion, all dressed up and washed?

Before I can go off thinking on this too much, Swaine turns to me and reaches for the pen I've put near me on the table. Without another glance, he quickly signs the contract and nods at me.

"Good doing business with you, Miss Davies."

I'm dismissed, and I'm fine with it. With Dorothy and Mable there, I feel itchy, as if I don't belong at the table. Which is foolish, of course, since I own a whole good chunk of the Prime Inn itself!

But I stand and nod my thanks at Joe. He's watched it all, and knows what it means—the electric is coming!—but he nods back. I like how we know what it means, that we'll be talking later on the next steps. I suppose if I need another man to talk to the electric men, Joe could do it, as my business partner. I hope it won't come to that. That I'll be enough.

When I get back to the General, there's commotion out front, where Yves has his posse moving most of his goods into my store. I hurry up, and sure enough, they're making a mess and spoiling the whole look.

"Why didn't you wait?" I say. "I've had this all set up pretty and fine for my first official day open after the party."

None of the posse pays me any mind. Even with Horeb and Gil back in their seats playing checkers and watching everything, I feel upside down. "You're messing with how I like it all laid out."

Yves turns around from behind the counter, which makes him look even shorter, and offers me a gummy smile. On his chest is a silver star, obviously crafted quick by Marie. I wonder if he woke her up just to get it fashioned right off.

"You said last night you want all zee goods," he says. "The sale of zee goods is to pay for my sheriff salary, ezz it not?"

"Well. Yes." I cross my arms around my stomach. Last night had so many decisions. They were like bullets, raining on me. I can only hope I remember everything I decided, everything I promised …

"Then it ezz good to start selling right away. We will ride out tomorrow," he says. "We need to find where zee Lakota are."

I've not yet caught Patrick or Jane to ask where my mother is, but it's enough to get Yves out of town. I'll manage the Lakota side next.

"Very good," I say, and move to the other side of the counter so Yves has to shift out of the way. A quick glance at the till puts my heart back in its place. Nothing has been shifted—I caught him before he could peek at the cash.

"And Matthias will stay," Yves says. He's still too close, the runny whites of his pale eyes dripping just so on his eyelashes that I can see them clump.

"What? Why?" I refuse to go looking at Matthias himself.

"If I am to be in zee country, riding, I must have a man here to watch for me. Ezz that not what a respectable sheriff would do, hmm?" Yves says. He looks mighty proud of himself, or his idea. He keeps on smiling. "What ezz they called?"

"A deputy," Arnold offers, bringing over a crate of canned milk and oysters in oil.

"But that's just …" I swallow the word *stupid*. "But he doesn't talk. How's he supposed to be a lawman here in your stead?"

Yves just shrugs and smirks at me, then turns to take stock of what Evan is hauling in next. Horeb's neck looks twisted to breaking as he peers up. It's cigars in painted boxes, and I frown at it. Since when has Yves had access to tobacco like that?

Well, never mind. It's mine to sell. When I turn back, Yves is watching me, and he shakes a small finger at my chin.

"That ezz also why Matthias stays back. He will be sure you do not cheat me."

"Only someone who cheats would worry on that," I retort. Before he can rile me further, I stalk out of my own General and take in big gulps of summer air.

Everything is working out how I wanted. Maybe better. I'm getting Yves out of town. Even if Matthias stays, maybe I can just keep him busy with Helena as he has been. He won't bother me, and he won't be arguing with me, neither. As for my mother—

"Katherine."

Thomas Smith stands at the bottom of the stairs. It feels like I'm slapping eyes on him for the first time ever, with his tall black hat shining in the morning sun, and the silk patch over his eye. He's staring up at me as if he hadn't faced half the town down last night. As if there's not a speck of doubt about his integrity. As if he's the perfect match.

"What do you think this morning, with all the talk about the hospital last night?" he asks. "I didn't expect there to be so much division."

Division. Likely sown a bit by himself, I'd wager. It would be something I'd do, if I were him. Allies are important.

I walk down the stairs slowly to meet him. This way Horeb and Gil might not hear everything either, and we're away from the eyes of Yves, too.

"I still say it's a grand idea for Flats Junction," I say. "And I'm mayor now."

A slow smile rises, wrinkling the firm flesh of his cheeks. "What of us? The night's troubles have not changed your mind, I hope?"

It's a chance to get out. He's not offering it, but it's there in his question. Half of me yanks my heart backward, as if I could run away from him and be free of needing a man. But I pull back at the feeling just as hard. He's everything I've been looking for in a husband. There's no expectation of love, and we both know that. It's not as if I'm joining with him expecting it to be something beautiful or happy or more than a transaction.

I don't think I've ever really thought I'd have love anyway. Not really.

Might as well latch onto what I do have.

It's better than nothing.

"Hm," I say, remembering how Thomas and Yves spent an hour chatting closely. "And you've made some additional headway with Swaine yourself. I suppose that will come in handy if the Army is helping build the hospital and pay for electric now."

"Isn't that what you wanted, my dear?" he asks. "A hospital, electric, and more?"

"It's all exactly what I've wanted."

"Then we shall start our plans tonight," he says. "If I might take you to supper?"

"How about we eat alone, in my back room?" I offer. It's too late to remember I don't need to give my body. We are already engaged. Old habits, I guess. And it'll tie him to me a little bit more. His one eye darkens as he understands my meaning. A tiredness winds itself through my sinew. Or maybe it's resignation. Or maybe I'm just finally feeling the end of the energy that's propelled me this far. Maybe I'm finally able to rest and feel like I won't lose everything I've built.

The panic of last night flows out of me.

It's all working out. Everything will be fine—I'll make sure of it. In the end, I'll make a mark on this place bigger than my father ever did.

As I walk into my General with Thomas at my side, I send up a hope to the clear blue of the sky stretching across the whole town.

If I'm given one thing, just the one, let it be this.

Let it be that I matter.

The End

HISTORICAL NOTE:

As the penultimate book in the Flats Junction series, *Trader 1884* continues the ongoing saga between the three main protagonists (Kate, Marie, and Jane) and their families as they attempt to preserve the lives they've built and create a bigger legacy at the same time. It is my hope that their overlapping lives and experiences have continued to paint a picture of how the territories and land west of the Mississippi was developed, and how towns either prospered or failed based on the strengths or weaknesses of the people who lived together.

While a town called Flats Junction never existed at the very real intersection of the Milwaukee Road railroad lines in what is now South Dakota, there was indeed a fort on the Missouri called Fort Randall, which existed—with all the buildings there mentioned in *Trader 1884*—until 1892, which is also the same year tick-borne illness was discovered. There was indeed electricity running out to Deadwood by the Black Hills Corporation, and the idea of having a stationary doctor or nearby hospitals instead of "horse and buggy" doctors to serve the population was beginning to take off in the States, where the scars of hospital mortality rates were not as fresh as they were in Europe.

Kate's aspirations to be mayor were not completely outlandish, though they certainly would be considered impossible in more "citified" areas of the country or states where voting laws had been ratified in state constitutions. The first female mayor in America was officially elected in 1887 in Kansas, but settlers in the Dakotas were attempting women's suffrage and political engagement before the territory became a state. Emma Smith DeVoe, who worked closely with Susan B. Anthony, hoped to include women's rights to vote in the South Dakota state constitution in 1889, but the legislation for women's suffrage wasn't ratified in time. I like to think that the "lawless" parts of the territory would have been able to act a bit more loosely, even making Kate mayor without an official vote, as Flats Junction was still part of a territory, with a different set of legal rules. This is, after all, part of the fun of writing fiction!

But the attitude against women was still rife with low opinion of women's abilities. This is pictured when Patrick and Jane stand off against Thomas, and the corrupt doctor's supporters in town speak against women in general, as well as against Jane personally. In fact, Jane knowing about medicine may well have been even more out of the box thinking than the notion of Kate taking over politically.

Thus, Kate would need to get married to hold down a hefty powerful position. Society would have expected it—*demanded* it—and she would not have been wrong to tie herself to a man who could boost her esteem. Marriage for love was still considered a luxury, and Kate is, if anything, extremely pragmatic if not a bit mercenary about her choices and decisions.

As in *Outcast 1883*, health and medicine play a large part in the drama of the west. Not only was there still distrust in doctors and science, but it was extremely easy for charismatic con men to bamboozle folks with promises of cures and big plans. This is where the notion of "snake oil" comes from, or as the premise of classic entertainment such as *The Music Man*. Thomas is such a man, coming in with his enigmatic eye patch and fancy clothes and posh accent. He also doesn't have the same baggage as Patrick—the history of cutting off limbs and failed surgeries and death. Like Professor Harold Hill, Thomas is able to fool many with his smooth-talking ways, even as the evidence mounts against him.

As for the violence against Helena, this exemplifies how easy it was for men to harass women, but also how towns would rally around their girls. Her position as a tradeswoman, young as she is, would put her in a separate class of women. She would not need a chaperone to operate or walk from place to place, and would not be required to marry to operate a dressmaking shop, as it was considered a respectable profession for a female. But it also made her vulnerable, with some presuming because she didn't have a husband that she was "fair game" or easy to 'seduce'. She also would have had to continue operating if she wanted to survive and thrive—there was no space in active society for a woman to really deal with any PTSD or lasting mental health side effects from the many types of assault. In many a way, marriage was an escape from those kinds of overtures—married women were, generally, left in peace more so than unmarried girls.

Marriage aside, I continue to strive for as much historical accuracy as possible without devolving into nonfiction. As always, data about cost, clothes, tools, methods, medicine, the types of food available by train or in the local prairie, and the color of ostrich feathers and a thousand other details are correct for the 1880s, which we now call the Gilded Age.

That said, it was not my intent to make this book about politics or the 'patriarchy' though I have discovered, in writing, that these themes have inevitably—by nature of history—wound themselves into the lives of the characters. In the end, as always, I simply wish to entertain and offer an escape to the past. Maybe it will help create fresh appreciation for the knowledge we now possess of medicine and the human body. Maybe it will just have you form a bit of a crush on one of the characters (I have a few myself!).

There is one more book left to tie together all the little pieces and strings, and leave our characters where I mean to let them go. I cannot wait to show you how medicine and disease, death and birth, and the hope to build something big and bold shape Jane, Marie and Kate as they search for a place to belong in their corner of the world. I suppose that desire—*to belong*—has not changed one bit, even after all this time. Fancy that.

With affection—Sara Dahmen

harvesting herbs in the garden, Wisconsin

AUTHOR'S ACKNOWLEDGEMENTS:

I struggle to write 'bad guys'. It may come from an inherent belief that all people are probably good instead of evil, or I just like to focus on the happy parts of life instead of the underbelly. But we all know there are nasty people out there. Vindictive, unkind, with a mean streak that can be hard to see until it strikes.

Thankfully, I have no such people behind me and the Flats Junction series. Instead, it's the opposite, which is the most fantastic gift an author could receive.

To Ben Coles, thank you for not only helping me keep the structure of this trickier novel in shape, but for seeing the long game of this entire set of books and the intellectual property behind it. Without your vision and belief, these novels would be languishing in some forgotten corner of the world … and likely my desktop. Also, a sincere thanks to the team of editors, producers, designers, and artists at Promontory Press, who make the books lovely and figure out how to make my artwork on the pages look fancy.

To my manager, Noah Jones, who keeps me sane amid the juggling of the many projects—both book and film—and always has a strategy for talking me off the ledge when I get frustrated by the amount of patience needed to navigate the entertainment industry. To Bonnie Nadell, who doesn't blink when I beg her to read not one—but two—novels at a crack, and is ready to take on anything, even if it's one of my crazy ideas. And to Laura MacDonald, my agent at Gersh, who handles all the weird requests we get and makes sure contracts are airtight.

There are many who have put wind beneath the wings of the Flats Junction books—the rallying around this property by the many producers, executives, and creatives in Hollywood never ceases to astound me as we inch toward the finish line of production.

To my book club, which consists of my dear friends, who cheer me on every book endeavor, big or small. I can't tell you how much I'd flounder without you all.

For all the extended family—thank you for showing your enthusiastic interest and delight whenever a new book is out. It is like Christmas every time I see one of my books on your side tables.

To my children: Will, Hannah, and Jack, who are old enough to see that when I don't have time to write I'm not a very patient person, and are beyond understanding when my deadlines mean I sometimes need to write at the community pool instead of swimming in it with you—may you all find as much happiness in your jobs as I do with mine.

Forever, to my husband John, who not only supports this writing endeavor of mine wholeheartedly, but who urges me to keep reaching further with it. I'd have given up a dozen times if he was not there to remind me with utter confidence that "you'll figure it out, you always do." And I do, but mostly because of him and his unwavering, magnificent love.

BIBLIOGRAPHY:

Black Elk, Linda S. *Culturally Important Plants of the Lakota.* Sitting Bull College, Fort Yates, ND; 1998

Bruton-Seal, Julie & Matthew Seal. *Backyard Medicine: Harvest and Make Your Own Herbal Remedies.* Castle Books, New York; 2012

Bynum, W.F. *Science and the Practice of Medicine in the Nineteenth Century.* Cambridge University Press, Cambridge; 1994

Chevallier, Andrew. *Encyclopedia of Herbal Medicine.* Penguin Random House, New York; 1996

De la Forêt, Rosalee & Emily Han. *Wild Remedies: How to Forage Healing Foods and Craft Your Own Herbal Medicine.* Hay House, Inc., Carlsbad, CA; 2020

Gilmore, Melvin R. *Uses of Plants by the Indians of the Missouri River Region, Enlarged Edition.* University of Nebraska Press, Lincoln; 1977

Hertzler, Arthur. *The Horse and Buggy Doctor.* Harper & Brothers, New York; 1938

Lavine, Sigmund A. *Wonders of Herbs.* Dodd, Mead & Company, New York; 1976

Peavy, Linda & Ursula Smith. *Pioneer Women: The Lives of Women on the Frontier.* University of Oklahoma Press, Norman; 1998

Pender, Rose. *A Lady's Experiences in the Wild West in 1883.* University of Nebraska Press, Lincoln/London; 1978

Sioux, Lyotanka. *Native American Herbalist's Bible.* Self-published; 2021

Steele, Volney. *Bleed, Blister and Purge: A History of Medicine on the American Frontier.* Mountain Press Publishing Company, Missoula, MT; 2005

Utley, Robert M. *The Indian Frontier of the American West 1846 – 1890.* University of New Mexico Press, Albuquerque; 1984

Wilbur, C. Keith. *Antique Medical Instruments.* Shiffer Publishing Ltd., West Chester, PA; 1987

Wilcox, R. Turner. *Five Centuries of American Costume.* Charles Scribner's Sons, New York; 1963

LANGUAGE GLOSSARY

POLISH

Babcia – Grandma

Co do cholery – What the hell?

Gówno – shit

Tak – yes

Zabije cię – I will kill you

Zamknąć sie – Shut up!

NORWEGIAN

Honning - honey

Mor - Mother

LAKOTA

čhaŋ wíziye – old man's beard (*clematis vitalba*) – a woody perennial vine also known as traveler's joy. It's a lichen and contains usnic acid

Čhaŋ wápe ǧí-wi – September

Hutkáŋ tȟáŋ ka – arrowleaf (or arrowroot) balsamroot resin (*Balsamorhiza sagittate*) a native sunflower, with multiple medicinal uses for the local tribes.

Iná – Mother

Pȟežíȟóta waštémna – sagewort (*Artemisia frigida*) or prairie sagewort, in the aster family, used for everything from coughs and colds to indigestion and more

Pilámaya ye ksto – Thank you (fem)

Sihasapa – the name of the Blackfoot Sioux band within the Lakota or Titonwan Sioux Nation

Tákuwe hwo? – Why? (masculine)

Taŋyáŋ yahí – It is good you have come

Tȟózi - green

Tókša akhé waŋčhíyaŋkiŋ kte – Surely, I will see you again.

Uŋglákčapi – the herb echinacea or purple coneflower

Waŋńa – Now! (command)

Wapiyekiya - medicine

The Flats Junction Series

Tinsmith 1865

Medicineman 1876

Widow 1881

Outcast 1883

Trader 1884

Stranger 1886

To connect with Sara,
visit www.saradahmen.com.

Find her on Twitter at @saradahmenbooks,
on Facebook, or Instagram at @housecopper.

To learn about Sara's cookware line
inspired by her research for Flats Junction,
visit www.housecopper.com.